Love Me At My Worst

ADRIAN J. SMITH

EREKA PRESS

Love Me At My Worst

CHAPTER
One

THE HANDLE on the door jostled, and Isla's heart thrummed along steadily as she crouched down. The kids' eyes were glued to her, the weight of what was about to happen resting on her shoulders. The handle twisted down. The heavy door cracked open.

Isla pushed up with her toes, her thigh muscles tightening as she demanded them to move. She jumped forward, shouting, "Boo!"

Andry's hands flew into the air, her jaw dropping as the scream reverberated through the classroom. Her dark brown eyes were wild with sudden fear, her face contorting as the suddenness rocked through her. Her entire body leaned back as she tried to catch herself. Isla reached forward and wrapped her arm around Andry's waist to tug her back so she didn't fall.

Laughter erupted behind Isla as she backed away from the door, a grin overcoming her face and her body, relaxing the muscles she had spent days ignoring. Andry crossed her legs, pushing down on her thighs as she leaned over to catch her breath and steady herself, her fingers still wrapped around Isla's wrist to steady herself. But when Andry looked up, she wasn't mad—she was elated.

Isla put her hands to her mouth, trying to contain her own laughter. Her heart still raced with the thrill of success, joy bubbling in the top of her head through the excitement. She wanted to keep it there, wanted to dig her fingers into the happiness she found and keep it right in front of her so she could see it, experience it, live into it. It had been the simplest prank, but it had been so worth it. She'd asked Shannon in the office to give her a heads-up as soon as Andry was coming to the classroom. And the plan had delivered.

The kids roared with laughter as Andry's eyes gleamed through the joke, her hands clapping together slowly before she locked her eyes on Isla properly. Isla's heart stuttered at that look, but she couldn't linger on it too long. Andry reached up and wiped her cheeks as if tears were falling down her face, her lips curled into a smile still as she let out a laugh herself. Isla snorted when Andry leaned in to wrap an arm around her shoulder, tugging Isla into her side as the sudden shock calmed down.

"You got me good that time!" Andry pointed at the kids. "Were you all in on it, too?"

"No!" They shouted, shaking their heads, child-like giggles still filling the classroom. Isla loved to hear that sound, and this had been the perfect way to fill the room with as much joy and lightness as possible.

Isla was still laughing, real tears forming in her eyes as she tried to catch her breath. It would have been so much better if she'd had time to capture video of it so she could share it throughout the rest of the school, so she could rewatch it with them and let that same joy and happiness fill her multiple times. The other teachers and staff all loved her antics, for the most part, but especially when they involved Andry. The kids enjoyed it, too.

"You're crazy," Andry said, turning to Isla again, not letting go of her shoulders as they stood next to each other. Isla was so warm and filled with the connection she felt standing next to Andry in front of her sixth-grade classroom.

"She got you so good!" Graham shouted from across the room.

Andry nodded and gave Isla a tight squeeze with her hand, but didn't let go again, her fingers wrapped around Isla's upper arm as she continued the side hug. "She did. Ms. Walsh has a particular talent for scaring me, doesn't she?"

They all agreed just as Isla's timer went off at her desk, the *beep beep beep* almost hidden by the voices in the classroom. Isla turned her focus on the students and straightened her shoulders as she walked over to her desk, recognizing the need for a shift in focus even if she'd rather linger in the burst of joy she'd created. The pull to switch back into teaching mode and teach the kids how to make that transition as well took hold of her, and she knew she had to follow it. It was the start of the school year, but they would have it down pat by the end.

"Time's up for the test, but you all knew that already. Hand in your tests, and line up so you can go to recess."

The movement in the room was suddenly less about the scare prank and far more about the excitement of getting outside in the sunshine and running off some of that energy kids were notorious for. It couldn't have been more perfect timing. The kids grabbed their jackets from the hooks along the wall and lined up. Andry stepped to the side and next to Isla as the kids did their thing.

The energy in Isla's chest and hands still vibrated after such a successful prank. As soon as the line leader for the day was in place, Isla ushered the kids out the door. Andry walked with her, still shaking her head.

"That really was a good one." There was a lightness to Andry's tone that Isla was envious of—she wanted that ease of being in the world.

"Just wish I'd gotten video." Isla kept her eyes on her kids as much as possible, unable to really look at Andry and recognize everything she was missing out on.

"There's always next time." Andry winked at her as they got

to the doors to the playground. The kids waited until Isla moved to the front of the line and opened it for them to run out. The para-educators were already outside and waiting for the students to join them.

Isla crossed her arms over her chest as the last kid raced through the door. She leaned against the wall and watched them from the window. Andry gave her an odd look, but Isla shook her head before pushing off and starting back toward her classroom. No way did she want to discuss what was going on internally. That was a mess that couldn't be untangled in the thirty seconds they had.

Andry followed, her steps quick to keep up. "Did you call me all the way down there just to scare me?"

"Maybe?" Isla tossed a smile over her shoulder as Andry raised an eyebrow at her, falling back into the joy she'd created.

"You're insane."

"Some days." Isla pressed her lips together firmly as they stepped into the classroom. She collected the papers and stacked them together to put on her desk for later, distracting herself now that she didn't have the excitement of a prank to live into. She would be up late grading those later that week since she'd rather spend the time she was in the building with other people instead of alone, even if it wasn't with the vibrancy of a prank just pulled.

Andry watched the kids play outside through the window, distracted. The knock on the door was sharp, and Glo, the other sixth grade teacher, came into the room. Isla smiled at her as she eyed the two of them.

"Did you scare her again?"

"I did." Isla chuckled a little, so proud of herself for that one moment that had managed to relieve all the stress that had been building up the past month—if only it would last longer than a few seconds. The school had become her sanctuary and so had these people in a way that she had never expected.

"She hid behind the door and jumped out at me," Andry added. "Kids thought it was hilarious."

Glo laughed. "I bet they did. We could hear you scream all the way in my classroom."

"Of course you could." Andry's cheeks tinged pink, and she folded her arms together, slightly embarrassed.

Isla watched her carefully, making sure that she hadn't crossed the line. She was always wary of that since Andry wasn't only someone she would call a friend, she was also the principal, and that was a thin line they had to walk every day.

"I'll get you back though, just you wait." Andry pointed at her and winked again, the easy grin not leaving her face.

"I know you will." A smile lit up Isla's lips, but she wasn't quite feeling it like she had been. The overwhelming sadness she had become all too familiar with in the last few months settled into her chest. She hated it, despised that she hadn't been able to work through it and go back to being her happy self. That had been the entire point of the prank—to give her something else to focus on and maybe remind herself that joy *was* achievable.

Glo and Andry talked briefly before Andry caught her eye. "Recess is almost up, Isla."

"Right." Isla straightened her shoulders and made sure that her façade was in place. She had successfully managed to make it through the start of the school year without anyone finding out what was going on, and she planned on keeping it that way for as long as she could.

～

In the sea of people Isla was surrounded with daily she couldn't be more alone. As the school day finished, she sent her kids off for the weekend and strained to avoid the silence settling into her heart. Her life had been far too quiet lately. For weekend after weekend, all she would do was crawl into her bed and not come out until halfway the next morning, sliding through her days off work by merely existing.

Then again, no matter how hard she tried to be present in the moment, she failed miserably to keep herself there longer than a few minutes at most. She stayed in her classroom as the last few voices echoed through the hallway, packing up her things to head home for the weekend.

Maintaining the facade took everything in her. Isla halted her movements, glancing out the window as kids ran to their parents. Andry walked the playground as she usually did, her light brown hair down around her shoulders and her voice loud as she talked with kids and parents alike. Isla envied that confidence, the ability to have everything in her life be calm.

It hadn't been calm since late summer, since Wil had—Isla tensed, her shoulders so tight that it hurt—since her forever friend had started dating her stepmom. Isla clenched her jaw hard, not just her stepmom, but the woman who had raised her and abandoned her. Wil wouldn't do that—at least, Isla kept telling herself she wouldn't. But facts were facts, and she hadn't seen Wil in months and the phone calls and the texts were few and far between and there was a damn wall right between them.

Andry laughed loudly at something, and Isla blinked, coming back to herself. She had to get out of there. She grabbed her bag and made her way to the staff parking lot, tossing her bag into the passenger seat. When she shut the door, Andry stood next to the car, that big perfect grin on her lips, one side pulling higher than the other, her dark brown eyes filled with that lightness Isla longed for, and her hair moving in the wind.

Isla's heart stuttered, and she pulled herself together as quickly as possible, curling her lips upward and shifting her stance so she could pretend just a little longer. Andry shoved her hands into the pockets of her tan slacks as she stood casually, no weight on her shoulders. "That prank was exactly the laugh I needed today. Thank you."

"Oh." Isla blinked in surprise, but she warmed at the thought. She'd been selfish in why she'd pulled it, but to find that Andry got as much out of it was a balm to her aching heart. "You're welcome."

For the eight years they had worked together, they had been work friends—friends while in the building and doing school-ish things, but never outside the building. Isla inwardly frowned at that thought. In the eight years she'd been there, she hadn't made any friends. She'd relied on Wil for everything she needed, and now, she didn't have that.

"You'll have to tell me someday how you managed to convince Shannon to help you with that one." Andry's hand was on her arm again. Isla flicked her gaze down to the touch, her heart thumping hard at just how easy it was for Andry to do that.

"That's a secret I'll never tell." Isla raised her gaze up, meeting Andry's in the tight space But she would tell. She and Shannon were work friends, perfectly capable of laughing and getting along while in the walls of the school, but as soon as the bell rang, they went on with their own lives like they didn't know each other.

Isla shifted at that uncomfortable thought, shoving her hands into the pockets of her jeans and rocking up on the balls of her feet. She shook off Andry's touch, as much as it pained her. She wasn't looking to change their relationship. What she wanted was to have Wil back in her life, right by her side, like nothing had changed, like she hadn't been asked to sacrifice their friendship for love she would never be invited into.

"Do you have plans for the weekend?" Andry asked.

When Isla looked back up to meet her gaze, her world shifted again, becoming solely about the two of them. "Nothing out of the usual."

It was the best non-answer she could give. Had Andry asked last school year, she would have expected Wil to come up for a visit or her to go to Denver, but some kind of antics would be had, alcohol would be involved, and she would come home with laughter still bright in her memory. But now that Wil was dating Lynda, she didn't want Wil to visit or to talk to her. While she missed her forever friend, she wasn't prepared for the hurricane of emotions that would sweep her off her feet if they did talk, or heaven forbid, get together.

"Katie's working on applying for colleges this weekend." Andry frowned, pulling Isla from the impending chaos she'd found herself leaning toward. "I'm not looking forward to that experience."

"Well, she's your only kid, so I'd imagine not." Isla grasped onto the topic, digging in to talk about anything but herself.

"Yeah." Andry looked far off, not elaborating, and Isla suspected there was another reason entirely that brought up mixed emotions, but she didn't want to pry either. She wasn't sure she had the bandwidth to deal with someone else's problems right then. "Having her out of my house next year is going to be quite an adjustment."

"It will be." Isla hadn't ever experienced that. She was the oldest, so she'd been the first to leave, but she understood the feeling of an empty house, the unending quiet like a black void. That awkward moment when she swore the other person was still there, but they weren't.

"I think Glo is organizing one of her get-togethers again. You going to go?"

Isla shook her head. She'd gone to one or two of those when she'd first started there, but it was definitely for more experienced teachers who had been jaded by the systems in place. Isla didn't want to add that to her problems, so she delicately bowed out any other time she had been invited.

"Yeah, I'm not going to go either. Too much complaining."

"You know, we could always have our own get together and change up the personality of the group so that it's more positive." It was an idea she hadn't had before, but it would get her out with people and perhaps make friends, which was something she had neglected in the last eight years. Now she didn't have a choice but to navigate that.

"That's not a bad idea." Andry raised her eyebrows as she thought, her dark eyes seeing something that Isla wasn't privy to. She nodded her head after a few seconds. "I'll see if I can work it out."

"I think it'd be good." Isla folded her hands together. They were standing awfully close, and she'd lowered her voice so that no one else could hear. It was a habit she had picked up when she started teaching since children heard everything.

"Yeah? I'll figure it out then." Andry reached out and touched Isla's wrist. "Have a good weekend. I'll see you Monday."

"Yeah. See you then."

Andry walked away with a small wave. Isla waited until she got back to the gate on the playground to get into her car. She buckled her belt and slowly backed out of her space. Isla took the quick drive home, passing by cars and businesses. She almost didn't see anything as she went, so caught up in her own depressing thoughts.

When she got to her apartment, she dropped her keys on the kitchen counter and her bag on the side of the couch. Isla collapsed onto the other couch cushion and closed her eyes, pinching the bridge of her nose. The noise from the school faded in her ears and her memory, and she knew she was going to be cast into the silence of another long weekend with no one to see and nothing to do.

To be fair, she had planned it that way, but that didn't make it any easier as the hours ticked by. She stared at the television even though the screen was dark. She took deep breaths and fell into herself. No matter how hard she tried to sleep lately, she couldn't manage more than a few hours. She would just lie in bed, and when her alarm went off in the morning, it was like she hadn't even managed to rest.

When she checked the time on her watch, it was already

after nine. Dragging herself to her feet, Isla went to the bathroom and took a long shower, sitting in the bottom of the tub as the water sluiced over her body until it ran cold. When that was done, she dried off, got into pajamas, and lay in bed in absolute silence until she must have fallen asleep.

CHAPTER
Two

"HOW DID THIS WEEK GO?" Larisa asked, her typical opening question for therapy day.

"Fine," Isla responded habitually. She knew she wouldn't get away with that kind of answer, but it would at least delay the inquiry a bit longer—though not by much.

Larisa didn't even say anything this time, she just pinned Isla with a serious look.

Isla wrinkled her nose and stared down at her hands in her lap. It was always harder than she anticipated to dig deep inside herself and share. Choosing the easy out, Isla met Larisa's gaze. "It's been about the same. I played a prank on my principal this week. That went well."

"Oh? What kind of prank?" Larisa seemed only halfway intrigued, as if she'd already figured out that this information was a distraction.

Isla hesitated in continuing, choosing to shorten the story so they could get to the point. Someday, she wished this would be easy. "Nothing elaborate. I jumped out at her from behind my classroom door. The kids got a kick out of it."

Larisa nodded, still keeping that steady gaze on Isla. She didn't write anything on her notepad, though she rarely had in the few short months Isla had been seeing her. Isla swallowed the lump in her throat, not sure where to go from there. The last time she had been in they'd talked about work—that was her safe bet, but she knew they had to go deeper than that. She needed to sort out her feelings about Wil and Lynda, she needed to find some sort of balance with them so she could still have her forever friend in her life.

"You have a pretty good relationship with your principal, right?" Larisa interrupted her thoughts.

"Yeah, I've worked with Andry since I started full-time teaching. She's great, and always there when I need her." Isla folded her hands together, brushing her thumb along the edge of her palm as she waited for the other shoe to drop. It seemed she was always waiting for that, ever since she was a kid. Something would happen that would tear everything good away from her. She'd never thought that would happen with her forever friend, but it had finally come. They weren't friends anymore, at least not like they had been, and Isla wasn't sure they'd ever find that tight connection again. Loneliness ate away at her, and if she focused on it too long, she'd devolve into uncontrollable tears.

"What are you thinking about?" Larisa's voice was gentle as she pried.

Isla refused to raise her gaze from the floor, digging deep into her thoughts. What did Larisa see that no one else could? Granted, she was trained in this sort of thing, so that was expected. The silence in the room held, Isla sitting in it as she parsed through exactly what she wanted to say. All in all, she was there for a reason, and as difficult as it may be, they did have to talk about it.

"That I miss my best friend."

"You miss her?"

Isla nodded, tears brimming in her eyes in an unexpected way. She wasn't someone who cried, and never about these things. She'd rarely cried in the last fifteen years, but she hadn't realized how hurt she was. "Wil hasn't called or texted in two weeks."

"Two weeks?" Larisa looked dubious.

Isla shook her head. "That's abnormal for us. We usually talk every day. Maybe we'll miss a day here or there, but it's always at least once a day."

Larisa stayed still, those deep blue eyes piercing Isla as if she was waiting for Isla to say something else, to continue on. When she didn't say something, Larisa shifted and prepared her next question. "Do you know what's going on?"

Isla nodded, although the move was so small she wasn't sure Larisa would pick up on it. That tension in her chest tightened again, making it difficult to breathe and working its way up her throat and around her neck. It hurt almost as bad as the situation she found herself in.

"What do you think happened?"

"Wil started dating someone," Isla mumbled.

"Is it normal for her communication to drop when that happens?"

Isla shook her head, unable to meet Larisa's gaze. "It's usually the opposite."

"Then what's different this time?"

Isla clenched her jaw tightly, her fingers strangling each other as she clasped her hands. She had to force her gaze to move from the floor and back to Larisa's face. This was why she was there, and it had taken them six weeks to get there, six weeks for her to feel comfortable enough to potentially trust another therapist. Her breathing increased, short rapid breaths as she mulled the words through her head multiple times just to force herself to say them.

"Wil started dating my stepmom."

Larisa's eyebrows rose up, disappearing behind her blonde bangs. She cocked her head to the side and shook her head. "I'm sorry. Your best friend is dating your stepmother?"

Isla understood the disbelief. Hell, she was still struggling to believe it. "It's a long story."

"Well, that's what I'm here for."

There wasn't an easy or short way to get through all the complications in that statement, or all of the emotions that Isla was fighting. Failure had haunted her personal attempts to parse them out in the past. With a deep breath, she started at the beginning. "Wil's been my best friend since kindergarten when she moved in with her grandma. She lived right across the street from me, and we were inseparable."

"So this is the person you've known the longest in your life?"

Isla nodded, fresh tears biting at her eyes and making them hurt. *I don't want to cry.* She sucked in a breath. "My dad and Lynda started dating when I was seven. Other than Wil, the only other person is my sister."

"I see you giving more weight to meaning making with Wil than you do your stepmom from our past conversations—you care more about your relationship with Wil. And now that's been thrown to the side. Would you say that's true?"

Isla's chest constricted tightly because she hadn't been ignored. They had asked and called and wanted her to be on board with it all. Making eye contact with Larisa, Isla said, "I don't think that. They...well, Wil...wouldn't be in a relationship with Lynda if I didn't approve of it."

Larisa studied her, that unwavering gaze unnerving. She shifted back in her seat, her eyes never leaving Isla. "But do you approve of it? Are you okay with it?"

Isla sucked in a breath, her stomach twisting. She had approved of it, but that didn't mean she was okay with them being together.

"Isla?"

"No, I'm not okay with it." Her voice was a whisper, barely audible in the silent room.

Larisa eyed her, not moving. Isla swam in the confusion of what she'd just said because she'd told Wil the exact opposite.

She'd even ventured to tell it to Lynda the one short time they had spoken since then. But outside of an initial meetup in Fort Collins, Isla hadn't been able to bring herself to see Lynda again or call or text her, slipping back into the silence she had kept for so long.

"I hadn't spoken to Lynda in five years, not until all of this happened, and I was very comfortable with that."

"Why is that do you think?"

Isla gnawed on the inside of her lip, Lynda's stoic face coming to mind, her red lips and pinned-back hair, always prim and proper like she should be. Her stomach soured, not just from the feeling she was about to admit but because admitting it wasn't acceptable. "Because I don't like her."

"You don't like her as a person or who she is to you?"

"Who she is to me. I'm sure she's a very acceptable person for others." Isla's heart fluttered, for the first time not admonished for feeling something so unsavory. Lynda was put on a pedestal as the savior of the family, taking on two orphaned kids to raise them, but Isla hadn't wanted that.

Larisa shifted her legs, uncrossing and recrossing them. "Does your sister talk to her?"

"She does, though not as often as she used to. I think she feels torn between us, not sure where the lines are or how to navigate them."

"Have you told her not to talk to Lynda about you?"

"No, but I think it was implied." The guilt she had avoided before found her, twirling in her stomach and in her chest. She hadn't wanted to ruin their relationship, and she'd worked hard for years not to do that. But inevitably, she had failed at that too.

"And why don't you talk to your stepmother anymore?"

Isla collapsed. Tears built in her eyes, and she had no concept of where to go from there. She just wanted to break and fall apart on her own without anyone there to witness it, but they still had twenty minutes to go in her session. Why was she paying for this torture session?

Her heart thumped against a constricting chest. Nothing was going to be able to solve this, not unless she said the damn words, but she wasn't sure that she trusted Larisa enough. It hadn't been long enough yet.

"Isla." Larisa's tones were cool as she brought Isla back around to the present moment. "When you came to see me the first time, it was because of this. We've skirted around the issue since then, but I'm encouraging you to be more open. It's the only way real work can happen. Why don't you talk to your stepmother?"

Isla locked her gaze on Larisa's blue eyes. She held it. She took deep centering breaths like she had been taught when she was a teenager, when Lynda had forced her to go to therapy even though she didn't want to. For years she'd thought it was a bunch of bullshit, and yet that had been the first place she'd run as soon as she needed help, as soon as Wil wasn't available.

"It's not because of Wil." She had to protect that relationship as she had so many times throughout her life. Everything was Lynda's fault. It always had been, and it always would be. Then again, Lynda hadn't forced her to go to therapy this time, Lynda hadn't thrown her into this turmoil. She'd managed to find it all on her own.

"Then what is it because?"

Isla pulled her lower lip between her teeth, gnawing again on the flesh there until it hurt. "I'm not really sure."

"You can do better than that." Larisa remained frighteningly still, not even shifting in the chair.

The tension in the small room intensified, and Isla wasn't sure she'd be able to breathe through it any longer. "I don't know."

"You know," Larisa cooed confidently. "Take a minute to think about it."

Isla did exactly that. She closed her eyes, she remembered everything that came to the forefront of her mind. Dad introducing Lynda, the way she was so entranced with her in the beginning. The way she liked seeing her dad smile and hearing him laugh again.

But it was so clouded with that moment. With the wailing Isla had woken sharply to. The police officers standing at the door. Her heart raced as the grief erupted in her again. When Dad had died, Lynda had taken a week off work, but that was it.

Isla clenched her jaw. After that week, there was nothing. No crying, no heart-stopping moments, no special things to remember him by. Isla pulled herself back to the small room, opening her watery eyes that stung with the pain of unshed tears.

"She didn't care." Her voice broke, words barely forming through the thickness of her saliva as she strained to speak.

"Didn't care about what?"

Isla raised her gaze, staring directly into Larisa's eyes. "That Dad was dead. That we were hurting because of that." Larisa's face morphed from stubborn probing into absolute pity. Isla despised it. She hated receiving that glance from anyone. Her defenses went up, and she scrambled to protect herself from it. She focused back on the floor, unable to look at the pity in front of her. "It doesn't matter anyway."

"It does matter," Larisa put her hand up. "What are you feeling? Right now."

"Embarrassed." Isla drifted her line of sight to the small table next to Larisa's chair.

"What else?"

Isla held the silence. She hated these kinds of questions. It always took her forever to answer, and then guilt would eat away at her for not knowing what she felt within the first few seconds. She shook her head, her heart aching at the thought that finally popped into her mind, the feeling swiftly following. "I'm mad."

"You're angry?"

Nodding, Isla tried to make herself as small as possible. In all the intervening years, she had never said this. Wil had told her it was fine at one point to be mad at her dad for dying, but that wasn't it. She had been initially but not anymore. Now she just felt utter sadness that he was missing everything in her life. Pinpointing the anger that seemed to be focused in the center of her forehead, Isla dragged it back and pulled it together, forming it into something tangible. She wasn't mad he died anymore. He hadn't been able to control that.

"Who are you angry at?" Larisa rephrased.

"Myself." Isla clenched her eyes. It was true, but it also wasn't the real person she was mad at. For some damnable reason, she couldn't say it. She couldn't force the words to leave her lips.

"What are you mad at yourself for?" Larisa had so much patience. It had taken them weeks of figuring each other out and balancing the silence and press for questions. She must have held that silence too long this time because Larisa prompted her again. "What are you mad about?"

"She was supposed to be there for us, and she wasn't."

Larisa's eyes lit up, as if she suddenly had an answer for why they were there. "You're talking about Lynda? Or your mother?"

Isla's heart sunk. "Lynda. Lynda was supposed to be there. She was supposed to care. She was supposed to replace him when he was gone, and she didn't."

Wiping at her cheeks, her hands came back wet. When had she started crying? Her shoulders shook, racking with sobs as she tried her best to contain the sobs. Larisa snagged a box of tissues from the table and set them next to Isla on the couch, but she refused to touch them—her own damn stubbornness getting in the way. She didn't want to be weak, and she certainly didn't want to be crying over some decades-old hurt.

"Take some deep breaths," Larisa encouraged from the chair across the room.

Isla pulled herself together, staying fully in the quiet Larisa allowed. She wiped the snot on the back of her hand. She shook her head and finally forced her gaze up to meet Larisa's eyes. Compassion. She was surrounded with compassion. It wasn't pity like she'd thought, but care. Isla clenched her jaw against it, not ready to accept it.

"I think we made some real progress today, but we are out of time. I want to make sure that you're okay to go home—that you're going to be able to take some time for yourself."

Isla nodded, folding her hands together again. Her eyes burned from the tears. When had the time passed so quickly? Last she'd looked they had twenty minutes left, but she honestly couldn't account for where the minutes had gone.

"I'll see you next week, okay?"

"Yeah. Okay." Isla pressed her hands down her thighs and awkwardly stood up. She squared her shoulders and left the small room with her chin down. She didn't want to see anyone in the waiting area. She didn't want anyone to know what she had just been through. She wouldn't be able to survive another one of those looks.

CHAPTER
Three

"CHRIS, I know it's rough right now, but we really have to find a time to talk about this—" Andry stopped, taking a moment to attempt to change her tone from annoyed to pleading without begging. "It's for Katie. Please call me back after school."

She blew out a breath as she stepped into the hallway of Elbert Elementary, the place she had come to call her second home throughout the years she had worked there. The halls were quiet this early in the morning, but after leaving early Friday to meet with a no-show Chris, she'd needed to come in to finish some work up for the week.

Soft tunes haunted the halls and surprised her. Andry squared her shoulders as she stood at the vertex of corridors, debating which way to turn. She could go to her office, or she could investigate which teacher was in already. Moving on instinct, Andry stepped down the hallway.

As she walked to the end, farther away from her office, she realized she was going directly to Isla's sixth grade classroom. The notes of the music sent a shiver through Andry's spine. The volume was enough to be heard, but it wasn't obnoxiously loud, and Andry suspected that Isla would turn it down before everyone else arrived for the day. Her lips quirked as she stepped closer to the door, ready to check in on her favorite teacher.

She'd noticed that Isla had been coming earlier and earlier to work throughout the last few years, but this took the cake. It was nearly six in the morning. Andry stepped quietly to the open door and leaned against the doorframe, a smile resting on her lips and her stomach warming as she watched. Isla stood at the front of her classroom, organizing something—probably for later that day. Her hips swayed to the beat of the music, a slow glide from side to side.

Her bright blonde hair was pulled tightly back in a ponytail that sat at the base of her neck. She had on jeans and flats that day, a blue T-shirt that would rival the color of her eyes as soon as Andry could see them. Hiring her had been worth the risk. She had nailed her interview with Andry. She may have been young, but she was hyper-organized and never missed an opportunity to connect with her students or other staff.

In fact, Andry often sent new hires her way just so she could break them in and teach them the ropes before sending them around to the rest of the school. She just had the kind of personality that said anyone could talk to her and be listened to. Though Isla was skimpy on details about herself and often avoided talking about her life growing up other than her *forever friend*. Andry loved that they called each other that.

Andry stayed still, watching Isla work. It was rare that she got to have a significant amount of one-on-one time with her teachers, and she missed that, but ultimately, she had an entire school to run. Her lips curled upward, remembering Isla's suggestion of another evening group get-together, one that was low-key and would allow more of that connection from principal to teacher. It deserved further investigation.

Stepping into the room, Andry broke the ice. "You're not going to scare me again, are you?"

Isla jumped, her shoulders tightening as she spun around with her hands up, her eyes wide, and her mouth open. Andry immediately put her hand out and shook her head. She'd never intended to scare her—not then anyway, though she had thought about getting Isla back for some of the pranks she pulled.

"Take a breath," Andry murmured, coming in closer now that Isla seemed to calm once recognizing her.

Isla did as she was told, holding a hand to her chest as she clasped her elbow with her other hand. She shook her head. "Jesus, Andry!"

"I didn't mean to scare you. I swear." Andry was fully inside the classroom in an instant, standing right next to Isla. She put a hand on her upper arm and squeezed, trying to reassure her that all was right in the world.

Isla stepped into her slightly before all the tension in her shoulders released and she plastered a smile on her face. "You're evil. You know that, right?"

Andry chuckled. "I promise you it was unintentional."

"Sure it was. Just remember, payback's a bitch." Isla laughed lightly, but it didn't sound like she meant it.

"Oh, I'm sure it is." Andry sobered and stared into Isla's eyes. She didn't seem quite as relaxed as Andry had thought she would be. That tension was still riding in her gaze, in the lines of her face, across her clenched jaw. Had the scare truly been that awful? Andry hedged for a moment before she gave in to instinct and asked, "Are you okay?"

"What? Of course I am. You just scared the shit out of me." Isla twisted back around to the table in the front of her classroom where she had been getting something ready.

Andry pressed her lips together firmly, trying to decide where that line was for them. She wanted to be the person Isla could come to with any problems she had, but at the same time she was Isla's boss, which meant that line could get sticky, not to mention, Isla had never come to her before. Still, Andry was pretty sure there was something else going on. She stepped in close and bent over the table to look at what Isla was doing.

"Tests?"

"Yeah. I need to hand all this back to the kids today and get ready to start evaluations for the end of the quarter."

"That's four weeks away." Andry blinked at her in surprise.

Isla shrugged. "You know me, I like to be on top of things."

"How much can you actually get done before then that you haven't already done?" Andry held her travel mug of coffee tightly as she continued to look down at the tests in front of her. Most of them were decent grades from what she saw, but that didn't mean anything for how the class was going.

"There's always something to do," Isla murmured as she finished the last of the stack. "What are you doing here so early anyway?"

Andry sighed heavily and frowned. "I left earlier than I planned on Friday, so I had to come in today to make up for that."

"What'd you leave for?"

"I was supposed to meet with Chris." Andry's heart twinged with pain. They had been married for seventeen years before Andry had to call it quits. Chris hadn't taken the separation and subsequent divorce well. That decision still haunted Andry every day.

"Bet that was a fun meeting."

"Would have been...if she'd shown up for it." Andry rolled her eyes and sat in the chair at the table, leaving Isla to stand and continue on with whatever she was doing.

Isla hissed. "That's hard."

"It'll be harder when we do finally get together, because there are deadlines looming that can't be missed." Andry sipped her coffee and looked up at Isla, those bright blue eyes locking on her. "Not the least bit curious what this illustrious meeting was about?"

"Kind of." Isla cracked a smile. "But I wasn't going to ask."

Andry's lips twitched upward, and she tilted her cup at Isla in a silent toast of understanding. "Finances. Katie needs her financial aid filled out for college applications, and we need to figure out how to buy her a car."

Isla snorted. "I remember that talk. I got my first car when I was sixteen."

"Really?"

"Yeah. My stepmom insisted that I didn't need a brand-new car, so I got a newer used car. I was so affronted by that fact, but in the end she was right. I was a pissy teenager who did *not* need a brand-new vehicle to screw up."

Andry laughed. "Katie will definitely be getting a used car, but I understand the sentiment. Stepparent is an interesting relationship to have to deal with."

"It is." Isla trailed off, not raising her gaze again.

Andry canted her head to the side, studying Isla carefully. She was normally bright and perky, but then again, they were also normally in a room full of other people. Andry honestly couldn't remember the last time they were alone together without prying eyes and ears. It was the first thing she could remember Isla sharing about her family, too. Something personal, and she wanted to know more. "Did you have issues with your stepmom?"

"Some. But who doesn't with any parent?"

"True. I loathe the day that I start dating again, or Chris does, and Katie has to figure that out." She hadn't even dared trying more than a date here or there when Katie was at Chris' or a friend's for the night. She wasn't ready to have that conversation with Katie yet.

Isla's face fell, her gaze downcast and her shoulders drawn. "At least she'll still have you to be her solid foundation."

"Absolutely. I'm not sure she could get rid of me even if she wanted to."

Isla smiled, but sadness swept through it, marring it. That was what had stolen over her before, but this time it consumed her. Andry leaned forward and set her travel mug on the table, immediately wanting to comfort.

"Is everything okay?" Andry asked.

"Yeah, it's fine. Just a tough weekend." Isla still didn't look her in the eye, and her voice wavered slightly, as though she were about to cry.

"Sorry to hear that." Andry paused, needing to say more, anything to pull Isla out of herself and give Isla a reason to finally trust her. Andry wanted to know what was going through that mind underneath the surface. "I'm here to listen if you need to talk."

"I know that. Thanks." Isla gave her a brilliant smile, her eyes lighting up again as if nothing of the last few seconds had happened.

Andry took that as a sign that the conversation was over. She doubted Isla would come find her if there was a need, but at least the offer was on the table, and she was glad to see even the half smile. Andry's phone buzzed in her pocket. Frowning, she reached against her side and grabbed it, seeing Chris' name. Her heart sank. She couldn't listen to one thing, could she?

"Chris." Andry frowned as she held her phone up so Isla could see. "I'll talk to you later."

"Yeah." Isla didn't look up as Andry stood and walked out of the classroom.

She answered as soon as she was out of the door. "I asked you to call *after* school today."

"Well, I thought you wouldn't be busy yet." Chris had a bite to her tone, the sound of the engine starting in her car.

Andry rolled her eyes. "You didn't show up on Friday."

"Shit," Chris muttered. "I'm so sorry about that. I totally spaced it."

Right. Of course she had. She had done that constantly throughout the final few years of their marriage, which had been a major part of their separation. But it wasn't the only reason Andry had filed for divorce. "We need to find time this week to fill out the financial aid stuff."

"I know. I know. It's just a crazy week."

"Every week is a crazy week." Andry reached the main office and juggled her phone to grab her keys. As soon as the lock clicked, she pushed the door open and grabbed her phone to hold it securely to her ear. "Katie was expecting you." Perhaps it was low to use their daughter to guilt Chris, but Andry couldn't find it in herself to care.

"I'm sorry." Chris' voice changed as the sound switched from her phone to the Bluetooth.

Andry unlocked her office and dropped her bag onto the desk before plopping heavily into her chair and clenching her eyes tight. "This is something we have to get done so she can go to college."

"I know it is." Anger seethed into Chris' words.

"So we need to get it done." Maybe if she said it enough times it would stick in Chris' brain.

"Do we have to do it together?"

Andry's shoulders tensed sharply. She bit her lip and looked at the lightening sky outside. "We don't have to do the financial aid stuff together, but we do have to figure out the car issue together. Unless you don't want to go in on half of it."

"No, I do. I've got the money."

That hadn't been why she'd made the comment, but of course, that was the way Chris would take it. She never took anything Andry said lately as anything less than an attack on her. Andry clenched her jaw to keep from arguing back. That was the distinct advantage to no longer being married. She didn't have to feed into it.

"When can you find time to meet with me?"

Chris groaned, her blinker sounding loudly through the phone line. "Thursday."

"Fine. Why don't you come to the school? I've got a late meeting I need to be here for."

"What time?"

"Five."

"I'll be there. I promise."

"See you then." Andry hung up and clenched her eyes, her heart thundering. She wasn't sure how much longer she could take this kind of relationship with Chris. It hurt too damn much to see who she had been when Katie was little versus who she had become in the last decade. She was a completely different person, someone who didn't prioritize her family anymore. And the worst part was it wasn't even because she was spending all her time at work.

The likelihood that Chris even showed up Thursday was going to be slim, and that was what hurt the most. The next ultimatum would be that Andry would figure it out and just give Chris the cost and see if she coughed up the money. She worried paying for Katie's college would be that way in the end. She hated that Katie was stuck in the middle of everything. She deserved so much better than either of them could manage to give her.

"Andry," Isla's voice was gentle, defusing the tension in the room.

Andry's eyes snapped open, finding Isla standing in the doorway to the office. In an instant, every defense she had was up. "How long have you been standing there?"

"Long enough." Isla's lower lip quivered as though she was nervous. She shouldn't be. Andry had shared with her enough of what had happened that the conversation she'd heard should be no surprise. "I'm sorry she's being so difficult."

Andry shrugged it off, embarrassment filling her as her defenses fell. She hated being this vulnerable in front of one of her employees, but at the same time, Isla had always been a little bit more than that, hadn't she? Andry shared things with her that she hadn't with anyone else, and she begged for Isla to share in those same ways—especially since her divorce.

"I just hope we can figure out how to work through it for Katie's sake."

"That's the best thing, really. You...uh...forgot this." Isla stepped into the office and set Andry's coffee on the desk. She leaned against the edge of it, her palm flat on the desktop. "Can't have you being under-caffeinated for the day, now can we?" Her half-attempt at a joke was appreciated.

"No one would enjoy that."

Isla let out a little chuckle, already seeming much better than she had minutes before.

"Thanks for bringing it down here. I would have gone to get it."

"This way you don't have to make the walk."

Disappointment hit Andry squarely. She would have loved to do that. She would do just about anything for Isla, and that morning, she sensed they both needed the companionship more than the gentle teasing. It was simply their presence together that made the day already better than it had been, which surprised her. She hadn't expected that, but now that she had Isla back in her sights, she didn't want her to go.

Andry leaned back in her chair with the coffee between her fingers. "What were you listening to?"

"Oh!" Isla cheeks tinged a rosy color. "Just something my forever friend told me about. I'm not sure if you remember Dido."

"I remember." Andry's lips quirked upward, her heart fluttering. She couldn't take her eyes off Isla's face, the sweet shy glance Isla gave her that could almost come off as coy. "I was a decent fan of hers back in the day."

"Well, I like listening to her music first thing in the morning. It's a great way to wake up the day." Isla stayed on the edge of her desk, her fingertips only touching it now.

Andry dragged her gaze back up Isla's arm to her face. She couldn't fault her for that logic. She was just about to speak when Isla shifted off the desk and brushed her hands down the front of her thighs. Andry's voice caught in her throat, and Isla interrupted her.

"I've got to get back." Isla was already by the door before Andry managed to wrap her head around the fact she was practically running from the room. Isla wasn't okay, that much she knew.

"Don't forget, Isla. I'm here if you want to talk."

Isla's cheeks filled with pink again, only this time there did seem to be slightly less hesitation than before. "I'll keep that in mind."

As Isla left, Andry rested in her chair, her mind still on the young woman. She let out a sigh as she took another sip from her coffee. She hoped she would be able to deepen that connection, and that someday—preferably soon—Isla would trust her enough to share.

CHAPTER
Four

ISLA'S HANDS trembled with nerves as she pulled onto the interstate. As much as she liked days like today, she hated them at the same time. It was never easy. Her heart raced, and she'd thought about turning back home a dozen and three times already. She'd left fifteen minutes later than she normally would, which she knew would only irk Lynda, but that wasn't the reason she'd done it.

She just couldn't force herself to leave any sooner.

Because until that moment there was still a chance that they would cancel and she could stay home all day in her warm bed and block out the world and all of the problems she was having. That would be ideal, wouldn't it? Biting her lip, she picked up her speed and tried to center her mind and slow her breathing.

Snagging her phone, she tried calling the second person she could think of. The first currently caused just as much tension as Lynda did. When her sister, Aisling, didn't answer, she gave up and called Wil. If they were going to mend whatever was broken between them, then they were going to have to talk it through at some point.

Wil's voice echoed through her speakers. "Hey, sis."

Isla nearly cried at the comfort that term of endearment

caused for her. She had let this go on too long between them. They'd worked through some of it when they were younger, but she never thought that her forever friend would end up shagging her stepmother.

"Hey," Isla answered. "I'm driving down to Fort Collins."

"I know," Wil answered. "Lynda left an hour ago."

Isla cursed under her breath. Of course Lynda would leave hella early and she would leave late. They were two people who never could come together easily, even before her dad had died. Isla clenched her jaw and switched to a different topic—avoidance at her best. "I was thinking about pulling another prank on Andry."

"Yeah?" Hesitation entered Wil's voice. "You don't think they're getting excessive?"

"No. I've hardly done any this year."

"But last year—"

"Was last year, and this year is brand new." Isla turned from Interstate 80 onto 25 and headed straight south toward Denver. She should just drive all the way and meet up with Wil. That would be a far more pleasant conversation than the one she was destined for.

"All right." Wil paused, the sound of dishes clanging in a sink. "What were you thinking?"

"I'm not sure. I know I want it to be a bit more of a scare prank than a showoff kind of prank." Isla set her cruise control as she got up to the right speed, crossing the state border and officially driving into her home state of Colorado.

More clanking of dishes sounded through the line. "Have you thought about dropping something from the ceiling on top of her."

"Oh, that'd be fun. Halloween is coming up soon so there's loads of things built for that. I wouldn't even have to create something."

"Don't want to drop like a bucket of water on her when she opens the door?" Wil snickered, no doubt remembering the time they had done that to Isla's dad. It had been hilarious, and he was such a good sport about it.

Isla chuckled. "No, I value my job too much for that one, I think."

"Your job or your friendship?"

Isla wrinkled her nose at being called out so blatantly on that one, but she couldn't deny it, not that she'd admit it either. Pressing her lips together, Isla thought it through. She and Andry had gotten closer throughout the years. She had a way of getting under all of the walls that Isla put up, but she wasn't someone Isla would consider a close friend, not like Wil was. "My job for sure. I think Andry would find it funny and would be a good sport about it, but not if she had to work in wet clothes for the rest of the day."

"Maybe on the last day of school then."

"Ha! That's an excellent idea. But for now..."

"Now..." Wil interrupted "...you just drop something on her like a spider or a clown face."

"Spider is a great idea. I'll have to get into the main office to do it and warn the admin so they don't freak out when it happens." The plan was already spinning in her head, the details of what needed to happen. It was a great break from the tension that she had gotten into the car with and one more step in the avoidance that she loved.

"Are you going to get a video of it this time?"

Isla raised her eyebrows as she thought it through. "I can try, but no guarantees."

"You do that."

Pulling off the highway toward the small coffee shop in downtown Fort Collins, Isla started to take those deep steadying breaths again. Wil must have caught on because the chatter died down. She always loved that Wil understood her so well. She'd longed for that same connection with someone else along the way, someone that was more romantic. Chances of that seemed doubtful at best.

"You almost there?" Wil asked.

"Yeah." Isla worried her lip, her fingers tightening around the steering wheel and her shoulders tensing. She didn't want it to be that way, but there was no way around it. She and Lynda had sixteen years of pain to work through, and that wasn't going to happen without apprehension or hurt on both sides. But they were making an effort, which was a start.

"Do you want me on the phone until you go in?"

Isla debated it. She hated putting Wil in such an awful position, to have her feel torn between herself and Lynda, but she also knew that there would be no contest. If she said the word, Wil would choose her in a heartbeat. She trusted that friendship more than anything else in her life. Wil had been the only person who had never left her.

"No, I think I'm good. I'm just going to park and walk down." Isla clenched her jaw hard, her heart hammering as she did exactly what she'd told Wil she would do. She found a spot a few blocks from the coffee shop, downtown Fort Collins bustling on a day like today.

"Okay, sis. Remember, I love you."

"Love you, too."

She nearly cried when the call ended. She hated feeling so vulnerable, and the conversation hadn't even started yet. They hadn't really dug deep into their issues yet, and Isla knew they would have to. Today had to be that day, if any of this was going to work out for Wil.

Not hesitating, because if she did she was going to stay in the car and never get out, Isla pocketed her keys and started down the sidewalk toward the coffee shop. She saw Lynda before she even got inside. She'd picked a table close to the window, a mug of coffee in her hands as she stared at someplace off in the other direction. Isla's stomach roiled hard, bile threatening to slip up her throat.

With a newfound determination, Isla stepped into the coffee shop. Lynda straightened her shoulders. She wasn't dressed to the nines like she was going to work, but she was still classy. In beige slacks with kitten heels, Lynda had on a white button up and casual blazer that didn't button in the front. Her makeup was perfect, as always, and her hair was pulled back by a large clip at the nape of her neck.

Her gaze softened when she eyed Isla standing a ways off. Isla wished she could return that softness, but she hadn't been able to manage that in years. Her knees felt like jelly as she came toward the table. Lynda watched every step she took, holding a smile that seemed somewhat out of place.

Isla slid into the chair and folded her hands. She was about to speak when a barista came over. "Can I get you something?"

"Oh, um...just a chai latte. Hot, please."

"Any espresso?"

"No." That was the last thing Isla needed. The caffeine would throw her even more into overdrive. Her hands were already shaking, which she didn't need Lynda to see, not that she would notice anyway. Isla inwardly cringed. She had to stop thinking that way and give Lynda the benefit of the doubt.

"How was the drive?" Lynda asked, sipping her drink.

"Fine," Isla answered and then chastised herself. "It was good, easy. I'm sure you had more traffic than I did."

"Construction is taking forever along I-25."

Isla's lips curled upward. "It is, but it'll be good when it's done."

They fell into an awkward silence, Isla wishing she had something to do with her hands already because she wanted to twist them together in her lap. Lynda waited patiently, something she had always been extremely good at. It was rare for her to lose her temper or say something out of turn except when Wil had been involved when they were kids. Isla glanced down at the table in front of her.

"I suppose we should talk."

"I'm here to listen," Lynda stated, her voice clear and calm.

"You can talk about whatever you feel I need to hear, but I'm only here to listen."

Isla hesitated. Reminding herself again that this was why she was there, that this was the entire purpose of driving down and meeting up with a woman she hadn't spoken to until recently. That five-year gap of silence had been during a critical part of her life, a part when she needed a mother, an adult who could help her answer questions, someone to rely on, and she hadn't had that. It had been her choice, but that didn't make the absence hurt less.

Taking a deep breath and choosing to make different decisions than she had before, Isla centered her focus. "I guess I didn't feel like you cared when I was growing up."

She risked a glance up into Lynda's gaze, seeing the massive hurt that flashed through her eyes. It stunned Isla. Lynda had always been so closed off when she'd been younger.

"I know you'll say otherwise," Isla quickly corrected, always hating to be the one hurting others and bringing them into her own drama. "But that's what it felt like."

Lynda pushed her mug in front of her, holding Isla's gaze before she nodded. "I didn't do a good job sharing with you. When your father died, I was thrown into parenting in a way I never thought would happen."

"You agreed to be our parent—"

"I did," Lynda interjected. "But I never thought I would do it by myself. I wasn't prepared. I didn't do a good job making up those gaps, and you're the one who suffered for my failures."

Isla's heart thudded wildly. She never thought in a million years that she would hear Lynda admit that. She had spent hours and days and years looking for some kind of emotion from this woman, that her father's death had affected her, that she was just as devastated and ripped apart as the rest of them, but she'd never shown an ounce of that.

"That hurt me so much growing up."

"I'm so sorry." Lynda reached out, covered Isla's hand on

the table, and gave her a gentle squeeze. "I'm so sorry that I hurt you, that I couldn't be the parent you wanted and needed."

Isla's eyes misted over, her nose stopping up. She had waited so long to hear that, to have that kind of validation. "I never wanted you."

"I know, Isla." Lynda frowned. She drew in a deep breath and let it out slowly, her back straightening. "Trust me, if I had a choice in the matter, I would have picked him over me to stay any day. You and Aisling deserved him, and he was an amazing father."

Isla wiped her eyes with the backs of her hands as her drink was set in front of her in a fancy mug. She couldn't even grab it. She met Lynda's eyes, a depth of understanding floating through her that she never had before. Isla coveted it. She held it close to her heart, not willing to let it go.

"Aisling never seemed to have that issue with you."

Lynda cracked a smile, grabbing her coffee again. "Aisling isn't like you. She's very much like your dad. You, however, I suspect take after your mother, which means that you and I are similar in some ways that Aisling and I aren't."

"What do you mean?" Isla furrowed her brow, finally getting up the courage to grab her own drink and take a sip.

"You're stubborn as a horse, Isla." Lynda grinned again. "And you don't share much in the way of what you're thinking and feeling. You keep everything very close to you unless you completely trust someone, and I think there's only one person who fits that bill."

"Wil," Isla murmured.

"Yes, and I don't want you to lose that with her."

At least they were both on that same page. Some of the tension in her shoulders eased. Isla nodded her agreement. "I won't let that go with Wil."

"Good. You should tell her that because I think she's still a little afraid it might happen, especially with..." Lynda trailed off, clearly grasping for a good way to phrase all that had happened in the past few months.

"You dating my forever friend?" Isla raised an eyebrow in a direct challenge. "Because yes, ideally that wouldn't have happened, but Wil has had a crush on you for years, and it's never gone away. No one else she's dated has ever matched up to her fantasies of you."

Lynda choked, her cheeks reddening. She slowly raised her eyes, locking her gaze on Isla's face. "Excuse me?"

Isla smirked, enjoying the fact that she could finally share this, that she could use it against Wil but also for her in some ways. Isla wasn't going to repeat herself. She wanted to keep that fun tension instead of the awful feeling she'd had in the middle of her chest moments before.

"I get it," Isla started. "I really do, but I really don't like it. It's going to take me a bit to get used to it."

"I think we're all working through that right now." Lynda finished her drink, and Isla still had almost all of hers left. "I'm glad you were willing to meet with me today. I know it's not easy, but I do think that this is the way to get to know each other again." Her stepmother suddenly seemed to become as fragile as glass as she added, "If that's something you'd like?"

"I suppose." Isla raised her eyebrows. She was doing it for Wil to begin with, but now she at least felt as though she was doing it for herself, too. If she could resolve some of this, then perhaps she wouldn't have such awful downward spirals. She just had to hope that it would be enough.

CHAPTER
Five

"WHAT'S GOING ON?" Andry's voice was soft.

Isla's heart stuttered. Her classroom was quiet, the kids long gone for the day, and she had taken to finding anything and everything to keep her there as late as possible. By that point, it was a struggle to keep herself busy, and she'd been straightening up for the last hour. Normally she would have buzzed out of there as quickly as possible to escape any of this, but for some reason, today, she couldn't bring herself to do that.

"Just straightening up for Monday." Her voice was breathy, surreal almost. It didn't sound like her when she spoke. She turned around to find Andry staring at her with those dark brown eyes, the look on her face full of concern.

"Isla." Andry's tone dropped. She stepped inside the classroom, although there couldn't be that many people still around in the school.

Isla swallowed hard, wondering if this would be her doom, if she was finally going to be called out for her depressed mood and the fact she was barely keeping herself together. She stared down at Andry's feet, the tennis shoes so well worn that they must be at least a few years old at that point. When the door clicked shut, Isla tore her gaze upward, once again meeting Andry's soft brown eyes full of sympathy.

"What's going on? Really." Her voice was so warm, and Isla wanted nothing more than to fall into her. It was the first time she wanted someone other than Wil to talk to, someone who wasn't connected to the pain, and Andry had always been there for her.

Isla had to work hard to resist it, to not give in and spill all the drama that was going on in her life. Andry's hand against her arm was warm. She stared down at her fingers, closing her eyes, and reveling in the touch. Aside from Andry, no one had touched her in months. Not adult to adult, not giving comfort or plea- sure. She shivered at it, that stone in the pit of her stomach growing bigger, but she didn't pull away. She wanted that connec- tion, even if she wasn't ready for it.

"Isla, I'm worried about you."

"I'm fine," Isla squeaked out, guilt racking her that someone would be so concerned. "I promise, just a bad day."

"Are you sure that's all there is?" Andry was so sincere.

Isla's chest cinched tight as she held back a wave of emotion she didn't want to identify. She had spent years perfecting how to put up a front of joy and happiness, that masquerade as the well- adjusted kid who wasn't orphaned at thirteen, and yet here she was nearly in tears because her life was crashing down around her.

"You know what? Let's go out tonight. We can get dinner and some drinks, my treat."

"Andry, we can't do that. You're my boss." Isla blinked away the tears, thankful that Andry had given her a pause in the conversation, whether she meant to do it intentionally or not. It took her longer than she would have liked to realize that Andry still held onto her arm, then Andry dropped her hand slowly, so it slid down Isla's skin to her wrist.

Andry nodded. "I *am* your principal, which means it's important to me that my teachers are getting along well. Come on. Katie's gone overnight to Fargo for a speech meet, and I've got nothing to do myself. You'll be entertaining my poor old soul."

"You're hardly old." Isla gave the rebuttal before she could think. She enjoyed being this close to Andry, feeling the heat from her fingers against her skin, knowing that someone may just be seeing under the surface image she presented to the world. Yet, somewhere deep in heart, she wished that Andry's concern wasn't solely based on the fact that they worked together but on something more. It had been years since she longed for that, and it warmed her that it would come up with someone she so obviously trusted.

"Come on. We can go to the Rib and Chop House."

"It's Friday night and you want to go to the hottest date place in town?"

"I thought you young kids preferred places like The Office." Andry stepped back and winked. "It's your choice, truly, but I could use the night as much as you, I think."

Isla canted her head to the side, looking Andry over fully for the first time since she came into the classroom. The concern was still there, the wrinkles around her eyes making it known. Her lips were slightly parted, and her nostrils flared as she waited with full anticipation for Isla's answer. Nodding slowly before she knew what she was doing, Isla agreed. "Rib and Chop House it is."

"Want me to drive?" Andry shifted her bag, the blazer she'd worn that day still on her shoulders. Her breasts pushed against the button, and Isla wondered if they would pull apart the sides of the blazer and just what the button up shirt looked like underneath.

Isla smiled slightly. "Are you scared I'm going to get drunk on you and drive home?"

"Can never be too careful." Andry's voice made it light, but the paleness in her cheeks said something else entirely.

Isla wanted to come back to that, but for now, she was going to have to live with getting out of this building. "You can drive if you want, or I can meet you there."

"Let's meet there. I'm giving you fifteen minutes before I call in the school resource officer to find you." Andry turned on her toes and walked out of the classroom, the bubble of hope and intimacy that Isla had felt popping in an instant.

She couldn't find her voice as she stayed in her classroom, staring at the open door and into the hallway. Fifteen minutes was barely enough time to make it across town from the school to downtown Cheyenne. Her heart pattered lightly in her chest as she struggled to get her body moving to do what needed to be done. In rapid sequence, she shoved all the things she would need that weekend into her bag and closed up her classroom. She was the only one in the parking lot when she pulled out. Andry had been right—she needed this night out more than she'd thought she did. She needed a friend, someone who wasn't tainted by the drama that her past held.

~

Isla's stomach filled with butterflies as she stepped through the doorway with Andry. They had never done this before, not the two of them alone anyway. They'd gone out with groups of other teachers and staff surrounding them, acting as a buffer. But now that it was just the two of them, Isla wasn't sure what to say. Every awkward moment in her past relationships came back to haunt her in an instant.

They sat at the table and ordered drinks. Isla gripped the menu tightly, staring at the words but not easily comprehending, nerves making the words seem to bend and swirl. They made small talk about the different options until they ordered, and Isla's hands shook as she handed the menu back over to the waiter.

Andry looked so calm, sipping her beer and staring at Isla as if she could read every nuance. Isla had been happy to escape the deep questioning in the classroom, but she may have put herself right into a situation where it was unavoidable. The war between wanting to be in someone else's presence and hide everything away tugged at her heart again. What was she even supposed to say?

"Are you going to tell me what's going on?" Andry wasn't accusatory. Instead, she was soft, imploring.

Isla shook her head slowly, staring at the tabletop and the beer that had been set in front of her. She hadn't even taken a sip yet, and it was her favorite microbrew. She hadn't even told Larisa everything.

Andry's hand was suddenly on hers, prying its way between the fingers of her clenched fist so she had to relax. Isla flicked her gaze upward and looked Andry directly in the eyes. Her heart thundered, the confession on the tip of her tongue.

"Whenever you're ready, okay? I'm not going to make you talk, but I want you to know that I'm here to listen."

"It's nothing, I promise." Isla tried to deflect, to turn down the heat that was rising in her cheeks and avoid once again.

"It's not nothing, and I can see that, but I also see how uncomfortable you are." Andry's hand vanished, and Isla missed the touch. She stared at her empty skin, the ghost of Andry against her a mere memory now, and she hated it.

"It's just some family issues." God, she didn't know how to do this. She really was like Lynda.

"With your sister?"

"Somewhat with her, mostly with my stepmother. It'll take some time to figure it all out, but we're working on it, I promise." That was as good as she could give for now. Certainly more than she'd been prepared for.

"Oh, I understand that." Andry leaned back in her seat, her gaze unwavering as she looked Isla over. "Family is an adventure when it comes to communication. I never thought I'd end up a divorced middle-aged woman, but I did."

"Divorces happen," Isla mumbled and finally took a refreshing sip from her ice-cold beer. "Sometimes they're for the better."

"Doesn't make it easy."

"It doesn't." Isla had wished at times that Lynda and her father had divorced before he died. Then they would have gone to her grandparents, but she hadn't been given that luxury, and she'd been stuck with her stepmother for the rest of her life. "Neither does staying married in some situations, I suppose."

"True." Andry's nose wrinkled slightly when she smiled. "I couldn't stay married to Chris any longer. She has a beautiful heart, but she wasn't putting in the effort for us anymore."

Isla was about to say something but stopped. Andry's tone was so sad, and there was a hint of pain underlying it all. She shifted in her seat, searching for hints in Andry's features. "It's hard to be stuck with someone who doesn't show their love."

Andry's lips parted in surprise, her eyes wide. "It really is."

Isla understood that deeply. It had been her biggest issue with Lynda from the beginning. She'd always been far more interested in Isla's dad than in his daughters, and she'd never been interested in Wil. At least not until recently. Isla bit her lip. They'd never managed to find a balance in that kind of relationship. She'd grown up ignored and pushed to the side while Lynda had worked to advance her career and never seemed to pay half a mind to the fact that she'd lost both her parents before she even got a chance to know them properly.

Isla knew she had to say something, anything to change the direction of her thoughts and move to a safer topic of conversation. Taking another sip of beer, Isla searched her memory for something to grasp onto. "My last ex-girlfriend was similar. We were fine for a while, but then she was far more interested in hanging out with her friends than she was with me. That was the slow end to the relationship."

"Was there a fast one?" Andry raised an eyebrow, pushing her long brown hair over her shoulder.

Pursing her lips, Isla thought back to that relationship. They'd been together throughout college and a few years beyond it. They'd been dating when she'd started working for Andry, but it hadn't lasted much beyond that. "No, unfortunately. I think we both hung on way longer than we should have."

"I think that's what happened to Chris and me too, except when there's a marriage to dissolve and a child in the middle of everything it's much harder."

Isla nodded. "It's more complicated for sure. I think the problem is that there's not something definitive to point to and say this is what's wrong and this is how to resolve it. When there's the slow degradation of a relationship, we're stuck in the midst of it barely even noticing it falling apart around us."

Andry was still. "That was deep."

Isla chuckled softly, not sure where to go from there. It was exactly how she thought about her relationship with Lynda. It wasn't entirely Lynda's fault that they hadn't spoken in five years, but it started well before Isla made the decision to stop trying. She had tried, for years, to keep some sort of connection with her for Aisling's sake, but when there was little in the way of reciprocation, it was impossible to keep going. Isla took a long pull from her beer as the appetizer was set in front of them. "I can be deep sometimes. I'm not all fun and pranks."

Andry chortled, the sound warm across Isla's skin. "I never thought you were just fun and games, Isla."

Isla's stomach tightened with pleasure. Andry's voice had dropped, sending shivers across her skin. Was this more than friends going to dinner? Isla couldn't be sure, but the strange part was that she wouldn't mind if it was. "But I do have some damn good pranks in there, don't I?"

"God, you do." Andry laughed, leaning forward, the smile lines creasing on her face and making her even more beautiful than before.

A lightness took over Isla, filling her completely. The conversation had turned. They'd talked about deep trauma without naming it, and it was the first time Isla had said that to anyone outside her immediate circle in ages. The closeness between the two of them intensified, and it didn't take Isla long to realize it was good. She smiled, and it reached her eyes. Her chest wasn't as tight.

"I'm planning another one for you already," Isla added, not willing to give any more hints, but she was pretty sure Andry would already suspect that.

Andry shook her head slowly, leaning in again and reaching for Isla's hand. This time the touch was like fire. Before it had been all for comfort, but this time it left Isla's stomach flip-flopping like a fish out of water. Her breath was ragged, but she didn't move her hand from the table or from Andry's.

"I always expect you to pull something on me."

Isla's lips curled upward. "Well, you'll have to start getting me back just as good as I get you."

"Is that a challenge?" Andry's eyebrow rose again as a light blush reached her cheeks.

Laughing, Isla took a sip of her beer and realized far too late that Andry was still holding her hand. This wasn't a date, was it? Andry hadn't been divorced that long, though they'd been separated for years from her understanding. Isla pried her hand away, unsure of where they stood with each other. Or where she wanted to stand.

"I think it is," Isla answered, raising her chin up when their food was set in front of them. "And I *love* a good challenge."

Where the hell was this flirtatious woman coming from? Isla hadn't seen her in years, and definitely not since that past summer when Wil had dropped the bomb in her lap. For the first time since Wil had called to ask her about dating Lynda, Isla felt free from that drama.

"You're bad." Andry winked and dug into her steak. "I'll think of something to match your creativity, I'm sure."

"I can't wait." Isla grinned broadly. This was exactly what she had needed. Andry had been able to turn her awful day into something that lifted her up and she hadn't even tried. All Andry had done was notice. How had it been that simple?

By the end of the evening, Isla couldn't stop smiling. She bumped her shoulder into Andry's as they left and went to find their cars. Andry swiftly stole Isla's keys from hand and shoved them into her own pocket.

"I'll drive you home," Andry murmured.

Isla's eyes lit up. "I'm not drunk."

"No, but you had a couple more than I did, and I don't mind. I can come get you and your car in the morning when you wake up." Andry looped her arm through Isla's and walked a little farther down the street.

"I can drive," Isla protested, ignoring how difficult it was to articulate without slurring.

Andry sighed heavily, closed her eyes, and stopped to face Isla. "Please just let me do this."

Isla halted, that same flash of something crossing Andry's face as earlier when they were talking about her divorce. Isla tensed but then relaxed. "Yeah, sure."

"Thank you." Andry started walking again, Isla's arm still looped with hers. "Just text me in the morning when you want me to get it with you, all right?"

"Sure."

They got to Andry's SUV, and Andry opened the passenger door for Isla, helping her inside even though she didn't need it. Isla almost stumbled when Andry's hand rested briefly on her lower back. The attention Andry gave her was something she hadn't experienced in a long time, and it felt amazing. They weren't doing anything they shouldn't, but there was a hint of it, of more. With the door shut and Isla sitting in the car by herself while Andry walked around to the other side, she bit her lip. Why was she thinking this? Why was she allowing herself the pleasure of this inane dream?

With Andry sitting next to her, Isla tried her best to push those thoughts to the side and ignore them. Andry was merely being a good friend and principal, and it was completely unethical. Larisa would have a field day. She wasn't in a good place for a relationship to start anyway, and certainly not with the one person she had come to trust over the years. But damn she wanted exactly that.

CHAPTER
Six

"HEY, MOMMY!" Katie stepped through the front door to the house.

Andry jerked her head up, her brow furrowing. "You're home early."

Katie shrugged. "Reagan gave me a ride."

Andry's stomach clenched. She never liked the idea of Reagan driving Katie, which was probably why she hadn't texted or called. The kid had way too many accidents, and Andry had heard through the rumor mill at school she was drunk for half of them. "How did it go?"

"Not great." Katie sighed and dropped her bags next to the couch before flopping onto the cushion next to Andry, resting her head on Andry's shoulder. Andry held the precious moment tightly, keeping the tears from her eyes knowing it would be sooner than she wanted that Katie would be gone. "Reagan and Kolby broke up on the way there, and it was a mess the rest of the trip."

"I'm sorry, baby." Andry stroked her fingers through Katie's hair. She couldn't say she was surprised, though. Most high school relationships didn't make it beyond senior year, and since

Kolby was at college, they had done well to make it through the summer. "But how did your debates go?"

"Oh, I placed."

Andry looked down, finding a giant grin on Katie's face. Laughing, she shook her head and rolled her eyes. "You couldn't have started with that?"

Katie shrugged but giggled. "I'll text Mom and let her know in a minute."

"Good. When you go to State, we should celebrate when you win." Andry kissed the top of Katie's head and shifted.

"What are we doing for dinner?"

"Hell if I know." Andry stood up and walked into the kitchen. She hadn't quite planned for dinner yet. Her mind had been completely caught up in her dinner the night before, the long drive home, and the fact that Isla still hadn't texted to go get her car, and Andry—stupidly—hadn't gotten the courage to text her either.

She pulled open the fridge door and stared blankly inside, seeing nothing that she could put together for a meal.

"What'd you do this weekend?" Katie asked.

Andry jerked at Katie's voice, the fridge door shaking as she straightened herself back up. She glanced over her shoulder at Katie, her dark curly hair looking just like her other mother. "Not much."

"Hmm...I don't buy that." Katie reached into the fridge and pulled out the to-go container of food, shaking it in front of Andry's face. "Where'd you go?"

"Rib and Chop House."

"Oh! My favorite." Katie took the container and plopped down at the kitchen table. "Oh...steak. You *do* love me!"

Andry didn't have the heart to say anything. She shut the fridge and leaned against the counter as Katie dug into the cold leftover steak. She may have Chris' hair, but she had Andry's deep affection for a good steak.

"So who'd you go out with?"

"Isla Walsh."

"She still teaches sixth grade, right?"

"Yeah." Andry crossed her arms, just enjoying being in Katie's presence for longer than a few minutes. Since she had hit her senior year running, they'd barely had time to spend together. Katie seemed to pick every extracurricular she possibly could that year.

"You go with anyone else?"

"No." Andry's voice dropped before it rose.

"So was it a date?" Katie lifted her gaze, locking their eyes together.

Andry's heart hammered hard, pushing against her ribs. Cold rushed through her, and her hands got clammy. It had definitely not been a date, and yet, she still couldn't stop thinking about it. Andry bit the inside of her cheek. "No, it wasn't a date."

Katie's eyes narrowed, as if she detected everything that Andry was trying to hide. "You and Ms. Walsh went out together, by yourself, to the hot date spot for you middle-aged single-ites, and it...wasn't a date?"

"No." Andry waved her hands in front of her. "That's not what happened. We went out to dinner after work like two adults who work together do."

"She's your teacher."

Andry sighed, her cheeks heating even more. How was she supposed to get out of this one? They hadn't gone on a date even though there were definitely date-like elements to it. Katie dropped the piece of steak into the container and leaned back into her chair.

"Mom?" A line creased in the center of Katie's forehead before she relaxed and her eyebrow rose. Her eyes were locked on Andry, defiant and confident.

"We didn't go on a date." Andry spun around and opened the fridge again, really hoping she would find something that would keep her hands busy. She needed the distraction more than anything. She grabbed the open bottle of white in the side of the fridge and reached for a glass.

"Did you *want* it to be a date?"

Andry's stomach dropped. She had wanted it to be a date, but she couldn't figure out if she'd wanted that date to be with Isla or someone else. She hadn't had enough time to think it through, but since the divorce was final, she'd wanted nothing more than to move on and start over—maybe even fall in love again. She loved her life the way it was except for the deep longing for a strong relationship like she'd once had. She swallowed hard, raising her glass to her lips and turning to face Katie with the calmest look she could manage on her face. "What would you think if I did go on a date sometime in the near future?"

"With Ms. Walsh?" Katie wrinkled her nose, put off by the thought.

Andry shook her head before taking a quick sip of wine to cover her nerves. "Just a date in general, with someone I may meet in the future."

Katie rubbed her lips together, eyeing her mom suspiciously. "Are you dating someone?"

"No." Andry laughed, an undertone of nerves in it. "I wouldn't do that without talking to you first."

"So...is this *that* talk?" Katie raised an eyebrow, her shoulders falling in on themselves.

Andry hated the fact that she couldn't figure out what Katie was thinking or feeling. This was a conversation they hadn't really broached since Chris had moved out. Chris wasn't dating, Katie had filled her in on that much—not that she'd wanted to know—but Andry also had more of her life together than Chris did.

"I don't know." Andry chugged half her glass of wine. "Do you want it to be?"

"Mom." Katie tilted her chin down. "Do you want to date Ms. Walsh?"

"We're talking about dating. We're not talking about Isla." Andry squared her shoulders, her defenses coming up in an instant.

"Well...if we're talking about dating, I guess since I'm dating and you're dating, we could always double." Katie's lips quirked upward, her eyes lighting deviously.

"Oh my god, I need more wine." Andry turned suddenly and snagged the bottle. She pulled the cork and refilled her glass. She took another long sip before eyeing her daughter over the rim. "There will *never* be a double date with me and another woman and you and whoever. I'm not doing that. You're not doing that. I'm drawing that line right here right now."

Katie dissolved into a fit of giggles. "Mommy! Oh my god! Mom! I was joking."

Andry's jaw clenched hard, unable to hide the smile that wanted to blossom on her lips. She waited until Katie calmed down enough to actually talk. "In all honesty, how do you feel about me potentially dating?"

Katie stilled, her eyes wide, but she shrugged one shoulder up and down. "I think I'd be okay with it. I guess you'll have to do it in order for me to know."

That sounded like the worst experiment on the planet, though at least Katie was thinking about it. She had always been a smart one, very aware of her emotions, which Andry had been thankful for, but it also caused some issues along the way too. Andry moved to sit next to Katie at the table. "Please let me know if it bothers you, okay? We'll figure it out as we go."

"I will. I promise."

"Good."

Katie whipped out her phone when it sounded. "Mom's coming over."

"What?" Andry frowned. "What for?"

"Financial aid."

Andry held in her grimace—barely. She stared down at her

wine glass, debating whether to finish it or dump it. "When is she coming?"

"Now." Katie flicked her gaze to Andry's face, her jaw suddenly tense. "I can tell her not to."

"Andry silently cursed in her head. "No, it's fine. Get the computer set up, will you?"

"Yeah, sure," Katie said flatly.

As soon as Katie was out of the room, Andry sighed and rubbed her temple. She slowly stood up and dumped the wine down the sink and put the rest of the bottle back in the fridge. She skulked her way to the bathroom to brush her teeth and give herself a few minutes to get her head on straight. She hadn't expected Chris to actually show up for this. She expected to have to work from memory to fill it out herself.

Andry splashed cold water on her face and then dried her skin. She rolled her shoulders and stepped out of the bathroom right as Chris came through the front door. She held out her arms, and Katie ran into them.

"I placed for finals!"

"That's awesome, kiddo." Chris gave Katie a tight squeeze, looking at Andry over her shoulder. "We did good with this one, didn't we?"

"Yeah, we did," Andry answered, her voice low with emotion. If there was one thing she and Chris would always connect on, it was their mutual love for Katie. "Come on, let's get this over with because it's going to take hours."

"I set up the laptop on the kitchen table," Katie chimed.

"Thanks, baby." Andry walked right to the table, knowing that Chris would follow. Chris had only been over a few times since she had moved out of the house, and it was odd to have her presence there again, her boisterous personality and loud voice.

Andry sat down heavily, really wishing she had figured out dinner beforehand and managed to eat something, but then again it would keep Chris' visit shorter if there was no food involved. The three of them sat around the table, and Andry pulled up the website that they needed to fill everything out.

They spent nearly two hours bent over the computer, Katie abandoning them halfway through. By the time Andry hit the submit button, her brain was fried and the wine she'd managed to drink before Chris showed up had lost its sweet effect.

"We do need to talk about a car," Andry murmured, looking over her shoulder to find Katie attached to her phone.

"I don't have money for a car." Chris looked guilty, her gaze sliding to the floor. "I can maybe throw in a few hundred."

"What happened to the savings—you know what? Never mind." Andry sighed heavily. "I'll figure it out. Her birthday is in December, so we still have a couple months to get some cash in.

"Andry..." Chris pursed her lips, her hands folded across her lap. Her face fell, her eyes looked down, and the air around her darkened. When their eyes locked again, shame swam in her gaze. "...a few months isn't going to make a difference."

"How bad is it?" Andry fisted her hands and ground her molars together. Chris' refusal to say was enough answer in itself. She'd never been the one who was good with finances, but to have wasted away the twenty thousand she left the marriage with in two years was over the top. She hit her fist against the table. "I'll figure it out."

"Thank you," Chris muttered. "I don't want her to know."

"She's not stupid. She's nearly an adult, and she's always been in tune with what's going on, you know that. I'm not going to hide it from her, and frankly, you should tell her something is up. As much as you can, anyway."

"Typical," Chris scoffed, the shame morphing into defense.

Andry's shoulders tensed, her stomach tightening, and her jaw clenching. "What do you mean? You think she doesn't know something is up? I've tried to keep her out of it, but I just can't anymore."

"Look, I'm always going to be there for her, you know that."

"But are you?" Andry glared. "Because it's taken me dozens of attempts to get you over here to fill out these forms, to corner you to have a conversation about a car for her birthday, and you're barely coming through on any of that."

"You always have to make me out to be the bad guy, don't you?"

"Jesus." Andry's raged inside, barely holding it in by a tether. She seethed. "Do you really think I do that?"

Andry stood up, her hands shaking as anger pooled in her chest. Her heart smashed a little more. She'd never thought Chris could be so cruel, but this took the cake.

"Just leave." Andry rubbed her forehead, holding her ground. "We're done here, just...go."

"Is Katie coming with me tonight?"

"Ask her. She's practically an adult. She can decide." Andry locked her eyes with Chris as she stood up.

Chris' lips parted like she was going to say something but stopped. She tried again but stopped one more time. Andry sighed heavily and pointed toward the door. She didn't even have words to speak at this point. But she did know that she didn't want to fall into the same old argument that they always seemed to have.

Thankfully, Chris stepped out of the kitchen, leaving her alone. Andry couldn't help but listen to the conversation between Katie and Chris and the soft rejection of their daughter to stay with Chris for the night or the week. Andry covered her face with her hands. They knew why. They all knew, and Katie had gone over there a few times but had largely avoided Chris when she could.

Chris' drinking had changed all of them, and there was no coming back from that. But they did need to move on.

Andry busied herself by cleaning the kitchen, waiting for Katie to come in and talk to her. But this time, she didn't. The television echoed in the living room, and Andry was grateful for the break. Another deep conversation with her daughter had to happen, but she needed a few more minutes herself.

Sticking the dishes in the dishwasher, Andry sighed heavily. She hated this. They should be better at this by now, shouldn't they? But Chris refused to pull her head out of her ass. Andry shoved another plate into the dishwasher.

"Damn it." They couldn't even have one conversation without Andry getting upset.

All she wanted was the love and adoration that they'd once had, all those years ago when they'd met, when they'd decided to start a family, when they'd been silly in love and before the damn drinking started. She loved Chris, the Chris she'd met. But this Chris wasn't that woman anymore, and that hurt as much as losing her wife.

Andry dragged in a deep breath and let it out slowly. She hated that she always seemed to fall into these thoughts when she ran into Chris. Her heart sank. She had to be the one to change that. And she wanted to—desperately. Their marriage was over, and any semblance of what they once had was gone. Andry wasn't going to stand for being second best anymore, and she wanted to put her heart out there again. She would let go of the Chris she loved if it meant her heart was free to find love again.

CHAPTER
Seven

ISLA STOOD on Andry's desk, up on her tiptoes to reach the strings she needed to attach so that when Andry opened the door to her office, the spider would drop perfectly. She should have sprung for the automatic one, and she cursed her cheapness and creativity throughout it all. This was taking far too much time and the PTA meeting was ending soon.

She wove the string between her fingers, tying a secure knot, though it took her several times to do it because her hands trembled—they'd been doing that on and off all day. Isla squatted down to slide off the desk. She was just about to reach for the door to leave when she stopped short, her fingers tight. She clenched her fist and stared up at the spider, her heart running wild in her chest. She couldn't leave. Cursing under her breath, Isla moved to the back corner of the office and whipped out her phone. If she was going to be stuck there, then she was going to make the most of it.

Setting up her phone to record everything as soon as Andry entered the room would be perfect. She could share it around with some of the other staff if Andry was fine with it, and then they could all have a big laugh over it. Isla dropped the phone three times before she managed to get it sitting upright without her jittery hands messing it up. Isla hit the record button after checking the time and shifted into the far corner against the wall with the door so Andry wouldn't see her when she came in.

Isla slid down the wall to the floor, bending her knees and resting her head on them as she took deep steadying breaths. She was stuck in the room for as long as necessary, until Andry came in. She waited for her heart to slow its thrum, but it didn't. Frowning, Isla closed her eyes and concentrated harder on calming her body.

She should have thought about the fact that she wouldn't be able to leave once she'd set everything up. She should have anticipated that this would happen. But she'd failed again. Which was odd. Usually when it came to pranks like this, she had everything planned out because everything mattered and something undoubtedly would go wrong. Guess this was what was going wrong this time. Isla clenched her eyes as panic reared its ugly head again.

I have to get a hold of myself.

With a shuddering breath, Isla blew out hot air and tried to figure out which muscle group to relax first. The room closed in on her. She clenched her eyes tight, her nails digging into the flesh of her palms until it felt as though it was piercing skin. Surely, she wasn't doing it hard enough for that. She squeezed even more, her heart racing to the point that it felt as though it was going to gallop out of her throat and into the world without her. She couldn't do this now—not when she wasn't someplace safe, when she wasn't alone.

Her chest tightened, and it was hard to breathe. Isla tried to swallow, but something caught in her throat making it damn near impossible. Fuck, she hated this. She couldn't stop it. She'd missed the damn window to get hold of herself and stop this from happening. Tears stung her eyes, and she knew in an instant that they were going to fall down her cheeks, furthering her embarrassment. Here she was, curled in a ball on her principal's floor, unable to move, and stuck where she absolutely didn't want to be.

She gasped in a breath, her heart racing so painfully that it hurt. It had been ten years since she'd had a full-blown panic attack, since Wil had held her in the middle of the night when she couldn't control herself anymore. Swallowing as she gasped in a breath, Isla struggled to get any semblance of control.

She was pathetic. She couldn't think of any other word that would define her in that moment. The weight of the world was on her shoulders because of the damn situation she found herself in. Cringing, Isla tightened her grasp on her knees and buried her face in them. At least that way, she wouldn't have to see anyone when they found her because they *would* find her. There wasn't enough time to get her shit together and get out of the office before Andry came in.

The doorknob jiggled. Isla barely heard the noise through her thundering heartbeat and rapid breathing. She turned against the wall even more, trying to hide from the inevitable. Her hands and feet tingled from the lack of circulation, from the struggle to keep herself together, and she wished she could form a void underneath her that would suck her down and away.

The spider dropped.

Andry screamed.

Isla didn't even see it, tears streaming down her face and onto her shirt. Laughs echoed through the corner edges of her mind as Andry talked to someone. Isla couldn't figure out who it was, so she gave up on attempting. Instead, she curled in on herself even tighter in the corner of the room. Everyone was about to find out. They were going to see her. They were going to know everything. There wasn't any hiding it anymore.

Andry continued to laugh, her voice loud as she came fully into the room. Isla couldn't see where she was as she cowered down.

"Isla Walsh is one of the best pranksters I know," Andry said, still chuckling as she dropped something heavily onto the desk.

Isla swallowed hard, staying as still as possible. Maybe Andry wouldn't see her. Maybe she could hide away in the corner until they were all gone, and then she could escape to her apartment and never see the light of day again. She'd be able to come back the next day and not be embarrassed to the point of needing a comp day.

"Yes! She's amazing with the kids. One of the best teachers I've ever worked with, truly."

Why couldn't she hear who the other person was? Why couldn't she figure out who they were? Everything in that moment centered on Andry.

"I can't believe she managed to do this—" Andry's voice hitched for a moment, and Isla knew she'd been made. "—yeah, I'll have to get her back. Um...do you mind excusing me? I've got some work I need to catch up on, and I'd like to get out of here before Katie goes to bed."

Isla had no idea how much longer it was because Andry left the office, her voice quieting down as she stepped into the main office area. Her heart rate really picked up then, which she'd thought was impossible. She had to escape.

"Isla." Andry's voice was so soft and gentle, it shocked her nerves. When had she come back?

The click of the door and the lock on it blasted through Isla as though her fate was sealed. She was doomed to be put on leave now. The kids deserved so much better than what she was giving them, and she couldn't afford to keep faking it.

Andry groaned as she sat down, the heat of her body against Isla's side surprising. Andry's hand wrapped around hers where she still clung to her knees. Andry was on the floor with her, scooted against her. Her breathing was steady and calm in a way Isla longed for. She'd always wanted that ease, and she'd never been able to find it.

"Isla, I want you to take deep, even breaths. Come on."

Isla said nothing, doubling down on the embarrassment as it swam through her with free rein. Her mind spun a million thoughts a second about what was going to happen next, from her firing, to being put on leave for mental health issues. Her nose stopped up, the snot lodging in the back of her throat and making it even hard to breathe.

"Come on, Isla," Andry murmured, her voice that low, tender sound that Isla had longed to hear for years. She'd never gotten that kind of connection or comfort when she'd grown up. She'd always been left on her own to deal with whatever was thrown her direction, and she had been thrown more than she could handle.

"Breathe in." Andry paused. "Breathe out."

Isla shuddered as Andry continued the mantra. The words were the only thing in her mind, circling around and around as she fell into the steady breathing that Andry commanded of her. When the intakes became longer and she slowed her breathing, Andry squeezed her hand and fingers, prying them from Isla's knees.

"Relax your muscles, Isla. Start with your hands."

Isla wanted to shake her head, the same pain cycling back into her heart, but with Andry so close to her, she couldn't avoid the calming effect of it. She just wanted to be left alone and not have witnesses to this breakdown.

"Isla," Andry cooed. "Relax your fingers."

Isla stretched her fingers out before letting them curl naturally.

"There you go."

Hot tears raced down Isla's cheeks, burning their trail down her face and cementing her depression. There was no escaping it this time, and she might as well figure out how to calm down enough to at least figure out what was going to happen with her job. Because she needed it. She couldn't move in with Wil anymore because Wil meant Lynda, and Lynda meant—her heart rate picked up again.

"Uh-uh. Isla, listen to what I'm saying. Relax your hands

again, and then move that up your arms. Deep, slow breaths only."

Isla did as she was told, keeping her face buried in her knees until the muscles she was trying to relax were in her shoulders and her neck. Then she had to move, and she would have to lift her face and see the pity written all over Andry's. She wasn't sure she could handle it.

Reaching up, Isla pushed her hair behind her ear. She opened her eyes and stared at the legs of the desk in front of her, narrowing her focus on them so she didn't have to see Andry. She couldn't bring herself to look at her. Isla scrunched her nose and clenched her eyes tight.

"There you go," Andry soothed. "You're doing great."

Andry relaxed next to her, her legs stretching out on the floor as her back leaned against the wall. It wasn't until that moment that Isla realized Andry had been just as tense as her. She'd been so surrounded by the black hole that was her panic that she couldn't even begin to focus on Andry.

"Who...who was here?" Isla managed to ask, needing to know who else she was going to have to avoid as soon as she got her ass out of here.

"One of the parents, but she didn't see you, don't worry."

Isla didn't take any comfort in that. It would be impossible for her to walk through the halls without knowing that someone out there had seen her like this. Isla dropped her forehead to her knees.

Andry made soft circles against her back with her hand, her fingers digging in every once in a while as she twisted the circle up or down. Isla wanted to tell her to stop touching her, to leave her alone, but she couldn't bring herself to form the words. Her nerves were still on fire, ready to go at a moment's notice, and the exhaustion was seeping into her bones.

"I'm so sorry," she whispered.

"Don't ever be sorry about this," Andry answered. "I wish you would tell me what was going on." The plaintive tone of

Andry's voice made telling the truth tempting, but Isla was already ashamed of how exposed she was.

"Nothing's going on."

Andry snorted lightly. "Sure, it's not, and you didn't just scare the shit out of me with a spider jumping from my ceiling."

That did bring a slight quirk to Isla's lips, but she dropped it quickly. Blowing out a breath, Isla shook her head. She shifted, trying to motivate her body into standing. "I'll get going home."

"Don't even think about it." Andry put a firm hand on Isla's shoulder. "You're not going anywhere, not yet."

Isla tensed again. She wasn't used to this. No one had taken care of her. Lynda was supposed to, but she hadn't. She'd been abandoned and left on her own to deal with everything. Andry would be nice tonight, but tomorrow was a different story. "I just want to go home."

"I know." Andry sounded confident, as though she understood.

Isla raised her chin and looked over into Andry's brown eyes. She looked...*concerned*. Isla had no idea what to say or do, but her body refused to decide if it wanted to move or melt into the floor. Eventually she gave up trying.

"What happened?"

"Nothing," Isla's immediate reply came. It was so swift she didn't even have to think about it.

"Isla..." Andry groaned. "Look, I know I'm just your principal, but I do care about you."

Isla's chest tightened and breathing became hard again. Caring meant leaving, and she didn't want Andry to leave her. She whispered, "I know."

"Then trust me. Please."

Tilting her chin up, Isla locked her eyes with Andry's. The panic in her heart stilled. She clenched her jaw tightly and nodded, not moving her gaze from Andry's face. "Okay."

"What happened?"

"I panicked."

Andry nodded as if she already knew that. Their hands were locked together tightly, and Isla had no idea when that had happened, but she held on firmly, using the touch to center herself. She hated this. She hadn't had panic attacks since she was a kid. Lynda hadn't known what to do with her, and Wil had more often than not been the one to find her. She hadn't ever thought it was because Lynda didn't want to help her, but it was all because Lynda had no idea what to do with her at the time. Andry was different. Her voice was calm, the care was in her gaze, and Isla knew she could trust her. She wanted to be able to take that leap. Squeezing Andry's hand, Isla tried to silence her doubts and rampaging thoughts.

"I'll be fine soon, I promise."

"I know you will." Andry offered her a half-hearted smile. "But until then, until you're better than fine, I'm going to be right here, okay?"

"Yeah, okay." Isla was nearly in tears again. She hated how she felt after these things, so caught up in the moment that she couldn't parse her way through to see the end. "Can we...can we just sit here?"

"For as long as you want."

"What about Katie?"

"She's almost eighteen. I think she can forage through the fridge for dinner and manage to survive."

Isla's lower lip quivered, her eyes watering. Lynda had made sure there was dinner for her and Aisling every night, even if she hadn't been home to eat it with them. "You should be with your daughter."

Andry canted her head toward the side. "Does that mean you're coming home with me? Because I'm not leaving you here alone, and I'm not even sure I want you going home by yourself any time soon."

Panic swelled in Isla's chest again, but it wasn't the same kind as before. This was panic over being a burden. If she was a burden, then she would lose their friendship because no one could handle the trauma she came with.

"Hold on, stay right here with me." Andry tightened her grasp on Isla's hand. "We can go there when you're ready, but let's get you back on your feet first, okay?"

"Yeah, okay." Isla focused on the touch again, on relaxing her muscles like Andry had told her to. "I'm so tired."

"I bet." Andry chuckled lightly. "What do you say we give it a few more minutes and then we go back to my house? I can order us some food, and you can pick at it as I'm sure you'll do. We'll put on *Pride and Prejudice* with Keira, and then we'll zone out for the rest of the night."

Isla wasn't sure what to say. It honestly sounded like the perfect night, aside from the panic attack that landed it for her. She nodded slowly, breathing out a sigh of relief. "That sounds good."

"Good." Andry didn't move. "Just tell me whenever you're ready."

"Okay." Isla stayed where she was, closing her eyes and steadying herself even more. She had been here so many times in the past. She'd honestly thought she was done with them. Licking her lips, Isla looked deep into Andry's eyes. "Let's go."

"You're ready that fast?"

Isla shrugged. "To be honest, I don't think I'll ever be ready to move."

Andry smiled. "Well, as much as I would love to stay here on the floor with you for the rest of the night, I think my knees and butt will start to protest soon."

"Exactly." Isla exhaled slowly. "Thanks, Andry."

"Anytime, Isla. Please believe me when I say that."

"I do." And Isla meant it. For the first time, she had someone to trust other than her forever friend, someone she just might be able to get close to. And she wanted that—desperately. But she knew it wouldn't last—it never did.

CHAPTER
Eight

THE AIR HAD a chill to it as Isla stood outside right before the last bell of the day. Her heart thundered, knowing exactly what was going to happen in the next ten minutes. She'd agreed to it—stupidly—because she wasn't sure she wanted to be there anymore. Andry walked around the playground like she owned it.

Kids ran up to her to give her hugs, parents caught her attention and had quick conversations before snagging their kids and departing from the playground. Isla wrapped her arms around herself and drew in a shuddering breath as her own kids filed out the door and walked away. That was the biggest advantage to teaching sixth grade. Her students didn't need her to wait for parents to arrive like the littles did.

Andry caught her attention, raising her hand in Isla's direction and giving her a full looking over. Ever since that night last week, Andry had kept a close eye on her. They had done exactly what Andry told her was going to happen. They went back to her house, ordered dinner, and watched historical romances until nearly one in the morning. Isla had stumbled her way back to her apartment that night, barely able to keep her eyes open and had triple the amount of coffee the next day. Her heart warmed at the thought, though. Andry had done everything possible to keep her distracted but also keep the space open for talking if that was what she wanted. Isla nodded at Andry and turned on her heel to go back inside the building.

By the time she got back to her classroom, her cellphone had a message on it. Her stomach clenched before dropping, and when she looked up, she found none other than Lynda standing in her doorway. She had on a nice pair of slacks and a teal colored blouse with a cardigan over her shoulders.

"So this is the classroom." Lynda's lips quirked into a smile as she stepped inside.

Isla's shoulders tensed, her worlds colliding as Lynda came closer. She had a small smile on her lips, and Isla had to calm the panic that reared its ugly head again. She purposely stayed still, wanting a few extra seconds to catch her bearings before she allowed Lynda in even more. "Uh...yeah. I would have met you at the door."

"I figured you were busy still, and it gave me a chance to wander the halls."

That irked her, even though it shouldn't, and she knew that. She didn't want Lynda to have freedom in her world—not yet. Isla twiddled her thumb over her fingertips, trying to figure out what to do and say next. Lynda had never been in her classroom before. Isla had never offered because by the time she'd landed herself a job, they weren't talking anymore—or barely, anyway. "Well, this is it. It's not much."

"Hey, Ms. Walsh!" Alice ran into the classroom, her backpack jingling as she raced through the door and around Lynda.

Isla's cheeks heated with embarrassment as she looked at Alice with curiosity. "Did you forget something?"

"I wanted to talk to you about that history project."

"What about it?" Isla flicked a glance to Lynda, hoping that she didn't comment on anything.

"If you're busy...I can always ask tomorrow."

"No, it's fine. This is a visitor to the school today. Lynda...

Walsh." Isla stuttered over her last name, realizing all too late that Alice would figure out the connection immediately. Curse Lynda for never changing her name back after her dad died. They'd only been married a few years at that point, and she could have easily done it.

"Walsh?" Alice's eyes lit up. "As in..."

"My stepmother, yes." Isla nodded. "What questions did you have about the project?"

"Um..." Alice turned and faced Lynda full on, eyeing her over carefully. "Isn't she a bit young to be your stepmother?"

Lynda's lips curled upward, her eyes lighting, but she tilted her chin into her shoulder to hide the reaction. Isla flicked her gaze back to her student.

"Alice," Isla corrected. "The project."

"Right. You wanted us to build a 3D model, but I don't know what to make."

Isla pursed her lips. "You need to decide that. It can be anything related to the ancient Greeks before the year one thousand. I can't tell you what you're going to build."

"Oh." Alice frowned.

Isla knew that look well. She was always trying to find out the best way to get the best grade possible, and Isla had taken to withholding answers in order to get her thinking more. "You have a week and a half to get it done, so I would start doing some research and see what you're interested in."

"I guess." Alice shifted uncomfortably, looking over Lynda before back at Isla again. "Thanks, Ms. Walsh."

"See you tomorrow."

Alice left the classroom, and Isla was plunged into silence with Lynda again. She nervously shifted her stance as Lynda focused on her and came forward. "Ancient Greeks?"

Isla shrugged. "Standard history lessons."

"I'm glad you found something you love, truly." Lynda's lips curled upward into a small smile. "That's all I ever wanted for you and Aisling."

Doubtful, Isla grunted as she moved to her desk and shifted some papers around. She'd never felt she could explore her passions when she was growing up. "I don't think that's quite true."

"Why would you say that?"

"You always pushed me to get better grades."

"Because you could do better than you were."

"It was a struggle just to get to school most mornings, even though school was a safe place that I didn't have at home." Isla grimaced, realizing the words had slipped from her mouth when she hadn't meant them to.

Lynda froze on the spot, their eyes locked in a battle Isla wasn't sure she would win. Isla was about to step forward and apologize, try to backtrack the conversation, but Lynda held her hand up to stop her.

"I deserved that," Lynda murmured.

Isla wanted to stop the pain flowing between them, put it back in the box she'd torn it from. This discomfort was more than she could handle, and she hated being the cause of it. Her instincts to avoid kicked in.

"Isla, do you—" Andry stopped short in the doorway to the classroom, her eyes wide and lips parted. "Sorry, I didn't realize you had someone in here."

Isla shook her head, the lump in her throat getting bigger by the second. She threw Andry a "help me" look and hoped she'd see it and step into the situation. Thankfully, she did, because she came farther into the classroom and held out her hand to Lynda. "I'm Dr. Murphey. It's good to meet you."

Lynda blinked and suddenly her perfect face was back in place, and she held her hand out. "I'm Lynda Walsh."

Their fingers connected, and Andry shot Isla a curious look. "It's really good to meet you then. I'm Isla's principal."

"Ah." Lynda pressed her lips together hard. "Not the first time I've had a run in with her principal."

Normal people would expect that Lynda would know who

Isla's boss was, but their relationship was anything but normal. Isla hadn't had a moment to even begin to tell Lynda about her day-to-day. Andry stepped back and crossed her arms over her chest. "Are you visiting for the week?"

"Just the evening," Lynda supplied. "I live in Denver."

"Oh." Andry's eyebrows rose up again.

Isla inwardly cursed. She hadn't told Andry anything about her life growing up or the fact that her stepmother actually lived close by. "Lynda came up to see the classroom."

"First time?"

Isla knew Andry was prying, but she let it slide because her added presence was a different kind of tension in the room—one that she could handle. "It is. We haven't managed to find a minute for Lynda to come visit. She works in investing and is rather busy."

Isla shot Lynda a look, one that meant it was the truth but also relating to their earlier moment of spilled beans. Lynda hadn't been there for her, and Isla wasn't going to let that piece of information drop now that it was out in the open.

"I'm a bit of a workaholic, as I'm sure Isla could share with you." Lynda waved her hand slightly, placing a perfect smile on her face. "I'm afraid I wasn't around as much as I should have been."

The gut punch was unexpected. Lynda had never admitted that before, never stepped up to say she was part of the problem. Isla's lips parted in surprise, her gaze locking on Lynda's impassive face. She still didn't look like she'd meant it, but words had weight, didn't they?

"Oh, I understand that. Now that Katie—my daughter, she's almost eighteen—is getting older, it's so much easier to slip into staying late because she doesn't need me home when she's home anymore."

Lynda gave a wry smile. "It's a pleasure to watch children grow into adults, isn't it? And Isla has done a beautiful job of that. I'm very proud of her."

Isla's heart raced. She'd never heard those words from Lynda. What was happening? The world spun as she gripped onto the edge of her desk, leaning against it. Andry came closer, standing next to her, the silent support she'd come to expect lately and had begun to crave.

"I am too," Andry added. "She's one of my best teachers in the whole school, but don't tell anyone else I said that."

Isla lifted her chin, staring into Andry's eyes. Andry freely gave praise, but she'd never heard those words with quite that tone before. Isla moved to look at Lynda, who seemed to be beaming. What planet had she been dropped off on? Because this wasn't the one she grew up on.

"Right, anyway, I invited Lynda up today to see the school and where I work."

"An excellent idea." Andry stayed put.

Isla had given her an out if she wanted it, but she stayed firmly in place right next to her. In fact, they stood close enough that if Isla leaned a little farther to the side, they would touch. "I thought I'd give her a tour of the building and then maybe we could go on a walk?"

Lynda nodded, keeping her hands to her sides. "That sounds like a good idea. It's been a long time since I've stepped foot in an elementary school. Since Aisling's last day."

"Some days I never wanted to leave," Isla murmured, her voice low. "School was the safest place I ever had after..." she trailed off, not wanting to explain to Andry what she was talking about but knowing that Lynda understood the unspoken words deeply.

"Yes." Lynda nodded and wrapped her arms around herself as if to protect herself from the bad memories. "I understand that."

Isla breathed out relief, a moment of connection between the two of them that she could handle. They had both lost something that day, and they would never get it back. "Do you want to join us for the tour, Andry?"

"Oh." Andry's eyes widened. She locked her gaze on Isla, no

doubt trying to read between the lines and figure out exactly what Isla wanted. Isla gave her a slight nod to indicate the offer was real. "Sure."

"Good." Isla stood up and walked toward the door of the classroom. "This is my room. I've been here the last seven years since I was moved to sixth grade. I actually had Andry's daughter in my classroom."

"I'd forgotten about that." Andry smiled, and they shared a look.

When Isla looked back at Lynda, her heart skipped a beat. In all the years that they hadn't spoken, they had each missed so much. Wil knew everything, but Lynda was left squarely in the dark about anything Isla had done since junior year of college. Lynda's smile faltered, as if the same realization hit her.

"She was one of my best students," Isla commented, still not taking her eyes off Lynda.

Andry laughed. "You were *not* her favorite teacher."

"Of course not. I have high expectations for my students. They have to work to earn their grades."

"Exactly." Andry touched Isla's arm. "Where are we starting?"

"Oh, I don't know." Isla glanced at Lynda. "Let's just walk the halls."

Lynda silently moved toward Isla and Andry, as if she wanted to ask another question but hesitated. It didn't take them long to walk the school, Andry's easygoing presence a life saver for the forty minutes they were there. But then she left. "Want to take a walk?"

"Sure."

Isla breathed in the fresh air as soon as they stepped outside. She started down the street with her arms crossed. The playground was nearly empty, only a few straggling students playing with their parents. Wind whipped around her as was typical that time of year in Cheyenne. She blew out a breath, trying to decide where to start with Lynda.

"I know I wasn't the parent you needed," Lynda said, her

voice so quiet that Isla wasn't quite sure she heard her. "You needed your father, but beyond that, I wasn't the stepparent you needed."

Isla wanted to talk her off the ledge, to make it so Lynda didn't think so harshly of herself, but she resisted the urge. She had felt that way for years, and it wasn't her place to make Lynda feel better. "You weren't. You were cold, absent, and I couldn't ever figure out what you wanted."

"To not be there." Lynda's face pinched tightly with her brutal honesty. "You were young when I started dating your father, but I never thought...none of us ever thought he would die. I wasn't ready to be a parent, and I'm not very good at it."

"I don't know about that." Isla bit her cheek because she dove right into what she hadn't wanted to talk about. "You and Aisling seemed to get along well."

"Yeah." Lynda stopped walking as they reached the end of the block. "Because Aisling is exactly like your dad when it comes to personality. I understand her. But I don't understand you, and there were so many times I wanted to walk away because it was so fucking hard."

Isla snorted. "You've been hanging out with Wil too much if you're cursing like that."

Lynda gave her a sly smile, but the confession rang true between them. Once again, Isla resisted the urge to placate and avoid. They continued down the sidewalk, Isla sending Lynda looks every so often as they went.

"I was unprepared for parenting," Lynda continued, "and no amount of studying or reading or talking to therapists made me good at it. I did want to leave, Isla, but not because of you or Aisling. I was scared of what it meant to be the only person you had left and what I would have to do to be an effective parent. And I couldn't leave you two because despite what it may have looked like or felt like for you, I do love you. I have since before I even met you."

Isla cocked her head to the side, her brow furrowing. Her

heart raced, and she couldn't process what Lynda was saying. She'd never heard those words from her. "What do you mean?"

"Your dad would recount stories about you and Aisling when we were dating, and I fell in love with you then. By the time I met you, I was already in love with how much joy and happiness you brought to your father." Lynda rubbed her hands together nervously before locking her gaze on Isla's. She whispered, "You're so much like him in some ways, and in others, you're so much like me."

Isla's stomach twisted, her heart racing. She'd thought that before, but to have Lynda say it as well confirmed it. "I'm like you?"

"In some ways, yes. We have a dark streak in us that Aisling and your dad didn't, a place we don't let anyone into if we can help it, but Isla, it's so worth it to let someone in—even if it's not me."

Isla was so uncomfortable. She shifted and started walking down the next block, needing the time to think through everything, though she suspected she'd be weighing that comment for a long time. They walked in silence down half the block before Isla dared say something again. "I needed *you* after he died."

"And I failed to be there for you," Lynda said, so sure of the comment.

"You did." Isla was nearly in tears again, but she didn't want to cry in front of her. "I had no one else growing up except you."

Lynda stopped walking again, reaching out and touching Isla's arm. "I wasn't a good parent for you, Isla. I know that, and I'm so sorry that I didn't see what you needed and work harder to fill that space. You needed support, comfort, love, and I didn't give that to you."

It wasn't entirely true. Isla hadn't gone without all of that, but when she'd been so lost in grief, Lynda hadn't even noticed. When she'd been thrown to the winds of depression again, Lynda had sent her to a therapist and let them figure it out. "You didn't care."

"I did. I do. I do love you. I'm just not very good at showing you that I do."

Isla drew in a ragged breath. She kept her shoulders tight, even though she wanted to move in and wrap her arms around Lynda like she was a little girl again, like she had on Lynda's wedding day, when they'd been so happy, when her dad had been there. Raising her gaze, Isla couldn't stop the tears as they fell down her cheeks.

"I didn't meet your needs," Lynda said softly, her voice nearly carried away by the wind. "I'm so sorry that I couldn't give you what you needed."

"I miss him so much." Isla wiped her cheeks furiously, trying to get the tears away from her.

"I do, too. Every day. Your dad was the first person I ever loved, and I never thought anyone could live up to him." Lynda touched Isla's arm. "He was the best dad around, wasn't he?"

Isla nodded.

"He knew exactly what you needed, when you needed it, and he never hesitated to stop everything to be with you."

"He didn't." Isla smiled through her tears. She'd always put her dad on a pedestal after he died. He wasn't perfect, and she had to work hard to remind herself of that because it was too easy to blame all of her problems on Lynda, but she didn't deserve that either. Lynda had only been there by circumstance, and while no one was perfect, she had done the best with what they had all been handed by fate. "He did love you, though. I remember him coming into my bedroom late one night with Aisling to tell us he was going to ask you to marry him."

"He did?" Lynda's eyes watered, her cheeks reddening.

"Yeah. He took us the next day to buy you the ring." Isla glanced down, finding the wedding ring on Lynda's right hand, the sapphire in the center of the diamonds still brilliant and beautiful. Reaching out, Isla took Lynda's hand and studied the ring. "He loved you."

"Your dad was a man who loved with everything he had, and he never held back."

"No, he didn't." Isla stilled, dropping Lynda's hand. She wanted to be like that, to be able to push past the blocks in her life to be exactly who her dad had raised her to be. Someone who had love, who gave love, and who wasn't afraid to risk it all for family. Here she was doing the same thing for Wil and Lynda. If she couldn't do this, then she would never know what true love was.

CHAPTER

Nine

I NEED DRINKS.

Andry stared at the text message, her stomach clenching and worry working its way up into her chest again. Isla had been off that day when her stepmother had been there. Andry had to resist helping out more. Her go to was always to take care of the people she loved, but that had hurt her in the past and she was on her own because of it. Pursing her lips, Andry debated what to do.

Inviting Isla to her house could easily violate boundaries, not that they hadn't already done that post-panic attack, but those had been special circumstances, right? Andry hovered her thumb over the keyboard, debating what to say. They could go out somewhere, but she loathed the idea of being surrounded by people that night. She needed a break from it after the week she'd had. She might be lonely but being in a sea of people would only exacerbate that.

Come over.

She pushed her phone into her back pocket after sending her reply and stared around the house, already warming at the thought of company. Katie was gone again, but this time she was at Chris' for the night. Andry swallowed hard at the messy state of her house and started to pick things up quickly. She had no doubt that Isla would show up in the next ten minutes, ready for exactly what she had asked for.

Andry was just setting the jackets in the closet when the knock came from the door. She opened it, finding Isla shadowed in the evening light, her eyes wide, her full lips quivering, and her hair around her shoulders. Andry's stomach fluttered with arousal. Isla was stunning, there was no doubt about that. Almost all the boys in the upper grades knew it, and some would frequently come back to visit their old teacher when they reached junior and high school, hoping that she would pay them some kind of attention.

"Am I allowed in?" Humor glittered in Isla's eyes as she looked up from her spot on the stoop.

"Uh...yes, of course." Andry had to clear her throat, embarrassment hitting her full force once she realized she had been staring and hadn't managed to catch herself quickly enough. Inviting her over might not have been the best idea. Andry moved to the side and held open the door while Isla stepped into the house. Isla touched her fingers softly to Andry's arm as she came in, a shiver running right up Andry's spine.

"Thanks," Isla whispered as she walked by Andry. "I didn't...I didn't have anyone else to call."

"It's no problem." Andry's stomach hadn't stopped whatever it was doing, and that annoying voice in her head was far too loud. She needed to shut it up because Isla was her teacher, and she couldn't be thinking about her like that, especially with the state that she was in.

Andry led the way into the kitchen and opened the fridge. "I've got white wine, and that's about it."

"No vodka?"

Andry shook her head, cold washing through her. Hard liquor had been Chris' choice of drug, and she'd unknowingly avoided it since their separation, even opting for beer, which she preferred even less than liquor.

"White wine it is then." Isla stepped next to Andry as she straightened up with the bottle in hand.

She set the bottle on the counter while rummaging through the drawer for the corkscrew. Isla was so quiet it was unnerving. Add in that look with the feelings swimming through Andry's stomach, and she knew she was in trouble. Yes, she had wanted to find love again, but she hesitated to find it in someone like Isla. All she had done for years was take care of Chris and it wore her out. Years of being a caretaker and living into that role had been her undoing, and she wouldn't put herself into a position like that again. But damn, Isla was adorable when she looked like a walking mess. Andry poured two glasses and handed one over to Isla.

Their fingers brushed, and tingles raced through her and up into her chest, settling in her breasts. *Yeah, that's going to have to stop immediately.* Andry nodded her head toward the back door. "Want to do a late fall campfire out back and tell me why you desperately needed drinks tonight? I figured you'd be hanging out with Lynda more."

Isla snorted and rolled her eyes. "No. She went back to Denver. I didn't invite her to stay the night."

Andry's forehead wrinkled as she moved toward the back door, wrenching it open. "But you invited her for the day?"

"Kind of?" Isla sighed as she followed.

"What do you mean *kind of?*" Andry put her drink on the small table between the chairs that sat adjacent to the fire pit she'd bought right after her divorce was finalized. She certainly hadn't used it as much as she'd hoped, but they didn't have many more nights when it would be warm enough for this. Isla moved with her and pulled the grate off the firepit so they could fill it up with wood and paper. It'd been so long since someone had been there to help her. Even Katie didn't want to sit out there with her most nights, and just having the calm presence of another adult was unexpectedly comforting.

Isla hummed, bringing her wine glass to her lips as she sipped and dropped a log into the pit. "Before this summer, I hadn't spoken to Lynda in over five years. Lynda and I didn't really get along, and as soon as Aisling finished college, I was out. I didn't need her anymore, so I stopped talking to her."

Andry recalled how stiff Lynda had seemed in the classroom and the way Isla and she had kept their distance. She put another log on the fire and grabbed some of the paper she had lying around to get everything set up. "I bet that was a hard choice to make."

"No, it was easy, actually. Not much different from what it had been." Isla rested her hand on Andry's shoulder for a brief second before she slipped down into one of the lawn chairs and wiggled to get comfortable. "My panic attack was because I'd agreed to let her come up here."

"Oh?" Andry raised an eyebrow, letting the silence steal through them. She had wondered, but Isla hadn't shared that day and she'd let it slide because there were enough emotions running through them at the time. "So she asked to come?"

"I offered when I saw her the other week in Fort Collins. I didn't think it would happen so soon. She usually works constantly, so I didn't think she'd ever take a day off to come up here."

"You saw her in Fort Collins?" Andry was confused, as if she was missing a piece of the puzzle, the most important chunk of it to understand the whole story. Andry snagged the torch and lit up the fire, settling next to Isla in the other lawn chair. She stretched out her legs as the flames licked at the wood, catching. "Isla...if you haven't talked to her in five years, why now?"

Isla tensed, every muscle in her body tightening sharply. Fear stabbed in Andry's stomach that she may have just pushed her into another panic attack, but luckily, she remained calm. Isla took her time answering, spinning the wine glass on her knee as the logs really caught and flared to life. Isla continued to stare into the liquid.

"My childhood sucked."

"I suspected it did." Andry sunk into the conversation, putting her heels up on the edge of the fire pit to relax and just enjoy the company of another adult, someone she was finding she deeply cared for.

"What?" Isla lifted her chin, those bright blue eyes locking on Andry's face.

Andry shrugged slightly, looking Isla's smooth face over. Sunlight faded out west of town, and the fire cast a beautiful glow against her skin. "You never talk about growing up. That's usually a pretty good sign that it wasn't the greatest."

"I loved my dad. Really, I did." Isla gave her a wan smile and went back to her drink. "He was the best dad on the planet."

"Most parents are that way for their kids." Andry was still waiting for the other shoe to drop. Isla was neatly avoiding whatever it was, and Andry was practiced enough to see it a mile away. When Isla didn't add to her comment, Andry decided to push. If they were going to be better friends and if she was going to dig deeper into this relationship—whatever it turned out to be—then she wanted to know more about what made Isla who she was. "Why do you use past tense?"

Isla's eyes were filled with tears. Without hesitating, Andry put her glass down, leaning over the small table, wrapped her arms around Isla's shoulders, and tugged her in for a hug. She held on tight as Isla let sobs tear through her, as they racked her body and made it difficult for her to breathe. Andry rubbed her hand up and down Isla's back and nuzzled her face into Isla's shoulder, closing her eyes. To have her arms full felt amazing, and her heart gave a sharp tug to remind her of that.

Andry hadn't thought the night would go this way, but she was glad to see the outpouring of emotion. Isla couldn't keep that bottled up any longer. It wouldn't be good for her. Andry held her close. When Isla had calmed enough, Andry finally found the question she wanted to ask.

"Did you stop talking to Lynda when he died?"

"No." Isla cleared her throat and wiped the tears from her

face. Isla sat back in her chair, her hands shaking when she picked up her wine again. "My dad died when I was thirteen. Lynda raised me and Aisling after that."

"Your stepmother? What about your mother?" Andry's heart rapped hard, already knowing the answer to the question. It was either because Isla's mother was unfit or it was because she was dead, and she suspected the answer before Isla even said it.

"My mom died when I was four, when Aisling was born. I don't really remember her much despite Dad trying. But Lynda didn't know her, so when he was gone..."

"There wasn't anyone to help you remember her." Andry's heart broke at the thought but reveled in the tie between them strengthening.

"No one but grandparents, and we only saw them once a year."

"Oh, Isla." Andry pulled her in for another hug, this one quick. "I can't imagine how hard that was on you."

"It was, and Lynda didn't really seem to care about me. She and Aisling were fine, but when it came to me, it didn't seem like she cared at all. I couldn't...I just couldn't live up to her standards, but it wasn't like she ever explained them to me either." Isla rubbed her palms across her thighs, easing the stress and tension out of her body.

"She favored Aisling?"

"Well, I saw it that way, but I guess..." Isla sighed heavily "... after talking to her today, I'm not sure that's what it was. I think she and I are too alike, and it was easier for her to talk to Aisling because she's like Dad."

"That would make sense. Katie is exactly like Chris in some ways, which means I know how to talk to her better than Chris does. Well, and Chris isn't really in a good state to have any deep, meaningful conversations with Katie anyway." Andry frowned into her wine glass. She hadn't been able to talk this frankly with Chris in ages, not to mention sitting to have a glass of wine together to enjoy company.

Isla tilted her head and reached out to touch Andry's arm. "What do you mean?"

Andry's breath caught in her throat, and she pulled herself together as quickly as possible, using her principal face. Her stomach was tight and her chest constricting as she made eye contact with Isla. She shouldn't have let that slip. "Nothing. What about Lynda? Why are you talking to her now?"

Isla held Andry's gaze for another moment before sighing heavily and falling in on herself again. "My forever friend, Wil, and she are dating."

"You're shitting me!" Andry tensed, her eyes wide, and her heart racing. And she thought her secret was bad.

"No." Isla scowled. "Wil's always had a crush on her, for years, but I didn't think this would ever happen. But I can't talk to Wil without feeling some sense of impending doom. I hate it. I really do."

"No wonder you're struggling so much right now." Andry set her glass down and added another log to the fire. They should have s'mores or something, but since this was an unplanned girl's night, she hadn't been prepared.

"Yeah. So I'm talking to Lynda so I can play nice with Wil, but also...I'm just tired of being mad at her, you know?"

"I understand that completely." She really did. She was tired of being mad at Chris, tired of the tension that came up any time they were in the room together. Andry reached for Isla's hand and squeezed lightly. Giving up her anger was a goal of hers before Katie graduated high school, but ultimately, she knew it was probably going to take Katie's four years of college to accomplish that one.

"I want everything to be easier," Isla whispered.

"It can be, with a lot of work." Andry knew she was talking as much about herself as she was Isla and her situation.

"Yeah." Isla trailed off, and she sucked down the rest of her wine. "I'm sorry about the other day, really."

"What day?"

"The spider day."

"First, that was one of the best damn pranks you have pulled on me so far, but second, don't worry about it. That's what friends are for, right?" Andry knew as soon as the words were out of her mouth that she shouldn't have said them, even if she was considering them to be truer by the day. She had to remind herself that Isla was her teacher and that added in some extra boundaries Andry had to navigate and keep in place, but it felt so right in this situation. Not to mention, Andry really needed a friend, too.

"Yeah, that's exactly what they're for, which means I should probably have a conversation with Wil."

"That's true." Andry's lips quirked up. "But tell me about Lynda, not her personally, but when you were little, was she okay? Before your dad passed away?"

Isla frowned, a line creasing deeply in the center of her forehead.

"I mean...Katie brought up dating to me the other day, and I just...I don't know how it would be for her to have a stepparent to add in there." Andry had been thinking about that conversation a lot. The loneliness and pang from Katie being away at college was already hitting her, and if Katie was gone, she had far less excuse to hold off on dating.

"You went from dating to marriage quick," Isla teased, her voice lighter even if the smile didn't fully reach her gaze. It was at least a good sign that they were moving in the right direction.

"Well, I mean...I guess." Andry's cheeks heated and she finished off her wine. She was going to need more depending on the turn this direction took. "Do you think I should date around before I date seriously?"

"It's whatever you want to do." Isla covered Andry's hand this time, their fingers lacing. Isla looked nervous, her lips pulled tight, and her eyes narrowed, but she didn't let go.

Andry's heart hammered in her chest at the touch, warmth seeping deep into her bones and her body in a way it hadn't in years. She missed this, the connection, the communication, the ease of it all. She hadn't had that with Chris in a very long time.

"Do you want to date?"

Is she asking me out? Andry's stomach flopped then flipped. Her heart was in her throat as she parsed through the words again before hearing them as Isla meant them. "I've been thinking about it more often lately, and with the conversation with Katie, I guess, yeah. It wasn't planned, but she thought when we went to dinner the other night that it was a date and so the conversation came up."

Isla chuckled, but the sound didn't ring quite true. Andry's palms sweated, and she struggled to not jerk her hand back from Isla's grasp. She had no idea why she wanted to do it other than she was embarrassed that Katie would think that—or was it because she'd wanted it to be a date somewhere in the back of her mind? Cursing herself, Andry clenched her jaw and swallowed hard.

"Did you like Lynda when your dad and she started dating?" Andry had to keep the conversation going because wallowing in her thoughts with Isla holding her hand was going to be her undoing.

"It was different. I was really young when they were dating. I don't think Dad introduced her to us until after they were serious and had been dating for months. He mentioned her to us, but we never met her until he was ready to propose." Isla scrunched her nose and closed her eyes. "He did take us to pick out her rings before he proposed as a way to get us involved. Katie's in high school and nearly in college. It's going to be a completely different experience for her. And you're divorced, not widowed."

Andry wasn't sure how different that really was, since it was still introducing a potential parental figure into Katie's life, though parenting would be far harder with Katie being older, if not impossible. "I guess, but when did you and Lynda start to have issues?"

"When Dad died. She wasn't really involved with parenting until then."

"Until she had to be, you mean?"

Isla nodded slightly. "Lynda was really young. She's about twenty years older than me, and I don't think she was ready for that role."

"But she got stuck doing it anyway."

"Yeah. Shit happens."

Andry laughed at that. It was one of the truest statements she had heard, and it rocked through to her core. Squeezing Isla's hand, Andry rested back in the chair and bent her knees as she shifted the position of her feet on the rim of the fire pit. She had imagined her life in a completely different way than it had ended up. Not that anything was happening with her and Isla, but it was certainly a start to dissolving the loneliness she'd never thought she'd have.

"What was good about having Lynda in your life?" Andry wanted to pry more, but she was also genuinely curious how this would affect Katie in the end. Her daughter had been her priority for so long, but if she was an adult, she didn't have to be anymore. That wouldn't happen instantly, but it would happen sooner rather than later.

"I guess the biggest is that when Dad died, we got to stay in the same house with someone who was young enough to raise us and not die."

Andry wrinkled her nose. "That's morbid."

"Well, when your mom dies when you're four, conversations about death and dying are pretty commonplace. Dad was worried about it, I'm sure, which is why he made plans for what would happen if he died." Isla didn't let go of Andry's hand as she set her empty wine glass on the small table.

"Good thinking on his part." Andry and Chris hadn't really thought about it all that much, but having it affect a family like that it would make sense. "But there wasn't anything else about it?"

"She was really good at helping with math homework." Isla shrugged. "My goal for now is to forgive her and forgive myself. Then maybe we can find some sort of neutral ground."

"Not a bad idea." Andry wasn't sure if Isla was being flippant on purpose or if she was really struggling to find something good to say about Lynda. Surely it couldn't have been that bad, right? Andry reached for her wine glass. "Do you want any more?"

"Yes." Isla grinned up at her.

Andry left the tension in her wake. Just how much depth did this woman have? Andry dragged in a deep breath as she headed inside. Her shoulders relaxed as she poured each of them a second glass and searched to see if she had stuff for s'mores hidden in the pantry. She wanted to make Isla happy, ease some of the discomfort she'd come to the house with. It didn't surprise her that she wanted to take care of Isla, that's what she always did. But this time felt so different from before. This time she enjoyed it.

CHAPTER
Ten

"I'M WORRIED ABOUT YOU."

Wil's voice was clear through the phone, and Isla wasn't sure how to take it. She was worried too, but she hadn't managed to admit that to anyone. Although she was pretty sure that Andry knew it, and she was glad she could rely on that relationship because she needed it. "There's nothing to worry about."

"Ha! That's amusing." Wil sounded like she was driving, the echo of wind and the sound of her voice farther away than if she was holding the phone right next to her ear. When the distinct clicks of her blinker echoed, Isla knew for sure Wil was in her car. Her tone turned somber when she spoke again. "I am really worried about you."

"I'm fine. I promise you." Isla frowned, hating that she automatically pulled back so much. Normally Wil would be the first person she called if she was struggling, but with everything going on, Wil couldn't be that person anymore. Even if Isla wanted her to be.

"I remember you saying your therapist banned that word when we were in high school because it doesn't tell anything about how you're actually doing."

Isla groaned and rubbed her temple. She folded into her

couch, pulled the blanket up tighter around her chest, and closed her eyes. Wil would remember that, wouldn't she? Nothing ever slipped by her. Isla clenched her jaw before finding an answer. "I don't know what you want me to say."

"I want you to say what you're feeling." Another blinker echoed, and Isla frowned into her phone. It was late Friday night, and she was exhausted from the week. With Lynda's visit and getting close to the end of the first quarter, she was running herself ragged emotionally and physically.

"I'm *fine*." She was, actually, and she didn't know how else to explain it. Her night with Andry had done her wonders, and she'd truly found relief from the drama encroaching around her.

"Isla..." Wil's voice brooked no argument, the warning in her tone clear.

"Nothing is going on." Nothing except Wil dating Lynda when she knew how Isla felt about her. Or Lynda suddenly showing interest in her for the first time ever, or the totally inappropriate feelings she was sometimes having for her principal and maybe newfound friend. Isla pressed her lips firmly together.

"Bullshit."

Isla sighed heavily and changed the topic. "How was your week?"

"Oh, we're not avoiding this. Nope." Wil chuckled. "You're going to talk to me whether you want to or not because I have it on good authority that you're not doing as well as you think you are."

"And who the hell would have told you that?" The rest of Isla's defenses immediately rose to protect her, and she was ready to stand up, pace, and make sure she knew who was talking behind her back.

"Lynda. Who else?"

Isla cursed silently. The two of them teaming up against her wasn't going to result in anything good. They'd been careful not to talk about all three of them together, but it had to come up at some point, didn't it? "What did she say?"

"Not much, honestly."

Isla wanted to growl. Getting used to the two of them talking to each other was taking more effort than she'd anticipated. She didn't like it. She was so used to Wil being her confidant when it came to Lynda. Now it felt as if Lynda was spying on her to boot. "What did she say?"

"Truthfully, *not much*. She did tell me I needed to come visit you soon so you couldn't avoid me."

It didn't sound like any Lynda that Isla knew, but then again, she didn't really know Lynda. "What does that mean?"

"It means you need to let me into your apartment in about two minutes."

Isla's heart skipped a beat and then sped up. Her leg muscles were poised, ready to run to the front door to see her forever friend standing there. Instead, Isla stayed motionless and stared at the door in question. "What?"

"I'm just driving over the College Street bridge right now."

"What!" Isla immediately sat up, her feet planted on the floor. Her heart raced. "You're in Cheyenne?" Energy coursed through her like it hadn't in months, and she vibrated from it.

"I am, and I should be at your place in less than two minutes."

"What the hell, Wil?" Isla launched up and immediately raced around her apartment to clean things up so she didn't look like the absolute slob she had been. Normally, she wouldn't care, but it was worse than normal and Wil was already concerned about her. And it was possible she'd been letting too many chores slide recently. "When did you leave?"

"Ugh, not soon enough, but I took 85 to avoid the nasty traffic."

"Oh my god. Are you seriously here?" Now she was excited for the first time in months.

"About to turn onto Pershing." The amusement in Wil's voice was evident.

Isla still didn't know what to say. She ran toward her

bedroom to grab a pair of sweatpants so she wasn't just walking around in her underwear and T-shirt like she did when she was having a shitty day or week. Which had been almost every day and week for a while.

"In the parking lot."

"Holy crap."

"You hide all the sex toys yet?"

"Shut up." Isla ended the call and opened her front door to look out at the parking lot. Wil wasn't there. Not only was she not there, but it took well over another three minutes for her to pull into the parking lot. She had lied about how close she was.

As soon as Wil stepped out of her car, Isla ran down the stairs from her apartment and straight up to Wil, wrapping her arms around her in the most comforting hug she had had in a very long time—almost. The one Andry had given her definitely topped this. Wil held on tight, not letting go as she buried her face in Isla's neck. They stayed there, way longer than was appropriate, but Isla hadn't realized just how much she had needed this. She needed her forever friend, the one person who had been with her through just about everything.

"Fuck, I missed you," Wil muttered. "I'm not doing this again. This was way too long."

Isla pulled back and punched Wil on her shoulder. "Well you went and got a girlfriend and a new job in the same month. What did you expect?"

"Ugh, not to lose you." Wil still hadn't let her go.

Isla stayed put, pressed against her forever friend. She clenched her eyes shut tight as tears started to form. She hated that she did that so easily now. Sniffling, she straightened up and broke the embrace. "How long are you staying?"

"All weekend! And you better bet we're getting hammered tonight." Wil shifted to the trunk and pulled open the hatchback. Along with her backpack of clothes and the pillow she always brought with her when she could, there was a huge box filled with bottles of liquor.

"I would like to be alive by the end of the weekend," Isla said with a laugh.

"Yeah, yeah. We won't drink it all, but I do expect we'll get good and drunk tonight."

"You're an idiot." Isla reached for the backpack and pillow, leaving the awkward box carrying to Wil. They walked together up the stairs to Isla's apartment, setting everything down in the living room. Wil ran to the bathroom while Isla dragged her stuff into the bedroom where they would both stay like they'd always done since they were kids.

She was mixing two screwdrivers when Wil came back in and touched her arm lightly. "You eat dinner yet?"

"No," Isla said easily. She'd completely forgotten about eating, which was a habit she was falling into again. "Want to order something?"

"Yes. I'm starving. Skipped food in favor of getting on the road quickly." Wil took her drink and a long sip from it. "I'll even pay for dinner."

"What? Is your new job paying you that well?"

Wil shrugged slightly. "It pays enough. Better than what I was making, but not a ton more."

"Well, more is better." Isla chinked their glasses together and walked toward the couch to sit on it. She grabbed her phone and ordered their favorite go-to dinner whenever Wil visited. "So... you really didn't drive up here because your..." Isla choked on the word "...because you were worried, did you?"

"Damn straight I did. Well, queer. Damn queer I did." Wil gave Isla a big old grin before chugging half her drink. "You've had me worried for months now, and frankly, it's about time we hashed this out."

"There's nothing to hash out," Isla mumbled as she stared into her drink. She hadn't worked through what to tell Wil about moving forward. She still felt stuck back in that call that night, the questions, the need, the desire in Wil's voice. Isla hadn't been able to deny her the one thing she had wanted since they were teenagers. But giving Wil permission had come at a huge personal cost.

"You are such a bad liar." Wil shimmied deeper into the couch, her nice loafers already discarded under the coffee table and her ankle crossed over her knee. She eyed Isla carefully, expecting an answer of some sort.

Isla balked. "So I played that spider prank we'd talked about."

"Don't think that gets you out of the conversation."

Isla groaned, setting her drink down heavily on the table in front of her. "Fine. What do you want to talk about?"

"What is going on? Really and truthfully. I need to know."

Her stomach swirled. She'd never hidden anything from Wil on purpose before, but she had internally put a distance between them since Wil had asked to date her stepmother, since she'd said it was more than just a fling. Isla blinked at the sudden tears as the loneliness she had caused herself slammed hard into her. She had been the cause of it all, she had no doubt of that, but it had been self-preservation.

"Isla," Wil cooed, leaning forward and touching her hand. "I still love you."

"I know." Isla sniffled. "I love you too, sis."

Wil's lips curled upward, the smile reaching her dark brown eyes. "Good. So let's stop the bullshit and get to the point. I know this is because of Lynda and me—"

"I don't want you to stop seeing her. Not because of me."

"All right..." Wil said slowly, though she looked far from convinced. "But that doesn't mean you can pull away from me either. You're the only family I have left, and I'm not going to let you go that easily."

Isla's lips twitched and she nodded, finally raising her gaze to make eye contact. "You're my family, too."

"Good. Now that we've established that. What's next?"

"I..." Isla looked across at the window, the blinds closed to keep the light out. The scent in her apartment was stale and musty, as if she hadn't cleaned or taken care of anything in weeks

—which was accurate. She had closed in on herself hard. It was why she was back in therapy—because she knew she needed to get out and stop this self-destructive behavior. When she locked her eyes on Wil again, she shrugged as she took the risk to share what she had avoided. "It hurts."

"Me being with Lynda?"

"No, not that so much as anything with Lynda. You know, she was never really there for me, Wil. I waited years for her to be the parent I wanted her to be, but that wasn't within her capabilities, was it? She was an absent parent, but I don't think it was because she chose that." Isla couldn't stop the words from tumbling out, the dam finally smashed to smithereens. "She was thrown into this as much as I was, and I never gave her a chance, because let's face it—she's not Dad, and she never could be."

Wil blinked, her eyes wide. "Did you just have a therapy session all to yourself there for a second?"

Isla chuckled a little. "Yeah, I guess I did. I just...when she came up here the other day, it was the first time I truly saw *her*, I think."

"Oh?" Wil cautiously took a sip of her drink. "And what did you see?"

"Me. And it was fucking scary." Isla laughed. "When did I end up so much like her?"

Wil's laugh rang through the room, echoing off the walls and filling Isla with the companionship she had longed for. "You've always been like her. Probably why she and I get on so well."

"That's TMI." Isla shuddered.

"You're an idiot," Wil fired back. "But an idiot I love. You're both insanely focused and driven. I like to call it tunnel vision. You get stuck on one thing and don't think about or see anything else. But here's something else I want you to consider."

"What?" Isla pulled away cautiously, the tone in Wil's voice not lending to the idea that she was going to like anything that was coming.

"You and Aisling weren't the only ones struggling with the fact your dad died."

Isla furrowed her brow and wrung her hands together. "What do you mean?"

"Lynda isn't..." Wil paused, her gaze at the ceiling before she shifted again and finished her drink in one fell swoop. "Lynda loved your dad with everything she is. I know they weren't together for very long, but there is no doubt in my mind that when she falls, she falls hard."

Isla knew what Wil was saying without the words being necessary. They were in love, and she was going to have to make a monumental effort to be okay with their relationship moving forward because it wasn't going away any time soon. A stone filled her stomach, weighing it down. She grabbed her drink and raised it up to Wil's empty glass. "To love?"

Wil's cheeks reddened as she lifted her empty glass so they could clink. "To love."

Isla took a sip of her drink, and Wil leaned forward and stole the glass from Isla's hand, taking a long sip from it.

"We need more!" Wil stood up and went to the kitchen.

Isla let out a breath, her heart racing as she leaned down on her knees and closed her eyes tightly against the onslaught of emotions running through her. She had to make this work. Somehow, someway, she had to figure this shit out because she couldn't be without Wil in her life. Isla stood up when their food was delivered, grabbing the bags from the driver and bringing them to the coffee table.

Wil sat down heavily and set Isla's drink in front of her even though it had only been halfway drunk to begin with. Isla picked through the food and put it all out, snagging the plastic silverware so she could dig into the cheap Chinese she had ordered. Wil groaned as she took the first bite.

"Damn this is good. I should have eaten before I left. I know, but I just wanted to get here."

Isla laughed a little. "You're always starving."

Wil narrowed her gaze. "Not always."

"Sure." Isla rolled her neck. Today was going to be the start of a new day for her. Moving forward, she needed to be better than she had been, and she needed to give Lynda and Wil the benefit of the doubt. That was going to be a bitter pill to swallow after all these years, but she could manage it, especially if it meant Wil was going to be happy. "So what are we doing the rest of the weekend if you're stuck here with me?"

"Oh, I don't know, but we're definitely going to be drunk tonight and tomorrow."

Isla rolled her eyes. "Are you leaving Sunday or Monday morning?"

Wil narrowed her gaze as she thought. "We'll figure that out later."

"Good. I could use some time with my forever friend."

"Always!" Wil bumped her shoulder into Isla's.

One step at a time, that was all Isla had to remind herself. Fixing things with Wil was going to be far easier than fixing them with Lynda. Today was about the two of them. She could figure out Lynda tomorrow.

CHAPTER
Eleven

ISLA WAS HUNGOVER, but hell would freeze over before she admitted it. She struggled to get through the day, and she'd used the lunch period to try and reset herself to be a better teacher and focus on the kids more than she had that morning. Wil had left in the wee hours before the sun rose, and it had been one of the best weekends she'd had in a long time.

By the time the kids came back in after recess, Isla was beat. Her feet were dragging, and despite the extra coffee she'd had that day, she was barely managing to push through. She sat down at her desk as her kids did some reading time, quiet music filtering through the speakers she had set up in the classroom.

She had to blink three times at her computer to bring it into focus. She had two hours left until the end of the day, and she planned to leave on time, crawl into her bed, and crash until the next morning. She could afford not to get any work done that night. She grabbed the mouse on her computer to wake it up and start inputting some grades, but it didn't work.

Hitting the spacebar on the computer, she confirmed the issue was with the mouse itself and not the computer. Frowning, Isla glared at the mouse in question and gritted her teeth. The last thing she wanted to do that morning was play techie to fix her computer so she could get what little work done that she could manage.

Ducking down, Isla followed the cord to the computer tower. She pursed her lips as she found it attached and fully plugged in. Wondering what could possibly be wrong, she popped her head back up to find Andry standing at her doorway, her arms crossed, and her eyes directly on Isla.

Her stomach fluttered, that gaze direct and complete in some way she couldn't quite put words to. Andry's lips quirked upward in the corners, and even from across the room, Isla had a sinking feeling that something was up, but she couldn't stop staring at the beautiful woman in her doorway. This wasn't an ordinary visit. If it was, Andry would have come in and started talking to her already.

Isla tried her mouse again to no avail. Andry started laughing, and she moved from the door and sauntered across the room like she owned everything in it and more. Isla waited patiently to see what was going to happen, her finger absently clicking on the mouse to get the computer to work, as if it was going to magically be fixed in the next few seconds.

"Having an issue?" Andry's voice was so smooth, like the wine they'd drunk at her house all those nights ago.

Isla's stomach flopped, her heart racing and her mind clouding even more. If she wasn't struggling to keep up that day, she would have easily figured out what was going on. She liked that direct stare. She wanted more of it. It wasn't a look of compassion or pity, but it was filled with excitement and—dare she think—a thrill she longed for. One she definitely couldn't have with Andry.

"My mouse won't work," Isla said, keeping her voice low so as not to disturb her students. She risked a glance toward them, and all eyes were riveted on the two of them. She gave them a curious look before turning her chin up to Andry again. "I was going to put in a work order request for it."

"Oh, I think we can figure it out, don't you?" Andry came

around the desk, leaning over Isla's shoulder and down to the computer.

Isla's heart fluttered, her eyes back on the computer screen before she flicked it over to her students who were still watching her. Did they see this, too? Did they see her cheeks red with arousal or did they simply see the principal helping a teacher?

"Did you see if it was plugged in?" Andry's tone was low, quiet, her breath on the side of Isla's face even though she wasn't that close.

"Yeah." Was her voice breathy? What was happening to her? If they didn't have an audience of twenty kids, Isla would be doing something entirely different.

"Hmmm." Andry looked up at the classroom. "Did any of you mess with Ms. Walsh's computer?"

"No!" Most of them answered with shakes to their heads.

Something was up. Isla couldn't figure it out, her brain moving far too slow for things to make sense in that moment, but she really wished she was completely with it. Andry was pulling one over on her, she knew it, but she couldn't figure out what the hell was going on either. And between the hangover and the arousal, she wasn't going to be able to parse through it.

"Andry," Isla whispered, turning to look directly into those eyes. But all that did was give her a fuller view of what she desperately needed to avoid. "What's going on?"

"Oh, I think we can fix this problem real easily." Andry reached for the mouse and flipped it over.

It took Isla longer than she wanted to admit to focus on the mouse. Her brain clicked slowly once, then twice, and she narrowed her gaze at the piece of technology. A piece of scotch tape was pressed tightly over the light on the bottom of the mouse, preventing the laser from sensing movement. Laughter bubbled up in her chest inexplicably, and she reached for it, ripping the tape off and shoving it onto Andry's arm. "You pranked me!"

"I did." Andry looked up at the classroom and winked. "And it was a good one."

It was the simplest prank Isla had seen in a long time, and she was impressed by Andry's ability to pull it off. Clearly the kids had known what was happening, so she was going to have to figure out how Andry managed to get in her classroom and put tape on the mouse without her knowing.

Laughing, Andry walked out of the classroom with a wave and a bow to the kids. Isla had to work hard to get the class under control again, but she managed to get them to finish their reading time and move on to the next subject for the day.

~

Exhaustion hit Isla as soon as the last bell rang for the day. She managed to get her kids off where they needed to go, and then she picked up her bag and shoved it full of all the work she knew she wasn't going to do that night. She closed up her classroom and headed out to the parking lot, keys in hand so she could get home, take a hot shower, and sleep for the rest of the night.

She stopped short when Andry spotted her and started in her direction. Her stomach did the same fluttering thing it had done earlier that day, and she was thrown right back into that moment —to Andry leaning over her shoulder, to Andry's breath on her cheek, to the scent of Andry's shampoo. Her heart rate rose, pattering away like she couldn't control it. Because she fucking couldn't.

"Hey," Andry said, her voice deep as she reached Isla. "Taking off for the night?"

"I'm beat," Isla answered truthfully. "Wil came up for the weekend, and we may have stayed up drinking a little more than we should have every night that she was here."

Andry smiled slightly, her cheeks red, but Isla couldn't tell if that was from the bite in the fall air or if it was from something else. "I hope you didn't mind the prank today."

"Mind it?" Isla chuckled and shook her head. "I loved it. It was brilliant. I'm still not sure how all the kids figured it out."

"Oh!" Andry's eyes twinkled with mischief. "They had no clue, but I think they suspected something might be up."

"Well, for the record, I did, too." Isla winked and then chastised herself for it. She was flirting! She definitely should not be doing that with her principal.

"What tipped you off?" Andry stepped in closer, Isla's back against her car.

Her heart thundered, and it was getting harder to breathe. "Oh um...you didn't have any reason for being in my classroom."

"Really?" Andry shook her head. "I'll have to come up with a better one next time."

"Will there be a next time?" Isla raised an eyebrow, trying to catch herself, but it was so hard. Everything was moving at lightning speed whereas most of the day it was like molasses. She couldn't handle being catapulted into it. Andry's hand on her skin startled her, and she looked down to see Andry's fingers wrapped around her forearm, sure and warm. She was doomed.

"Do you want there to be? Because I think it's your turn." Andry winked and then turned to smile at a student who passed by.

Isla had nearly forgotten they were standing in the middle of the parking lot at the school, her entire vision had become this woman. Not her principal, but someone far more intriguing than that, someone who held the reins for the next few moments.

When Andry turned back to her, Isla stuttered. "What do you mean it's my turn?"

"Well, this was payback for the spider in my office, so tag, you're it." Andry winked again and shifted her stance to walk away.

Isla reacted in an instant, reaching out and grabbing hold of

Andry's hand to pull her back. Her entire body was tense with the moment, every fiber of her being tuned in to what was going to happen next. She could barely breathe the words that were on the tip of her tongue. "Are you challenging me to a prank war? Because you *will* lose."

"I'm pretty sure I can bet on that." Andry grinned, the smile reaching her eyes before it hit her lips.

"Are you sure you want to do that?"

"More than anything." Andry stepped away from her again, but Isla followed this time, moving to the sidewalk and away from her car. She shifted as a few lingering students walked by with their parents.

Isla cleared her throat. "Are you sure you know what you're asking for?"

"Absolutely." Andry put her hands on her hips, moving her blazer to the side as she stared Isla down. "Do you know what you're getting into?"

Isla had no clue, truthfully. Her body was telling her one thing, and her mind was so slow to catch up she couldn't even make sense of it—not yet at least. This had ramped up out of nowhere, hadn't it? Her gaze flitted all over Andry's face, trying to figure out exactly what they weren't saying, but she couldn't untangle her way through the conversation because she was still so damn tired and hungover.

"Andry," Isla lowered her voice, but she stopped there, not quite sure what she was going to say this time. The challenge Andry had issued was direct and clear, but she wasn't sure how much she could push back on that either. She was brilliant when it came to pranks, that was nothing new, but how much of a strain would it put on their tentative friendship, not to mention the fact that Andry was still her boss?

"Yes?" Andry asked, her face falling slightly, as if the teasing had been pulled out of it.

"Um...did you want to get dinner this week?"

Andry blinked, clearly confused by the turn in conversation, but Isla hadn't figured out what else to say or what she wanted to say. Not that this was any better because it almost sounded like she was asking Andry out on a date, which she wasn't, *was she?*

"I mean...I'm too tired to go out tonight, but maybe on Friday or something?"

Andry canted her head to the side. "I think I could manage that. I'll have to talk to Katie first and see what plans are in the works for this weekend."

Right. Isla cringed. She'd forgotten. Andry's birthday was coming up, and of course she would want to spend it with family instead of her. Still, perhaps her next prank could revolve around that if she could pull something together quickly. "Sure, if you have time and whatnot. I just...I'm sure Wil won't be coming up again this weekend, so I'm free if you have time."

Again, Andry cocked her head to the side, her hair blowing in the breeze and her eyes locked on Isla's face. Heat kissed Isla's cheeks as embarrassment swam through her again. It wasn't a date—she had to keep reminding herself that and had to make sure that she made that clear. When they went to dinner, it couldn't be a date night place, even though it would be a Friday night. Isla cursed. She wasn't making this any better.

"Let me check with Katie. I want to make sure she's doing okay before I make any plans, okay?"

"Is something wrong?" Isla immediately stepped forward, ready to help out wherever she needed to. She loved Katie like she did all of her students, and she didn't want her to suffer unnecessarily.

"No, nothing's wrong." Andry waved her hand in front of her. "I just like to run our schedules by each other so that we can plan to spend time together when we can, that's all."

"Okay. Phew. You had me worried for a minute there." Isla moved the back of her hand across her forehead in an over exag-gerated sign of relief. She was so on edge, and she needed to stop immediately. She was going to fall into whatever mess she was about to create, and she couldn't do that, not when she'd seemed to find her feet again after a few days with her forever friend. "Anyway, I'm going to go home and rest up for tomorrow."

"See you then." Andry winked again, and Isla's heart fluttered this time.

Her entire body was warm with pleasure, and she couldn't control it. She wanted to stop it immediately. To go down that path wouldn't lead anywhere good. Isla spun on her toes, her body dizzy from whatever the hell was going on with her. She got to her car, and when she turned the engine and looked through the front windshield, she was met with Andry's unwavering stare.

"I'm so screwed," Isla muttered to herself. She raised her hand and gave a half-wave and half-smile to Andry as she pulled out of her parking spot and didn't look back. She couldn't look back. She had to separate herself from whatever was going on because she needed to think clearly. This—whatever this was because she hadn't figured that out yet—was a bad idea. She knew it from the instant it had popped up. It would be the end of her, and especially with everything she was going through just then, it would be a really bad idea to get any of those ideas in her head.

Isla got home and parked her car. She pressed her forehead to the steering wheel and took a few deep steadying breaths. She was insane. It was as simple as that. She wanted to get out of her depression, not jump into a relationship of any kind, and certainly not a relationship with her boss. Nope. That was a bad idea on all fronts, but she would take the interest in something like that as a really good sign that her depression was finally working itself out of her. At least in small bits at a time.

The resolution with Wil that weekend had done each of them wonders, and Isla was already making plans for the next time they could see each other. It had to be sooner than the last time because she couldn't go that long again. They needed each other, hands down. Isla smiled at that thought and grabbed her bag as she got out of the car.

On her way up the stairs to her apartment, she put all thoughts of dating and relationships into the back of her mind. What she needed now was to get her head on straight with help from her therapist and confront her problems. Then, and only when she was ready, could she explore the possibility of dating again, and that was years off if she had any say in it.

CHAPTER
Twelve

ANDRY SAT in her car in the parking lot of The Office, the biggest date spot in town for young adults, and her heart hammered relentlessly. She'd already talked herself in and out of dinner that night so many times she'd lost count, and it was a push from Katie that had landed her in the car and thus in the parking lot outside.

She was too far in at this point. She couldn't stop thinking about Isla all week, and the prank proved it. She'd never allowed herself to stoop to that level with another teacher before. She let them play as many pranks on her as they wanted, but she'd always maintained the boundary that she was the boss and they were her employees. Somehow, Isla had weaseled her way underneath that wall.

Andry grimaced and looked down the parking lot to the door. Isla was inside already. She'd texted when she'd gotten there to put their name on the list for a table. Andry shuddered as she took a deep steadying breath and let it out slowly. Her goal for the night was to put some of those boundaries back up and stay in the frame of boss and employee. She couldn't allow herself to put that on Isla when she already had so many issues going on.

Pocketing her keys, Andry got out of the car and walked toward the building. Her shoes felt as though they had bricks in them. Something in her told her this was a huge mistake, that she would regret it, but she couldn't stop the disaster from happening. Stepping through those doors, Andry stopped short at the sight of Isla waiting on one of the small benches in the entryway.

She was gorgeous, her bright blonde hair pulled back in a ponytail, her blue eyes dark in the lighting of the hall, her jacket wrapped around her shoulders as she gave Andry a beautiful smile. Andry was doomed. Her stomach flopped as she moved to sit next to Isla and rest back, her pussy clenching when their thighs touched on the small bench that was crowded with people.

"It shouldn't be too much longer," Isla stated.

Andry barely heard her, a loud buzzing sound in her ears over the realization that just hit her. She liked Isla more than she liked any of her other teachers, which she knew, but it was also a different kind of attraction. Isla was someone she wanted to get to know more outside of teaching. Andry rested back into the bench and clenched her jaw to try and bring herself back around.

"How was your week? I haven't seen you much since Monday." Isla bumped her shoulder against Andry's.

A shiver ran through Andry at the touch. "It was busy. Had some issues to work through, but nothing major."

"That's good." Isla gave her a hard look, probably wondering why Andry wasn't sharing more than that or continuing the conversation.

Andry hated it, but she did need to put some walls back up between them. She had taken too many down, and the fact that she was interested in dating again shouldn't mean that her attention was turned solely on Isla. There were plenty of other queer women in Cheyenne who she could date if she wanted, or she could even go outside of Cheyenne. Gritting her teeth, Andry silenced the voice in her head. "How was yours?"

"Better." Isla smiled. "I think I'm making some good progress with sorting out issues, and I did talk to Lynda again."

"Did you?" Andry raised an eyebrow. Talking about Isla's stepmother seemed a safe way to avoid any deeper conversations that could lead them down a dangerous road. "How did that go?"

"Pretty well, I think. I'm trying to talk to her at least once a week now. I need to call Aisling and let her in on everything. I'll do that this weekend sometime."

"She doesn't know?"

"I didn't want to get her hopes up if it wasn't going to work out. She's been smashed in so many ways by this."

"Always trying to play the role of big sister?" Andry chuckled lightly and stretched her legs out in front of her.

Isla's smile faltered slightly. "I try to be a good sister, yes. I try to avoid being her parent, which she yelled at me plenty for when we were growing up."

"I can see how that would play out, especially with your unique situation. Katie always wanted to be a sister, but we never had any luck after having her." Andry rolled her shoulders. "So when she was about eight or nine we gave up."

"You wanted more kids?"

Andry flinched at the age-old hurt brought up. It didn't sting as much as when she'd been younger, but it still hurt. Deflecting was the easiest way out. "Don't you think it's a bit odd to find teachers without kids? I mean, they are our world."

Isla shrugged. "I don't know. I don't have any, and don't really intend on it. My school kids are my kids, and that's enough for me."

Andry frowned slightly, her eyebrows raising. "I guess that was a bit judgmental of me."

"But not an awful judgment. There are a few of us out there, you know."

"I suppose."

"Isla?" The hostess came out into the waiting area.

Isla stood up immediately, and Andry moved slower. They

hadn't even gotten to the meal yet and Andry was already strug-gling to keep everything surface level. They followed the hostess into the restaurant, sitting by the large windows that gave them a perfect view of the parking lot. With drinks ordered seconds later, Andry stared over the menu. She'd eaten there several times throughout the years and had a particular love of the bruschetta chicken meal. When she glanced up to see if Isla had decided yet, she was startled to find Isla's gaze locked on her.

"What are you having?" Andry asked, her voice wavering.

"I like the pork chop with apples and onions."

"Good choice." Andry's heart thundered again when Isla's stare didn't move. It was as if they weren't actually in a room full of other people, but it was just the two of them, sitting together intimately while they discovered what else they could have hidden behind all those layers.

Isla leaned forward slightly. "I wanted to compliment you again on that prank you pulled on me. If I hadn't been so tired, though, I wonder how long it would have taken me to figure out."

Andry shrugged, lifting her drink to her lips as she eyed Isla over the rim. "We'll never know, will we?"

Damn. She was flirting—again—and she couldn't stop herself. She needed to because this was a road that would lead nowhere good, and she had to be the one to pull back on it. Isla certainly wouldn't like her, not like that. She'd been a friend to her, someone she could rely on during this trying part of her life, because her usual support system was mixed up in the drama. That was all this was. Andry wanted to believe that, so she swal-lowed it down and repeated it in her head.

"I don't know. You pulling one over on me is something I never expected."

But had she hoped for it? Andry silenced the question in her mind, refusing to be the one to ask it even if she desperately wanted to know the answer. Andry had known when she planned it that it was a departure from her norm, that she was moving outside the boundaries of a relationship with a teacher, but she hadn't been able to resist either.

"How long did it take you to think of that?"

"Oh, not very long." Andry stared down at the table between them. "It may or may not have been a prank that I played in college on the dean."

Isla's eyes bugged out, her lips parted in shock. Andry gave a subtle but firm smile, knowing that Isla was probably completely surprised by that tidbit of information, but it was true. She had at one point been the one who pulled pranks on her teachers, and her family, and any of her friends who would allow it. She'd even pulled a few good ones over on Chris once upon a time. Over the years, she had lost that desire for fun.

"April Fools used to be my prime day," she confessed.

"Are you kidding me?" Isla narrowed her gaze.

Andry's stomach started that flip-flopping again, the butterflies also working in there. "No, I'm not. I used to be very adept at pulling pranks."

"I'll have to up my game if you truly meant to challenge me."

"Oh." Andry barely remembered that moment in the parking lot—well, the conversation they were having. She definitely remembered standing there with Isla so close to her, touching her arm, and the fact that their voices were hushed until Isla got in her car and that long look Isla had given her before she'd pulled away. "I mean...that was...we don't have to."

"Oh no! I fully expect it now." Isla leaned forward and touched Andry's hand briefly, heat searing through her skin and into her chest. "The game is on."

Andry shivered, needing to get Isla's hand off her arm because it was way too intimate. That boundary needed to go back in place, and she had to be the one to put it there. She shifted her hands from the top of the table into her lap.

When the plates of food were put in front of them, Andry

was forced to sit up more and lean in close to Isla. She dug into her dinner, her mind swirling with different ideas of how she could keep up the walls when they just seemed so determined to fall down.

"So what will you do next?" Isla asked.

"For what?"

"For a prank." Isla giggled and eyed Andry over as if she found the entire situation amusing.

Andry licked her lips and set her fork down, drinking the water she'd asked for after finishing her one and only beer of the night. "Why would I tell you what prank I'm going to pull?"

"You won't. I know that. But I'm trying to sit here and judge what kind of tricks you have up your sleeves." Isla laughed lightly. "How good are you at this game?"

"Oh lord." Andry shook her head. "I'm not as devious as you, I promise. The whole spider thing was on a different level than what I'm used to."

"But old dogs can learn new tricks." Isla raised her eyebrows in quick succession.

Andry laughed. "Did you just call me old?"

Isla lifted one shoulder and dropped it. "I think both of us are well aware of the fact that you're older than me. I was twelve or thirteen when Katie was born."

"Jesus." The gut punch was hard, and Andry groaned. "You're a baby."

"Compared to some, yes, but not compared to you." Isla leaned in again, her hand resting on top of Andry's. "You're *not* old, Andry."

Oh the way Isla said her name. Andry's mouth went dry, and she had to reach for the water to wet her tongue. If Isla kept this up, she was going to be doomed to flirting whether she wanted to or not, but Andry had to admit, it was nice being the center of Isla's attention. It was nice to feel this close with someone again, and with Katie's blessing to attempt dating again and see how it went, she was far more interested in trying that out than she had been a few months before.

"I'm pretty old to start dating again." Andry inwardly cringed, the topic of conversation taking a dangerous turn, and she was the one who had instigated it. She didn't want Isla to think this was actually a date, especially since they hadn't talked about that and it couldn't be—not with them working together.

Isla cocked her head to the side. "How old are you, really?"

"I'm forty."

"And you think forty is too old to date again?" Isla didn't look convinced, and truthfully, with the statement out in the open, it sounded pretty damn far-fetched.

"It's not that I'm forty, really. Age...well, it's not the issue so much as the fact that I have a kid who's about to transition into adulthood, and I'm divorced, and I'm looking forward to retirement."

"Retirement?" Isla pulled a face, her nose scrunching. "You're years away from that, assuming you even retire the earliest you can."

"So, it's a thought in my head, you know."

"You're an idiot." Isla laughed lightly. "Just look at my step-mother, for instance. She's fifty and just started dating again. By your standards, she's ancient."

Andry winced. "I didn't mean it that way."

"Well, the two kids she raised have been out of the house for years, and we're well on our way into adulthood. She's even dating my best friend, so the age gap between them is massive, and they don't seem to have too many issues with it."

"They're not?"

Isla froze. She took a sharp breath before holding her finger up in front of her. "They're not, but I really don't want to discuss that tonight."

"You're the one who brought it up," Andry reminded her.

"Because you brought up dating and how old you think you are." Isla smiled as the waitress came over with their check.

Before Isla could reach for it, Andry snagged it and put her card on it, handing it back to the waitress before she left. She gave Isla a hard look. "Starting over is hard."

"It is. I'll give you that one." Isla sighed heavily. "But think about it this way, Andry... Will it be worth it in the end?"

"I don't know if it will be." Andry was hit with the reality of that statement. That was her fear, wasn't it? With Chris, despite the hardships, everything had been worth it because they had Katie, but would another relationship be the same? Andry couldn't fathom that possibility.

"Think about it." Isla grabbed her leftovers as Andry signed the bill. "And thanks for paying for dinner again, you didn't have to do that."

"I wanted to," Andry commented before shoving the receipt in her pocket.

They stood up, put their jackets on, and walked out of the restaurant together. Andry made her way toward her car, realizing belatedly that she had accidentally parked next to Isla. When they reached the vehicles, Isla put her food on the passenger seat and then came around the car, her arms crossed over her chest as she eyed Andry up and down.

"What are you doing the rest of the weekend?" Isla pushed.

"Don't know. Sleeping before next week, that's for sure, but other than that I don't have any major plans in place."

Isla smiled, the darkness partly obscuring those subtle changes in her face. Andry wished they were back inside where she could see everything. She leaned against the side of her car, her hands shoved into her pockets.

"What about you?"

"I've got some grading to catch up on after taking last weekend off."

Andry nodded slowly, understanding. Isla stepped in closer, and the tension in Andry's chest rose. When she raised her gaze, she realized just how close Isla was, that she'd shifted and was moving to lean against the car with her. Andry struggled to breathe, her entire body telling her one thing while her mind told her something else. It would be so damn easy, but she wouldn't do it. She couldn't let herself take advantage of this situation.

"I need to figure out what decorations I'm doing for Halloween."

Andry chuckled wryly. "I gave up on figuring that stuff out as soon as I became principal."

"I enjoy it." Isla faced Andry, their shoulders touching. "Lynda was never super big on the holidays, so Aisling and I would decorate for them. Lynda always said it was something about her not having time to figure it out."

"I can understand that." Andry smiled. "Having teenage kids is hard, and when you're thrown into it, I can't imagine the learning curve on that one."

"Steep, I'm sure." Isla's voice lowered, and she reached out to put her hand on Andry's forearm.

Andry desperately wanted to turn and lean into the touch. She started to move in that direction before her brain caught up with her. She pulled away and stood up straight.

"I'll see you on Monday, Isla. Thanks for inviting me to dinner." Isla seemed surprised by the action, but Andry had to put some physical space between them. They both needed it, but she needed it more. Andry squared her shoulders and said the politest thing she could think of. "We'll have to do it again sometime."

"Yeah." Isla gave her a smile, but it didn't quite reach her eyes.

Guilt twisted Andry's insides, but she couldn't back down now. She needed to back away and put space between them. "See you."

Andry got into her car, started the engine, and waited while Isla moved out of the way before she pulled out of the parking lot. She couldn't stay there and think. It would be way too tempting to get back out of her car, and Isla would know something was up then. She drove unsteadily through the side streets, taking her sweet time to get to her house. The entire time her mind was filled with moments from dinner, from the past months they had spent together. It all felt so damn good. She had to get her head on straight because what had happened that night couldn't happen again.

CHAPTER
Thirteen

ISLA CLAPPED her hands loudly to get her class's attention. They finally clapped with her. They were restless right before the lunch period every day, but she had something special planned for them today. She'd had less than a week to plan it, and it was perfect. Even with the way they had left dinner on Friday, Isla couldn't resist the call of a flawless prank.

"Hey, you all, I've got an idea fizzling around in my brain, and I want to know if you want to help me with it."

"What is it?" One of the kids asked.

Isla put her hands on her hips as she stood in the front of the classroom. "Many of you know that it's Dr. Murphey's birthday today, right?"

A few girls squealed and some of the boys groaned.

"But I was thinking we could all sing Happy Birthday to her *in style*."

"In style? What does that mean?"

Pleasure and excitement built up in Isla's chest. These were the kinds of moments she lived, the prank that was about to be pulled, the anticipation that everything was going to go well. She rolled her shoulders as she walked over to her classroom door and shut it.

"I was thinking that we could stage a fight in the lunchroom. Dr. Murphey is right across the hall in her office, and we can send another adult to run and get her. Then when she gets to the lunchroom, we can all break out and sing Happy Birthday to her."

"That's awesome, Ms. Walsh!" Graham said, and Isla could see her own excitement filling him as well.

"Now, here's the deal. I've told the other teachers that we're going to sing Happy Birthday, but I haven't talked to them about the rest of the idea, so this is going to be a prank on everyone. I'll need at least two or three volunteers to stage the fight, and when I mean stage, I *mean* stage. There will be no breaking of any of our school rules, okay? No touching each other with any part of your body, and no using harsh or mean words."

"I want to do it!" Graham raised his hand, nearly bouncing out of his seat.

"Me too!" Jaxon added.

A few more joined in, but Isla picked the first two to answer. Her stomach twisted suddenly, a moment of doubt pushing through that perhaps this wasn't the best idea. Andry had been so stilted after dinner that it left an uneasy feeling in the pit of her belly. Pushing past it for the thrill, Isla told the other kiddos involved to really amp up the tension. They talked about how the whole plan would work, and then they lined up for lunch. As she walked down the line of kids, Isla smiled at them.

"Now, here's the deal everyone. This is only going to work so long as we don't break character and no one figures it out, all right?"

When she received confirmation that they all understood, Isla took them out of the classroom and down the hall toward the lunchroom. It was her break period, but she would gladly give it up for this. It was the perfect way to celebrate Andry's birthday with a big bang, even if they were on treacherous territory in terms of their personal relationship.

They entered the cafeteria, and the kids went to get their

food, not wanting to stop up the lunch procession even though they were the last ones for the day. Isla kept her phone in her hand, ready to start recording as soon as she got a chance because this was something that she was going to want to share with anyone she could.

As soon as the last kid got their food, and they had put all their trays on the table, Graham shouted, "What are you talking about!?"

His voice rang through the lunchroom, ushering a silence through it. Everyone turned their eyes on him, and Isla was filled with delight at how perfectly this was going. Pulling out her phone, she turned the camera on and hit record. She stayed in the corner of the room, wanting to hide away a bit so that the others didn't see her and think something was up.

"I didn't say anything!" Jaxon shouted back, standing up and moving toward the center aisle between the tables.

It was perfect. Damn, these kids knew how to act. Isla stayed still as the other kids in her class started to stand up and surround the two arguing, forming a circle that would make it hard for anyone to get in there. Isla cast a glance at one of the para-educators who came forward to see if they could stop whatever was about to happen.

"You sure did! Why would you say that? I can't believe you would say something like that!"

Isla laughed inwardly, knowing the boys were struggling to come up with an argument that had nothing specific in it, but so far, they were doing an outstanding job. Adults moved inward to try and stop them. Isla reached the first one she could and grabbed their arm.

With a wink, she said, "Go get Andry. We need her for this."

With a frown, he moved out toward the hallway. Isla crossed her arms and watched everything unfold beautifully. Andry came in, nearly running, as she jumped into the middle of the circle ready to do whatever was necessary, panic written all over her face in a way that only an adult would be able to read.

Isla stepped up and raised her hands so her class would be able to see her. She dropped her hands, and in an instant, she started singing, "Happy Birthday to you!"

Everyone joined in, the entire cafeteria filled with small voices as they figured out exactly what was going on. Andry stood in the center of the crowd, dumbfounded before the realization that she had been duped again hit her. She shook her head and found Isla in the crowd, pointing at her with a huge grin on her face and a laugh bubbling up from her chest.

As soon as they were done singing, Andry clapped her hands along with the rest of them. "You all are amazing! I loved it! Thank you so much."

Isla smiled, clapping herself at the excitement surrounding her. Everything was perfect in that moment, and she didn't want to lose it. She needed more energy like that in her life, more of whatever could keep her moving forward instead of sliding back into the depression that had sucked so much out of her in the last few months.

All of the kids ran up to Andry, wrapping their arms around her middle as they gave her a hug and wished her a happy birthday individually. By the time they managed to calm everyone down enough to sit back down, the kids were severely limited in the amount of time they had to eat their lunch before running outside for recess.

Andry shook her head as some of the adults came over and wished her a happy birthday as well. Any other year, Andry hadn't made a fuss about her birthday, keeping the day as quiet as possible, but now the cat was out of the bag, and Isla was sure that other teachers would remember it and make sure Andry got the attention she deserved. Because she did deserve it. She was one of the best people out there, and Isla didn't know how she had been so lucky to end up teaching under her.

She was about to leave the cafeteria and all the fun and games to grab her own lunch when Andry caught her by the upper arm. She cocked her head to the side, laughter in her eyes as she shook her head. "You're brilliant, did you know that?"

"Not something you expected?"

"Not in a million years."

Isla's lips curled up into a smile, one of the few true ones she could remember giving lately. She shivered as Andry pulled her in, wrapping an arm around her shoulders, and giving her a side hug that meant more than she could have ever dreamed of. She needed that. Her cheeks burned, not with embarrassment, but with pleasure.

This felt so damn good.

Isla didn't want to give it up, so she leaned into Andry's side, moving her arm around Andry's back and tightening the embrace between them. It was intentional. It was slow. It was a beautiful moment between the two of them that she wasn't going to let go by without doing something about it. Isla melted into Andry's side as they turned to walk out into the hallway and leave the kids to finish their meals.

"Next year, I should figure out how to do something with your birthday and the PA system."

"You wouldn't!" Andry's eyes widened as she shifted out of Isla's grasp just before stepping through the doorway.

Isla missed the feeling of having Andry against her, the heat from her body but also the comfort that she derived from the simplistic touch. She didn't want to give that up for anything. Isla let out a breath before giving Andry a wicked grin. "This time I have a whole year to plan it, so you can bet that whatever I come up with, it's going to be epic."

"I'm trembling in my boots already." Andry laughed, a thrill rolling through Isla at the sound.

"You better be," Isla teased. They made their way toward Andry's office. It might have only been a birthday song, but it had been one of the biggest pranks she had pulled to date because most of it wasn't dependent on her. Her kids had pulled through beautifully. "You'll have to tell Graham and Jaxon that they did amazing. They planned that whole fight with only a minute's notice."

"I can't believe you convinced them to do that."

"Well, I laid out the ground rules." Isla defended. "They still had to follow all of our school rules while doing it, and you weren't there for most of the argument, but they couldn't find anything to argue about that wouldn't be breaking those rules, so they literally just stood up and started yelling questions at each other." Isla wanted to burst into laughter at just the thought of it.

"Are you serious?"

"Yes." Isla smiled. "I got it on video. I'll send it to you so you can see, but they were really creative with everything that they were doing in order to stay within the boundaries I gave them but still do what I asked them to."

Andry shook her head again. "My heart was racing so hard. I haven't had to break up a fist fight since I was at the high school."

"Well, you didn't have to break that streak today, did you?"

"No. I guess I didn't." Andry laughed as she stepped into her office. "Go eat your lunch, Isla. I've got actual work to do."

"Yes, Principal Murphey." Isla gave her tone a teasing quality to it, one that she knew would irk Andry but also tell her just how much fun she was truly having with this entire situation.

Andry chuckled as she walked through the main office doors and back into her office, stopping to tell the secretaries what had gone on in her absence. They were laughing loudly by the time Isla made it down the hallway and turned the corner to her classroom. It had been well worth losing some of her downtime to pull that one.

As she sat at her desk, she checked her phone. She wanted to call Wil, tell her about the prank, but something held her back. It wasn't because it was the middle of the day and Will likely wouldn't be able to answer.

It was Andry.

Isla took a bite of her sandwich and set it on her desk, rolling her shoulders as she stared at the phone again. She pulled up the video of the birthday prank and watched it carefully, her heart skipping a beat as soon as Andry entered the circle.

That...that was it.

Isla pursed her lips and leaned back in her chair before taking another bite of her lunch. What was she supposed to do with that? She hadn't thought about Andry in that way before this year, but they had been getting closer over the past few weeks and in the last month for sure. They'd gone to dinner just the two of them several times, and that wasn't something that they had done before in all the time they had worked together.

With her thumb hovering over the video, she texted it to Andry and then sent it off to Wil with a half-hearted joke in the comment. She needed to talk to Wil, but she had a feeling she knew exactly what Wil would say, which had something to do with the heart wants what it wants. But was it even her heart?

Isla certainly wasn't in any position to think about being with someone. She had to sort herself out first, but that didn't mean she didn't enjoy the flirting and attention that Andry had given her lately. She closed her eyes, remembering the way she'd melted into Andry's side when they'd shared that side hug in the cafeteria.

"Damn," Isla murmured to herself. She was completely enamored with Andry, wasn't she? There was no denying the flirting that had happened that weekend when they were at dinner, but Isla had just brushed it off as finally finding some sort of light in her life. She enjoyed the ease of the conversation. But they worked together, and Andry was her boss, and older than her, and she had a kid. Isla clenched her jaw.

She jerked with a start when a text message came through. She expected it to be from Wil or Andry, so when Aisling's name showed up on the screen, she was surprised. Frowning, she opened the message and read. *I'm going to Mom's for Thanksgiving.*

Isla's stomach dropped. That meant she would probably be

alone for the holiday. Everyone was gathering together, and despite the joy she had managed to find in the last few moments, it quickly vanished with the reality of the monumental task in front of her.

Wil would no doubt want to spend the holidays with her girlfriend, who also didn't have a whole lot of family around. Isla stared at the message again, trying to read between the lines. Aisling was never usually this blunt and to the point unless she thought there would be an argument. Isla would have to work through that one on her own because she didn't need to burden her sister with any more of her drama.

Taking a deep breath and the higher road, Isla wrote back, *I think that's a great idea. Let's get together soon. I miss you.*

She left it at that, the time on the clock telling her she had to get up and go get her kids from recess. She had barely managed to eat half of her sandwich, but it would have to do because she didn't have time to scarf down more of it.

She had to talk to Lynda and figure this thing out. Because she didn't want to be left out of what little family she had still remaining. She wouldn't let that be the outcome of all of this. And she definitely needed to talk to Aisling about everything going on. Texting one last time as she stood up, Isla set her determination in motion.

I'll call you tonight.

CHAPTER
Fourteen

"HEY!" Andry's voice startled Isla out of the quiet she found herself in. Her smile was pure when Isla turned to face her at the end of another long day. "We're doing drinks tonight at Scooters."

"Who is *we?*" Isla narrowed her gaze, her stomach fluttering. For days now, she had been sitting with the fact that she may like Andry more than was appropriate, and it hadn't gotten any easier in that time.

"A few teachers. Something low key, I promise."

Isla canted her head to the side. "*Which* teachers?"

"The fun ones you like. I promise." Andry laughed lightly as she pulled away from the door. "Be there at seven, and make sure you eat food first."

"All right," Isla mumbled to herself as she finished packing her bag for the weekend. It had been a long week, but she was still riding the high from the fake fight she'd managed to pull with her students, and from the conversation she'd finally had with Aisling and Lynda which had put a thought in her mind about the holidays. She wasn't ready to share it with them yet, but maybe soon. She was headed the right direction, and that was what mattered.

With other teachers at the bar with them, at least Isla would have a buffer between her and Andry, which would help her figure out if earlier that week was a fluke. She straightened her back and pulled her bag over her shoulder. She had just over two hours to eat dinner and get ready for the evening out, and she planned to make the most of it.

When she got to the bar, she saw a few cars she recognized along with Andry's. She'd specifically shown up late, not wanting any extra time alone with Andry if she could avoid it. That wouldn't do either of them any good, especially if Isla's suspicions that she had a crush were correct.

As she stepped inside, the warmth hit her first but so did the rumble of voices and the trill of laughter. She recognized Andry's laugh immediately. Looking from side to side, she finally saw them at a table in the back. With a deep breath, Isla made her way in that direction, finding the only seat left was one right next to Andry. Cursing her luck, Isla slid into it and smiled at all the greetings she received.

This was a much younger crowd than the gathering that they usually had for teachers. It was exactly what she had been looking for earlier that year. Isla ordered herself a drink and smiled at Andry's bubbly one in front of her. Isla had no doubt that Andry would drive each one of the teachers home if she had her say in the matter, not wanting any of them to drive while intoxicated.

"Glad you could make it," Andry whispered into Isla's ear over the din of the crowd and music.

"Me too." And it was the truth. Isla had thought about just not showing up, but Andry hadn't really given her a moment to decline the offer, and she wasn't willing to risk a text or phone call from her.

Conversation picked up quickly and lasted for about an hour before the first of their crew begged off. Andry made sure that her husband was going to pick her up before she let her go. Isla loved that about her, the fact that she wasn't willing to let anyone put themselves in danger unnecessarily along with everyone else on the road. It was considerate, but it also took effort on her part and showed how much she truly cared for her employees.

Within the next hour, Isla was caught off guard as the last of the other teachers left and she was alone with Andry. She shuddered as she'd just ordered another drink, and she knew without a doubt that Andry was going to insist on driving her home that night. Andry shifted on her seat, their thighs brushing under the table and another shiver ran through her. Isla cursed it. She didn't want this. Neither of them needed this to be the situation they found themselves in.

Isla tensed but then took a deep breath and relaxed herself. "I take it you'll be driving me home."

"Damn straight." Andry winked and sipped the soda that she'd been ordering all night.

The thrill that rose in Isla's chest wasn't expected, but she did like it. She wasn't used to this kind of attention from anyone other than Wil and maybe some of the people she had dated in the past, although the longest relationship she had ever been in was a little over half a year aside from the one in college.

"Did you have fun at least?"

"What does that mean?" Isla looked up at her.

"With the new group. You said you'd wanted a different group, one that wasn't just *old people complaining about teaching.*" Andry's voice took on a whine as she did an exaggerated impression of Isla's complaint.

"Oh my god, I didn't say it like that." Isla rolled her eyes, her smile coming easily. Every time they were together, she found herself more and more relaxed. The only other person she felt that comfortable with was Wil.

"No, you didn't." Andry laughed. "But it *was* your suggestion."

"Fine. I'll take credit for that at least." Isla touched the top of Andry's hand, the skin smooth and warm against her fingers.

Her shoulders shifted down, the constant tension in her chest lightening. She'd been doing more of that lately—touching Andry in small ways. She didn't seem to mind, but Isla knew they were pushing the limits of decorum.

Andry shifted again, the brush of the denim against the denim of Isla's pants sending little fingers of electricity running through her. Isla bit back the groan that wanted to erupt. It seemed they were spending nearly every weekend together lately, with the exception of the one Wil had been there for. Isla leaned over the table, her elbows on it as she looked at the crowd in the rest of the bar.

"Are we staying longer or going home?" Isla suddenly asked, trying to figure out where they stood with each other. She needed some ground rules, but she had no idea how to ask without Andry thinking there was something else going on.

"It's whatever you want and need." Andry leaned back and out of Isla's immediate line of sight.

But it did cause Isla to have to question what it was she wanted, something she typically wasn't good at doing. She had taken to working through that, to learn how to be better at expressing what she needed, especially as she navigated these conversations with Lynda and the rest of her family.

Shifting and turning in her chair so she faced Andry full-on, Isla gave her a smile. "I'd like to stay a bit longer." *Get to know you better.* But she didn't add in that last part. She needed to keep space between them, so she kept those words to herself.

"Sounds good to me."

"Where's Katie wanting to go to college?"

"Who knows." Andry gave a small smile. "She's applying to about four schools I think, maybe five. They're all in the Rockies, though. She shouldn't be too far from home."

"But sometimes it's good to leave home, you know, get out on your own a bit."

Andry lifted a shoulder in a half shrug. "Did you leave?"

"Yes, but I didn't leave the state. Wil and I went to CSU, so we weren't far from Denver, not that we went back often." Isla stayed where she was even though the position was awkward. She wanted to see Andry's face, to note her reactions and understand what was going through her mind. "Once I was out of the house, I left it all behind."

"You had extenuating circumstances." Andry raised an eyebrow, her gaze locking on Isla's face.

"I did," Isla agreed. "And I pushed those circumstances so I didn't have to deal with problems I didn't want to touch with a ten-foot pole."

Andry's lips curled upward. "Well, at least you can admit that."

"Admitting it was never the issue. Figuring out what to do about it was."

"Isla, I've known you for eight years, and I never knew your father died when you were barely a teenager or your mother when you were a little kid. You don't talk about your home life other than Wil and Aisling."

Her lips parted in surprise at that. She hadn't realized how much they hadn't been a part of her life, that she'd kept everyone at such an arm's length. She knew she'd done that in relationships in the past—it was why most of them failed—but she hadn't thought she had done that with everyone else. But it did make sense. Sighing heavily, Isla grabbed hold of her drink and took a long sip. "I don't want to do that anymore." She wanted more—connection, friendship, and maybe even love.

"I'm glad to hear that."

"Being an orphan sucks. Don't need to add to it, right?" She tried to lighten the mood, but she failed at that one. The look on Andry's face told her as much.

"It's certainly a cross of yours to bear, but the real question, I guess, is do you want it to define you?" Andry raised one eyebrow and stared Isla over. "Because how you choose to define yourself is the story that people will hear."

Isla hated that Andry was right, and she had let it be her

story for far too long. She had been working slowly on that, but no one had said it to her as beautifully as Andry had in that moment. Isla smiled to herself and then focused back on the present moment.

"And what's your story, then? Old and divorced? Or are you starting a new life in the way you want it to be?"

Andry's confidence faltered, her full lips parting as her eyes dropped to Isla's mouth. "That's not nice to do."

"What? Turn the conversation back on you?" Isla giggled slightly. "It's a good question."

"It is." Andry sighed. "It's hard to get away from the past, isn't it?"

Andry's phone buzzed. She stared at the screen for a moment before silencing the call. Isla caught the name on the screen before Andry turned her phone over—*Chris*. Perfect timing there for sure. It was only another strong reminder for Isla that she wasn't ready for this kind of relationship. She was better off on her own, truthfully. Dealing with exes and stepchildren wasn't for her.

"I don't want to be the old, divorced hag who stands on the front porch and yells *get off my lawn!*"

Isla snorted. "I can't see you doing that."

"Oh, I've done it, not to any kids passing by but definitely to Chris when she was making a fool of herself one night. Thankfully, Katie wasn't there to witness that." Andry rubbed her hands together then sipped her drink. "I got really unhappy after my divorce. I never thought we would end up separated."

"No one thinks they'll end up divorced when they get married. No one thinks they'll end up widowed before they're in their eighties either." Isla clenched her jaw at her own comment, realizing once again that Lynda had been out of her element and that her dad's death had an impact on all of them. "I probably should have been nicer to Lynda growing up."

"You don't strike me as someone who was mean."

Isla chuckled. "No, I left that to Wil. She was such an asshole to Lynda."

"Really?"

"Yeah. Long story." Isla shifted on her chair, but Andry's phone vibrated again.

Sighing, Andry shot Isla an apologetic look before flipping her phone over to see who was calling. Once again it was Chris. "I'll be right back."

Left alone at the table, Isla rolled her shoulders, finding the tension that had been in them all day was gone, and she was pretty sure it wasn't the alcohol. She'd drunk with Wil and the tension was still there at the end of it all. The only difference had been Andry and the gentle conversations that they seemed to manage.

Isla pursed her lips and pulled her own phone out. She had a few missed texts from Wil, but it wasn't anything that she couldn't answer the next day. She drew in a deep breath and let it out slowly. If she was going to make a difference in her life going forward, rewrite her own story in other words, then she had to continue to do things differently than she ever had before. She'd started that with Andry, but she needed to do more of it.

"Sorry about that," Andry muttered as she slid onto the chair again.

"Don't worry about it." But the entire mood had shifted. Andry was withdrawn, her face tense and her shoulders looked so tight. Isla was about to suggest they stay longer to work that out, but she wasn't even sure how they would manage that. "Did you want to leave to go deal with whatever's going on?"

"Might be best," Andry mumbled. "I'm sorry to cut the evening short."

"It's not short." Isla sent her a brilliant smile. "In fact, I think we stayed here way longer than anyone else. It was a good night."

Andry nodded, but she didn't say anything. She stood up, throwing a few bills on the table for a tip. Isla did the same and left her half-consumed beer in place. Grabbing her jacket, she put it on and shoved her hands in the pockets, not quite sure where they were going to go from there. No matter what, she wanted to see the dark cloud that was over Andry vanish and never come back.

The car was cold when they got inside. Isla stayed quiet while Andry drove toward her apartment, tension filling all the empty spaces between them and more. She wanted to say something that would take that away, that would break it, but she was at a complete loss for words. When Andry pulled up into the parking lot, Isla shivered and turned to her.

"Whatever it is, I'm pretty sure it'll turn out fine."

Andry furrowed her brow, throwing the car into park. "It's nothing I haven't had to deal with before."

"See? So you should be an expert at it." Isla smiled, but it was forced. She was trying to pull out the silver lining and failing miserably.

Andry grunted but didn't add anything to the conversation. "I'll see you Monday, Isla."

"Right." Isla pulled her lips into a tight smile and grabbed the handle on the door. "See you Monday."

As she walked up toward her apartment, she forced herself not to look over her shoulder. But when she got to her door, Andry was already pulling out of the parking lot and onto the main road. Isla leaned against the door and let out a sigh. Just when she thought she was making progress, it all came crashing down again. It was probably a good thing. She didn't need to fall any harder for her boss.

CHAPTER
Fifteen

ANDRY CLENCHED her jaw as she got out of her car at the used car dealership. Chris was supposed to be there, but she was pretty sure she'd be late. With a deep breath, she set out to find the car for Katie's birthday, with or without Chris. What she was going to do to afford it if Chris didn't show up was anyone's guess.

She looked at a bunch of cars before Chris finally showed up, parking. Andry's stomach tightened at the sight of her. This was going to be a battle of a day, she knew that, which had been part of why she'd avoided it for as long as she had.

"Hey," Andry said, greeting her ex-wife stiffly. She took deep, slow breaths to try and dissipate that built up tension.

"Hey back," Chris answered, much smoother, as if there was no tension between them. She was so fucking good at pretending there was nothing wrong—Andry envied that ability. "Find anything good so far?"

Chris would act as though she'd planned on being there late. Andry kept that thought to herself. They didn't need to hash out those things anymore. That was a conversation for the past. Right now Andry wanted to get the car purchased and figure out what she was going to do with it until December when she could give it to Katie. "There are a couple I was going to test drive."

Chris raised an eyebrow. "Let's do it then."

"I'm driving," Andry quickly answered. She wasn't about to let Chris behind the wheel of a vehicle that wasn't her own, and if she could prevent that from happening, she would.

Hurt flashed across Chris' gaze before she acquiesced. "Fine."

They went inside to get the keys, then took the car out onto the streets, driving through town and bit onto the highway to test it out. It seemed like a fitting first car, enough to get Katie through the first few years of her adult life.

"This is a nice car," Chris said, sliding around in the seat next to Andry.

Andry kept her mouth shut, looking at Chris for any sign that she was drunk but coming up completely empty. She assumed Chris was always drunk, but they hadn't talked about the late-night call and Andry was determined not to bring it up. They hadn't really talked about Chris' drinking other than the fact that Andry had called her out on being an alcoholic and told her she had to change. She hadn't, at least not from what Andry had seen.

"It's got low mileage too," Andry finally added to the conversation. "The price is a bit more than I was hoping for."

"What is it?"

"Fifteen thousand."

Chris wrinkled her nose in that way that Andry used to love, but now it irked her more than anything. When had she fallen so out of love with Chris, almost to the point of complete dislike? Sighing, Andry swallowed hard and pulled back into the dealership.

"I think this is the car for her."

"Me too. Let's get it set up."

They breezed through the paperwork and financing. Andry had to take out a loan to cover her portion of the costs, but Chris had somehow managed to throw in cash. With the conversations they'd had surrounding the vehicle before then, Andry couldn't have been more surprised, and she wanted to ask, she wanted to question and dig for the truth, but it wasn't her business anymore.

"What do we do with it now that we have it?" Andry shoved her hands into her pockets, the keys burning a hole.

"We can keep it at my house."

"She'll see it." Andry shook her head. "If the idea is to make a big deal out of her eighteenth birthday, then we give it to her on her birthday."

Chris pursed her lips. "We should just give it to her now."

"You agreed to wait."

"What difference does a few months make?" Chris rolled her eyes, scoffing at the same time.

In the grand scheme of things, a few months didn't make a big difference, but she and Andry had agreed years ago that this was how it would happen. Renegotiating that wasn't on Andry's to-do list for the week or even the year. She didn't have the energy for it. "I can see if I can find some place for it."

"Where?" Chris' voice grew louder, catching the attention of some of the workers nearby.

Andry wished she could shush her, but she couldn't. "I've got a friend who lives in an apartment. I can ask her to leave it there. That way someone is watching it, but it's not where Katie will find it."

"You have a friend?" Chris raised an eyebrow sarcastically. "Ye who shall never have friends."

Andry steeled herself against the hurt she knew was coming. Their entire relationship had always been about Chris and her friends and Chris and her family, and that fact wasn't lost on Andry. "Come off it, Chris. I don't have the time for this today."

"No, but you have the time to go to your friend's house. Is this really a friend?" The taunt was clear, and Andry's entire body tightened at it.

"I'm not having this conversation with you. I'll call her and see if we can leave it there." Andry's stomach was in a bundle of knots as she walked away from Chris and back toward her car. She needed a break, and she hadn't been able to catch one. Chris had thrown this shopping trip on her at the last minute while she was out and having a good time. She'd been relaxed and comfortable for the first time in years, and then Chris had ruined all of that with an incessant need to talk right then and there.

A quick phone call with Isla was enough to let her in on what was going on and get permission to bring the car over there. Andry tightened her grip around the keys in her pocket as she walked back toward Chris.

"Come on. You're driving your car."

"I can drive the new one."

"No," Andry firmly stated with a glare. She wasn't going to let Chris into this vehicle if she could help it. She'd now spent hours in a financial office getting a loan for it, and Chris was privy to that. She wasn't going to let Chris ruin anything with her name on it, not while she had control anyway.

Andry got behind the wheel and let out a sigh as Chris stalked to her car. This was the longest day ever, and she couldn't wait for it to end. She needed a break after this. Andry took the most direct route to Isla's, realizing far too late that now Chris was going to know where Isla lived. She couldn't quite name why that thought disturbed her. They wouldn't be there long—she would make sure of that.

Pulling into the parking lot, Andry parked next to Isla's vehicle and pocketed the keys again. She could always give Isla the spare set at school on Monday, which would be a better choice than walking up to her apartment and giving them to her now, especially with Chris already parking and getting out.

"Why are you being such a stickler about me driving the car?" Chris' voice was loud and carried through the breeze.

Andry cursed. She'd always been bold when she spoke. She'd never been able to keep her voice tempered. Even talking

normally she was loud. Andry moved closer, trying to ignore the
fact that Chris was going to have to bring her back to the dealership and she wasn't going to be able to avoid being in a moving
vehicle with her.

"Andry!"

"We can talk about this later," Andry answered, getting to
the car but having to walk by Chris first. Chris put a hand on her
arm to stop her.

"No, talk to me now."

"Not now." Andry refused to glance up toward Isla's apartment. She refused to acknowledge that Chris was about to make
a fool of herself in front of one of Andry's employees and that
she had willingly walked into this drama and brought Isla into it.

"Now. I've been trying to be nice to you all day, but you're
not giving me any kind of break."

Andry clenched her jaw, all the muscles in her shoulders,
neck, and back tightening in an instant. They had been through
this so many times, and as much as she could resist diving headfirst into an argument, Chris was equally adept at dragging her
down into one when she least wanted it.

"You don't deserve a break." Andry plowed forward with
everything she had held back.

"Why not? You divorced me. Isn't that enough?" Chris' eyes
narrowed.

"I divorced you because you refused to acknowledge the fact
that you're a drunk and you refused to work on any of our problems. I gave you plenty of chances over the last ten years to get
your shit together and start paying attention to your family and
you refused to do a single thing toward that." Andry poked her
finger into Chris' shoulder. "So don't talk to me about how *I*
divorced *you*."

"You did divorce me. You served me papers while I was at
the school."

"How else was I supposed to find you? You vanished from the
house, and you refused to pick up your phone. You were so

drunk that I couldn't even get you to pay attention to our daughter. You know, the kid that we made and raised together, the one who adores you to a fault."

"Don't bring Katie into this." Chris' voice dropped.

"How? You've hurt her more times than you can even count because you're so drunk that you don't even know the damage that you're doing." Andry crossed her arms, determined that she was going to make her point now. "You never think about her, do you? I've asked you for months to come up with a plan to buy a car, you tell me that you have no money, and then suddenly you have a ton of cash on hand to buy a car? What is this? Where did you get it from?"

"It's none of your business."

"No, it is. Where did you get it from?" Andry knew she shouldn't have asked the question. She knew she shouldn't have pushed that far, but she couldn't stop herself.

"My pension, all right? I cashed out a chunk of my retirement to pay for the car."

Andry sucked in a sharp breath before slowly shaking her head. "How much do you have left of it?"

"Nothing." Chris put her hands out to the sides. "There, you win. I'm a failure at this thing we call life and parenting, and I just continue to prove it." Chris closed in on herself, her shoulders falling, her eyes watering, and her head shaking. "I'm a drunk failure."

"Chris." Andry stepped closer, touching Chris' elbow. "What are you going to do about retiring?"

"Hell if I know. It doesn't really matter, does it?"

"What about Katie's college?"

The sheepish look Chris gave her was more than enough explanation to know all that money was gone too. The only thing left was what Andry had managed to stash away without Chris' name on it. She knew she should have fought harder during the divorce to control those funds and get Chris' name off everything, but she'd only been trying to be fair.

"Katie knows I don't have anything to give her."

"What?" Andry frowned, her gaze piercing into Chris'. "You told her?"

"She deserved to know. It was the money we'd set aside for her."

"What did you tell her that you did with it?" Andry needed to know, as if the excuse that Chris came up with would be some kind of reason that would wash everything away, but she knew it wouldn't make a lick of a difference other than to piss her off even more.

"I told her that I spent it because of some very stupid decisions that I've made in the past, but I'm trying to make better decisions from now on. One of those was being honest with her about the mistakes I made."

Warning bells went off in Andry's peripheral. She eyed Chris over, truly looking at her without as much judgment as she had before. She clenched her jaw, not sure if she wanted the answer to the question she was about to ask, but it needed to be out there. "Are you sober?"

Chris reached into her pocket and pulled out a small circular chip. She handed it to Andry. Hesitating, Andry fingered the chip, staring at the dark blue color with the triangle on it and the circle in the center of that with the number six printed. Andry dashed her tongue across her lips and flipped the coin over in her hand.

"What does this mean?"

"It's my six-month chip. I got it last week."

"You've been sober for six months?" Andry wasn't sure she could believe it, although she desperately wanted to. This was everything she had wanted for Chris and more. "Are you telling me the truth right now?"

"Yes." Chris didn't smile. In fact, her face remained so passive that Andry wasn't sure what was going on behind her gaze.

"Why didn't you tell me you were going to meetings?" She stared down at the chip in her hand, again in awe that she was even holding it, something so precious and something to be completely proud of Chris for.

"I didn't think you would believe me."

Well, Chris had her there. She probably wouldn't have believed her, but this was proof. Not only that but she was acting differently in some of the small ways. Not like she had when they first met and got married, but she was acting differently than when she'd been at the height of her drinking, right before Andry had filed for divorce.

Andry curled her hair behind her ear, everything shifting in an instant. "You're right. I probably wouldn't have."

"It was after we were divorced, but I hit rock bottom. I was drinking in my car at school, any chance I could get, and I couldn't handle it anymore. I could have lost everything, and I very nearly did. At least this way I still have my school, not that it's much consolation compared to what I did have."

Andry's lips parted in surprise. Never in all the time since they had separated had she thought Chris would admit this. Her heart raced. Stepping in, Andry wrapped her arms around Chris' shoulders and pulled her in for a hug. She closed her eyes, clenching them tight as she held on. She'd needed this more than she'd ever thought possible. Andry whispered, "I'm proud of you."

"Thanks." Chris let out a little chuckle. "I know it's not much, but six months is more than I've ever managed before."

"It's a lot. It is. I know it is." Andry stepped away and handed the chip back. "Thanks for sharing this with me."

Chris lifted her shoulder in a slight shrug. "You deserved to know."

"You didn't have to tell me. I know how hard this has been for all of us."

"It has been." Chris raised her eyes, tears in her gaze. "Thanks for trusting me."

Andry wasn't sure she would take it quite that far, but it was at least something to bring them slightly closer than they were before. "Come on, let's go get my car."

She moved around Chris' vehicle, and just before she slid into the passenger seat, she glanced up to see Isla standing outside her door to her apartment in the covered stairwell. Her heart leapt to her throat, making it impossible to breathe for a second. She couldn't see enough detail in her face, but the fact that she hadn't come down there, hadn't said anything, meant more than any words could. Andry clenched her jaw tightly as she slipped into the car like she hadn't seen Isla standing there. She closed her eyes as soon as Chris was behind the wheel and let Chris drive her back to the dealership.

CHAPTER
Sixteen

THE KNOCK on Isla's door was a surprise. An hour had passed since she'd walked back inside after watching Andry and Chris argue in the parking lot. She'd originally thought she'd go down there and talk to them but thought better of it when their arguing was loud enough to reach her ears. She shuddered at the memory as she reached for her doorknob.

Andry stood on the other side, sheepishly with her hands in her pockets and her chin dipped down. Her brown hair was pulled back in a ponytail, but it didn't look as kempt as it usually did. Isla tried to figure out exactly what was going on and what she wanted to do with that.

Clearly Andry was there to talk about something. Andry had been there so much for Isla lately, and even though it was still a struggle with her depression, she wanted to scrape enough together to be the friend Andry needed right now—even if what had happened in the parking lot a little more than an hour ago panicked her. Isla kept her mouth closed, staring at Andry as if she was going to explain everything and leave a second later.

Andry cleared her throat, and their eyes locked in an intense stare. Isla remained silent, still not sure what to do. She was so out of practice with this. She'd thought Andry had her shit together until she saw them arguing, that Andry had come out the other side of the divorce unscathed. On second thought, she knew that was unrealistic. She didn't want the image she had of Andry to be rebuilt either, not with the way her mind had been taking their relationship in the last few weeks. This was the more authentic version of Andry.

Andry's lips quivered as she spoke. "I wanted to apologize about earlier."

Isla raised an eyebrow, taken aback by the start.

"Can I come in so I'm not doing this outside?" Andry's voice was gentle, heartfelt almost.

Hesitating only for another second, Isla moved to the side and let Andry step in. Her heart raced as she heard the click of the door. Drawing in a deep breath, Isla watched as Andry stopped awkwardly just inside, her hands still shoved into her pockets. Everything moved in slow motion, and Isla stepped closer, leaving the only exit behind her in a burst of confidence.

"Like I said, I wanted to apologize about what you saw. I tried..." Andry pressed her lips hard together, stopping herself before starting again. "There's a lot mixed up in my relationship with Chris, and I think unfortunately you got a front row seat to that today."

Isla sighed and walked around Andry, plopping down onto the couch where she'd sat earlier, steeped in her memory of that day. She patted the cushion next to her and rolled her shoulders slightly to try and ease out of her own issues and focus on Andry's.

Andry came over, sitting stiffly next to Isla. She didn't relax into the cushions and remained slightly hunched, her hands clasped tightly between her legs as she leaned over them with a curve to her back. Isla pulled her feet under her, turning her entire body to focus on Andry. The turmoil running through Andry was obvious, but Isla wasn't able to place where exactly it was coming from—if it was from the argument with Chris or if it was from the embarrassment at having witnesses.

"Chris is a drunk," Andry finally started. "It wasn't the only reason we divorced, but it was a starring reason in that. She never wanted to admit it, and she never wanted to deal with it. She's been a drunk for close to ten years, but it wasn't until the last five before we separated that it got really bad—especially at home."

Isla reached out, sliding her fingers over Andry's wrist and pulling her hand to rest it on Isla's knee. She folded their hands together in a tight grasp. Even if Andry didn't understand exactly what Isla had witnessed that day, Isla could still give her some support for this. Dredging up old hurts wasn't for the faint of heart.

"I finally convinced her to move out. Or rather, I gave her an ultimatum. Katie didn't want to see her at all that first year, no matter how hard I tried to tell her Chris was her mother, too. I didn't know what to say to her because I had to walk this stupidly hard line of protecting our daughter but also trying to keep the relationship between them alive when it was the last thing I wanted to do."

Isla hadn't spoken yet, but that didn't seem to deter Andry any. Andry needed this time to vent. Isla bit the inside of her cheek, looking Andry directly in the eye to make sure that Andry understood she was paying attention.

Andry sighed, nearly in tears as she went to speak again. "It's been so hard to balance all of this."

Isla understood that. She'd been there and seen it throughout the years with Lynda and her own family. Any time there were tough emotions, she and Lynda would shut down. They would tune everything out. They would avoid with the best of them, but Andry wasn't doing that. She expertly navigated the complications.

"I just... today she told me she's sober. I almost can't believe it." Andry reached up and wiped her fingers under her eyes, looking as though she was surprised to find she was telling the truth.

Isla touched her hand, curling her fingers around the side and holding on tight, giving Andry whatever support she could manage in the moment. Andry deserved that at the very least. Everyone needed someone they could rely on, and if that was going to be her for just that one night, Isla would give her whatever she needed.

"But I saw the chip, and she's been acting...different." Andry covered Isla's hand with her own, squeezing tightly. "I never thought she'd do it. I never thought..."

Andry trailed off, tears sliding down her cheeks. Isla slid forward, wrapping her arm around the side of Andry's neck and tugging her in for a hug. She held on as Andry cried into the front of her shoulder, as sobs racked through her, shaking her. Isla closed her eyes, breathing in Andry's scent, filled herself with it along with her own sorrow.

If Andry could reconcile with Chris, even just a little, then there had to be some hope for her and Lynda. Lynda had never done anything unforgivable, and since Isla had contacted her again, they were working toward bettering that, weren't they? Isla sucked in a deep breath, clenching her eyes against the onslaught of emotion.

She hadn't expected this. The waves of unease in Andry's past had rocked through her when Andry and Chris were outside, but this wasn't what she had wanted. She hadn't even thought Andry would show up, and then when she had, she'd never anticipated this, not her own turmoil. Isla tightened her shoulders, threading her fingers through Andry's hair as she gave whatever comfort she could.

"I'm so sorry. I shouldn't be dumping this on you." Andry's voice was muffled.

Isla sucked in a deep breath. Neither of them should be here, and certainly not in this position, but over the past few months, Andry had been there for her, and Isla wanted to respond in kind. Isla shifted, and Andry moved, their faces close.

Isla's heart skipped a beat. Their breath mingled, and the

tension in Isla's chest wasn't because of the argument she'd witnessed. This moved lower, across her breasts, to the pit of her stomach, and between her legs. Her gaze dropped to Andry's brown eyes, then to her lips, wet from when her tongue had dashed across them in her upset.

It was only that thought that turned Isla's stomach. She couldn't take advantage of this, not to mention Andry was her boss, and she wouldn't put herself in that situation—neither one of them. But the draw to move in, the tightness in her chest, the heat that moved through her body was so damn tempting. She hadn't felt it that strongly in well over a year.

Andry locked her gaze on Isla's, the same realization flashing through her. Isla saw the moment it hit her. Neither one of them moved. They stayed perfectly still, lips slightly parted. Andry took shallower breaths, and once again, Isla dropped her gaze down to her mouth. It would be so easy, not just in the physical action, but to fall into someone who she knew cared about her. Maybe not in that way, but Andry did care. They were friends first and foremost, and Isla wasn't willing to give that up. But to fall into something deeper—oh she could dream about that for eons.

"Andry," Isla whispered, the silence shattering, the moment broken. Isla broke eye contact purposely, her hands in her lap, putting some space between them. She dragged in a breath of cold air.

Andry shifted awkwardly on the couch, wiping her eyes again. The distance between them seemed like a chasm larger than Isla had ever felt before. She didn't want to let that go, but she also wanted to let Andry have some time to gather herself.

Instead, she couldn't stop herself from speaking. "When I was growing up, I had three parents who loved me. My mom, my dad, and my stepmom, and I'm not sure until recently that I could ever admit that last one, so please listen to me when I say this."

Andry had her full attention on Isla.

Her heart raced, the confession on the tip of her tongue in a way she wasn't sure she was ready for, but she knew it had to be said. "I never wanted it because I always felt like I had to love one more than the other, simply because of the circumstances I was born into. Katie didn't choose this."

"I know she didn't," Andry whispered.

"She didn't, and that means you have to love her and you have to let Chris love her. You can't stop their relationship, you can't prevent it, you can't even show your distaste of what Chris does because Katie will pick up on that, and she is damn lucky to have two parents alive who love her and want what's best for her." Isla blinked away her own tears, determined to get this out without breaking down completely. "I *never* had that."

Andry stilled. They looked each other over, silence filling the space between them and dragging them inch by inch back together. "You deserve it."

"I know, but it wasn't in the cards for me. Don't let Katie suffer because you two can't get your shit together and keep it together."

"I won't." Andry's hand covered hers again.

Isla let out a shuddering breath. She turned slightly into the couch, putting the physical distance between them that they needed. "Right, so do I get keys to this car in case I need to drive it somewhere?"

Andry blew out a breath. "Yes, I'll leave you with a set of keys. I'm hoping to get plates for it in the next week or two."

"Take your time," Isla answered, relaxing completely. She knew without a doubt that what she was about to say next was true. "It's not going anywhere and neither am I."

"Well, that's good news, I suppose." Andry followed suit and relaxed into the couch. "I'm still waiting on the next prank you'll pull."

"Are you?" Isla raised an eyebrow, their easy teasing coming back now that the tense moment was done with. It was jarring, and she still couldn't get that look out of her mind, but they couldn't talk about that—not yet.

"Truthfully?" Andry crossed her arms, giving Isla a stern look.

"Yeah."

"How often did you find yourself in the principal's office growing up because of pulling these kinds of stunts?"

Isla snorted out a laugh at Andry's absolute look of indignation. She hadn't thought that was where she was going with that. "Not as often as you'd probably like to think."

"Are you sure?"

"Yup." Isla got a wicked grin on her lips. "I didn't get caught. Now I don't care if I get caught. Sometimes it's rather nice to get called to the principal's office, you know."

"Oh lord." Andry rolled her eyes. "Not another teacher who's determined to keep getting in trouble. Never could leave all that behind, could you?"

Isla leaned in, energy zipping through her. "Never."

CHAPTER
Seventeen

THIS WAS Isla's one and only chance to pull something like this, and she was all aflutter with anticipation as she prepared. She stood at the copy machine in the main office. She'd already made dozens of photos before even getting to school that morning, and it had been with Katie's help that she even had the images to do this. She hadn't anticipated the number of teachers who would want to participate in the *little* prank she had going on. Isla snagged the paper copies of the photos and moved into Andry's office while the rest were being made.

Everyone else was already setting up, kids helping out too, but they only had the morning while Andry was out at a meeting. She'd be back just after one. Isla only had forty minutes to get this done in the office, which was cutting her time quite short. She knew she was pushing it.

Isla got to work. Tape, paper, stick. She repeated that, not concerned that the papers would inevitably fall down later. That would only add to the chaos that was about to ensue. She giggled to herself as she put up one of her favorite photos of Andry. It most definitely *wasn't* her professional photo for the school website. It was one where she was giving Katie a full-on smile after she'd taken her first few steps, so it was easily close to eighteen years old. Katie had told her the story of each picture when Isla had gotten them from her the week prior.

Isla pulled off another piece of tape and stuck up the next photo, one with Andry blowing out birthday candles. All the pictures were in black and white because Isla had been too cheap to pay for color when she'd ordered the majority of them. She'd only needed extras because as soon as she'd started putting them up others wanted to join in.

Andry wouldn't be able to walk into the school and avoid what Isla was doing. And she would know it was Isla as soon as she saw it. Going as quickly as she could, Isla ripped tape, put it to paper, and tacked it onto whatever surface she could find that would take the tape.

It was beautiful. When she finished with Andry's office, she went out into the main office to find it finished as well. She giggled to herself as she stepped into the hallway, adding more pictures to the ones that were already there. Some of the staff who had extra time were adding to them, too. She wished she'd had time to get up on some sort of ladder to hang images from the ceiling.

She'd have to remember that next time.

Isla walked through the hallways, peeked in classrooms and saw that every single class had participated in this *little* prank of hers. Andry was going to pee herself she would laugh so hard. Having so many of the staff and kids involved was perfection.

Isla made it to her classroom and snagged the poster board that she had made up for the front doors of the school where Andry would come inside. In fact, she'd made one for each door so that parents would see them when they got to the school that day too. She walked down the hall to the front of the school and plastered it on with packing tape. It said in bubbly letters, "We love our principal!" along with a collage of the photos that were hung around the school.

Katie had wanted to see it all, so Isla took pictures as she went. She texted the pictures over to Katie and then pocketed her phone. Isla couldn't be more pleased with herself.

She stepped into her class just before the kids returned from their music lessons and physical education class. Isla stood at the front, prepared to go into her planned history lesson for the day. They were all privy to the joke, so there was very little talk about the pictures.

It took another two hours of teaching and keeping the kids focused before Isla and the class heard Andry's tell-tale trill of laughter down the hallway. Isla turned to her kids with a big grin. All the kids looked at Isla, silently asking for permission to go out and see Andry. She put her finger to her lips as Andry's laugh continued. "Line up quietly and efficiently."

The kids moved as if they had been waiting all day for this one moment, which Isla supposed they all had. She peeked her head out of the door as Andry spun around and looked at all of the photos. Isla had added words to them, things like *you're our star* or *blow out those bad thoughts*. Andry seemed to be reading each of them as she went even though there were only twelve different photos with words.

Isla filed her kids out of the class and lined them up against the wall. Other teachers did the same as Andry walked. The cheering and the clapping started. Isla hadn't planned for that. The kids laughed right along with Andry, her cheeks a colorful bright red that brought joy to Isla's heart. This was what she had hoped for.

Seeing Andry the other week, completely shattered and broken in front of her, she'd known she'd have to go big with this next prank. It had to be something that would make her laugh hard, but also something that would make her feel loved and appreciated. Some of the kids stepped forward with cards, especially the little ones in the school. Isla hadn't even thought of that.

By the time Andry made it down to her end of the hall, she pinned Isla with a serious look. "I take it this was all your idea."

Isla got caught in that look, her entire body listing forward as a grin blossomed on her face and her eyes widened. She'd never been happier than in these moments, and she longed for them, to make Andry smile and have just as much joy as she did.

"Katie helped," Isla answered, her voice breathier than she'd anticipated.

"Oh, I'll deal with her when I get home tonight."

"I think she's coming here after school. She wanted to see my handiwork, and the pictures I sent her probably don't do it justice." Isla was grinning from ear to ear, happy to see Andry in such a relaxed state.

"How did you get her to help you out?"

"Not as hard as you think it might be." Isla shrugged. "But you should go see your office."

"What did you do?"

She winked and played innocent. "Nothing you shouldn't already expect. Come on, kids! It's time to get back to work!"

Isla filed her class back inside. Andry followed for a moment, gasping when she saw what the inside of the classroom looked like. "In here too!"

"Every class participated, Dr. Murphey." Isla spun around as her kids sat at their desks. "Maybe you should go check out how creative they all got."

"You're incorrigible."

Isla laughed as Andry pointed a finger at her and walked out of the class. They could hear echoes of her loud voice as she visited each classroom, praising the students for their creativity and talking about how surprised she was to see it all. It took tremendous effort to calm her students and finish out the rest of the day.

When the bell rang, she ushered them out the door and then made her way down to Andry's office. She'd been summoned. She stepped into the principal's office, her palms slightly clammy. "You wanted to see me?"

"Shut the door," Andry said, standing up from her desk. "What on earth possessed you to come up with this idea?"

"No clue, really." Isla looked Andry over. She didn't appear mad.

Shaking her head and crossing her arms, Andry let out a little chuckle. "How did you get everyone on board?"

"I didn't really. I got a few other people on it, but as soon as the pictures started going up, everyone wanted to join. I think we all needed a little celebration of you to tell you how much we all love you." Isla flashed Andry a smile.

Andry stepped forward, coming far closer to Isla than would be normally appropriate and certainly closer than Isla had thought she would after the night of the car incident. Isla held her ground, crossing her arms and raising an eyebrow at Andry. She wondered just how much closer Andry would get, if she would end up in the same state that Andry had left her in that night.

"Well, I certainly felt the love," Andry's voice dropped low, seductive almost.

Isla's breathing quickened, her entire body telling her to shift forward and her brain jumping in to tell her to stay still. She panicked for an out, for a shift. Looking directly into Andry's eyes, Isla grasped the first topic she could think of. "How was the meeting?"

"Like any other meeting, longer than necessary and pointless, but there were some good parts to it." Andry stayed put, not moving.

Isla knew she liked to be out on the playground when the students and parents were, that it gave the parents a time to see her that wasn't just when problems arose with their children. But today they were in her closed office, and Isla couldn't stop the feelings rushing through her, the joy, the happiness, the gentleness. She had done something good for Andry, and she could see it in her eyes without even trying to look too hard.

"Katie should be coming soon," Andry added. "You were

right, she wanted to see everything in person, but she couldn't get a ride over here until later."

Isla grinned. "Guess she really does need the car, doesn't she?"

"She likes to think so, but she's managed so far without one." Andry snagged Isla's hand, squeezing lightly. "Thanks again for letting me keep the car at your place until her birthday. I want it to be a big surprise reveal."

"I'm sure it will be." Isla deliberately dragged her gaze down Andry's body and arm to their joined hands, but Andry didn't let go, not like she expected her to. Isla loved it. She didn't want the moment to end even though she knew it had to, and probably sooner rather than later.

"And thank you for that night. I didn't realize how much I just needed someone to talk to." Sadness crept over Andry's eyes, the bow of her lips dipping slightly. But she didn't move, staying right next to Isla, as if she wanted to know this was all okay.

Isla's smile faltered slightly, but when they locked their eyes together again, she was at home in Andry's look. She wanted to be there for Andry, to be the one Andry could confide in. Despite the other feelings mixed in, Isla had loved being the person Andry had come to. "Anytime you need that, I'm here for you."

"Same goes for you." Andry squeezed her hand again, their fingers lacing unexpectedly.

Isla couldn't figure out what was going on. This was more intimate than it should be. There was more touching, and as much as their conversation was light and general, the undertones raged with unsnapped tension, and it just kept pulling tighter. That night, on her couch, over a week ago, Isla had been damn sure they were about to kiss, but she'd pulled back. Andry had shifted. Everything had broken around them, hadn't it?

"I'll remember that." Again her voice was rough, husky, barely above a whisper. Heat filled her from the touch. Isla swallowed hard, her lips parted as she struggled to come up with something else to say. "I'll get this cleaned up before the morning."

"I don't envy you that job." Andry's eyes glittered with humor.

"Part of the downfall of playing a prank, but this one was well worth it." Isla finally listed forward on her toes, bringing them even closer. How much could she pull out of Andry? It was beyond clear to her that the attraction between them went both ways, and she wanted to play with it, tease it out and see what it looked like under all those layers of job descriptions, duties, and friendship.

"I suppose it is, but you're right, the cleanup is usually well worth the prank itself."

"Especially if I get to hear you laugh that hard again." Isla winked, adding a little more flirt to her tone.

Andry's cheeks instantly tinged pink with whatever thoughts or memories were running through her head. "Was I that loud?"

Isla would love to hear just how loud Andry could be, and when the grin hit her, it wasn't because of the prank. "Everyone heard you, Andry. That's why we all came into the hallway."

"My god." Andry closed her eyes, hanging her head and shaking it. "I'll never live that down, will I?"

"I'm sure you'll do something else that'll erase this memory, and if all else fails, the kids do eventually grow up and out of this school, so in about six years, not many of us will remember it anymore."

"But you always will, won't you?" Andry's look was direct and sure.

Isla stuttered. She'd had a teasing comment back, but Andry seemed so serious all of a sudden, and she couldn't look away, she couldn't bring it back to that type of flirting. "I'll always remember it."

"Hey Mommy!"

Isla snapped her hand back, her chin downcast as she

stepped away from Andry like they'd just been caught in the act of something far more intimate than a simple conversation. *Because it was.*

Andry crossed her arms and eyed Katie over as she came into the office with hesitation in her step. "Hey, baby. Did you see Ms. Walsh's handiwork?"

"Some of it! You'll have to show me the rest." Katie's eyes were not full of innocence, as though she had known exactly what was going on in that room before she came in.

"Let's go do a quick tour then. Ms. Walsh has to take it all down soon." Andry tossed Isla a look, her principal face perfectly in place.

Isla lost her breath, because underneath that mask, she knew exactly what was behind the look. They'd been unexpectedly interrupted in a moment that they shouldn't have shared. Isla nodded and flashed Katie a smile. "Better go quick. I don't anticipate I'll be here all night doing this."

"Let's go." Katie eyed Isla carefully before shifting out of the door.

Andry allowed herself to be led out of her office. Isla released a pent-up breath as soon as she was alone. She gave them a head start in the library by taking down all of the photos in Andry's office and the school offices, although the admin team had already started on some of that as well. It was going to take her a good couple of hours, but like she'd told Andry, it had all been worth it in the end, especially with that interrupted moment in the office.

CHAPTER

Eighteen

ANDRY GOT into her car ready to take Katie to school. She sighed, putting her coffee in the cup holder and pulling on her seatbelt. She put the car in drive and took her foot off the brake.

"What's going on between you and Ms. Walsh?"

Andry slammed on the brake again, the entire car jerking forward. She clenched her jaw and glanced over at her daughter, her beautiful black-haired blue-eyed daughter, who looked exactly like her ex-wife. Katie's question had been direct and pointed, and Andry guessed her curiosity had been ramping up for the last week since Katie had walked in on them in her office.

Shifting her car into park, Andry turned in her seat to look her daughter over, thoroughly. Was she mad? Was she struggling? Was this simple curiosity? Was she scared? When she couldn't answer any of those questions, Andry pushed the button on her seatbelt, indicating to Katie that they were going to be there for a bit.

"Why are you asking?" Andry took the slow way into this conversation, wanting to know exactly where Katie was coming from.

"Because it seemed like there was a whole lot going on in your office the other day."

Having her suspicions confirmed didn't sway Andry's curiosity as to what exactly Katie felt about it. Andry's stomach fluttered before it tightened, and she struggled to keep her body relaxed. Katie stayed locked in her seat, her backpack at her feet. The air in the car was uncomfortable. Katie had a habit of picking these moments, when they were both trapped with no escape, to have these deep conversations.

"I'm not dating Isla." Andry chose to use her first name, specifically wanting to see what Katie would do with it. Since Isla had been Katie's teacher all those years ago, she had done her best to maintain that professional level of relationship between them, but Katie was older, and Andry couldn't deny that there was more between her and Isla than it seemed from the outside. Katie just had an insider's viewpoint.

"That's not what I asked," Katie mumbled, her eyes glued to her hands folded in her lap.

"Then what are you asking, because I'm not sure I understand, and I want to know what's going on." Andry could wait her out. She would gladly send Katie to school late if it meant they were able to have this conversation.

"I don't know." Katie shuffled her feet on the floor.

Andry held the silence, using it to her advantage, needing Katie to know that she was listening and was going to hear everything that she said.

"Are you dating?"

"No, I promise you that we're not."

"Do..." Katie licked her lips, her thumb pressing down on the top of her hand. "...do you want to?"

That was a question Andry hadn't toyed with answering and had successfully avoided thinking about it in depth since the last prank Isla had pulled. She needed to navigate this conversation very carefully because she didn't want to tell any untruths, and depending on Katie's reaction, she didn't want to give her any false hope either.

"I think Isla Walsh is a very attractive woman." Andry played it safe.

"Mom!" Katie whined.

Andry couldn't stop the smile that touched her lips, but she sobered up pretty quickly. "I think I'm ready to consider dating again. I don't know if that'll be with Isla or someone else. Right now, Isla is going through some things and what she needs most is a friend. I can be that for her."

"But you're her principal. Isn't that why you and Mom couldn't work at the same school?" Katie was so damn smart sometimes, and very good at putting two and two together when the dots didn't always connect easily.

"Yes, it is, and should Isla and I decide to do anything going forward, that will have to be a point of discussion, but we're nowhere near that, Katie. Okay? We're not dating, and it's not even a topic of conversation right now."

"But you want to date her?" Katie wasn't going to let go until she got the exact answer she wanted.

Andry pursed her lips, leaning fully into her seat. "Yes."

"Ms. Walsh?" Katie raised her thick eyebrows and pinned Andry with a look that said she meant business.

Sighing, Andry lifted Katie's chin and shifted the entire dynamic of the conversation. "What I'm saying is that I think I'm ready to date again. That's going to have to be enough for now because I can't answer any of the other questions."

"Because you don't want to or because you don't know?"

"Because I don't know." Andry tried to be as honest as possible, but even then, there were limits to what she wanted to share with her only child because she was a child. She didn't need the drama of adult relationships, not yet anyway. "Okay?"

"Okay. But...just give me a heads up about who it is, will you?"

"I'll do my best."

"There's not that many lesbian-leaning women your age in this town." Katie's cheeks flushed red.

Andry shook her head, chuckling lightly. "Thanks for calling me old, kid."

Katie shrugged. "I call it like I see it."

"That you do." Andry shifted back into her seat and put her belt on before putting the car into reverse. "But let's get you to school, okay?"

"Sure thing!" Katie was back to her happy self, the relief from the conversation having an almost instant effect between them. Andry couldn't have hoped for anything less than that.

"You leave on Thursday morning, right?"

"Yeah. The bus leaves at like five I think."

"Perfect," Andry mumbled. She hated getting up so early in the morning to bring Katie to and from places. Not because it was Katie and she needed it, but because she was anything but a morning person, despite being in teaching for the last twenty years.

"I can see if I can hitch a ride if you want."

"No, I'll take you." Andry reached over and touched Katie's hand. "I won't see you for four days, so I'll want to see you off properly."

"Just don't embarrass me, okay?"

"Every time, baby. It's my job to do that." Andry laughed as she continued her morning routine. Katie looked absolutely appalled by the fact that she couldn't tell if Andry was telling the truth or not.

∾

The idea hit Andry hard. She swiftly slipped out of her office, having the time that day for some miraculous reason. She made her way down to Isla's classroom and the substitute that had come in for a couple hours while Isla was gone for an appointment.

Hands on hips, Andry noticed they were just sitting there reading in silence. She stood at the front of the classroom until she had everyone's attention, the kids' eyes riveted to her. She hadn't said a single word, not even to the substitute. Everyone looked at her confused.

"I have a proposal to make to you all," Andry said, her voice clear as she kept her hands on her hips. "And I think it might be an idea that you'll like."

When none of them said anything, Andry pursed her lips and eyed them each carefully.

"We all know that Ms. Walsh is really good at playing pranks on me, right?"

They all nodded their heads, their eyes bright as if it were dawning on them what was about to happen.

"Do you want to help me play a prank on her?"

"Yes!" They burst with excitement, the energy in the room intensifying.

"Good." Andry clapped her hands and risked a glance to her substitute. "So, it's still relatively a warm day outside, and we're going to have to make this quick and do it quietly. Do you all agree to that? I want no talking in the hallways as we move."

"Yes, Dr. Murphey."

Andry moved her hands together and squinted at the kids. "First thing we're going to do is stand up."

When the kids had all listened and were standing behind their desks, Andry made an *okay* sign at them. "Perfect! You are all doing wonderful with this already. Now pick up your chair. I want you to line up and follow me."

Andry led them all outside by the fastest route. They all stared at her like she was a bit crazy, but that was normal, and she knew she hadn't given them a whole lot of explanation. With a deep breath, Andry shoved her hands into her pockets.

"Okay, I want you to leave your chairs here, and we're going to walk silently back into the classroom."

Back again they went. Andry vibrated with excitement. She

had thought about pulling this prank so many times on her teachers when she was growing up, but she was finally going to do it.

She liked Isla, more than she was willing to put words to at the moment, but that very tense moment in her office had turned that part of her thoughts in a direction Andry was very willing to go. When all the students and she were back inside the classroom, she stood at the front of the class. They all mingled, still having no idea what to do.

"I need you to work in pairs. Grab your tables and bring them outside, be very careful with the legs, okay?"

The kids worked together, Andry helping them around the corners and through the doors as they went—primarily through the classroom door, which was the smallest one to get through. She put her hands on her hips as she watched them put the tables upright outside.

"Now set it up like you're in the classroom and make these windows—" Andry pointed to the windows that were to their class "—as the front of the classroom."

"This is awesome!"

"So cool!"

Andry smiled brightly as the kids went to work setting up their outdoor classroom. It was perfect. Isla was due back in the next fifteen minutes, and the kids would be nowhere in sight. Not to mention the timing couldn't have been more perfect because there was no recess scheduled before they would bring all their things back inside.

Andry moved to the substitute, speaking quietly with her. "Just continue to teach them like normal. They're just finishing up reading time, right?"

The sub nodded.

"Then what a perfect day for them to read outside." Andry walked away, a lightness in her step.

She flashed her card to get back inside, making her way to her office. She had a full fifteen minutes before she went back to the classroom to see Isla's reaction. It would be absolutely perfect.

She sat at her desk, unable to focus on anything other than the prank she was about to pull. It was one of epic proportions, especially for her. The kids were going to get a kick out of teasing their teacher, which added joy to it, and this was certainly something they would remember for years and years to come.

Andry glanced at them outside, finding that most of them were studiously reading their lessons for the day. At least they were good listeners. It was one of the better classes that they had, and she'd known that going into this idea. Isla had all-stars for students, and they didn't have the same issues that some of the other classrooms did.

But what was she going to do about Isla? Especially concerning the conversation that she'd had with Katie that morning. Katie hadn't made something out of nothing. When they were in her office after the last prank that Isla had pulled, there was something more between them, something that was deep and tension-filled.

That brought Andry right back to that night with the car. That night had been so full of every drama she had experienced in the last few years but in a much calmer fashion. Having Isla hold her hand and comfort her while she'd shared everything had been more than she could ever ask for. That moment was what Andry craved. Attention, but also comfort and support from someone she knew had her best interests in mind.

But then there was *that* moment. The almost-kiss, as she'd come to call it. It would have been so easy to give in to every physical desire she had because damn did she have those. Yet with the state Isla had been in, and the fact that they were there because of a fight she'd had with Chris, she'd been glad when Isla had broken the moment. But damn had she dreamed about it since.

Days.

Nights.

Any time in between that she had a chance to stop and think about Isla and that was right where she found herself. Even now, as she sat in her office trying to get work done, she was distracted by Isla. *Ms. Walsh.* The sixth-grade teacher she had hired eight years ago right out of college. A risk, but so worth it.

Would that also apply to more?

Andry wanted to find out, she wanted more than what they had, and she could sufficiently say that now. Katie had been right to call her out. Andry shifted uncomfortably before she stood up and walked slowly toward Isla's classroom. It was almost time, and this prank held more weight than a mere joke. It held with it anticipation of something new, something that would bring her immense joy. All she had to do was wait for Isla.

CHAPTER
Nineteen

ISLA SAT in her car and let out a deep breath. Therapy always stole the energy from her. It was supposed to—at least that's what she told herself every time she went. And she'd come back with a fuller understanding of what was going on between her and Andry, not to mention Larisa's push to rely on that relationship instead of putting the weight of her life in Wil's hands. It was a crush—but it was teetering on the brink of being far more than just that. She trusted Andry, which wasn't something she could say for many people in her life.

Trust was the be-all and end-all of any relationship.

As soon as that trust was broken, she booted people out of her life faster than they could come up with a rebuttal. She'd always been that way, which was why her circle in life was so damn small, and why it was so difficult for her and Lynda.

Forcing her way out of her car, Isla flashed her badge against the door to get inside the building. She built herself up with each step as she went, preparing to teach for the rest of the day before she could go home and crash for the night. She was desperate for it. Squaring her shoulders, her shoes clicking as she walked down the empty hall that was alive with energy, she let it seep into her bones.

Isla grabbed the handle for her classroom, taking one last second to steel herself for whatever she was going to be greeted with. Pushing the door open, she stepped inside and stopped short. A rush of breath left her lungs as she stared at her very empty classroom. She wasn't sure she had ever seen it so empty before, even when she moved into it each fall and out each spring.

"What the..." Isla stepped inside, skimming over the empty space on the floor where her students should be, where their tables and chairs should be.

Moving toward her desk, she stopped when that was gone too. Isla glanced back at the door, her heart racing as the silence permeated the dark recesses of her mind. Panic swelled in her chest, tightening against her ribs before she calmed it down. She needed to figure out what was going on quickly. The resounding rap made her jump three feet back. The knock on the window from outside and when she was greeted with Andry's bright smile and face, Isla knew all was well.

Behind Andry sat her entire class, perfect in their seats as they watched her reaction. Busting out in a laugh, Isla put her hands to her mouth and dropped her purse on the floor. Tears filled the corners of her eyes as she shook her head at them, laughing. Moving to the window, Isla opened it wide and pointed at the kids.

"You are all crazy! Oh my god." She laughed again, making eye contact with Andry.

Immediately, Isla left her classroom and headed outside. She put her hands on her hips as she walked out, a smile she hadn't been able to wipe away on her lips. "What are you doing out here?"

"We're pulling a prank on you, Ms. Walsh!" Jaxon laughed. "Just like we did with Dr. Murphey."

"Well, you succeeded! I can't believe... How did you get everything out here?"

Andry faced her. "We did it carefully and quietly, am I right?"

"Yes!"

Isla giggled again, a hand over her stomach as the tightness that had been there when she'd entered the school was completely gone in the flash she'd had coming into her class- room. She had never expected something like this. Andry grabbed her arm and pulled her a little closer.

"They completed their lesson for the period, too, because I told them we weren't coming out here to have fun."

"You guys!" Joy overwhelmed her. Isla shook her head again, covering Andry's hand with her own to keep herself upright. "I can't even believe you did this. I'm still in shock. You definitely won this round."

The kids were laughing and chattering amongst themselves. Isla looked over each face. They seemed so pleased with the fact that they had been able to pull one over on her, the self- proclaimed queen of pranks. Never had she expected this. She still couldn't even wrap her mind around it.

"All right." Andry stepped forward and clapped her hands to get their attention. "Now, we have to put everything back together, right? Let's do it the exact opposite way we brought it out. Tables first!"

The kids moved efficiently, pulling the chairs out from the tables, and they started to move back inside. Andry went with them and Isla followed.

Isla was still in a state of shock, apparently. She couldn't even find words to speak, and her focus was completely gone. It was a good thing it was lunch soon because she wasn't going to be able to focus without that small break and the kids probably weren't either. When they had the tables in, the kids went back for the chairs.

Andry touched Isla's arm lightly as soon as they had a moment without kids running by them. "Are you okay?"

"Yeah. I'm perfect." Isla lifted her gaze to meet Andry's, making sure that Andry knew everything would be fine. It had to be because she didn't have another option. "Do you have time after work tonight?"

"I don't. Your lunch?"

Isla nodded. It was a shorter period of time and had to happen in the school, but it was better than nothing. "Sounds good."

"I'll come to you," Andry added. They would have fewer interruptions if they did this in her classroom rather than Andry's office.

Isla went back into her classroom, helping the kids set up the tables and chairs where they were supposed to be. She had them sitting and starting their math lesson within record time. She hadn't thought that they were going to be able to focus that well.

Another hour and she had the kids lined up for lunch. Taking them down to the cafeteria, Isla caught Andry's attention as she went. Once the kids were dropped off, Andry caught up with her, a lunchbox in her hand.

"Ready?" Andry asked.

Isla nodded, not sure she could trust her voice to speak just then. She hadn't ever been the person who was willing to say a whole lot out loud, and the fact that Andry was the person she was going to talk to was something else entirely. It was pushing the boundaries of their professional relationship, but they'd already done that several times that school year. Still, it was an uneasy feeling in the pit of Isla's stomach, and she knew it was going to stretch her habits.

The dark cloud loomed over her head, and Isla knew it was there. She hadn't ever been able to get rid of it, but lately it seemed full and closer to her than ever before. She'd usually been able to avoid it or make it disappear behind a bright fake sun, but not lately. Andry let her be in silence as they walked down the hall to her classroom. She shut the door as soon as they were inside.

Relief flooded her, seeping into every crevice Isla didn't know she had. Heavily, she walked to her desk and sat down, pulling out the lunch she had packed last night. She set it on the table as Andry settled in across from her, where her students usually sat when she had to talk to them individually.

Andry eyed her over before pulling the zipper and taking out a sandwich. "You want to tell me what's going on?"

"Yes," Isla answered clearly, even though she was still scared to let someone else in. Isla dragged in a deep breath and let it out slowly. "I wasn't at a doctor appointment. I was at a therapy appointment."

Andry cringed. "What if I told you I already suspected that? Which is why I didn't hesitate to approve the time for you to go."

Cold washed through Isla. She hadn't thought it was so obvious. She'd thought she'd done a better job at hiding everything, but then again, Andry wasn't just anyone. "I try to make the appointments after school, but it's not always possible."

"Hey now." Andry softened her tone immediately, reaching out to touch Isla's shaking hand. "I understand, okay? Stuff happens in our lives and sometimes we need to go talk to someone who's a bit smarter than us and way more removed from the situation. I get it, and I'm not going to stop you from going to an appointment."

"Thanks, but... Well, that's not really why I brought it up." Isla fiddled with the baggie of cucumbers she had brought, still not eating anything.

"Then talk to me. You know I'm here to listen."

If only it was that easy. Isla hated being this vulnerable in front of anyone, and the fact Andry was her boss added an element of insecurity to that. But she trusted Andry, and she had to keep reminding herself of that. This was a woman who had shown up every time Isla had needed her, had switched things around to be there for her.

With a deep breath, Isla locked her eyes on Andry's face. "I know you are. That's why I'm sitting here."

Andry gave a slight nod but kept silent, waiting for Isla to continue.

"You know I have issues with my stepmother, Lynda. It's not just...they're not simple issues, and it's all coming back up again because she and my best friend are dating. I can't escape her anymore, and I think...well, I realized that I was doing a whole lot of avoiding in that relationship. It's not just her fault that she was a crappy parent when I was growing up. It's my fault because I didn't let her be a good parent, no matter what she did or said."

"It's really easy to blame someone else for your problems, isn't it?"

"Yeah." Isla smiled slightly. "I built up my dad like he was the best dad on the planet, and he was a really good dad, but he wasn't perfect. And I never really looked at things from Lynda's perspective. She never took a starring role in parenting because Dad always did that. She was a stepparent, but when she was all we were left with..."

"You still didn't give her permission to have that role," Andry finished for her.

Isla nodded. "I didn't. I didn't want her. I wanted my dad."

"What kid wouldn't?" Andry's hand was on hers again, and Isla had no idea when that had happened. She was so close to tears again, but with one hard swallow, she knew she could keep it all in.

"No one would want to lose their parent, and I lost both of mine."

"But you still have one."

"I do," Isla agreed, probably for the first time in years. She'd never liked that comment, but it was true. Her dad had made sure there was someone in her life who would take care of her and love her, and Lynda had done that to the best of her ability. When she was a kid, she'd hated thinking that, but now it was nice to know she wasn't alone. She had been loved, even beyond death. "Seeing you and Chris the other night really hit home for me."

"How so?" Andry gave Isla's hand a gentle squeeze before she went back to eating her lunch.

Isla picked at hers, still not actually eating anything. This was the hard part to say because it was such a sensitive topic of conversation all around. "You weren't fighting about the actual problem."

"Which is what?"

"You both love Katie, and you need to stop fighting against each other loving her more because it doesn't matter. You both love her."

Andry straightened her shoulders, pursing her lips, and nodding sharply. "You're right."

Isla stuttered. She hadn't expected Andry to agree with her so quickly, and that meant she had to steer back toward the real topic of conversation—her revelations from therapy, at least the ones she was willing to share. "I never gave Lynda the benefit of the doubt. To me she was always the woman who couldn't live up to a ghost."

"She never stood a chance."

Isla's heart dropped in the simplicity of Andry's words. She hadn't done anyone any favors growing up, but that was all changing, and she was working on that day by day. This was one of the ways. "She didn't, and I want to give her one, but it's so damn hard some days." Isla dropped the pretense that she was going to eat and shoved her food back into the bag. "So therapy today was hard, but a good hard, and I do want to make a change in my relationship with her."

"So do it, but do it slowly. Going all in is hard to keep up with." Andry sent her a tender look.

"I am." Isla gave Andry a soft smile, her heart picking up its pace now that the heavy conversation was out of the way. She had done what she wanted, which was to share with Andry. "I do have to say that the prank you pulled today was epic, and it was exactly what I needed to get my day going again."

"Happy to oblige." Andry put her fingers to her forehead in a half-salute.

"It was brilliant, really. I think the kids are going to be talking about this one for decades to come." Isla laughed lightly.

"I hope they do. I'm not sure I have another prank like that in my line up."

Isla winked, the temptation to flirt too strong, and now that she'd admitted her crush to herself, she didn't want to resist it anymore. "You can find one, I'm sure of that."

Pulling out her food, Isla finally started eating. Her stomach was settled, that uneasy feeling was gone, and she was more comfortable and happy than she could remember being in a long time. She was doing well in making those changes—her therapist had even told her that—but it was still hard and a fight nearly every day to make sure she was staying on track and not slipping back into old habits. But she knew that with Andry's help, she could conquer this. She had to because there wasn't another option.

CHAPTER

Twenty

ANDRY CAME into Isla's classroom unexpectedly halfway through the morning. Isla spun around and made eye contact before Andry beckoned her out with a curl of her finger. Frowning, Isla turned to the class. "Work on the first page of your assignment. I'll be right back."

Isla stepped away from them and out into the hallway. Her heart pattered rapidly, the seriousness in Andry's face, the graveness, washing away any jokes Isla might have made. Andry shut the door as soon as she was in the hallway.

"What's going on?" Isla asked.

"Alice's mom is on her way here, and she asked for some assistance in breaking the news that Alice's father died of cancer about an hour ago. I've got the school counselor coming in on this, but I think Alice would really benefit from having you there because you're her teacher."

Isla sucked in a breath, all the muscles in her body going rigid. She hadn't ever thought she'd be dealing with this, not in this way, and she could already feel her panic rising. She wasn't sure she could. Andry's hand on her arm brought her back to reality, the ringing in her ears coming to a sharp stop.

"I need you on this. Alice knows you better than she knows me." Andry's voice was so clear and strong. Isla latched onto it.

"Yeah." Isla swallowed around a lump in her throat, unable to clear it. "Yeah, I can do that."

The words didn't match with what she was feeling because she was anything but confident. Sucking in a deep breath, Isla glanced at her classroom door.

"He's had cancer for years, but she wasn't expecting it to happen this morning." Andry squeezed Isla's arm again. "Hunter is going to take over your class for the next hour. Fill him in on what he needs, and then bring Alice down with her things, will you? I'm going to set up a plan to break the news."

"Yeah," Isla answered again, not sure what to say. She would agree to anything Andry told her just to get out of the situation. She rolled her shoulders as she stepped back into her classroom, picking up right where she'd left off, going through the motions of the science lesson, and pushing the thoughts of what was about to happen as far from her mind as possible.

Hunter came in thirty minutes later when he'd finished up his library class. Isla filled him in quickly on the rest of the lesson, and he seemed confident enough to move forward with it. Pursing her lips, Isla moved to Alice's desk and bent down. Her heart thundered so loudly she could barely speak.

"Alice, I need you to grab your backpack and come with me."

Alice's bright blue eyes lifted to Isla's face, and they both knew. There was no hiding anything. Alice's eyes watered, but she snagged her backpack from her cubby and left with Isla in tow. They walked down to Andry's office. The room was filled with people—stifling. Isla's breathing was shallow, and she knew she should be taking deeper breaths, but she couldn't manage to do that.

A live wire shot through her, and her hands were shaking, her feet unsure as she stood. Alice's mom was already there, and they both sat at the small table in the corner of Andry's office. Her face was pale, but her eyes puffy and red, her lips dry and cracked. Devastating grief was painted across her. Isla had seen that look on Lynda. Everyone else—Andry, Isla, and Keri, the school counselor—stood on the edges of the room and watched. Isla could barely focus.

"Daddy died this morning, baby." Her voice cracked, the words barely leaving her lips, but they all heard her through the echoing quiet.

Isla clenched her eyes shut, the bright lights from the police cars, Lynda's wail as soon as the words had left the officer's mouth.

"He loved you so much."

Hot tears filled her eyes, and they streamed down her cheeks, burning her skin. Isla had no idea if it was her now or her then. Alice's mom clenched Alice's hand tightly—Aisling clinging to Isla for hours, so tightly that Isla could feel the pricks of her recently cut nails digging into her flesh, but she didn't say a damn thing about it.

Alice cried, snot filling her nose and stopping up her ability to breathe. Andry squatted down next to her, speaking low. The words were washed away and there was just a loud ringing in Isla's ears, her heart pounding in her chest so hard that she swore it would break out. The office around her was dark, like the sky that morning. She needed Wil. She needed that steadying presence to hold her because Wil would understand, wouldn't she? She had to.

Andry stood back up, stepping away from the mother and daughter and giving them some space. Isla had always had too much space, never able to find anything but space. Aisling had clung to her, yes, but after a few weeks, Isla spun in an orbit completely her own, everyone else going on around her. Spinning on her toes, Isla left the office.

She walked straight out the front doors of the school, the cold fall air nipping at her cheeks. She leaned against the red brick wall of the school, her hands on her knees as her tears fell helplessly to the cement below. She dragged in a ragged breath, barely able to get enough air into her lungs to function, to stop seeing the dark spots floating across her vision, to stop the onslaught of memories as they swarmed her repeatedly.

Lynda wailing.

Aisling's grip.

Bright police lights.

Bringing her hand up to her mouth, Isla bit down on the side of her thumb. A new pain speared through her, this one completely physical and totally outside the events of that day. Clenching her eyes tight, Isla straightened her back and put her head against the wall. She counted her breaths.

In—One. Two. Three. Four. Five.

Out—Five. Four. Three. Two. One.

Again.

Isla lost track of how many times she repeated the process, but eventually, when she pried her eyes open, the bright sun shone on her. It wasn't nighttime. It wasn't early morning. The police weren't there to talk to her—not again. With a deep breath, Isla relaxed her fists first. Glancing down, she saw the outline of her teeth in her skin. She rubbed it with her other hand, trying to make the redness vanish.

She had to get back inside before anyone noticed, but first she had to make sure that she could walk into her classroom and teach for the rest of the day. Her kids would be the perfect distraction, but she still needed to give them what she could of herself. Isla lifted her fingers to her neck and counted her pulse. Once it was calm enough, she dropped her arm back down and shook out her hands as guilt ate away at her stomach. She'd left Alice, just like everyone had left her.

Standing up straight wasn't as hard as she had thought it would be. Isla shook her hands out again and turned on her toes to the front door. She wanted to go to the office, hug her student and comfort her the exact way she'd needed all those years ago, but she couldn't bring herself to do it. Not just yet, not when she would bring too much of her own grief into the moment. Wiping her eyes, she let out a short breath and walked right inside and back to her classroom, glancing down the hall toward Andry's office as she passed.

~

Isla dragged herself into her apartment. As soon as she shut the door, she sank to the floor. Tears flowed down her cheeks freely and she let them. This was the fastest way to get it out of her system, and she needed that. She'd made it through the day, the kids hadn't questioned anything, and she was well on her way to being able to deal with this without the pressure of work and school.

Knocking on her door vibrated through her.

"Isla, open up." Andry's voice was filled with worry and maybe even a tinge of fear.

Shifting around, Isla forced her body to move even though she didn't want to. She stood up, her things left abandoned on the floor. She didn't have the energy to deal with them first, and the second startling knock let her know there wouldn't be time for that anyway. The knob was cold on her hand as she turned it and opened the door, finding Andry on the other side, eyes wide, lips parted. Andry shook her head slowly.

"I'm so sorry I asked so much of you." Andry stepped forward into the apartment, her arms open wide.

Isla didn't even hesitate. She wrapped her arms around Andry's back, holding onto her tightly as she buried her face in Andry's shoulder. The tears continued to flow, her sobs tearing through her with a force she wasn't sure could be contained. But Andry did just that.

She held on tightly, her fingers rubbing up and down Isla's back in a soothing pattern. Isla tightened her grip, her fingers pulling at Andry's jacket until she could bunch it together. The metal from their lanyards and plastic from the badges dug into her chest, but she wasn't going to move until she was steady.

The door was still wide open as they stood right in the door-way. Isla didn't care, she closed her eyes and dragged in Andry's scent in an attempt to soothe her shaking body. She wasn't sure how long it took, but Isla finally let out a long sigh, her body sliding back to where she had been earlier that day.

"Thank you," she mumbled, suddenly aware of how inappro-priate this was. No one had ever held her like this before, no one but Wil. Isla had never allowed it. She'd always run away and hidden when she'd had these moments, when she was so over-whelmed by the memories and the past that she couldn't see her way through the dark.

Andry didn't move like Isla anticipated she would. Instead, she held on tighter, pressing her cheek into the side of Isla's head. The movements on her back, fingers gliding, took on a more purposeful move. Isla could tell Andry was getting ready to let go, but she wasn't ready yet—neither of them were.

"I hate days like today," Andry murmured. "They're so rare, but my god, what Alice is going through tonight."

"I know she's not okay, but is she..." Isla trailed off at a loss for words.

"She's strong," Andry whispered. "She was ready for it and even comforted her mom a bit."

Isla's lips quirked into a wry smile before she sucked in a shud-dering breath. She should have been there for her, but she'd been woefully unprepared for something like that. "I never should have left her like that. I thought I'd have..." Isla stopped, not sure what to say. Have her shit together? Not be affected by her student's trauma? Focusing in again, she resumed, "I remember being her. Everyone's going to look at her differently when she comes back, and they'll never look at her the same again."

"I know," Andry whispered. "It's a cruel world. Compassion one minute and pity the next."

Isla shuddered, not moving, her face planted into Andry's shoulder. Honesty—Isla had never expected to find it today. They stayed in each other's arms for a bit longer until a cold breeze blew up through the still-open doorway.

Pulling back, Isla ran her fingers under her eyes to clear the stains on her cheeks. "We should probably close that."

"Yeah." Andry shifted to the side, shutting the door behind her. "Go take a minute or two or ten. I'm going to order us some crappy food."

Isla nodded, happy not to have to make a decision. She walked to her bathroom and leaned over the counter. She didn't want to look at herself in the mirror. It would be so hard to see all that pain and heartache reflected at her, but she needed to do it. Steadying herself, Isla raised her gaze. Her eyes were red and swollen, along with her nose. She clenched her fingers around the edge of the counter and blew out a breath. Her hair was a mess, no longer in the neatly plaited braid she had put it in that morning.

She took the time she had been given, washing her face and taking her makeup off since it was ruined anyway. She pulled the braid out and threw her long hair up into a messy bun. Then she walked to her bedroom and changed into the comfiest pair of fuzzy pajamas that she had. When she got back to the living room, Andry was sitting on her couch with two glasses of water in front of her.

Isla plopped down next to her, far closer than she would have ever dared before, but she needed that touch to center herself, to bring her back to the reality she found herself in. Her voice was raspy when she spoke. "I had a flashback to the day my dad died."

"I'm so sorry," Andry whispered, their hands laced together on Andry's thigh. "I shouldn't have asked you to be in that room."

Isla didn't comment on that. If she'd had her choice she

would have preferred not to have been, but it would have hit her at some point anyway.

"Alice is going to have those moments, and we're going to be in them." A lump formed in Isla's throat, wanting anything but being part of someone else's tragedy. "She's going to be mad at him for dying, mad at herself for being mad at him, she's going to be pissed at her mom."

Andry shifted and broke her grasp on Isla's hand. She wrapped her arm around Isla's shoulders and tugged her in so they were pressed side-to-side. Isla curled in on herself and calmed in the circle of Andry's comfort.

"No one is going to blame her for that," Andry's voice was soft, her breath against Isla's head with each word.

"Someone will. It might be Alice herself who does. I wish I'd been there for her today." That lump got bigger, making it harder to swallow. Now that her own panic receded, the guilt she was racked with hit her hard.

Andry brushed her hand up and down Isla's upper arm. "You'll be there for her tomorrow."

Keeping her mouth shut, Isla closed her eyes and reveled in the feeling of being so close to someone, not just anyone, but someone who wasn't judging her for anything. She needed this more than she'd been willing to admit to herself, but now there was no denying it. Everything in this moment was pure comfort.

"I think Alice will do better than I did."

Andry hummed her agreement. "Different circumstances, and she'll have you there to help her through it."

"True, but she's stronger than I was."

"Isla." Andry dragged in a deep breath, lifting Isla's chin so she could look in her eyes. "You're incredibly strong. After today, I don't think there's anyone quite as strong as you are. You held yourself together through that meeting, and then through the rest of the day, and you did it all for the kids."

"Tomorrow I have to tell them what happened." Isla's heart thudded hard, Andry's closeness pushing against her. She blinked slowly, wanting everything to snap in that one moment, but instinctively she knew she wouldn't be able to handle it.

"And you'll manage that. I know you will, because you understand what Alice is going through better than she can even realize right now, and you know what to look out for." Andry left no room for debate, but Isla didn't have the energy for it either. She was glad Andry saw that in her, but she wasn't entirely sure it was there most days.

Isla shifted her chin back down and settled against Andry's side once more. She didn't want to leave this space she had managed to find. She wanted to stay here for as long as possible, knowing that Andry had her best interest at heart, that she would protect her while Isla shattered, even if she couldn't put herself back together again.

CHAPTER
Twenty~One

WALKING through the aisle at the store, Andry let out a long sigh. She had kept an extra eye on Isla for the last week and a half, and she had managed to handle herself well throughout it. Andry kept waiting for Isla to break down again, but she hadn't. Isla had taken hold of her emotions and she'd plowed through everything that was thrown at her that week. Seeing Isla's face when she'd shown up at her apartment had been heartbreaking. That amount of emotional catastrophe wasn't something a person could just shed in a day or two, but Isla had worked through it brilliantly.

She'd stayed with Isla until close to midnight, texting Katie to let her know she was on her own for dinner. They had been cuddled up together most of the night, and Andry had done everything in her power to take care of Isla as best as she could.

She couldn't imagine being a young kid and losing a parent, not to mention both biological parents and being raised by a stepmother. She swallowed back the thought as she grabbed a bag of *Reese's* and threw them into her cart. Thank goodness all the candy was on sale because this prank was going to have a touch of humor but also comfort involved, and she didn't want to overtax her budget.

The idea had come to her from watching one of her favorite crime shows the night before with a particular blonde who was constantly annoyed by a particular brunette. Andry smiled to herself as she snagged another bag of candy and threw it into her cart. They could all use some levity.

By the time she finished checking out, she had limited time to get to the school and get everything set up. Isla had another therapy appointment that day, which would give Andry the perfect chance to lay her plans while she took over the classroom for the hour and a half Isla would be gone. Only half of that time would be with actual students. She smiled at the thought of what was going to go down.

Andry parked close to the door that day, dragging in the bags of stuff she had bought and her coffee for the morning. Making her way to her office, she ripped open the candy bags and dumped them into a grocery sack to make for easier pouring. Then she took the other items she'd bought and wrapped them in Christmas paper—it was the only kind she had at the house when she had checked. With everything set up, all she had to do was wait.

Isla left midday through the kids' music class. Andry stole into her classroom with the bags in her hands, wanting to do this without the kids around so they could be just as surprised by the reveal as Isla would be. They were excellent kids and had been amazing the few times they had been included, but this prank was just for her and Isla.

Andry went to the desk that Isla used for her computer work and pulled open the drawers, dumping the candy on top of whatever was inside it. She took the few wrapped presents and laid them right on top so they were easy to find. All in all, it took Andry about five minutes to complete. She stood back and looked over her handiwork. Nothing would look amiss when Isla came back, but when she sat down to do her computer work, she would find a wonderful surprise. Andry figured at the earliest that would be at the end of the day when all the students were gone, if not tomorrow morning.

Rolling her shoulders, she smiled to herself as she went back to her office to wait for the right time to take care of Isla's kids until she returned.

∼

Andry hadn't heard anything from Isla about the desk, and when she got home that night, she settled into her couch with work on her lap, the television on, and the house completely quiet. She couldn't stop wondering about whether or not Isla had found the little surprise. She rested her head back on the couch and closed her eyes, imagining the different ways Isla could have found it, her reactions, and the laughter that she would have let out.

But if that had been the case, surely Andry would have heard about it before she left the school that day, right? Pursing her lips, Andry went back to work on her laptop. Thoughts of Isla plagued her, and she couldn't get them out of her head. She needed to know if she'd pulled off the prank.

She stared at her phone, as if Isla would magically text or call and let her in on the secret. Sighing heavily, Andry tried to focus again on the work in front of her. She forced her mind and her gaze to the laptop resting on her knees. She did like Isla—way more than she should—and the concern for her in the last week and a half had shown her that. Groaning, Andry ran a hand through her hair. She didn't want to end up in another relationship like she'd been in with Chris. She couldn't be Isla's caretaker—then again, Isla had handled herself all week, coming out of her depression more each day.

She was almost done with everything when her doorbell rang. Frowning, Andry shifted her laptop to the coffee table and stood up, stretching her muscles, which really should have been stretched an hour ago. Walking to the door, she twisted the handle only to find Isla standing on the other side. Her hair was down in waves against her back, her eyes bright as she stared up at Andry from the stoop, her hands shoved into the pockets of her jacket as she rolled up on her toes.

"May I come in?"

"Sure." Confused, Andry opened the door wider. Isla walked by her, the scent from her soap filling Andry's nostrils, enticing her irresistibly. She must have gone home, showered, and then come over here because that scent was fresh. Why would she do that? Her crotch clenched tightly as she shut the door. Had Isla been thinking about her during that shower? Andry had done that on more than one occasion recently.

They moved to the couch. Just as she was settling in, Isla stood up sharply, eyeing Andry with a joking sort of look. "Hold on a minute."

"Okay?" Andry answered, confused about what was happening.

Isla pulled the candy out of her pockets, dropping it onto the coffee table with a flourish. Then she went back for another handful, dumping it again. Andry smiled with amusement as Isla did it a third and a fourth time. Finally she put her hands on her hips, staring down at Andry with an eyebrow raised and her lips twitching as she held back a smile.

"Answer me this," Isla started, trying to control her face. She pointed down at the candy on the table. "Is this, and the millions of pounds of other candy in my desk, your idea of flirting?"

Andry's heart gave one loud, hard thud, stealing her breath right from her lungs. She hadn't thought Isla would be *that* direct. Dragging her gaze from Isla's face to the candy littering her coffee table and computer, Andry sat with the question for as long as she could, knowing that Isla would insist on an answer soon enough. When she looked back up, Isla was eyeing her down.

Andry pointed at the candy, barely holding in her own smile in much the same manner Isla had. She could play coy to Isla's bluntness. "You think that me giving you something sweet to think about is flirting?"

"Oh..." Isla's eyes glittered. She slid in next to Andry, so close that their thighs were touching, her hand on Andry's knee warm and sure. "...is this how we're going to do it? All right. I think something sweet is exactly what you intended on giving me, along with a reminder of you throughout the rest of the school year or however long it takes my kids to eat the rest of that candy."

Andry's crotch clenched again, and she slid forward, finding her stride. She covered Isla's hand with her own, the realization of exactly what she wanted to happen settling into her chest. "Are you saying it's *unforgettable?* Because you can bet your butt I don't want you to forget it."

Isla's lips curled up. "You *are* flirting."

"Was that ever in question?" Andry's breaths were shallow, the tension between them thickening in a way they hadn't allowed to happen before. She'd always pulled back, but now, she didn't want to. She wanted this tension to intensify and consume her. Isla wasn't Chris. She showed so much more self-awareness and strength of character, dealing with her issues in mature ways. Andry's lips tingled as anticipation of what was next built.

"Yes." Isla smoothly flipped her hand up, lacing their fingers so their palms pressed together.

Andry flickered her gaze down to their hands, her stomach dropping at the obvious intimate touch. They had skirted around this for weeks now, backing away every time it had come up, but this time, Andry didn't want to. She was so drawn to Isla, to the vulnerability she had shared, to the strength she had to keep on going when it was so hard. Andry admired that, but it was more than just that. She was attracted to it. And if she really thought about it, she'd been attracted to Isla more and more as they had gotten to know each other.

"When did you question it?" Andry asked, probing to figure out exactly what Isla was thinking and feeling because it wasn't normal for a boss to be the first one to admit that they had feelings for an employee. She would have preferred it the other way around.

"Every day," Isla breathed out, her voice quiet. Their gazes locked, and Andry held the tension, curious to see what it would do and what Isla would say next. "But I haven't exactly been thinking well lately."

"You haven't," Andry agreed. "And now?"

Isla's face fell, her eyes dropping back down to their still clasped hands. It took a second, but Isla smoothed her thumb along the side of Andry's hand, moving it back and forth and teasing the skin with gentle touch. Andry held in her shiver, still not quite sure where they stood in this moment.

Isla whispered. "I know what I want to think, but it scares me. Does it scare you?"

"Yes," Andry murmured, dragging the word out. Her body was a tightwire, waiting for her to snap and give in to exactly what they both wanted. "What scares you?" Unable to resist, Andry reached up with her free hand and wrapped a strand of Isla's hair around one of her fingers. She gave it a slight tug before dropping her hand back down. She shouldn't distract Isla from what she was thinking.

"Whatever's between us," Isla mumbled, finally raising her gaze back up to meet Andry's.

"What is between us?" Andry needed to know. She needed Isla to answer the question, to finally say what they had avoided so narrowly throughout the last few months. Something about had been different from the start of the year, and this was definitely it. She looked at Isla differently than she had before.

"Are you going to make me say it?"

Andry's lips curled up. "Yeah, I am."

Time paused. Andry couldn't drag her gaze away from Isla's beautiful blue eyes, from her slightly parted lips. They were both deeply broken souls, made from their past into who they were, and she wanted to see if they could fit together. Andry was ready to risk it.

"This is so different than any other relationship I've been in," Isla finally said.

Andry raised her free hand up on the back of the couch, using it to prop her head up as she looked Isla over. The intensity of her thoughts shifted. "What do you mean?" She cursed herself as she slipped back into caretaker mode and made sure Isla was perfectly okay before they did anything more.

"I'm different, and I'm not trying to be selfish, but I don't know how to say it other than that. I'm different than I was before. These past few months have been intense, but I feel like I'm coming out the other side, finally, and I feel like I'm finally seeing you—all of you." Isla's cheeks flushed pink, the color running down her neck and to her ears. "I don't want to mess this up."

"What makes you think that you will?" Andry's heart fluttered, hope flaring in her chest again. She'd seen it too, but now she could allow herself to say it.

"Because I only know who I used to be."

Andry dragged in a deep breath, noting their fingers were still locked together and Isla was still tracing her thumb back and forth. "Isla, what do you want from me? From us?"

Isla's movement with her thumb stopped sharply, and Andry missed the gentle pattern she had created. When she looked into Isla's eyes, the confusion was gone—replaced with a quiet sort of confidence that Andry had come to know from her—and she adored it. Isla slid in closer, her free hand skating down Andry's arm on the back of the couch, to her shoulder, tracing her collar bone before it dropped down to her lap.

Andry shivered as the touch left her, the wake of ripples shuddering through her. She closed her eyes, breathing in the moment of pure sexual energy between them. She hadn't felt this in so long, and she wasn't sure she would have allowed herself to feel it for anyone other than Isla, someone who had come into her life in such an unexpected way.

"I want us to try. I want to take care of you when you get upset and make you smile when you least expect it." Isla grinned, sliding in with a glint to her eye as she pressed her cheek against Andry's and whispered in her ear, "I want to kiss you." Isla's breath was hot against her.

Andry sucked in a sharp breath, her heart racing as she turned toward Isla. She had longed for this, not just sex, not just her taking care of a partner, but someone who could match her in seeking out answers and making changes to who they were. Their eyes locked, Isla's pupils wide, their noses almost touching. "Then kiss me. Please."

It was slow at first. The tender touch of lips to lips, the tentative shift in their relationship as it clicked between them that this was really happening. Andry threaded her fingers into the hair at the back of Isla's neck, the soft waves heavenly against her skin. She filled with tingles of anticipation, of hope, of pleasure. Moving in more, Andry held on and took everything as slowly as possible. She wanted to savor this.

Isla pressed in, just the slightest change of pressure against her mouth. Andry's eyelids fluttered shut. She was just about to sneak her tongue out for a taste when the door opened. Andry jerked back, covering her mouth with her hand and keeping her eyes closed as embarrassment burned through her.

"Uh...hi...Ms. Walsh." Katie sounded so surprised, so shocked, so put off.

Andry cringed as she tried to pull herself together.

"Hi, Katie." Isla's voice was bright as she shifted back on the couch just enough to give Andry some more space.

She knew she was going to have to turn around and look, that they were going to have to talk about this, that it had to happen now, but if she had the choice to run away and hide, she would *so* take it.

"Were you two...?" Katie left the question off, and Andry

imagined she was pointing at them, her brow furrowed as she stood stiffly. She still couldn't bring herself to meet her daughter's gaze.

Andry's cheeks heated impossibly more. Isla let out a little groan before moving off the couch to stand. "I think I'll take that as my cue to exit. I'll talk to you soon, Andry."

"Yup," Andry managed to squeak out, her voice breaking on the word.

As soon as Isla left, the door shutting, Katie swung around and plopped right into the place Isla had vacated. Energy flowed off her, intense and directed right at Andry. "Were you kissing her?"

Andry managed to look her daughter in the eye, ready to answer the question when Katie started in again.

"I thought you said you two weren't dating! Are you dating her? She's my teacher!" Katie's eyes widened in shock.

"Former teacher. She hasn't been your teacher for seven years, Katie." Andry bit her tongue, realizing far too late that she was getting defensive when she didn't need to be. Putting her hand out in front of her to stop them both, she let out a rush of air. "We're not dating, to make that very clear. But yes...we were kissing."

Katie went silent, a deep, contemplative expression crossing her features, and Andry feared it was only going to lead to more confusion, so she tried to head it off.

"I don't know what we're doing. We didn't exactly get a chance to talk about it yet. But I do need to talk to you about it before any decisions are made." Andry pinned Katie with a serious look. "How do you feel about me potentially dating Isla?"

Katie shook her head slowly, her eyes wide but unseeing, no doubt the image she had seen when she walked into the house was clear in her memory. She pressed her lips together, her gaze downcast as she wrinkled her nose a little. She shrugged before locking her gaze on Andry's, a mix of guilt and hope in her eyes. "I...I honestly don't know. I want to be okay with it."

"Well, let's talk about that a bit, okay?"

"Okay."

Andry braced herself for the conversation that would no doubt last the entire night and into the next day. She only wished she could find some time to talk to Isla in there, but Katie was her priority no matter what, and she had to believe that Isla would understand that.

CHAPTER

Twenty-Two

"I KISSED MY BOSS." Panic welled in Isla's chest, coming out in her voice. She had no idea what to say other than that.

"You did *what?*" Wil's shock reverberated through the phone.

"I *kissed* my boss," Isla hissed, her voice low as if she said it any louder the entire world would know. It wasn't even that good of a kiss either, but she was pretty sure that was only because Katie had come home. What she'd tasted of that moment left her wanting so much more.

"Okay. Okay. I'm going to need all the details."

Isla groaned, pulling into the parking lot of her apartment. She put the car in park and closed her eyes, leaning her head against the rest. "I don't even know where to start."

"The beginning," Wil answered. "Hold on."

Wil's muffled voice echoed through the line as she spoke to someone, and it didn't take too much work to figure out that she was talking to Lynda. Turning off the engine, Isla walked up to her apartment. Immediately, she pulled off her shoes and dropped her jacket onto the arm of the couch.

Energy burst through her, and she couldn't sit down. She couldn't define what kind of energy it was, either, which was annoying. She wanted to be able to know what she was thinking and feeling. Well, she knew what her body was feeling. Her lips still tingled along with the memory of Andry pushed against her, bringing back that distinct jolt of excitement.

The muffled tones from Wil continued. Isla frowned and walked into her kitchen. It was time to get her life back together. She put Wil on speaker and then turned on the water. Rolling up her sleeves, she started in on the dishes. Finally, Wil came back over the line.

"So...the beginning."

Isla wrinkled her nose. "I've known Andry for years, and I never...before this there was no indication that there was anything more than a principal-teacher relationship. She's very professional."

"So are you," Wil replied. "What changed?"

Isla wanted to tell Wil that it had to do with the shift in their relationship, in adding Lynda back into her life. That had been so much of it because she *couldn't* rely on Wil like she had before. That still stung, though not as sharply as before. Isla didn't want to make Wil feel any guiltier than she already did. But at the same time, she needed to tell the truth, and Wil needed to hear it. She had no idea what to say or how to say it without hurting Wil, and she hated that. It wasn't as easy to trust their friendship anymore, as much as she wanted to.

"When you told me you wanted to date Lynda, I wasn't...I didn't handle it well. Andry was there for me when I needed a friend and you couldn't be that friend." Isla grabbed one of the pots she had used to cook her dinner that week and stuck it under the water. She really didn't want to go into any more depth than that, but Wil might pull it from her anyway.

Wil sighed heavily, a pregnant pause before she finally spoke. "I had worried something like that might happen."

"It was impossible to avoid. You needed your time to get to know Lynda in the capacity you wanted, and I needed to figure out how I felt about it." Isla ran the soapy sponge against the metal.

"And did you?"

She could tell that Wil needed to know the answer, that a whole lot hinged on whatever Isla was going to say. "I did."

It never used to be this hard to talk to Wil—only when Lynda was involved. When they had been teenagers and Wil had admitted she had a crush on Lynda it had very nearly ruined their friendship, and when Wil had come back all these years later with the same problem in her hands, Isla couldn't risk their friendship because of it. Which meant she had to find a way to deal with it.

"I'm not comfortable with Lynda, but that has nothing to do with you," Isla started, taking whatever risks she had to in order to make sure Wil knew what was going on. "But I'm not willing to lose you because of her, and if that means I need to figure out my crap with her, then I will."

"Isla, you're an amazing woman. I'm glad you've had someone up there to help you with this, someone who isn't me and is a bit more removed from everything. I promise you. Don't ever feel like you only have room for one friend in your life."

"Yeah...I think I believed that for a long time." Isla smiled slightly as she set her pot on the stove to dry. "But not anymore, and Andry has been a wonderful friend to me so far this year. Therapy has helped, too."

"Well, good for that. But when did we get to the kissing part? Fast track me to that."

Isla giggled. "I've been playing these pranks on her, right? And she started playing them back on me. Well, there was also that time in her office."

"Whoa! Slow down, hoss. What time in her office?"

Isla's cheeks burned. "It was more than friends, and I think we both knew that. Nowhere near kissing, but it was close. But we did almost kiss on my couch once."

"She's been to your apartment?" Wil's surprise was evident.

"Yeah, and I've been to her house several times. Anyway, today Andry played a prank on me. She came into my classroom, and she filled my desk drawers with candy, all my favorites, and these other little gifts that were wrapped. One was a notebook with some inspirational sayings on it, one was my favorite kind of pens that I love writing with, a keychain, a new coffee mug, and a daily joke calendar."

"She put a lot of thought into that."

"She did." Isla found herself smiling again, unable to make it leave her lips. It warmed her that she could even begin to have this conversation with Wil but also the fact that Andry seemed to know her so well. "Andry has been upping the ante on her pranks. She even had the kids take all their desks and chairs outside so the classroom was empty when I came back from therapy."

"Oh I wish I could have seen your face!" Wil laughed loudly, and again Isla could hear Lynda's voice in the background.

It didn't frustrate her as much this time, which Isla took as a good sign. "I went over to her house today to tell her about the prank, and thank her for the candy—"

"All your favorites? True way to your heart, right there."

Isla sighed dreamily. "Yeah, and I just called her out on it. It was weird, but awesome, and I don't know, but I told her I wanted to kiss her, and then we were kissing, and then her daughter came home and—"

"Whoa! Her daughter?" Wil coughed. "You're going to be playing the role of stepmom now?"

Cold washed through Isla. She honestly hadn't fully thought that one through. They were just kissing, once, that didn't mean anything would go beyond that, would it? But she wanted it to, and she wasn't going to do anything to damage Katie's relationships with her mothers. Isla sighed, "Not her stepmom. We're nowhere near that. We're not even dating. We can't date. She's my boss!"

"Isla..." Wil trailed off and then started again "You're going to have to be careful with this one, okay? It's not just dating—it's figuring out where all the breaking points are that you can't see."

"I know. It's...tangled." Guilt sat in the pit of her belly. Isla turned off the water and dried her hands on the towel she kept on the door of a cabinet. Grabbing her phone, she went to the living room and sat on the couch, her hand covering her eyes as she rested the phone across the top of her chest. "I don't know what to do, but I do know I want to kiss her again."

"You need to talk to Lynda. I can tell you what it was like to date my boss, but you already know some of that. You're in the same shoes I was in. She can tell you what it was like from her perspective. All I can say is that you need to have an exit plan in place in case anything goes south but also in case it doesn't."

"What are you going on about?" Lynda's voice was clear through the line.

Wil chuckled and said loud enough for both of them to hear, "Oh look! Perfect timing. Here!"

A shiver ran through Isla. She wasn't sure she was ready for this conversation, but Wil was right, having that added perspective would really help her out in the long run.

"Isla?" Lynda's tone went from the easy one she'd used with Wil to something tight.

Isla hated that, but the same was true for her, and it was something they were going to have to work through. "Uh...hi..."

"Wil handed me the phone but refuses to tell me anything, so I have no idea what you two were talking about."

Isla swallowed the lump in her throat. Now was her chance. She'd wanted to deepen their relationship, and in order to do that, she had to take a risk. "I kissed my boss."

"Oh." Lynda's voice dropped, and she could almost see the look she slid to Wil, but then she didn't want to imagine that so she shook it from her head. "Both willing, I presume?"

"Yes, nothing...nothing nefarious was going on. I promise you that." God, it was so painfully awkward.

"That's good." Lynda spoke slowly, as if choosing her words carefully.

Isla was pretty darn sure they were both trying to figure out how to have this conversation and walk the line they couldn't see. They had to navigate back into something, and Wil was right, she had given them the perfect opportunity.

"We've been getting closer this school year, and one thing led to another, and I think...well, I think I'd like to explore this." Isla's stomach fluttered with nerves. Admitting that to someone other than Wil was hard and admitting it essentially three times in the same day was even harder.

"You need to be careful, like Wil said, and as much as I hate to admit it, an exit strategy is a good idea. Both Wil and I had one, though hers won out."

"Wil's a stubborn bitch like that sometimes," Isla teased. If there was one thing they could find common ground on, it had to be that. "It's hard to move schools in the middle of the year."

"Can you hold out until the summer?"

Isla pursed her lips, thinking. She hadn't honestly put much thought into it before. She'd mostly gone with whatever emotions had floated through her in the moment, but she had to think about Andry's career as well. This decision didn't only affect her. "I can try."

"That doesn't sound like you're confident."

"I'm not. We already kissed once...to wait now seems kind of pointless, doesn't it?" Isla scrunched her nose up. "I'm not royally screwing up my life and hers, am I?"

"Isla," Lynda's tone was so tender as it washed through her.

Isla had longed for that tone from her for years, and she'd never managed to receive it, yet now it came so unexpectedly. She smiled to herself, glad to finally have found something that she had wanted from Lynda, even if it was a little unexpected in terms of timing.

"I don't think you are, but this is one time when you need to plan. My understanding is it's far easier for a teacher to move schools than a principal, right?"

"Yeah, it is."

"Which do you want more? The school or the relationship?"

"I don't know. We just started... this is so new." Frustrated, Isla sighed. "I feel like we're trying to plan my future when I don't even know if it's the future that I want." Except she did know. She'd be stupid to choose the school.

"Then take some time to figure that out. You have it, right?" Lynda's question was pointed, but she was right. After she left Andry's, they hadn't even had a moment to talk about what had happened. Isla had wanted to give Andry the time to talk with Katie, who definitely had to be her priority.

"Yeah, I do." Isla pressed her lips together. "She's got a teenage daughter."

"Ah." Lynda's voice was strong. "And you're worried about your relationship within all of that?"

"Who wouldn't, with what I came from?" Isla knew the comment was harsh. "I mean... I don't..."

"Our circumstances were unique, Isla, and you're a teacher. You're already such a strong part of so many children's lives. I think you'll figure out how to navigate that easily compared to me. You're much better at it than I could ever hope to be. The fault in our broken relationship isn't entirely yours. Most of it rests with me."

Isla dragged in a deep breath, something cementing inside her that hadn't before. She needed to let go. Swallowing, she bolstered herself. "Don't be so hard on yourself, Lynda. I don't think any of us expected Dad to die and abandon us." As soon as the word was out of her mouth, Isla shuddered. She'd never quite thought of it like that before, but it had an air of truth to it. He had abandoned them all in some way, even if it wasn't his choice to do it. "I think it's time we put it behind us and go forward from here—as much as we can anyway."

"I'd like that," Lynda responded, her voice low but light.

"Good. And uh...thanks for the advice about Andry. I'll call and let you know how it's going, okay?"

"Please do, and if you need any more advice."

"Thanks."

"Oh! And Wil says she's crazy happy for you."

Isla snorted and scratched her head. "She's insane, but I'll take it. Talk to you soon."

Hanging up, Isla rested fully back on her couch and stared at her ceiling. They were right, she definitely needed to figure out where she and Andry stood, but first she needed some time to figure out exactly what she wanted from their relationship. At least more than just the desire to kiss her again. Because she had no doubt that she wanted that.

CHAPTER
Twenty-Three

ONCE AGAIN ISLA found herself standing in Andry's office while she was out at a district training. It lined up perfectly with her prep period, and she hadn't been willing to let it slide. She took construction paper and taped it over the window so Andry wouldn't be able to see in when she got back.

She had brought a small air pump that she plugged into the wall. Ripping open the first bag of balloons, Isla hit the pump and started in on her next prank. They hadn't quite talked yet about the kiss, and it had been days since it had happened. They'd both been incredibly busy, and Isla hadn't wanted to interfere with the conversation Andry was no doubt having with Katie.

Wrapping the end of the balloon around two of her fingers, Isla tied a knot and dropped it to the floor. This was going to take longer than she had thought it would, but it was going to be her big statement and exactly how she planned to get Andry's attention. Swiftly starting on the next balloon, she sat down in Andry's chair and went to work.

By the end of the forty minutes, the room was filled at least three feet high with balloons. Isla pulled the cord on the pump and stashed it to the side. She wasn't going to be able to open the door without an escape of balloons, so she sank to the floor on the side of Andry's desk and covered herself with balloons so Andry wouldn't be able to see her when she first came in. She only had a few more minutes, she was sure, before Andry would come into the office and the prank would be up.

The scent of latex filled her nostrils and made her stomach churn, but Isla pushed through it as she sank into the balloons and waited. She wanted this, desperately. The last few days she'd had time to think and feel, and she wanted to explore the possibility of what it would be like to be in a relationship with Andry. They were already kind of doing that anyway, weren't they? Dinner, drinks, nights watching movies at each other's places. They just hadn't made it official yet.

Andry's loud voice boomed under the doorway, and Isla tensed, ready for the reveal. Andry was laughing before she even got the door open, no doubt tipped off by the construction paper over the window. The rush of fresh air into the room was welcome, and Isla jumped up from her position on the floor, scattering more balloons in every direction as she moved.

"Isla!" Andry said through bursts of laughter. "How did you even think of something like this?"

Isla grinned from ear to ear as she stood in a sea of balloons that were falling out into the main offices. "Saw it on a video once."

"Oh my god, how many balloons are in here?"

"I bought over two hundred, not sure how many ended up blown up."

The office admins filed in behind Andry, excited to see what Isla had done since she'd kept the door shut this time. They shook their heads at Isla but seemed obviously amused as well. By the time they left, Isla only had a few more minutes before her prep period was done. She'd make up the work she'd missed out on easily enough. This had been worth it.

"This was brilliant." Andry stepped in closer, the door behind her still open. She clasped Isla's hands tightly and held on. "How long did this take you?"

"I could have done more if I had more time."

Andry rolled her eyes and shook her head, stepping in even closer and lowering her voice. She lifted both of her hands and smoothed down Isla's hair. "Your hair is all static-y."

Isla flushed, her giggle sounding slightly neurotic. "From sitting and waiting for you."

"Uh huh." Andry smoothed her hair down again, this time tugging lightly on the ends, her gaze dropping to Isla's mouth. "I've been wanting to talk to you, but this week got away from me."

"I understand," Isla murmured.

"Tonight? I was going to call you after school, but since you're here..."

Isla nodded slightly. "Yeah, tonight."

"Good." Andry's lips remained curved upward, and she leaned in like she was going to kiss Isla again, but a burst of voices from outside the office caught both their attention and they backed away from each other. Doing that in the middle of the school would be the worst idea, especially since they hadn't talked yet. Andry kept her voice quiet when she spoke again, "I'll see you tonight."

Isla's heart raced, trying to catch up with the exact place her body had gone. She should have been more careful. She probably shouldn't have pulled the prank, but it was definitely one of the ways they flirted, and Isla loved doing it.

"Andry!"

Isla shrunk into the background, trying to make herself unseen as more people came in to see her handiwork. She waited a few more minutes before she stepped toward the door. She slipped outside, the cool fresh air hitting her lungs in relief. That had been awkward and tense. She needed to cool off.

~

Isla expected the knocks this time, and she was still a jittery mess when they echoed through her apartment. Opening the door, nerves flew through her body, overtaking the desire she had to just lean in and kiss Andry hard to make up for the tentative and short-lived first kiss they'd shared days ago.

"Hey," Andry said, her hands shoved into the pockets of her jacket.

"Come on in." Isla held the door open until Andry was fully inside and dragging her jacket off. Isla had hoped she would because then it would mean she was planning on staying longer than a few minutes. That meant Isla still had hope.

"We've really got to talk."

"I know," Isla murmured, sitting on the couch to one side so Andry could put distance between them if she wanted it. Instead, Andry sat right next to her, hand on her knee like there was no strain between them.

Andry blew out a breath, her shoulders relaxing as she leaned back into the cushion. "I'm not quite sure where to start."

"Well, we kissed. We should probably start there." Isla pushed her sweaty palm across her jeans to try and dry it.

"We did." Andry turned to look Isla directly in the eye. "And for the record the only thing I regret about that was the interruption so soon, well, and who it was. I wish I'd been able to talk to Katie first."

Isla nodded slightly. "I understand. She's been through a lot of change in the last few years."

"Hmm yes and no." Andry licked her lips and then leaned in closer. "Chris and I were living pretty separate lives before we officially separated. Katie wasn't oblivious to that, and she wasn't all that surprised when we divorced."

"Still, it's an adjustment."

"It is, but it's been years since we separated, Isla. It's not like

I got divorced last week or even a year ago." Andry tightened her grip on Isla's knee. "I was already thinking about dating again and had already started that conversation with Katie, to an extent anyway."

"And how does she feel about it?" Isla held her breath, needing to know where the conversation was going. She'd thought they were going to talk about them and what they wanted, but like she'd known somewhere in the back of her mind, it was impossible to do that without talking about Katie first.

"She's okay with it, I think. As okay as she can be right now, but like you said it's an adjustment and it's going to take some time."

"I didn't meet Lynda for months after she started dating my dad. I think they were already talking about getting married by the time he brought her around to meet us." Isla flinched because Katie shouldn't have found out by walking in on them. That was probably the worst way to find out her mom was dating.

"You were younger than Katie, and Katie already knows you. I think she picked up on some of what I was feeling for you before I even managed to put it into words." Andry sighed and patted Isla's leg before moving her hand into her own lap. "Which brings us back to the kiss."

"Yes, the kiss." Isla couldn't drag her gaze up to meet Andry's. Her stomach churned with dread because she swore she could see the writing on the wall. "We shouldn't—"

"We should—"

They stopped, both chuckling lightly. Andry smiled and put her hand back on Isla's thigh. Silence filled the space between them before Andry finally broke it. "I like you, Isla, more than I should for a principal and her teacher."

Isla swelled with warmth, her entire body feeling lighter.

"But that doesn't mean we should do this either," Andry concluded.

"I know. It's complicated, and it breaks so many rules." Isla covered Andry's hand with her own, squeezing so Andry would understand that she knew what those complications were. Talking with Lynda had made those clear, and as difficult as that conversation had been to start, she was glad she had taken the risk.

"It does, and I think we need to be hyper aware of the decisions we're making. We can't..." Andry groaned. "I don't even know how to say this."

"Say what?"

"I want to damn the rules to hell." Andry's voice was nearly a growl as she locked her eyes on Isla with desperation.

Isla gasped, holding Andry's gaze. Could Andry really mean it? Falling back on the one question that Lynda had asked, Isla put it out there. "Can we wait until the end of the school year?"

"The thing is, Isla..." Andry started shaking her head "...I don't want to."

"What does that mean?"

"It means I want to be with you."

Isla's excitement bloomed. She moved in, pressing their mouths together in the kiss she had wanted from the start. She didn't hesitate, she didn't take her time, she went all in on the kiss that she wanted to make or break the moment. Isla traced Andry's mouth with the tip of her tongue before pulling back and smiling at her. "I haven't been able to think about anything but you for days now."

"We'll have to keep it quiet and be as careful as we can when we're at the school."

Isla nodded, already on board with whatever suggestions Andry had. They could figure this out and make it work with the two of them on the same page. Isla didn't say anything as she moved back in to kiss Andry again. Andry threaded her fingers in the back of Isla's hair, pulling her into the kiss as she deepened it. The last of those barriers fell away, bringing them closer than they had ever allowed themselves to go.

Isla didn't want to give this up, definitely not for the night. She pulled away briefly before diving back in, this time with her mouth open. It took the second time before Andry opened to her, their tongues touching for the first time. Heat and energy raced through Isla, washing out any of the previous fear she'd had that this was Andry coming to break her heart.

Lifting a hand to Andry's cheek, Isla held her close as their kisses deepened one at a time. It had been so long since she'd felt this comfortable with someone, and she had never felt quite this comfortable when in a dating relationship. Isla dragged in a deep breath and nipped at Andry's lower lip.

Andry laughed lightly and moved away slightly, her gaze full of humor. "You still smell like latex."

"Spoiler, so do you."

With one sharp pull, Andry's mouth was against hers again. This time it was passionate and deep, heated and filled with a frenetic quality. Isla groaned and pushed against Andry, hoping that it would give her exactly what she was looking for. Shifting on the couch, Isla slid onto her knees, putting one on either side of Andry's lap so she straddled her.

Andry's back pressed into the cushion, her chin tilted up. She dragged her fingers down Isla's back to her ass before sliding them up again and diving deep into her hair. Isla lowered herself down, keeping their mouths connected. She closed her eyes and reveled in the feel of being in Andry's arms, her safe arms, the protective circle that she'd created. Isla never wanted to leave. It was such a perfect and beautiful gift. She nipped at Andry's lip, pressing their chests together as she writhed on top of her.

"Isla," Andry murmured before kissing her again. "Just so you know, I'm not ready to go any further with this tonight, okay?"

"Got it." Isla kissed her again. "Wasn't even thinking about that."

"Good." Andry moved her hands back down to Isla's butt and pulled her tighter. "This does feel so good, though."

Isla chuckled seductively, her tone low. "Glad to know."

By the time Andry left, it was well past dinner. They managed to stop making out long enough to order and eat, but the goodnight kiss left Isla full of hope for whatever might happen between them. Still, she should probably put out some feelers for openings at other schools. The pressure weighing on her from the fact that Andry was her boss was heavier than she thought it would be. They would both be feeling it, and Wil and Lynda had been right. She needed an exit plan no matter which way this went.

CHAPTER
Twenty-Four

ANDRY KNOCKED on Isla's apartment door bright and early Saturday morning. She hadn't texted or called, but she had a feeling that Isla would be awake and ready for the day. Waiting in the chilly November air, Andry bounced in her shoes. Since they had broken through that barrier between them, it had been even harder to think about anything other than Isla.

The click of the lock sent Andry's heart pattering. To see Isla again outside of the school setting they were locked into was exactly what she had wanted. They had managed to keep everything low key that week at the school, but if anyone was paying close attention, they'd be able to see the slight smiles, the blushing cheeks, the whispers between them. Andry wasn't sure how long they'd be able to keep it hidden with the gossip mill that was any school, which added a layer of anxiety to every day.

Isla opened the door, her cheeks red with sleep, her eyes barely open, and her hair tousled around her shoulders. Andry nearly moaned at the beautiful sight. She'd never expected this. Isla furrowed her brow, drawing her gaze up to look Andry in the eye.

"What are you doing here?" Even her voice sounded lethargic.

Andry wanted to tell her exactly the reason she was there, but it was so hard to form words with a sleepy woman right in front of her, one with lips parted and ready for the taking. She was probably still warm. She groaned out loud. Andry's entire body was alive, ready to move and take, but she managed to hold it back—barely. These new-relationship jitters were stronger than she ever remembered them being.

"Um..." Andry wet her suddenly dry mouth. "Well...I was going to deal with the car today, but this seems like a much better distraction." Andry waved her hand up and down Isla's body, her tank top with no bra, her loose pajama pants around her hips, and her bare toes peeking out from under the pink flannel with gold thread in it.

Isla's cheeks turned pink, a definite blush compared to the sleepy look she'd had before.

"May I...?" Andry didn't finish her sentence, not quite sure how she wanted to. Did she want inside? Yes. Did she want to press Isla against the closest hard surface and kiss her senseless? Absolutely.

Isla moved the door open wider and stepped back from it. "What did you mean *deal with the car*? I thought you weren't giving it to Katie until her birthday."

Andry pressed her lips together hard, stepping inside the small apartment. That change of conversation told her exactly what she shouldn't be doing, which was letting her hormones get the best of her. "That was the plan, but since I have the registration and the car's already on the insurance, Chris convinced me that a month wasn't going to make much of a difference, and it would make it easier on my schedule, too."

"Oh." Isla moved to her kitchen, flicking the button on the coffee maker.

"I may have an ulterior motive for easing up my schedule, because if I don't have to take Katie to school every day or pick her up after her extracurriculars I'll have more time for other things." Andry stopped next to Isla, deliberately raking her gaze down Isla's body and then back up, meeting her gaze. The comment hadn't come off like she thought it would, though, because Isla didn't seem impressed or intrigued or even happy. Instead, she seemed wary. Cocking her head to the side, Andry went to speak.

Isla interrupted her thought. "Give me a second to get dressed."

"Hold on," Andry interrupted, trying to keep Isla there. She wanted to know what that was because she'd thought that Isla would be happy if they had more time to spend together. "Talk to me."

"I'd like to brush my teeth."

"Isla..." Andry took a deep breath and let it out slowly. "Don't run away from me."

"I'm not. I'm brushing my teeth." Isla pointed the way around Andry. "Help yourself to coffee when it's ready."

Andry didn't quite believe her, but she nodded and shifted to allow Isla through the small entryway. She wasn't going to get any further by pushing too hard. She leaned against the counter while Isla disappeared. What had she said that would have caused that kind of reaction? She'd thought Isla would be grateful for the extra time to spend together.

Crossing her arms, Andry closed her eyes to think while the coffee percolated. Time outside of school was difficult for them to find, and while they'd managed to catch a few moments over the fall, it hadn't been easy, and Andry really wanted that one-on-one time with her.

When Isla came back in, freshly dressed in tight jeans and a new tank top, Andry frowned. The sleepy woman she'd woken up was completely gone. Isla poured each of them some coffee and turned around to sip hers. Andry looked her over again, working hard to see what was happening under the surface, what Isla was avoiding.

Cocking her head to the side, Andry gave up. "What bothered you about that?"

"Nothing."

"Forgive me for not believing you." Andry raised an eyebrow at her, determined to get it out and needing to know exactly what Isla was thinking.

"It's nothing." Isla sighed and set her coffee on the counter, half-abandoning it. "Did you need the keys for the car?"

"Isla..." Andry stepped forward and snagged her hand, lacing their fingers. "Talk to me, please."

Pressing her lips together, Isla stared at some random place between them. Andry waited as patiently as she could for any kind of answer. She wanted to know where she had mis-stepped so soon into this.

"I remember what it was like when my dad started dating Lynda, which wasn't all that bad. But I do remember feeling like I didn't have enough of his time."

Andry's heart stuttered. She gave Isla's hand a firm squeeze. "How old were you again?"

"Eight."

"Katie's almost eighteen, and I love her dearly, but most of the time she doesn't want to be around me."

"She does." Isla raised her chin, defiance in her gaze. "She wants to know that her mom is always there for her."

"And I think she does know that. We've talked endlessly about this, every day since she interrupted us, and quite frankly before that, but she's going to be out of my house by the start of the next school year." Andry paused, another flash of hurt in Isla's eyes. Where had she gone wrong this time?

"Don't you want to spend as much time with her as possible?"

"I do." Andry shrugged. "But she has another mom, and she has friends, and in some ways, she needs to learn to live on her own a little and have some of that freedom now while it's safe. It's a balance where I have to give up the time I have with her."

"So why would you give her more?"

"Because she needs it." Andry brushed her thumb across the

top of Isla's hand. "She's growing up, Isla, and she's going to be an adult soon. I have to prepare her for that."

"But she needs you."

"Are we talking about Katie or are we talking about you?" Andry held firm, knowing the question was blunt and to the point, but she didn't have the energy to go ten rounds of circles that morning.

Isla winced. "I don't want to be the reason something comes between you and Katie."

Andry stuttered, the pure honesty and emotion coming from Isla was more than she had anticipated. "I'm not going to abandon Katie for you. She will always come first, at least until she's totally an adult and on her own. Katie and I have a good relationship that we work hard at, and I don't anticipate that will change just because you're being added into the picture."

Andry cupped Isla's cheek before sliding her hands around her shoulders and pulling her in for a hug. Isla held on, her arms tight against Andry's back as they embraced. Andry held the moment for as long as she could until Isla shifted back.

"I'm sorry. I'm so morose when I'm sleepy."

"I think you're sexy when you're just woken." Andry grinned when Isla blushed furiously. "And trust me, holding back on kissing you this morning was hard."

Isla snorted lightly. "Why did you?"

"I wasn't quite sure where we were on that whole thing just yet. We're still in that awkward have-to-figure-each-other-out stage." Andry stepped away slightly, but Isla grabbed her hips and pulled her back.

"I would have loved a kiss first thing this morning."

"Duly noted. And now?"

"Yes."

Andry smiled as she dipped her head and pressed their mouths together. It wasn't quite the hard surface she had originally thought about, but the counter would do for now. This kiss was gentler and calmer than she'd planned on as well, especially with the emotional confession Isla had just given her. Isla broke the kiss and winked at Andry.

"That was nice."

"Well, we can do that more often now." Andry kissed her again but quickly. "And I promise you that I won't forget about Katie or push her to the side as we navigate this, okay?"

"Okay."

"You'll have to trust me on that." One more kiss and Andry moved away, shuddering. If she stayed that close to Isla too long, she could very easily get distracted with the rest of her day, and like she'd promised Isla, she wouldn't do that. "But on that note, I do have to get the plates on the car and get the car back to my house. Chris is bringing Katie over around lunch for a special early birthday with just us."

"Sounds fun," Isla said, though her words didn't quite match her tone. "How are you going to do the big reveal?"

Andry shrugged as she snagged her cup of coffee. "I got a bow."

Isla's eyes lit up mischievously. What had Andry just walked into? "Want to maybe use up some extra balloons that your new BFF-sixth-grade teacher has left over from some ridiculous prank she pulled?"

Chuckling, Andry shook her head. "You're more than my new BFF." At Isla's confirmed nod, Andry added, "What are you thinking?"

"Fill the car with balloons, maybe snag a helium tank and tie some onto the side mirrors and wipers or something."

Andry pressed her lips together and closed her eyes for a second before nodding her head to the side. "Not a bad idea."

"Perfect. Drink up! We've got mayhem to complete."

Laughing, Andry took another slow sip of her coffee. "Are you not a morning person?"

"Hell no," Isla answered. "What would make you think that I am?"

"You're always bubbly when you come into work." Andry

couldn't tear her gaze away from Isla, even as she continued to drink her second cup of coffee for the morning.

Isla grinned and stepped forward, right into Andry's space in the small kitchen. She pressed against Andry's side. "That, my friend, is called Isla on the elixir of life. It's that very same thing you find in that cup of yours, and damn are you slow at drinking it."

Andry glanced down at Isla's mug, nearly empty. "How much of that do you normally drink a day?"

"All day every day."

"Are you serious?" Andry raised an unbelieving eyebrow at her.

"Absolutely!" Isla bounced on her toes as she leaned in for a quick kiss. "Come on, we have to introduce Katie into the world of pranks."

"Oh, she already knows how to do that."

Isla winked as she walked to the front door and slipped on her shoes. "Not my kind of pranks, I'm sure."

Andry sighed heavily. If Isla really was going to teach Katie that, then her future was going to be a lot more scare-inducing than she'd originally thought.

CHAPTER

Twenty-Five

ISLA'S CAR was warm as she pulled out onto the highway. Andry had sent her a picture of Katie with the car in all the standard poses, but also a small video of her opening the door to the vehicle filled with balloons. Chris had been in the background, and she hadn't looked amused, but Isla had gotten her kicks out of it.

With the holidays coming up, everyone had been suspiciously quiet about who was going where. Wil hadn't said anything and neither had Aisling other than that one text. Normally one or both would come to her apartment for the week, but now there was nothing being said. Isla winced when she realized belatedly exactly what they were avoiding.

They didn't want to come to her place.

Or at least they weren't sure how she felt about being with Lynda for a holiday. Rubbing her lips together, Isla clenched her steering wheel tighter. How did she feel about it?

They hadn't even managed to have a minute to discuss that at her last therapy session since she'd spent most of the time talking about Andry. Her therapist had seemed pleased, but also left the warning that she couldn't place all her hope and happiness in the beginnings of a relationship. It sucked to admit there was truth in that statement, but Isla had been very careful to determine what was giving her happiness and if it was solely based around Andry.

It wasn't.

She felt lighter and less bogged down than she had in years, and while Andry had been a part of that story, she wasn't the reason. Isla had stopped avoiding. She took great pains to make decisions to share, like that morning in her kitchen. She could have so easily walked away from why she was upset, but she didn't. It had been worth it to take that risk, and she wanted to do it again.

But that led her to Thanksgiving and the fact no one was talking to her about their plans. Normally, she was the first person on their list, but Thanksgiving was a little over a week away and somehow it had escaped her that they hadn't talked about it until then. She was sure Wil and Lynda would want to do the holiday together. They had become so close in the last few months, and Isla suspected they would be moving in together soon. She would have to prepare her heart for that announcement when she got a chance, but not today.

Aisling had texted the once and told her she was going to Lynda's that year, but there was very little conversation beyond that. Isla gnawed on the inside of her lip as she relaxed her shoulders and settled in for the drive down to Fort Collins. She had another meeting with Lynda to talk through some of their problems. The halfway point provided not only a reasonable drive for both of them, but also neutral ground to talk on.

Pulling into a spot downtown, Isla parked her car and got out. She pulled her jacket a little tighter around her shoulders as the chill in the air had picked up drastically in the last couple of weeks. She stopped short as Lynda pulled up in a parking spot a few down from her. Isla waited while Lynda got out, bundled similarly against the chill.

"Hey," Isla said, her voice soft. She wanted to be strong and confident, but it seemed every time Lynda was involved, she cowered behind the little girl she'd been when they met.

"Hey." Lynda smiled and leaned in before stopping.

Isla wasn't quite sure what she'd intended to do, but she was glad for the continued space between them. They started for the restaurant where they had decided to meet up, and once inside, Isla breathed in the scents and the warmth of the building. The steakhouse wasn't one she had been to before, but it was nice inside.

"There's two of us," Lynda said to the host.

Isla followed behind Lynda as they were brought to a table. She should probably have Wil come on one of these trips sooner rather than later because she had yet to see the two of them interact since they'd started dating. Isla pulled off her coat and slid into her seat, sighing when she settled in. She was going to make the most of this visit because while they had made progress before, they needed to take some drastic steps forward and quickly.

"How was the drive?" Isla asked, knowing Lynda's drive was at least twenty minutes longer than hers.

"Not awful, bit of traffic with all the construction, but it's not bad on the weekends." Lynda stripped her jacket off as well and straightened her shoulders. The pendant she wore that day was one that the girls had given her for a birthday—Isla couldn't remember which one—and she had rarely seen Lynda actually wear it.

Instead of brushing off the feeling like she normally would, Isla raised an eyebrow in Lynda's direction. "You're wearing the necklace?"

"Oh." Lynda pressed her hand over it instinctively. "I am. I'm not sure exactly why either. I was thinking of you a lot this week, and when I was getting dressed this morning, I saw it and put it on."

Isla's instinct was to reject the explanation, but there was no reason Lynda would lie to her. "No other reason?"

Lynda made eye contact before slowly shaking her head. "Honestly, no. It's beautiful, and I remember you and Aisling giving it to me when you were younger. You were so excited for it."

Isla pressed her lips together hard, still debating how much truth was in Lynda's statement or not. But Lynda had never lied to them, at least not from what Isla knew about or could remember. She could avoid with the best of them, but she never outwardly lied. Nodding, Isla studied the menu. "We spent hours at the jewelry store with Dad that day, figuring out the perfect gift for you."

"You did?" Lynda's face softened immediately. Isla had missed that after her dad had died. They all had sharper edges then.

"Yeah. It was a big deal." Isla found her lips curling into a smile, one unbidden but not unwelcome. "Same as picking out the wedding ring."

"I kept it for either you or Aisling, if you want it. I have your mother's, too."

Isla raised her eyes at that, shock echoing through her chest. "You have my mother's wedding ring?"

Lynda nodded slowly. "I wasn't going to give that up without letting you two decide on it. I have a few boxes of things that were hers that I kept for when you were adults."

"Like what?"

"Her wedding dress." Lynda said it so simply, like it was never a question as to whether or not she would have it, but this was the first Isla was hearing of it.

Her heart raced, and she sat completely still as the words moved through her again. All these years, she'd never thought she had anything of her mother's, but this woman held all those connections to her past. Isla was nearly in tears at the thought. "You have her wedding dress?"

Lynda nodded firmly. "And some books. I have all the family

albums from when you were little. I have a couple pictures of Aisling with your mom. I already gave those to her, but I kept a few copies in case she lost them along the way or if you wanted them. You just never seemed interested, but I didn't want to throw them out."

Isla shivered. She had photos of her with her mother, but she was pretty sure that Lynda would have some that she didn't even remember. She'd have to ask her grandparents if they knew the stories behind them because Lynda surely wouldn't know unless her dad had told her. "I'd love them."

"The dress, too?"

"No. I'd love to see it, but I think I'll let Aisling have first dibs on that. She'll probably get married first."

"And the rings?"

Isla paused, not sure what to say just yet. She shrugged and put as much trust in Lynda as she could. "Why don't you hold on to them for now?"

"Sure." Lynda crossed her hands in front of her, eyeing her carefully.

The waiter came over, and they ordered drinks and food. Then finally they were alone again. Isla cleared her throat, not sure where to go from there, but they did need to talk about certain things. "You changed when Dad died."

"We all did," Lynda answered. "But I didn't want to put my grief onto you and Aisling. You two needed your own space for that."

Isla furrowed her brow, thinking through everything Lynda had said word by word. It had been expected in a way, but there was something missing in there too. "We needed to see you grieve—at least I did."

Lynda's lips parted suddenly, but she didn't say anything. Her gaze dropped to the tabletop as she thought long and hard. Raising her chin up, she nodded. "You're right."

"I...what?"

"You're right. I didn't share that with you. You know, one of the first things I talked to Wil about was that day I dropped you off at school, the first day you went back. Principal Everette cornered me and threatened to take you and Aisling away if I couldn't prove that I had custody of you. I didn't have the papers on me, I didn't know I needed them." Lynda's eyes filled with tears, but she didn't shed them. "I was so scared. I went to a park, and I cried and screamed, and then I went home and I got those papers from the safe and put them in my purse. They have never left my person since."

Lynda shifted and grabbed her oversized purse. She rifled around in it for a second before pulling out very worn papers and handing it over to Isla. Isla's hands shook when the smooth paper touched her skin. The folds were worn, clearly opened and closed more times than she could count. She opened them carefully, finding simple paperwork leaving custody of her and Aisling to Lynda Walsh in the event of their father's death, and his signature at the bottom. The fancy scrawl was worn thin, the black ink faded, but Isla lifted a finger to trace over it.

"You still have them?"

"Every time I go to take it out and put it in the safe, I stop myself. I needed these so many times when you two were little. Every doctor's appointment, every therapist, every year at school, every special event—they became a part of our relationship, and to get rid of them..." Lynda locked their gazes together "...would be admitting the end of our relationship, and I didn't want that."

Isla's lips parted in surprise before she dropped her gaze back down to the papers. Their names were clearly written, all on one document. Lynda's signature below her father's, along with the notary's. The embossed stamp of approval was worn flat. Folding it back up carefully, Isla handed it over, and Lynda took it carefully, clearly confused.

"I don't want that either," Isla murmured. She steadied herself, ready to say what she had come there for. "You're the only parent I have left, and while I don't understand you half the time, you're the only one who knows what we've been through."

Lynda gave a weak grin, and she reached over the table for Isla's hand, giving it a comforting squeeze. "You're all I have left of him, and damn it, Isla, but you look just like him."

Isla scrunched her nose before she lifted her hands to wipe under her eyes. "I know. I hate looking in the mirror because of it."

"Don't. Please don't do that. Your father was so handsome, but you should love every bit about him that you are. You'll carry him with you forever, and it's easy for you to see that compared to Aisling."

Isla smiled, heat rushing to her cheeks. "Come to my place for Thanksgiving."

Lynda looked startled, her lips parted, her eyes wide, her eyebrows up. "Thanksgiving?"

"I assume either no one has planned anything yet because no one has talked to me and normally they have, or they're all going to your place and were just going to let me figure it out. But come to my place. Everyone. You, Wil, Aisling...we'll all do this together." Isla's heart raced, the decision made before she had time to back out of it, but as soon as the words were out of her mouth, she didn't want to change her mind. This needed to happen.

"Are you sure about this?"

Nodding, Isla shifted excited in her seat. "I am. I mean... I was just thinking that you, Wil, and I need to get together, and I haven't seen Aisling in months. I just... if we're going to be family, Lynda, then we need to figure out how to have the awkward family dinners, don't you think?"

"Yes." Lynda breathed out a sigh of relief. "We do. I know Wil will be thrilled for it."

"I'll talk to Aisling."

"Good." Lynda smiled. "I'm excited."

"Me too."

Lynda's eyes lit up like she remembered something last minute. She rustled around in her purse again and pulled out a small box, wrapped in paper. "I wanted to give you this but wasn't quite sure where we stood."

"What is it?"

"Happy birthday, Isla."

CHAPTER
Twenty-Six

ISLA SAT in her classroom the day before Thanksgiving break, her students restless and ready for the five-day weekend. She bent her head to do some paperwork when suddenly the birthday song randomly rang through her classroom. Startled, Isla looked around as the song played through once and then stopped. The kids all stared at her, just as confused. They shifted around, voices chattering as they tried to figure out what was going on.

"All right, hold on." Isla shifted to check the speakers she had set up near the windows. Often, she would play soft music while the kids were taking a test or doing their individual reading because it would help them focus. But the speakers looked completely normal and were turned off.

Furrowing her brow in confusion, Isla went back to her desk and sat down. "I don't know, you all. Try to focus on your math, okay?"

The kids mumbled but went back to work. She should have planned something fun for the day before the break, but she hadn't managed to find the time or the brain power for it. She was just about focused on her computer when the birthday song echoed through her classroom again.

Isla knew better. There was only one reason that would happen twice, and it wasn't by accident. She could almost brush off the first time, but the second? Not at all. Instead of getting up, Isla sat at her desk, looking around, as she tried to figure out exactly where the song was coming from, but it ended too abruptly.

Pursing her lips, she stared at her classroom, now completely disrupted. "All right, find me the speakers, people!"

The kids were immediately up and searching around the classroom. Isla stayed seated watching them work together and search under things. They came up with a lot of good finds, but no speakers.

Suddenly the happy birthday song blasted through the speakers again, and this time, Isla was able to pinpoint exactly where it was. The speaker was taped in the back corner of the room, under a bucket so that it would amplify the sound. Isla stood up and started in that direction, but the door to her classroom opened, and in came Andry.

Cautious, Isla cocked her head in Andry's direction, in her hands a serving plate with what looked to be a homemade cake on it. "Hey everyone!"

The happy birthday song continued to play.

"Did you know it's Ms. Walsh's birthday today? I don't suppose she told you. I thought we should have some cake!" Andry set the plate on the table, grabbing the paper plates and forks that she'd held under her arm and setting them down too.

Isla stood with her arms crossed, her stomach doing funny things. While she wanted to believe Andry was as good natured as she could be, the fact that the music was still blasting and she had that damn twinkle in her eye like something was up made Isla unsettled.

The kids joined in as the song repeated, suddenly everyone singing happy birthday to her. Isla couldn't stop the smile that found her face, and she faced her kids. Once they were done, Andry pulled out her phone and turned the song off.

"You snuck into my classroom and set that up?"

"I did." Andry looked pleased as piss with herself.

Isla shook her head slowly. "It took me a bit to figure out exactly where it was at."

"I'm sure. But I think these kids want cake, right?" Andry pointed at them like she was in charge of this show, which she was. With a glimmer of a smirk, Andry handed Isla a knife. "It's your birthday."

"Right." Isla took the knife slowly, trying to figure out exactly what was going on. This was wholly unexpected, and she needed to know for sure where they were going from here. Isla faced her classroom for a brief moment and nodded her head toward the front table. The kids all circled around it, and she bent down, the knife poised.

She slid it into the frosting and cut down, but the cake didn't cut. She tried it again, but it still didn't cut. Isla tensed, her chest tightening, and she looked up at Andry who had the biggest satisfied grin on her face.

"It won't cut!" Isla said loudly enough so all of the kids could hear because they needed to know what was going on, and she needed to make a big deal about it.

She took the side of the knife and scraped the frosting, revealing bright green and blue sponges underneath it all. The kids burst out laughing, and Isla found herself chuckling as well. She shook her head at Andry, putting the knife down and pointing at her.

"I'll give you this one. You got me good both times."

Andry clapped her hands with a laugh. "I do have cupcakes! Hold on."

While Andry left, Isla had the kids retrieve the speaker she had hidden so that they wouldn't have a recurrence of this prank any time soon. She set it up on her desk and had the kids settle into their chairs, packing up their bags for the day so that they would be ready to leave as soon as the bell rang. Andry finally came back with a tray of cupcakes, decorated with Isla's favorite candy right on top. These weren't store bought, and it took Isla a hot minute to realize that.

"Did you make these?" Isla warmed at just the thought and care Andry gave her.

Andry's cheeks flushed with red, but she was already handing out cupcakes to the kids along with plates and napkins. She was so distracted, and Isla let it drop until she got her own cupcake. She moaned around it. It was a *Reese's* cupcake perfect, peanut butter and chocolate swirled together.

"Oh my god." Isla stared at Andry with awe. Andry was looking at her, clearly waiting for the reaction. Isla was going to take all of these home with her, and she was going to eat them and not let any of her family have any. They were heavenly. "These are amazing."

Andry winked. "I do have some hidden skills."

Isla's cheeks heated, her mind going a completely different direction than the way Andry had intended. She said nothing because they were in a classroom full of sixth graders who were starting to pick up on those subtleties, but Isla desperately wanted to.

The flirting they were doing was no longer just in the pranks, and it was becoming more overt. Isla was going to have to get better about watching herself when they were in the same room and others were around to witness it. She had already heard some rumors start to fly that Andry was giving her special treatment, and if asked, she wouldn't be able to deny it.

"Did you really make these?"

"I did." Andry blushed and ran her hands along her thighs. "I enjoy baking when I need stress relief, and I like to think I'm not awful at it."

"These are hands down some of the best cupcakes I've had, and I'm pretty sure the kids all agree with that." Looking around the classroom, the kids were jabbering on about the cupcakes and the Thanksgiving break. They were excited, whereas thirty minutes ago they had been struggling to focus. Isla really should have planned something for them for the last day before the break, and the fact that she hadn't showed just how worn down she had become in the last few months.

She was never someone who would let the kids not have an experience of a lifetime. She took the expectation that her students were her life seriously, and since she didn't have a family at home, it was easy to make them her priority. But with Andry in the picture, with Lynda and Wil and Aisling all coming up on Thursday, she knew she needed to shift those priorities. But she couldn't forget to treat the kids like this again.

"I figured you hadn't told them it was your birthday." Andry leaned against the table, a cupcake at her lips.

What Isla would give to be able to lick the chocolate from her mouth, to kiss her and have that lingering taste of sweetness. Shaking the thought from her head, Isla turned back to her class. "You guessed right."

Andry chuckled. She lowered her voice to barely a whisper. "You're so private about random things sometimes."

"Birthdays weren't easy for me growing up." Isla cut Andry a look, checked to make sure the kids were distracted, and kept her tone quiet. "When you lose one parent, and then the second, birthdays become a reminder of what they're missing. Aisling hates hers, but that's because Mom died when she was born. For years she was convinced that she killed Mom no matter how many times we all told her otherwise."

Andry sucked in a sharp breath. "That's awful."

"It is." Isla nodded toward her students. "It's part of why I went into teaching. School was a safe place for me, but it was also me wanting these kids to have a better hand up than I did. So much has changed since I went through all of that, and I don't ever want my kids to feel the same disparity that I did."

When Andry didn't answer right away, Isla risked a look at her and was stunned to find Andry's gaze boring straight into her. Her breath caught, and she put down her second cupcake and shook her head.

"What?"

"You are an amazing and strong woman. You have to know that. You give so much of yourself when you didn't have much to start with."

Isla dragged in a deep breath, casting her gaze down. That comment unsettled her, forcing her to think about the hurdles she'd had to overcome and just how selfish she'd been lately. That wasn't going to be who she was anymore. "I give because we all should."

"You give more than most." Andry smiled slightly.

The alarm Isla had set to get the kids ready to leave sounded on her desk. She bent over and turned it off. Getting everyone's attention, she raised her voice over the children's voices. "It's time to clean up! Take your cupcake with you if you haven't finished it yet."

The kids moved swiftly, making sure their table space was clean and clear of any debris. Isla would come back through and wipe down the tables after they all left. Andry walked with her to take the kids out to the playground, but she continued out the door when Isla went back inside to finish out her day.

With the classroom quiet, Isla smiled to herself as she stared at the leftover cupcakes. She had no idea how she had ended up so lucky to have a principal like Andry. When she'd started teaching, it had been like being thrown to the wolves. She had felt like she had no idea what she was doing, and Andry had been supportive through every step of that. She couldn't have done it without her, and frankly, she wasn't sure she would have survived the last few months without her.

Sighing, Isla took a disinfectant wipe and started wiping down her tables from the mess the kids had left. They'd done a decent job cleaning, but she wanted to get all the food leftovers off the tables before they were gone for the next five days.

Andry knocked on the window, grabbing her attention. Startled, Isla glanced up and looked over at her before walking to the window and sliding it open. "What?"

"Don't go until I talk to you, okay?"

Surprised, Isla nodded, wishing they had more time to talk just the two of them. "Sure."

Andry walked away, and Isla closed the window and went back to cleaning up her classroom. She was just about done by the time Andry showed up in her classroom again.

"What did you need?" Isla tossed her hair over her shoulder as she stood up, her bag already packed and ready to go.

Andry moved in close, the door still wide open, so they left space between them. She lowered her voice to nearly a whisper, "Come over tonight for a proper cake and dinner."

Isla found herself nodding before she figured out what exactly she wanted and without thinking it through first. "Sure."

"Good. Be there by six."

"Okay." Isla smiled, warmed. It was the first time she had been able to spend her birthday with anyone in a long time, at least specifically for her birthday and not a combination birthday and Thanksgiving meal. "What are we eating?"

"It's a surprise." Andry winked. "Six."

"I'll be there," Isla called back, and she knew she would.

CHAPTER
Twenty-Seven

IT WAS rush time as soon as Andry got home. Katie had already managed to pick up in the living room and kitchen, but they still had to cook dinner. The cake Andry had made the weekend before was on the dining room table and out of the way while she pulled out pots and pans to get the meal started. Katie stepped in next to her, rolling up her sleeves and washing her hands.

"What are we cooking?" Andry asked, nudging her shoulder into Katie's. This had been Katie's idea, and she had taken point on planning everything.

"Scalloped potatoes to start, since those take the longest." Katie pulled out the bag of potatoes and set them on the counter.

"Got it." Andry went to work, the recipes burned into her memories from years of cooking.

Katie bent below in one of the cabinets, while Andry finished pulling out all the ingredients they were going to need. When she popped back up, she put the mandoline down in front of her.

"She'll love this meal, don't you think?" Katie commented as she grabbed the first potato and sliced off the end.

"Yeah, I think she will." Andry sent Katie a smile, glad to see that she was happy with the situation. She'd been worried about that, but as the week had passed, Katie had been more comfortable with it. Handing over another potato for Katie to slice up, Andry looked her over.

"We should use the fancy servingware."

"We can use whatever dishes you want, baby." Andry kept her hands in the water until she had them all done. Andry handed over the rest of the potatoes and leaned against the counter for a moment before starting in on the sauce they needed. Katie seemed so happy and relaxed. Andry smiled at her, brushing her hand along Katie's shoulders as she walked by. They put together the casserole dish for the scalloped potatoes and slid it into the oven with a timer set. Next up was the main part of the dish and the sides.

When they put the steaks onto the stove, Andry faced Katie again. "I want to make sure you're okay with this."

"Mom." Katie rolled her eyes. "You've asked me this a million times already. I'm not the one who's nervous."

Andry realized belatedly that she was gnawing on the inside of her lip, that her stomach was in knots, and that Katie was right. She was nervous, and it wasn't just about Katie's response to her dating again, but it was also about her dating again in general. It had been so long, and she didn't want to fall down the same path she had with Chris. Both Chris and Isla had clear mental health issues and family struggles, but there was one main difference between them: Isla seemed to be working on those far earlier than Chris ever did. Andry had witnessed her turnaround since the end of the summer, and while she looked tired, she was smiling easier and seemed much lighter than at the start of the school year. Sighing, Andry intentionally relaxed her shoulders.

"You're right," she mumbled. "I didn't think I'd be dating this quickly."

"You should have! You two are so cute together, a real live

OTP." Katie shook her head like her mother wasn't getting the memo.

"A real what?"

"One true pair." Katie rolled her eyes before she giggled lightly. "You need a couple's name, like Andra." Katie winced at that one. "Islandry? No, that's worse. I'll work on that one!"

"What are you even going on about?" Andry sent her daughter a side glance, trying to figure out if this was a joke or not.

Katie looked appalled. "How do you not understand fan language, Mom? It just means that you two are meant to be."

Andry wasn't so sure about that. Relationships were work and took way more effort than just existing. She was about to say as much when Katie interrupted her thoughts again.

"You'll get used to it and not be nervous for long. You've told me that since junior high. When people you love start relationships with other people, it changes things, but the strong relationships will make it through. And with change comes anxiety."

"Was I really that wise?" Andry frowned, trying to remember saying anything like that.

Katie snorted and laughed. "Sometimes you can be."

The knock on the door surprised both of them. Andry glanced at the clock on the oven, noting that Isla was a good twenty minutes early, assuming it was Isla. Wiping her hands on a dish towel, Andry started for the front door. When she pulled it open, Isla stood on the other side with a store-bought bouquet in her hand.

"You're early," Andry commented, but her stomach warmed, her heart fluttered, and she couldn't stop the smile from lighting up her face.

Isla shrugged. "I didn't have anything else to do, and I didn't think you'd mind."

"We don't!" Katie chimed, snagging the flowers from Isla. "These are beautiful."

"Yeah." Isla's cheeks flushed pink.

"You brought me flowers?" Andry squinted, trying to catch sight of them as Katie stole them away. When was the last time someone had given her flowers? Someone who wasn't in the PTA.

"Yeah," Isla said again, the blush deepening.

"Thank you."

"I'm going to put these in water. You two do...whatever it is you're going to do." Katie pranced off toward the kitchen, and they were left alone.

Andry awkwardly stood, her hands clasped together. The urge to step forward and kiss Isla was one of the strongest feelings she had, but at the same time, Katie was in the house. She wanted to respect the fact her daughter was there and this was new to everyone. Isla took the initiative and stepped forward, clasping her hand around Andry's arm.

"It's all right. I get it."

"Get what?" Andry's brows drew together.

"I have a stepmother, Andry." Isla raised an eyebrow. "At some point you are going to have to figure out how to have a relationship in front of her even if it makes everyone uncomfortable."

"Oh." Andry's voice dropped. Katie hadn't told them not to. In fact, she'd given them space to kiss without her in the way, not that Andry was going to initiate a make-out session or anything beyond a gentle hello. Giving in to desire, she swiftly moved in and pressed their mouths together in a brief kiss. "Happy Birthday."

Isla's lips curled up, the smile reaching her eyes. She moved in and kissed Andry a little deeper than before. "Great prank today."

Chuckling, Andry shook her head. "Last minute, but I think it sufficed."

"My dad played that one on me once."

"Did he?" Andry took Isla's jacket as she shucked it, and

hung it up with the rest of the coats before snagging her arm and wrapping it around hers.

Isla nodded. "He was the master at playing pranks on me and Aisling. I'm not sure if he ever did on Lynda. I don't think she would have found them all that amusing. She's so serious."

Andry lifted her shoulder in a shrug. "You never know unless you ask."

"True."

Andry suspected that wouldn't be a question Isla would pursue. Leading her toward the kitchen, Andry refused to let go of her arm. They stepped in just as Katie finished clipping the stems of the flowers and started putting them into a vase.

"I can do that if you want," Isla said, stepping forward.

Katie shook her head. "I don't mind. I actually enjoy it."

"Thought of becoming a florist?"

Katie snorted. "Hardly, but Mom so rarely gets flowers that it's a nice treat."

Isla stepped right up to Katie and leaned against the counter. "You know...you can buy her flowers."

Katie's look turned devilish, and a wash of fear moved through Andry. Just what exactly was Isla teaching her now? Because that look didn't bode anything good. Andry moved to the stove to check on the food before flipping the meat over to brown the other side. The kitchen seemed full again with three people in it, and that brought its own pang of sadness. It had been so long since something like that had happened.

She was glad her relationship with Chris was over—at least in that capacity—but every once in a while, the sadness would still sweep her off her feet and take her by surprise. She was lonely, not that it was something she wanted to actively fight to remedy. Having someone else with her in that sort of relationship was definitely something she wanted. Finding Isla had been a complete surprise.

Isla stepped in close to her and ran a hand down her shoulder to her fingers, curling their hands together. Touch lent Andry strength. She might be lonely for the normalcy of a relationship, but she wasn't ready to dive headfirst into those either. It just meant she was on the right path toward finding that again. She was opening herself to possibilities.

It wasn't much longer before they all sat down to eat. The conversation at the table flowed freely, Katie putting on her best show for Isla.

They had just cut into the cake and served it when Katie eyed Andry curiously. "You know...I never thought until now just how much younger Ms. Walsh is compared to you. You're robbing the cradle, Mom."

Andry's cheeks rushed with heat, and she slowly set her fork down and lifted her chin up, narrowing her gaze at Katie. "I hardly think—"

"How much of an age gap is there?" Katie looked directly at Isla as if she was going to answer that question without hesitating.

Isla shifted Andry a look of curiosity before setting her fork down. "Eleven years."

"Wow, really?" Katie turned her look on Andry, her lips quirked in that way that told Andry this was not going to be pleasant. She needed to end it as swiftly as possible.

"Where are you going with this?" Andry pushed back, using a much sterner tone than she had all evening. Katie was walking the line on being rude.

Isla winked at Andry before leaning on the table. "My step-mother is twenty-one years older than me, and I'm eleven years older than you. Fancy that. There was also a gap between my stepmother and my dad. Age gaps happen, and they work, or they don't work, but I don't think that's dependent on the age people are but more on how they handle themselves and the relationship. However, in the case of an eighteen-year-old...I would not recommend diving into a relationship with a twenty-nine-year-old. We can be vicious and need to be tamed by someone with a whole lot of experience."

Andry choked on her bite of cake. She shot Isla an incredulous look before glancing at Katie who looked horrified.

"I would never date someone who's nearly thirty—that's so...old."

Isla laughed, her voice filling the kitchen. "Good. I'm glad to hear that. If you're trying to poke at your mother, I think it failed." She went back to eating her slice of cake as if nothing had made a dent in her, but Andry could see under the surface that it had. She was stiffer, and while she smiled, it didn't quite reach all the way to her eyes.

"That was rude, Katie." She was absolutely embarrassed, but she wasn't going to let it continue without saying something either.

Katie shrugged. "It had to be said."

"No, it didn't. And if you have a problem with it, you should speak to me privately on the matter." Andry wanted to reach under the table and touch Isla's leg, let her know that she was there for support, but she hesitated because of Katie and the odd mood she was in.

Katie gave a defiant look but didn't say anything. Andry held the tension for another minute before going back to eating her cake, but the flavor of it didn't quite reach her tongue anymore. What had started as a good night had turned bitter. It wasn't much longer before she found herself clearing the table while Isla and Katie talked in the living room. She finished putting the dishes in the dishwasher and dried her hands before setting it to run.

Letting out a deep breath as she leaned against the kitchen counter, Andry tried to find an easier center. Katie had been excited to do the birthday meal and had even come up with the menu for it, but that last comment had thrown them off from a pleasant meal. Andry walked out into the living room to find Isla and Katie laughing about something. Having their ages so blatantly loud and in her face was unexpected, and she was unsettled by it.

"I'm going to stay the night at Mom's," Katie announced as soon as she realized Andry was in the room. "I'll be back Friday after the big family dinner over there."

Andry's heart sank. They hadn't talked about that being the plan. Yes, Katie was going to Chris' family Thanksgiving meal, but she'd been planning on staying with Andry until Thursday morning so they could have some time together through the holiday. She wanted to object, but it wasn't because she was going to Chris'. It was because there was something going on that was unsaid. She hated leaving so much unsaid between them, and she wanted to soothe whatever she'd upset unintentionally.

"Text me when you get over there, will you?"

"Sure." Katie stood up. "See you around, Ms. Walsh."

"See you, kid." Isla leaned back into the couch, clearly waiting for Katie to give them some time.

Katie grabbed her jacket and car keys, and after getting ready, stepped in to give Andry a hug. "See you in a few days, Mommy. Love you."

"Love you too, baby." Andry watched her go in silence, listening for the sound of the engine as it started.

Sighing heavily, she plopped onto the couch next to Isla and closed her eyes. Her shoulders were tense, more than she had realized, but now that Katie wasn't there, she couldn't deny just how stressed that had made her.

"She's worried about you," Isla murmured.

Andry scoffed. "She was rude. I'm sorry."

"Don't be. I didn't take it personally."

Sighing, Andry ran her hands through her hair. "I thought she was dealing better with this."

"Look." Isla grabbed Andry's hand and gave her a squeeze. "This is something that I understand really well, okay? So hear me when I say this. Katie's comfort with me is going to come and go in waves, likely for years if we continue dating. But even if we don't and you start dating someone else, it's going to be the same."

"What do you mean?" Andry looked at their hands, the thought of dating someone else so far-fetched that she couldn't even imagine it.

Isla hummed before trying again. "She's not uncomfortable with me as a person. She's uncomfortable with the shifting in roles and the change in dynamics. Until those are set and well-practiced, it's going to be unbalanced and difficult for her. Talk to her about it, but don't let her bowl you over either."

"Do you think she did that tonight?" Andry locked her eyes on Isla, still holding her hand firmly, not wanting to let go.

"No, not at all. I think she surprised you."

"I thought I had this all handled."

Isla let out a wry chuckle. "You've never done this before."

"True."

"So no, you don't have it all handled." Isla moved in and kissed Andry on the cheek. "I'm still here, and I'm still willing to be here while you navigate this if you want."

"I just... I didn't expect to find someone so soon."

"Things just happen sometimes." Isla's tone had gone from light and friendly to dark, and Andry was pretty sure they weren't just talking about Katie and her problem but the greater problem of life.

"They do." Andry used a finger under Isla's chin and raised her head up to make their lips meet.

Even with all the drama toward the end of the dinner, she still wanted the time they had together outside of school to do this and to figure out where they stood with each other beyond just principal and teacher. Isla moaned and moved in, deepening the embrace. Andry threaded her fingers into Isla's hair, pulling her closer.

Breaking the kiss for a brief moment, Andry whispered, "I'm so glad we get to do this."

Laughing, Isla opened her eyes and pushed Andry down onto the couch. "Me too."

CHAPTER
Twenty-Eight

HER PHONE RINGING SURPRISED HER. Isla reached down to see who was calling and smiled to herself as she answered, putting it on speaker as she pulled the apples over to start peeling them for the pie. "Good morning."

"Morning," Andry answered, her voice still a little rough from sleep.

Isla had spent the morning staring at the food in her kitchen and trying to find a method to the madness. She'd never cooked a full Thanksgiving meal by herself before. As nervous as she was, there was a plan, and if Isla was good at one thing, it was executing well-laid plans. She had a couple of hours before Wil and Lynda would show up, and an hour or two after that Aisling would come. It was going to be full in her tiny apartment, but well worth it in the end. She had to keep telling herself that.

"How was your night?" Isla chopped up the apple and dumped it into the pot on the stove.

Andry sighed heavily. "My house is too quiet without her here."

"You're going to have to get used to that sooner rather than later."

"I know." Andry sighed again. There was a longing there that Isla couldn't help but pick up on.

"You should come over today." If she was Andry, she wouldn't want to step within ten feet of the apartment that day, not with what they had to figure out within the family, but she didn't want Andry to be alone during the holidays either.

Andry chuckled wryly. "I think you have enough loose emotions on your plate today."

"Fine," Isla muttered. "But the offer still stands if you want to join us."

"Maybe next time. I think you should have this holiday with your family and figure out some things between you and them. Next time I'll come and add another crazy voice to the mix."

"You're hardly crazy," Isla whispered as she dumped the next apple in, but her stomach clenched tightly. Was Andry already thinking a year ahead? Where Isla would normally expect panic, instead she was filled with comfort.

"I feel that way sometimes. Especially with last night."

"Katie?"

"Yeah." Andry let out a dissatisfied grunt, and Isla knew she was struggling with it.

"Tell me about it." Isla continued to peel and chop apples, turning the heat on the stove while she did the last one to get it warmed.

"I want this, whatever this is with you, so please don't hear me saying anything as though I don't want to be with you, okay?"

"Okay." Isla's eyes wrinkled at the corners at the thought. They were barely into any kind of relationship, but it was nice to hear the commitment to it while they figured out where to go from there.

"I wasn't worried about how this would affect Katie, but then talking to you and how it affected you, and last night..."

"Now you're worried."

"Yeah."

Isla nodded even though Andry couldn't see her. She understood where Katie was coming from, and it had taken her years to figure out how to navigate that with Lynda, but they were making damn good progress so far. She dumped the sugar and spices into the pot and gave it a good stir so the apples on the bottom wouldn't burn. "I get it, where Katie's issues are coming from. Have you talked to her?"

"Not since she left."

"Well, you need to talk to her. Like you said, Lynda and I have some extenuating circumstances when it comes to our relationship, and that's what caused a lot of the strain. We're too alike in some ways and both of us would rather avoid big emotions. Don't do that with Katie. And don't let her avoid something. Unless you plan on becoming a nun, you will have to have this conversation."

"I know." There was a slight whine to Andry's tone, and it brought a smile to Isla's lips. "It's just so damn hard."

"Life is hard. Suck it up, buttercup."

Andry snorted a laugh. "Do you think everyone will remain civil today?"

"Of course. The only person I ever worried about not being civil was Wil, and she's seemed to figure her shit out for the most part. She's still brutally blunt sometimes." Isla was curious how that would play out with everyone in the same room. Lynda had been Wil's main trigger for her anger growing up, but with that issue resolved, perhaps it wouldn't be as bad as she was anticipating. "You could still come and witness the ensuing chaos."

"Oh, no. I think I'll stick at home with my glass of wine and leftovers from this amazing birthday dinner I had at my house the other night."

"It *was* excellent." Isla flushed at the memory, not just of the meal, but the closeness and connection she felt with Andry after.

"I'll let you get cooking. I'm sure you have a million things to do today, I just wanted to whine about the distance I'm feeling between me and Katie."

"Whine all you want. I'm here to listen." And Isla meant it. She wanted to be there for Andry in the same way that Andry had been there for her.

"Thank you for that."

Isla could have sworn she heard the smile through Andry's voice. They ended their call, and Isla lost herself in cooking. An hour earlier than expected, there was a knock on her door and the handle rattled.

"Wil! I have the deadbolt done up, hold on!" Isla called loudly from the kitchen out, hoping that Wil could even hear her. As soon as she got a chance, she dried her hands on a towel and went out into the other room to open the door.

Wil burst through it and flung her hands around Isla's shoulders in a tight hug. "Don't ever let me drive with this lady on the highway again."

"What?" Isla furrowed her brow, looking over Wil's shoulder to find Lynda standing behind her with a mischievous quirk to her lips. "What happened?"

"Speeding. Weaving in and out of traffic. No stopping."

Narrowing her gaze, Isla stepped back. "That sounds like how you drive."

"Shut up." Wil laughed. "So what if I was the one driving?"

Lynda shook her head as Wil stepped to the side finally allowing her into the apartment. "It was an adventure to say the least. I think I'll drive next time."

"Good idea," Isla added. "I always drive on the highway with that one." She moved her thumb over her shoulder at Wil and raised her eyebrows. Isla stepped in and wrapped her arms around Lynda in a gentle hug, reserved and a little hesitant. "It's good to see you again."

She was surprised to find that she actually meant it, so she held onto that comfort as she stepped back.

"It is. Thank you for the invitation. Aisling says she'll be a little late."

"I'm sure she went out partying last night."

"Speaking of!" Wil interjected. "We did bring booze."

"You always do," Isla laughed. "Go get it. I need to finish chopping yams."

"Want some help?" Lynda asked.

Isla eyed her down for a second before she nodded and walked to the kitchen. It was a small kitchen, so with limited space, there was nowhere to avoid Lynda. They had to talk to each other no matter what happened. Isla handed her a knife and cutting board along with a bag of potatoes while she took the yams and started to finish them.

"Skins on or off?" Lynda asked.

If she had remembered from when Isla was little, she would know that she loved to have the skins on in her mashed potatoes, but then again, Lynda had never been the most observant in the household. Isla had been frustrated with that a lot growing up, but she needed to learn to let it go. "Take them off. Neither Wil nor Aisling like them."

"Right." Lynda held her hands precisely as she started peeling.

An awkward silence fell between them before Wil came in, squeezing into the tiny kitchen to start putting drinks into the refrigerator. "We brought stuff for mimosas."

"Did you?" Isla tossed a look over her shoulder at Wil.

"Yup." Wil shifted a glance between Isla and Lynda, who was still quietly chopping. "Want one?"

Wil still hadn't looked back at Isla, observing Lynda with everything she had, and quite openly. Isla recognized the old pain that was coming up and pushing it back down. She needed to let go. "Yeah, sounds like a good idea."

"Lynda?" Wil asked.

"Sure."

The awkward tension filled the kitchen again, all of them going back to work without speaking. Isla held that tension in her stomach and then her chest. She had to be the one to break it. When Wil handed Isla her drink, she took a sip and winked at Lynda. "Much better than that nasty wine you kept in the house."

Lynda's shoulders tightened, and Wil froze in place. Isla faced them, her drink at her lips as she eyed them both over the rim of the glass while taking another sip.

"Yup. Vodka over that wine any day. Though...I do miss the free alcohol." Isla giggled. "Tell me, when did you figure out we were stealing it?"

"When you were sixteen," Lynda said in a rush, a hint of lightness to her tone. "I watered down the second bottle you stole in hopes it would dissuade you."

"Really?" Wil spun to Lynda, her eyes wide.

Lynda lifted her shoulder in a slight shrug. "It was your grandmother's idea."

"Well, it worked," Wil muttered, handing over the drink she'd made for Lynda and kissing her cheek. There was a radiance in her friend that Isla couldn't ignore. Lynda, as well, seemed to shine brighter with Wil's presence.

That was going to take Isla some getting used to, but she was willing to work on that. Wil's hand skimmed along Lynda's back as she stepped out of the kitchen and left.

Isla hadn't been able to drag her eyes away from it, and when she looked back up at Lynda, their gazes locked. Isla's heart shattered at the fear that shadowed Lynda's eyes. She said nothing as they continued to watch each other.

Setting her glass onto the counter, the thud reverberating through her ears, Isla said the only thing she can think of. "I'll get used to it. I promise."

"You're not okay with it," Lynda's voice was back to that low quality but with urgency and a tremor.

"I am, actually." Isla straightened her shoulders, looking out to see if Wil was lingering around. "I am. It just... there's a lot of adjustments right now, and it's taking some time to get used to the normalcy of things." Isla paused again, sighing heavily and diving straight in. "I can see how happy you two are."

Lynda's face was impassive. Isla longed to be able to read her better, but she just couldn't.

"You are. Wil has never been this relaxed in a relationship before. Well...most of her relationships were very short-lived anyway." Isla glanced toward the door to the kitchen. "And I've seen the changes in you, too. You're warmer."

The smile cracked through, and Lynda's shoulders dropped back, tension flowing out from her. "We are happy. It's nice to get to know her, since she spent most of her childhood hating me."

"Secretly loving you, you mean." Isla laughed a little. "Wil's crush on you was so big that she didn't know what to do with it."

"So she's said." Lynda relaxed her stance and focused back on the potatoes. "I'm glad you two seem to have repaired things."

"Just took me pulling my head out of my ass. I don't want you to hold back with her today, okay?" Isla touched a hand to Lynda's forearm to make sure she had her attention. "If you want to kiss her, do it. If you want to hold her hand, do it."

"Are you sure?" Lynda's voice wavered slightly.

"Absolutely." Isla glanced at the yams she was chopping but didn't go back to them. On impulse, Isla closed the gap between them and wrapped her arms tightly around Lynda's shoulders, dragging her in for a tight, authentic hug. She closed her eyes and breathed in her scent that hadn't changed in all the years she had known her. For once, it brought her comfort instead of rage.

She sighed into the embrace. Her heart pattered heavily when Lynda reached around her, holding her close, her hands moving circles against her back. Isla moved her face into Lynda's shoulder, dragging in a shuddering breath.

"I never gave you enough credit." Those words had weighed heavily on her for months now. She'd been able to avoid it until then, but with Lynda and Wil in her apartment, another holiday to come and go, Isla couldn't deny it anymore. She'd never felt quite this amount of comfort from Lynda before, and the gentleness with which Lynda held her made it all that much stronger. Isla snorted loudly before pulling back, the tears joining ones of laughter. "We also stole your entire bottle of gin."

"Gin?" Lynda's forehead creased, and she shook her head. "I don't drink gin."

"Dad's?"

Lynda frowned as she thought. "Probably."

"Well, leave it to Dad, then." Isla laughed. "We puked for days after that."

The realization dawned in Lynda's gaze as to what exactly Isla was talking about. "When I was at my conference, the one time I let you stay home alone for it."

"Yup." Isla giggled and turned back to the yams. "Such a mistake. I haven't been able to drink gin since."

"Why are you sharing all my damn secrets?" Wil mumbled as she came back into the kitchen area. "Also, when the hell is Aisling getting here? I still need to tease her about the football coach she was dating."

Isla groaned and rolled her eyes. "She should be here in the next couple of hours, but leave it alone already, she dumped him as soon as she figured out he was an asshole."

"Right." Wil shrugged. "Still want to tease her. Which reminds me...how is your boo?"

Isla rolled her eyes, but her cheeks flushed hot. "We're taking things slow."

"You and slow?" Wil shifted her gaze from Isla to Lynda before looking back at Isla again.

Isla nearly choked. "Lynda doesn't need to know about any of my exes, thank you."

"Sure, she does. She missed all the fun drama."

Lynda clicked her tongue. "I think you two were enough drama to last me for years."

Isla paused before she burst into laughter. They had given

Lynda a run for her money, especially Wil. Her chest rumbled with laughter as she finished the yams and Lynda finished with the potatoes. At least they were laughing already, the majority of the tension from the anticipation of the day easing within the first hour.

Isla couldn't have asked for more.

CHAPTER
Twenty-Nine

ALICE SAT QUIETLY the Friday after the holiday break, her head down and her arms crossed under her. Her eyes were closed, and through what looked to be a serene moment, Isla could feel the pain in her heart. It had been the first holiday without her father, and Isla remembered what that was like. In some ways those first holidays had been hard, but they weren't the worst. They were the ones she expected to be difficult.

When she took the kids out to recess, she called Alice's name to catch her attention and beckoned her back. "Come talk with me for a minute."

They made their way back into the classroom, leaving the door open as was standard practice when alone with a student. Isla slid into the seat across from Alice's as they looked at each other. She hadn't wanted to do this but seeing Alice in so much pain forced her look at the situation with a new light. She had to say something.

"My mom died when I was four years old," Isla stated quietly. As soon as the words were out of her, emotion choked up her throat, and she had to fight against it. Alice's eyes widened. "And when I was thirteen, my dad died."

Alice shook her head, her lips parted as if she was going to say something, but Isla held her hand up to stop her.

"I'm not telling you this so you can feel bad for me, okay? I'm sharing because I want you to know that I've been where you're at, and it sucks."

Alice's eyes filled with tears. Isla reached over the table and held her hand out so Alice could take it if she wanted. Instead, Alice wiped her cheeks clear of tears.

"I've been worried about you, and I know that school isn't where you want to be, but it's where you have to be. I'm here for you, okay? If you want to talk about your dad, if you want to just tell me how you're feeling, or if you just want to sit in quiet, knowing that someone else has been where you're at. That's what I'm here for, okay?"

Alice nodded. "Okay, Ms. Walsh."

Isla swallowed hard, that same pain as before coming back up. After the Thanksgiving spent with Wil, Aisling, and Lynda, the laughter, the memories, the joy she had found in that small meal spent together, she knew what she had missed out on for years, and she couldn't let Alice go through the same if she could avoid it. She would have given anything to have an adult, any adult, be there for her through all of this.

"I just wanted you to know that these first holidays are tough, and you'll figure out how to deal with it better as the years pass, but right now, everything is so jumbled."

"It really is." Alice brushed her hands against her cheeks again. "I'm so mad at him."

"Yeah." Isla gave a soft smile. "Yeah, I get that. I was so mad for such a long time, and that's okay too. Whatever you're feeling is okay, just make sure you're not bottling it up."

"I won't."

"Good. Do you want to stay in here for another minute or do you want to go out and play?"

Alice's gaze flicked toward the playground that she could see from the window, the kids running around outside as they played. "Just another minute."

"Tell me when you want to go back."

Isla shook the moment off, letting Alice take the lead. She ended up staying in the classroom for half of her recess and then deciding to go outside. Once Isla was cast into the silence of her empty classroom, she held her hand over her racing heart and closed her eyes, sitting with the hurt that she had willingly resurfaced. It was the first Thanksgiving that she hadn't felt like he was missing but fully present.

~

Isla was wrecked by the end of the day. Alice had looked at her randomly throughout the rest of school, and she'd forced a gentle smile to her lips in hopes that it was comforting. By the time she was able to leave, the sun was already close to setting and every muscle in her body ached from holding so much tension.

The knock on her door startled her, and she jumped fully before turning to find Andry standing there. Ease and comfort slid through her, warming her, except she couldn't walk up to Andry and wrap her arms around her in a solid hug like she wanted to. Isla rolled her shoulders, still trying to hold herself together.

"I got a call from Alice's mom."

Panic swelled. Had she crossed a boundary? Her heart raced, and she kept her jaw locked, not wanting to make the situation worse than it already was. "What did she want?"

"To thank you, but she wasn't sure she could say it to you directly." Andry scrunched her nose. "What happened?"

Isla's hands shook as she reached for her jacket and slid her arms into it. She wasn't sure she could stay there any longer and make it through the night. She needed to escape and release all the pent-up tension from the day. "Nothing, really."

"Isla." Andry stepped inside the door. "You're not okay."

It wasn't a question, which surprised her. After she swung her bag over her shoulder, Isla shivered at the intense look Andry gave her. She couldn't hide from it, and while she wanted to, she didn't at the same time. It was amazing to feel seen and heard. Isla pursed her lips and blew out a slow breath, choosing to ignore what her gut instinct told her.

"I'm *not* okay."

"Come with me."

Confused, Isla hesitated, but the warmth in Andry's gaze, the tenderness in it made the decision for her. She followed Andry out of her classroom, shutting everything and turning off the lights. They walked to Andry's office. As soon as they were inside, Andry packed up her bag and touched Isla's arm.

"What are we doing?" Isla asked.

"I'm taking care of you." Andry ushered Isla out of the office, then the building, and right into her car. Isla stared through the front windshield as Andry climbed in and turned over the engine. "We'll figure out the morning when we can, all right?"

"Okay." Isla's voice was despondent. She heard herself when she spoke, but it was so hard to add liveliness to it when she didn't have the energy. She had spent all her energy that day taking care of Alice, and now that she didn't have to do that, she was collapsing.

When they got to Andry's house, Isla took her bag inside and sat on the couch. Andry came back with drinks. "Katie is home tonight."

Isla nodded, though the impact of that statement didn't quite fully register.

"She says she's fine with us being together, but I know it's still a struggle."

"It will be in some ways no matter how long we're together or who you're with." Isla shifted her gaze to Andry. "She grew up with two amazing parents, so it should be a struggle. It's a testimony to how safe she feels with you."

Andry flushed. "I was telling you because you're welcome to stay the night here. I'm not sure what's going through your head right now or what you're feeling, but I get the sense you need company, and until I start to see a turn, I'm not sure I want you going home by yourself."

"Nothing bad will happen if I do." Isla locked her gaze on Andry's. She'd been suicidal when she was a teenager, and this was definitely not that. She was in a healthy space, even if it had been draining. "I'm not going to do anything stupid."

"I don't think you are." Andry's hand grazed Isla's thigh, and she shivered at the touch. "Want to tell me what happened today?"

"I couldn't let Alice sit there and think that she was the only one who had gone through this." Cold washed through Isla. She leaned against Andry and pressed her cheek into her shoulder, closing her eyes and breathing in her scent. "She looked so sad today."

"Yeah, she's struggling. Anyone would."

"When I was a kid, it was like no one cared. I mean, Wil did, and she understood it, and Aisling, and I guess Lynda now that I think about it years later. But when I was a kid, it just felt like no one understood and no one cared." Isla shivered, closing her eyes and breathing in Andry again. This was her comfort and her safe place, and she could trust it.

Andry dropped a kiss on her head. "I don't think no one cared."

"Me either, but I'm not sure they showed it well. And most people don't know what to do with an orphaned kid."

"They don't." Andry wrapped an arm around Isla's shoulder and pulled her in tighter.

She was warm and comfortable. She was safe. And it didn't even take a lot to remind herself of that. "Thank you for being here tonight."

"I'll be here anytime you need it," Andry whispered.

Isla breathed in peace, letting it settle into her chest. "What did she say? Alice's mom?"

"Hmm. She wanted to thank you for taking the time to share your story and connect with her. She said that she was really worried about Alice and how distant she's become and just what exactly is going through her head. Apparently, she came home from school today and they had a long conversation about everything, the first one since her father died."

Isla nodded slowly, heat rushing to her cheeks because it had all been worth it in the end. Sharing with Andry what was going on would be worth it too because she'd never been this close to someone before.

Katie came out of the bedroom, her brow furrowing as she stared at the two of them on the couch. Isla tried to curl her lips into a smile for a greeting, but she knew she didn't quite manage it. Katie plopped down on the chair across from the couch and eyed both of them, her elbows on the arms of the chair. She steepled her fingers together.

Taking a slow breath, Katie flicked her gaze from one to the other before landing on her mom. "Who died?"

Isla snorted at the irony. She'd read the mood perfectly, but how the hell was she supposed to explain to Katie what was going on? She wanted to cry.

"It was just a rough day," Andry answered, clearly skirting the real cause because she wasn't comfortable.

Isla shifted ever so slightly but remained curled against Andry. "My dad died when I was thirteen."

Katie jerked her head back in surprise.

"I have a student who lost her dad recently, and it's brought a lot up, but I'm also trying to work on my relationship with my stepmother, which is also bringing everything up again."

"Stepmother?"

Nodding, Isla shifted again, finding more confidence in her

voice as she continued. "My mom died when I was four. My step-mother finished raising my sister and me. It wasn't easy."

"Jesus," Katie muttered, her eyes wide with shock.

"Yeah, so today was tough, but tomorrow will be better. It has to be." Isla glanced up into Andry's eyes, hoping that she hadn't overstepped the line with sharing that. But she didn't want to be Lynda in a lot of ways, and if she and Andry were going to be in a relationship, then they needed to start forming a different kind of relationship than they'd had before. Katie deserved to know some of where she was coming from, which she had never gotten with Lynda.

"I'm so sorry."

Isla gave her wan smile. "I am too. No one should have to experience that kind of pain so young. They should have a life like yours, with two parents who love you dearly."

Katie scrunched her nose, but she didn't say anything. Isla suspected what she wanted to say, but they weren't quite on those terms just yet. Which was fine. They would get there, eventually—maybe. Isla stayed plastered to Andry's side for another hour until her rumbling stomach was loud enough to distract them. Together, the three of them moved into the kitchen to start cooking, and Isla couldn't stop laughing at the banter.

The pain from earlier vanished in the hours between school and evening. By the time Katie went to her bedroom, Isla was relaxed, and she had smiled a lot in the last few hours. Andry wrapped her arms around Isla and drew her in for a quick kiss.

"Do you want me to take you home?"

Isla flushed, heat rushing to her cheeks. "Did I pass the sanity test?"

"You seem more relaxed than before."

Snorting lightly, Isla smiled. "I am, thank you. And yes, I think taking me home would be best. I'm not sure Katie is ready for overnights yet."

"Me either." Andry kissed Isla's cheek. "I'll take you home, and then tomorrow we can go get your car, okay?"

"Okay," Isla whispered. She made their mouths meet. She took it slow this time but deepened the kiss and fell into the moment. Humming, Isla focused everything she had in that moment on the embrace. She wanted Andry to feel her thanks, to know how much she appreciated all that she had offered her, that she understood this was just for the two of them.

Andry broke the kiss abruptly, her breathing heavy. "Enough of that for now."

Isla kissed her loudly again. "But sometimes I don't want to stop."

Moaning, Andry moved in and pressed Isla against the front door, their bodies smooshed together. She slid a hand up Isla's side and back down to her hip. Her breathing heavy. Isla closed and opened her eyes slowly, locking them on Andry's brown eyes. "I don't want to either."

Andry's mouth was on hers again, heated, passionate. Isla struggled to keep up, her head spinning with every touch, with the lack of deep breaths. She clenched her fists against Andry's sides and held her close, not willing to let her go just yet.

Groaning, Andry pulled away again. "But we do have to stop, for tonight."

"I know." Isla kissed her soundly. "Thank you for being here for me."

"You've been there for me, too." Andry kissed her briefly before stepping away and putting some space between them.

"Have I?"

"In more ways than one." Andry blushed. "Come on, let's get you home."

CHAPTER

Thirty

ANDRY'S KNOCK on the door was firm mid-Saturday morning. She hadn't meant to be this late into the day, but when Katie had requested they spend some one-on-one time together, she'd texted Isla to make sure it was okay to wait on getting her car. It was so rare that she and Katie got a Saturday morning that she wanted to make sure she took the time while she still had it. Isla hadn't seemed to mind. The door snicked open, and there was Isla—beautiful, relaxed, and giving a sexual smirk a mile wide.

Andry's stomach fluttered with butterflies. Whatever had happened the night before had been exactly what Isla had needed apparently because she looked completely different than when they'd left the school. She loved seeing this part of Isla, the part that was open to whatever Andry had to offer. "Afternoon."

"Hey there." Isla leaned against the door frame, her hip propped up and her gaze locked on Andry. "Long time no see."

Andry's smile broadened. "May I come in?"

"Of course." Except Isla didn't move away from the door.

Andry cocked her head to the side, stepping forward and pressing herself against Isla to slide between her and the door. Their bodies brushed, breasts touching, heat searing through her. Andry sucked in a sharp breath until she made it inside. Isla turned around, shutting the door, that same saccharine smile on her lips.

"Katie wanted to go to breakfast this morning, and I couldn't resist."

"Where'd you end up going?" Isla shifted toward the couch and slid onto it, curling her feet under her.

Andry's stomach fluttered again. Something about Isla's mood was different, akin to their flirtation at the door the night before. It was subtly flirtatious, and while Andry had seen Isla flirt before, had experienced the full brunt of it, it had been nothing like this. She shuddered as she sat next to her, sinking into the couch and pressing her hand to Isla's thigh.

"We went to R&B. Katie loves it there."

"I'm not sure I've ever been."

Andry winked. "Then I'll have to take you sometime."

"Would that be a date? Like an out-in-public *date* date?" Isla's eyes were bright, and she shifted so she pressed more into Andry's side. "Because you know, you showed up here and didn't even greet me with a kiss."

"Oh really?" Andry raised an eyebrow, her heart hammering. What had gotten into Isla? "Is that the toll for coming in here?"

"If you want it to be." Isla reached up, curving her palm around Andry's cheek and chin, dragging her forward slightly. "I would love it if it were."

Chuckling, Andry leaned in and pressed their mouths together. Last night had been all heat when they'd kissed, the anticipation ramping up swiftly. But today was a warmth that spread into a heat. Andry had longed for connection like this for years. Sliding her tongue along Isla's, she allowed herself to completely fall into the kiss.

Isla threaded her arms around Andry's neck and tugged as she leaned back into the couch, pulling Andry down on top of her. Andry's heart raced, her mind spinning with a whir of possibilities and exactly what she wanted in the moment.

"Isla," Andry murmured. "What are we doing?"

"Whatever you want," Isla whispered, her lips pressing a line of kisses along Andry's chin to her ear where she nipped her earlobe.

Every part of Andry's body told her to fall into Isla, to give them what they both craved because she had no doubt that they both wanted this physical side of a relationship, but she still hesitated. She hadn't been with anyone other than Chris in so long, that her nerves worked overtime into her stomach.

Andry brushed her hand down Isla's neck and over her breast, massaging gently. She found Isla's hard nipple with the edge of her thumb and teased it. She knew this was what she wanted—she had for some time, but that didn't stop the nerves from roiling around inside her.

"Are you sure?" Andry asked, not confident that she was asking Isla instead of herself.

"Yes," Isla murmured, raising her hips up to buck into Andry. "Are you?"

That was the ultimate question. Andry swallowed the suddenly formed lump in her throat and raised up enough to look down into Isla's bright blue eyes. She was haloed by her golden hair, her entire body relaxed and warm. Andry's heart thumped hard. "Yes."

"Good. I absolutely love lazy afternoon sex."

Andry grunted as she bent down. "I can't remember the last time I had lazy afternoon sex."

Isla slid her fingers under Andry's shirt. "Neither can I."

This time when Andry kissed her, it was full of the same heat as the night before. She pulled on the memory of that, the softness, the sexiness, the tether that tied the two of them together. She had loved feeling that tether strengthen and tighten to the point that Andry wasn't sure she could go a day without thinking about Isla.

Isla scraped her dull nails up Andry's back, pulling her shirt with her as she went. Andry sat up and pulled it off, a smile on

Isla's lips that she never wanted to see vanish. She looked so damn happy. Andry bent down, pressing a trail of kisses down Isla's neck and over her chest and clothes. Her heart thundered when she pressed her palms fully against Isla's hips and pushed upward, taking the soft cottony material with her.

"There were some days I never thought we'd get here." Andry stared at Isla's skin the more she exposed, lifting the shirt over her breasts, finding them unrestrained as she went. Isla pushed up and tugged her shirt off, dropping it to the floor before she lay back down, her hair fluttered around her shoulders again.

Andry touched with tentative fingers. Isla's skin was fire, hot and burning as she teased her breasts with her hands. Isla dragged in a rasping breath. "When I met you, I never thought about this."

Andry let out a wry laugh. "I didn't either."

"This seems so surreal most days."

"Agreed." Andry bent down, twirling the tip of her tongue around Isla's nipple before covering it with her mouth and sucking. Isla dug her fingers into Andry's hair, tugging and writhing underneath her.

"I love that," Isla whispered, scraping her nails against Andry's scalp.

Andry didn't stop. She kept on with what she knew Isla liked as she settled in to the fact that they were actually doing this. She hunched her back, sliding her hands up and down Isla's sides to the top of her pajama bottoms and just underneath the elastic waistband. Impatient, Isla shifted and lifted her butt, dropping her hands to her hips and pushing her pants down.

Sitting up, Andry helped Isla pull her pants and underwear off, dropping them with her shirt. Isla was completely naked underneath her, and she was gorgeous. The hair between her legs was dark, the curls full as she parted her legs. Her scent hit Andry hard, and her heart skipped a beat as she struggled to drag her gaze away.

"You can if you want." Isla's voice was wispy, her chest rising and falling rapidly.

Andry pulled her lip between her teeth and scuffled down the couch more. What would make this better was if they were in a bed, some place they could both move and have the space to do whatever they wanted. Isla lifted her knees up, and Andry got a full whiff of Isla's musky scent with a hint of spice. She held back her moan but skimmed her hands against Isla's thighs, down to her center and back up to her knees again.

Her hands shook. She wasn't sure why, but she took her time feeling Isla's soft skin under her fingertips and calming herself down from whatever had upset her. She couldn't quite name it yet. Andry bent down and pressed a kiss to the inside of Isla's knee and closed her eyes. The knots in her stomach tightened, and her heart raced again. This wasn't anticipation like she'd originally thought it was.

Kissing farther down Isla's leg, Andry nuzzled her nose right into her curls. She took deep slow breaths, centering herself. Isla didn't move an inch other than to touch her breasts and arch her back slightly. "Please, Andry."

They both wanted this. That much was clear, and Andry didn't think that Isla felt like she had to, that Andry was pressuring her into anything. She pulled away slightly, and Isla grunted her protest. "You want this, right?"

"Absolutely." Isla's blue eyes locked on Andry's. "I want this. Do you?"

Her heart said yes, but Andry couldn't stop the niggling voice in the back of her mind telling her this was a mistake, just like the last time. She pursed her lips and closed her eyes, shutting that voice up as best as she could. Isla was nothing like Chris. Pushing past her own hesitations, Andry closed her eyes and moved back in.

She started slowly, tasting and testing to see what Isla liked and didn't like. Moving lower, Andry angled her gaze upward so she could see Isla's face, find her tells to see what was going on or

274 ADRIAN J. SMITH

not. She looked like she was in pure bliss. Closing her eyes, Andry focused all she had on Isla. She sucked, she teased, she gave everything she could over to her.

Isla keened, her voice carrying to Andry's ears, and she repeated what she had just done. Isla's legs twitched sharply, and Andry kept her pace and pressure. She risked one more glance at Isla, watching as her nose scrunched and her lips parted and her breath caught. Isla grunted, her stomach tightening and her fingers clenching Andry's hair tightly.

This was a moment Andry loved, the unraveling of her partner and the high it created, not only in Isla, but in herself. She took one last long lick, her heart calming down even though her body was tightly clenching and telling her to take it further. She hummed in her own satisfaction, pressing a kiss to the inside of Isla's thigh before she steadily relaxed herself. She just wanted her brain to shut up.

When Isla came down from her high, Andry cleaned her up and slid up on the couch to press Isla into the back cushions. She wouldn't be able to quiet that nagging voice in the back of her mind. "That's enough for today."

"What?" Isla blinked, obviously confused.

"I can't..." Andry sighed. "I thought I was ready, but I'm not."

"Talk to me. Tell me what's wrong." Isla brushed her fingers down Andry's arm and back up.

Andry blew out a breath, searching for the right words. "I want to make sure you're not doing this because I'm your principal."

Isla snorted a laugh even if she looked suspicious. "Hardly, though I almost *didn't* do it because of that. We've talked about that. What's really going through your head?"

Andry wished she could form words around it faster, but it was such a struggle. "I haven't been with anyone other than Chris since I was nineteen years old."

She shuddered, racked with the realization that she was afraid. Andry closed her eyes, sinking into Isla's arms. She was scared of what this would mean, of how it would change their relationship but also what would happen if she failed this again. She couldn't believe she was afraid.

Isla said nothing, just continued the trail of her fingers up and down Andry's arm. They were so close, Isla's naked body pressed against her firmly on the small couch. Andry wrapped her arm around Isla's back and pulled her in, pressing their foreheads together.

"I do want to be with you. I think I just didn't realize how much baggage I still had."

"We all have baggage," Isla said simply. "The real question is whether or not you'll let me see yours."

"I already have." Andry's heart thudded hard because the statement was true. She had told Isla more than she had anyone else, and she trusted that Isla would hold that sacred. Andry sighed and closed her eyes. "I'm just not ready yet."

"Then we don't do anything you're not comfortable with. I'm sorry that I pressured you."

"You didn't. That was..." Andry savored the memory of Isla coming apart against her mouth "...that was more than I could have ever asked for." Moving in, she stole a kiss from Isla's lips. "You just have to be patient with me."

"Always."

"Can we stay like this?" Andry moved her hand slightly, the edge of her thumb brushing along the underside of Isla's breast. Isla shivered. "I don't want to ruin what we have."

"Hardly ruined." Isla smiled and moved in, pressing their mouths together in a quick kiss. "Do you want to go on a proper date? You and me somewhere, not at a house?"

Andry's stomach swirled with excitement. "I would love that."

"Let me plan it." Isla fluttered her fingers over the edge of Andry's bra, the touch light and teasing, but not asking for more.

"I can do Friday. Katie wants to stay the weekend with Chris."

"Done." Isla kissed her again to seal it. "Wear something nice."

"Are we going someplace fancy?" Andry raised an eyebrow.

"Wouldn't you like to know." Isla giggled and dug her fingers into Andry's sides, tickling her. "It's a secret."

Andry cried out at the touch and moved against Isla again, pinning her hands above her head. They breathed heavily for a moment before she moved in swiftly and locked their lips in another kiss. Even if they stayed this way for hours, she would be happy. She truly had found someone interesting in Isla, someone she never thought she'd find.

CHAPTER
Thirty-One

ALICE STEPPED into her classroom early Tuesday morning, her eyes red and swollen. Isla's heart stopped short when she saw the look.

"Alice, what happened?"

She sniffled, dropped her bags at her table and moved to Isla's table, flopped down heavily and wiped her eyes. "My best friend is moving."

"Avery?"

Alice shook her head. "Avery is my best friend from school. This is Evelyn. Her dad's in the Air Force and they're PCSing."

Isla pursed her lips. She'd seen her fair share of kids come and go because of military orders over the years, and it was always a tragedy, but for this to happen so soon after Alice had lost her father had to be devastating. "I'm so sorry."

"She says we'll still talk when she moves, but I don't know." Alice sniffled. "We were helping them pack all weekend."

Isla raised her eyebrows, surprised that it would be happening so soon. Then again, they may have just waited to tell the girls. Alice breathed out, her shoulders collapsing in.

"What am I supposed to do?"

Isla drew in a steadying breath. "I think you have to be the best support for her that you can be. It's hard, I know, but she's moving to a whole new school in the middle of the year and leaving you behind, too. I'm sure she's feeling some of the same things that you are."

"Yeah." Alice pursed her lips and wiped her hands across her cheeks. "Her mom is a teacher, so at least at her new school, she'll get to see her mom every day."

"Is she?" Isla furrowed her brow. "Where does she go to school?"

"Irving."

Isla nodded and kept her focus on Alice as best as she could, but her mind was a whir of ideas and information. She brought herself back around to look at Alice. "Is there anything you can do that would help her move? Make it easier for her and maybe you in the process?"

Alice sighed. She took one finger and traced designs on the tabletop and shook her head, her eyes filling with tears again. "I just don't know."

"Think about it, because I think it'll help you both. I'll try to come up with something too, all right?"

Alice nodded. "Thanks."

"Thank you for trusting me with this." Isla put her hand on top of the desk to get Alice's full attention. "I know how hard of a year this has been for you, but I know you'll come out the other side stronger than you could ever imagine." Isla raised her eyebrows, hearing the words after she'd spoken to them. She had been told for years that she was strong, but she'd never believed it before now.

"Yeah."

They talked for a few more minutes before Alice left to go for breakfast. Isla leaned back in her chair, the weight of what Alice had shared settling into her. She licked her lips as she debated what to do. It would be an odd request, but with the timing, everything could be perfect. Unfortunately, if it all worked out, then she would be leaving little Alice as well, and that wouldn't do anything to help, but at least Isla could prepare her for that transition. It was a remote possibility that it would all work out anyway.

Besides, Isla had so much more to get done that day before she could really let all that sink in. But after the weekend, Wil's sage words of advice kept coming back to her. She and Andry were moving forward leaps and bounds even with slowing down, and she wanted to continue. Andry definitely did based on their conversations. She needed a plan because she wasn't going to ask Andry to leave.

Dragging in a deep breath, Isla glanced over at the phone in her classroom and pursed her lips. What harm would a phone call do? She scooted to her proper desk and turned on her computer, searching for Irving Elementary on their district website. Her heart stuttered when she saw the principal's name on the front page of the website—Christine Murphey.

That she had not expected.

Her heart thundered, and her hands shook. She wanted more with Andry, that much was for certain. She was willing to wait for Andry to be ready to move forward, and she hoped this coming weekend was going to be the start of that. Wil's words of advice filtered through her mind. *Have an exit plan.* If everything went well, she would want one, and even if it went bad, she would want one.

"Irving Elementary, this is Ms. Linda."

"This is Isla Walsh from Elbert. Is Principal Murphey in?" Her hands were sweating, her heart in her throat.

"She just stepped into her office, let me see."

Isla was put on hold, her stomach twisting into knots as she waited anxiously. Instead of Linda coming over the line, Chris answered. "This is Dr. Murphey."

She winced. Chris likely had no idea who she was, and this was such a precarious line she was walking. "Hi, I'm Isla Walsh. I teach sixth grade at Elbert. I was calling to inquire about a potentially open teaching position you have."

There was a long pause, and Isla's heart pounded, making it hard to breathe. Her hands shook, her head spun, and she had to grip onto the edge of her desk just to keep herself from reeling out of control.

"We do have an open position—or it will be when the new year starts. It's for teaching second grade."

Isla pursed her lips. She had done her student teaching in second grade, and while she hadn't hated it, she much preferred the older kids. However, if this would break some of those last barriers with Andry, it would all be worth it in the end. She had to trust that.

"How did you hear about it?" Chris seemed oddly suspicious, and Isla could understand why. They probably hadn't even opened the position anywhere yet.

"Oh, one of my students is best friends with one of your students, and her mother is the teacher." That was at least an easy question to answer. The reason why she wanted to move in the middle of the school year, which was so rare, was not going to be easy.

"Are you wanting to apply?"

"Yes." Isla stared at the clock, knowing the bell was going to ring shortly. "I'm looking to transfer, and I know it's unconventional to do that in the middle of the school year, but I would love to work under a new principal and gain experience from you as much as from here."

"You know that I have some familial connections to that school." Chris' voice was frayed, no hint of sarcasm or amusement in it.

"Yes," Isla answered, not quite sure what to say to that. She hadn't anticipated being called out so directly. "I realize it's unconventional—"

"It is," Chris interrupted. "Send over your resume, and I'll have a look at it, but I won't interview you without talking to Andry first."

"All right." Isla's stomach plummeted. That meant she was

going to have to talk to Andry about her plans, and she had a distinct feeling that it would not go over well. "I'm sure she'll give me a good recommendation."

"We'll see. Send your resume. I promise to look at it." Chris' tone had softened. "But I suspect you have the same problem I do."

"The first bell?" Isla questioned.

"Yes. Email me."

Before Isla could agree or say goodbye, Chris hung up on her. She pursed her lips and stared at the phone before jerking with a start when the bell reverberated through her classroom. All right. She could do this. She could apply for a job, get Andry on board, and not screw this thing up.

Isla sat on her couch, her computer on the coffee table as she built her resume. Wrinkling her nose, she snagged her cellphone as soon as she thought Wil might be home and called her forever friend. She really needed Wil's advice on this one because she didn't want to screw up something that hadn't even started yet.

"What's up, sis?"

Wil's voice was so welcome. Isla couldn't stop the smile from reaching her lips. "So much."

"Oh no, that doesn't sound good."

Isla let out a wry chuckle. "Do you have time tonight?"

"I always have time for you."

Rolling her eyes, Isla stretched her back. "I mean it. If you have a date or something, I don't want to disrupt it."

"You're not. I'll just chill in the bedroom for a bit when I get home."

Isla didn't miss the fact that Wil expected Lynda to be there when she arrived or at least to be there shortly. "Are you going to your apartment or hers?"

"Oh um...we moved in together, mostly. I'm still lugging my crap over since I have my lease until the end of the year."

Right. Isla sighed. Wil had mentioned that they wanted to do it, and she wasn't surprised. Still it stung a bit that she hadn't been told or wasn't asked to help them move. She had helped Wil move every time before then. "Good for you."

"You don't sound too happy."

"I am. I just... Why didn't you ask me to help you?" The hurt stung there more than anything. She knew Lynda would replace her in some ways, and she should if they were going to be in a relationship together, but it still hurt to have to deal with those shifts.

"I'm doing it slowly, sis. I promise. You can help me move out the big shit and clean up if you want. It'll be over the holidays, so you'll have time."

"Okay." Isla would have to take Wil at her word. She rolled her shoulders and glanced back at her computer. "I'm doing up my resume."

"Are you?" Wil sounded absolutely intrigued by that.

"There's a second-grade job that opened up at another school. I thought maybe I should try for it."

"Isn't moving in the middle of the year like a huge no-no?"

Isla pursed her lips, saving the file and emailing it over to Chris. "Yeah, but like you said, I need to have an exit plan."

"Is it going that well?"

"I hope so." Isla had been pretty sure that it was, but after the past weekend, she wasn't so sure about that anymore. Something had held Andry back, and she hadn't quite been able to figure out what that was just yet.

Wil grunted, her car turned off, her voice was louder when she spoke again. "What happened?"

"Not quite sure about that one."

"Like I always say...start from the beginning."

Isla sighed. "We were... things were getting physical, and she stopped it."

"Why?"

"She said she wasn't ready." Isla rubbed her thumb along her lower lip, remembering the kisses and the way Andry had touched her. She hadn't seemed to hesitate at all before she'd stopped everything. Isla stood up suddenly and walked to grab the items she'd bought and bring them back to the coffee table. She needed to prepare her next prank, and it was one that was going to take time and effort.

"Then she wasn't ready."

"Yeah, but we did stuff before she said that, and I'm worried she felt pressured into it."

"Then you need to talk to her, not me."

"I know." Isla groaned, pulling out the wrapping paper and pencils. "We haven't had time to do that yet. We have a date this weekend, and I'll be sure to talk to her then."

"Good. So this new job..."

Isla's heart sank, wondering if it was the right choice or not. Her words came out rushed. "It's at the school her ex-wife is the principal at."

"No shit." Wil's shock was evident, and Isla understood why.

If she could add one more complication in this relationship, she was apparently bound and determined to do that. She cringed. "I know, but it's hard to find a school with openings in the middle of the year, so this would be a perfect shift."

"You can't wait?"

"I don't want to. I want to take that complication out of the equation."

"By adding in another?" She hated hearing Wil validate her worries.

"I know. I know. I need to talk to her."

"Damn queer you do."

Isla whimpered. She really wasn't looking forward to that conversation. In fact, she wanted to avoid it as best as she could because it was going to be so hard. She didn't want to leave. She loved working with Andry, but there wasn't a doubt in her mind that if their relationship was going to continue that she was going to have to take this step.

"I'll talk to her," Isla gave in. "As soon as I find a minute."

"No, as soon as you talk to her next and not at the school."

"Definitely not at school."

Wil sighed. "Do you think you can work for her ex?"

"Depends on what she's told her ex about me and how bitter her ex will be about our relationship." A rock settled into the pit of Isla's stomach. This was going to be hard, but she could do it. She had to do it. "I guess I'll find out. At the very least, it'll be six months and then I can see if I can move somewhere else."

"That's quite the risk."

"It is, but I have to hope it's the right one to take."

CHAPTER
Thirty-Two

ANDRY STEPPED INTO CHRIS' house with Katie in tow. Her car already needed work, which wasn't unsurprising, so she'd taken the liberty to drive Katie over after school. She had her hands shoved into her pockets and pursed her lips.

"How's everything going?" Chris asked, moving around some of the papers on the coffee table as she tried to clean up.

Andry didn't care if the apartment was cluttered. That was just part of life, but she knew Chris liked to make an impression when she could. "It's going. Busy."

Chris nodded. "Want to stay for a drink?"

Narrowing her gaze, Andry eyed Chris and tried to figure out what kind of drink she was talking about.

"A soda."

"Right. Um...sure." Andry shucked her jacket. Katie looked elated. If they could manage to have a friendly conversation, then she would know she was well on her way toward moving on, especially if there wasn't any of that lingering hurt. Laying her jacket over the arm of the couch, Andry waited while Chris vanished into the small kitchen and came back with two *Sprites*. Not even caffeinated.

Chris sat next to her, relaxing into the couch with a subtle smile on her lips like she knew something Andry didn't. Not giving in to the temptation to ask, Andry stayed still. "How's everything going for you?"

"Same. I've got a second-grade teacher leaving once the break is up."

"Really?" Andry frowned, her brows drawing together. "Why?"

"Husband is military."

"Ah." Andry let out a sigh. "Forced move and she didn't want to live separately?"

"Who would?"

"Agreed." Andry took a sip of her cold drink. Katie went to her bedroom, doing who knew what, but she was a teenager with a cellphone and friends. It was good to see that she ignored Chris as much as she ignored Andry most days.

"You wouldn't happen to know anyone looking to apply, would you?"

Andry pressed her lips together and frowned. She didn't know anyone actively looking for a job in the middle of the year, which meant that Chris was going to have to find a long-term substitute. It wasn't out of the ordinary to have to do that, especially with maternity leave for some teachers, but that did mean it was going to put Chris in a bit of a tight spot. "Not really, no. I haven't taken an eval of who will still be there next year yet."

"Better do that soon."

There was that same damn look as before, the one that said Chris knew something that she didn't. Andry hated that, because she wouldn't just come out and say it like a sane person, she was going to make Andry work for it. "It's on the to-do list."

They fell into an awkward silence, Andry wondering not for the first time why she had agreed to do this, but she was still there. Katie was nowhere to be seen, so she brushed her hands on her knees and tried to come up with an excuse to leave.

"How's sobriety going?"

"Good, actually." Chris flicked her gaze to the short hallway that Katie had disappeared down. "I'm still going to weekly meetings, sometimes a couple times a week when I need to."

"That's good." Andry had always assumed that as soon as Chris sobered up that she would go back to being the person she had met all those years ago, but that hadn't happened. She still remained aloof and hard to read, someone who liked to toy with information and have the power in the relationship. "I'm glad you did that, really and truly."

"I am too." Chris put her drink on the coffee table. "I didn't realize it had gotten so bad until it was awful."

"What was rock bottom?" Andry wasn't sure she wanted the answer. She had hoped at first it would be their separation, and then some part of her had hoped it would have been when she'd served Chris divorce papers, but it seemed as though none of that had been the case. She'd always wanted Chris to sober up, but the dream that Chris would do it for her and Katie wasn't reality.

"Do you honestly want to know?" Chris stared at her directly.

Andry hedged, not quite sure what to say because she wasn't sure she really did want to know. Her stomach churned at the thought that it was going to be something absolutely awful, but her damn curiosity was insatiable. "Yes."

"It was Katie."

Andry smiled at that. At least it had been *one* of them.

Chris flushed, cheeks reddening and hands shaking when she grabbed for her drink. "She came over one night, and I was so drunk that I can't even tell you what we talked about. The next morning she was gone, and she refused to answer texts or calls, and I was too damn scared to call you. I realized that it was my fault, that if I wanted to be the parent she deserved, that I needed to shape up."

"That's it?"

"No, that's the nice version of the story. Melanie found me so drunk and hungover that she nearly called an ambulance. There was no going back from that. She said if I didn't figure it out that she was going to report me."

"Did you bring it to school?"

Chris frowned. "Never into the building, but in my car, yes."

Andry's stomach twisted. Maybe she should have called sooner, but she'd buried her head in the sand and ignored that it was a problem. She'd put kids in harm's way, and that was guilt she was going to have to work through. She didn't think that Chris would do anything stupid, but then again, being drunk while working was stupid. That guilt ate away at her insides while she sat on the couch with newly sober Chris, wondering if she'd made the right decisions again.

"I know how bad that is."

"It's awful," Andry answered, unwilling to soften the truth.

"It is. I was... I'm a drunk, and there's no ifs ands or buts about it, Andry. I fucked up, and it wasn't until I had the ultimate threat of losing everything that I had to step up and make a change."

The sting hit her hard and fast. She hadn't been enough. Andry blinked against the tears that formed in her eyes as that sting washed through her. She hadn't made a dent in Chris' drunk mind. Andry's marriage and their family were everything to her, but Chris' priorities had been elsewhere, and Andry hadn't even noticed.

"Don't think that," Chris murmured. "Losing you and nearly losing Katie should have been enough, but I'm a drunk, Andry. That's not your fault."

Andry lifted her gaze to meet Chris'. It was odd to her that after so many years and a divorce that Chris could still read her so easily, but that connection she had expected to appear wasn't there. Instead, she sat on the couch, still wondering what they had lost because there didn't seem to be any longing for it now.

"I wasn't strong enough to make different decisions than I did."

"But you stopped because of work."

"Because it was all I had left." Chris' eyes widened. "I had already lost you, and I don't blame you. It was totally me that caused everything."

Andry was inclined to agree because it would be easier, but Chris wasn't the only reason their marriage had fallen apart. They had both made bad choices in there, and while Chris' drinking was the final straw, it wasn't the only thing that broke the camel's back. "You weren't the only reason."

"No, I know that, but I was a lot of it. I didn't put in the effort."

Shock echoed through Andry, hitting her heart hard. She hadn't expected Chris to admit that.

"You were always begging for us to go to therapy or something, and I refused. That's on me, not you."

She hadn't come here tonight for this conversation, but she was willing to listen because she felt as though Chris needed to confess.

"Katie...I don't know what I'd do without her. Thank you so much for not turning her against me."

"It was hard not to at times."

"I imagine."

Andry gave a small smile, setting her soda on the coffee table. The tension that was in her chest disappeared. She hadn't even realized it was still there.

Chris shifted uncomfortably, her gaze not meeting Andry's eyes. Her voice was quiet when she spoke, "Do you want to...I don't know...maybe give this a go again? See where we land?"

Andry immediately thought of Isla, of the relationship they had tentatively started, of the hesitations still swirling in the pit of her stomach. It wasn't this. She'd thought it was at first, that it had been because of Chris and their long-term relationship that had ended so dramatically, but it wasn't. She didn't want to be with Chris anymore, and tonight made that clear. Andry looked Chris directly in the eye. "No."

Chris blew out a breath and halfway laughed. "I'm not sure I want to either. We were always really good friends."

"We were." Andry was thrown off kilter, trying to keep up with Chris' shift in mood. "What are you truly wanting, Chris?"

"I want to move on, figure out who I am."

"Then why don't you do that?" Andry folded her hands together, leaning against her knees. She glanced down the hallway to see if Katie was listening in, and she was glad to find they were still alone. "Try to be a better parent for Katie. She deserves the best from you this last year that she's with us."

"She does." Chris smiled, though it seemed far away as if she was stuck in her memories. "You're right, as always."

Andry's stomach clenched. Chris always did that, tried a power play and then tried to put the weight of the conversation and the decision on Andry. She'd hated that, and she'd thought it had been the alcohol talking for so long, but this conversation really only proved that it was who Chris was through and through. That was something Andry didn't want in her life. She wanted equals, partners, someone she could trust who wouldn't try to turn things for their benefit. Isla gave that to her.

"Thanks for talking with me tonight." Chris frowned. "I feel like this is the first real conversation we've had in a decade."

"It probably is." Andry shifted awkwardly. "It feels good in a weird way, like I understand you better than before."

"Yeah, I get that." Chris rolled her shoulders. "I guess I should just tell you. I got a call from one of your teachers today looking for a job."

"Which one?" Concern flashed through Andry. If she was losing a teacher over something she had done, then she wanted to know, and if they were secretly trying to leave in the middle of the school year, what else could it mean?

"Isla Walsh. She didn't say why she was looking for a job. I know you'd want to know that, but she'd heard through the grapevine that I had a mid-year opening and called."

Andry's stomach rolled. She held her breath tight in her chest, her fingers clenched on her knees, and she looked away from Chris, hoping against all hope that she didn't notice. She collected herself as quickly as possible. "What did you tell her?"

"To send me her resume. She emailed it over that night."

"What night?"

"Tuesday." Chris furrowed her brow. "What do you think of her?"

Andry blew out a breath. That rock in her stomach grew heavier. "She's an excellent teacher. I hired her right out of school, and it was worth it. She's been amazing. She was Katie's sixth grade teacher, remember?"

Chris frowned and shook her head. "I don't remember a lot that I should. But why would she want to look for a new job?"

This was the moment that Andry needed to avoid. She hadn't told Chris, and while Katie knew what was happening, it was clear she hadn't told Chris either. "She's got some changes in life, so she might just want a fresh start. You'll have to ask her if you decide to interview her."

"You're not opposed to me doing that?"

Andry wanted to say she was, she wanted to fight for Isla to stay as close to her as she could, but in the end, with everything that had transpired, she had to be willing to give in to what Isla needed. If they were going to be in a relationship, which they were already doing, then they needed to be able to work at different schools. Just like she had done with Chris all those years ago. "No, I'm not."

"Then I'll invite her for an interview."

"Good." Andry held the tension in her chest. She tapped her hands. "Well, I'll let you and Katie spend some time together. See you around, Chris."

"See you."

Andry stood up and left immediately. At the very least, her

conversation with Chris had revealed one thing. Their relationship was over long before they had separated. She dragged in a deep breath of cold air as soon as she got outside and let it out slowly. That was going to be a difficult conversation to have with Isla, but it was one they needed to start. Immediately.

CHAPTER
Thirty-Three

ISLA COULDN'T STOP STARING at Andry the entire dinner. She had definitely dressed up, in a slick pair of black slacks, a white oxford that had more buttons undone than she usually did, and a black blazer that was left completely open. Every time she shifted Isla swore Andry was about to expose more skin than she could handle.

Isla shivered in her seat when Andry's knee brushed against hers under the table. Those small touches had become more common as the evening wore on. The conversation had flowed so easily that she hadn't wanted to ruin it with talks of serious matters. She'd been nervous all night, and part of it was that. The other part was Andry—she was acting different. Maybe it was because it was their first official date, their first time out with a clear intention behind it, she wasn't sure, but Andry had a swagger to her that Isla found irresistible.

Isla's mouth went dry every time that she thought about undoing those buttons and pulling Andry's clothes off, but after the last time, she wasn't going to put any amount of pressure to be physical if she could avoid it. Andry smiled at her, their eyes locking.

"Tonight was fun," Andry's voice was husky.

It sent another shiver down Isla along with yet another touch of their legs. "It was."

Isla's heart raced as she tried to catch her breath. She reached for her water to distract herself because the looming heaviness of the conversation she had avoided all evening came down hard on her.

"You're good at planning dates."

Isla wasn't so sure about that, but she had put extra special effort into this one. Then again, with the bomb she was about to drop, she was pretty sure that Andry was going to think differently. There was no way to ease into that conversation either. Putting her glass down, Isla held her breath tightly before she loosed the words. "I'm looking for another job."

Andry's eyes widened, an eyebrow raised. She stayed nearly perfectly still, her forearms on the edge of the table, her gaze locked on Isla's, the one button revealing more curve of breast than Isla had ever seen her show off before. "What if I told you I already knew that?"

Isla pressed her lips together hard, dragging her gaze up from Andry's chest to her eyes. "You knew and you didn't say anything?"

"I found out last night. We didn't exactly have time to talk until now." Andry blew out a breath and relaxed into her chair, the mood from seconds ago shifting. "Why didn't you tell me before now?"

"I..." Isla stopped. She had avoided it. "I wasn't sure how you'd feel about it."

"I didn't know what to feel about it, truthfully, but I don't think it's a bad idea. I didn't think you'd be moving this soon."

"Me either," Isla murmured. "But the position came up, and I thought it would be worth it to apply. I didn't realize what school it was at before I called." That was her way of insinuating she didn't know Andry's ex-wife was the principal before, that she hadn't intentionally done that to cause issues.

Andry wrinkled her nose and leaned in again. "She doesn't

know that I'm dating, and she certainly doesn't know about you."

"Katie hasn't told her?"

"No, not from what I could tell. Katie is very protective, and I can't imagine she would say anything unless she was really upset about something, which I don't think she is." Andry paused, tapping her fingers on the table. "You could have told me, you know. I would have preferred to find out from you instead of from Chris."

Isla cringed. "I should have. I just...this is all so new, and I didn't want you to think that I was jumping the gun or something." That and she wasn't the best at having these types of conversations. She had done her best at avoidance for the better part of her life, and old habits were hard to change. But she'd brought it up, far sooner than she normally would have.

"Tell me honestly why you're looking for a new job." Andry lifted her gaze, the flirtatious moments from before gone and replaced with a quiet sincerity that drew Isla to her.

Dashing her tongue across her lips, Isla held the tension in her belly. She wanted to do this right, and she wanted to make sure Andry understood all her reasoning behind it, but she wasn't even sure that she understood it all yet. Taking another risk, Isla said, "I wanted to be able to give us the very best chance possible."

Andry's gaze was unwavering, completely locked onto Isla as she stayed still. Isla's breathing came in short, her lips slightly parted as she waited for any kind of response from Andry, anything to tell her which direction she should go next, if she had been honest enough.

"Andry?"

She cleared her throat and looked around, flagging down the waiter. "Let's go."

Confused, Isla sat still and observed everything about Andry's change in demeanor. Her movements were rigid and stiff, where they hadn't been before. Something had shifted, something drastic, but Isla couldn't name it—she couldn't put her finger on it. And not knowing scared her. Andry paid for the meal without hesitation, and she stood up, holding her hand out for Isla's.

With a ragged breath, Isla slid her fingers into Andry's. They walked out of the restaurant together, heading straight for Andry's car. When Andry opened the passenger door for Isla to get in, Isla put a hand on her shoulder to stop her. "What did I say?"

"Nothing," Andry answered, her tone clipped.

Isla tensed, holding the moment because she wanted an answer. "No, tell me."

"I..." Andry stopped and looked around them. There were several people walking by, moving swiftly from vehicles to buildings or buildings to vehicles. Andry moved quickly. She pressed Isla against the side of the car, covering her completely. She raked her hand up Isla's side as their mouths met in a sudden, heated kiss.

Isla moaned, arching her back. She slid her hand around Andry's back and tugged her in, the warmth from Andry's body heating her own. She closed her eyes and moved her hands all around Andry's back and hips, touching everything that she could manage to reach. Andry broke the embrace, breathing heavily. Isla was just about to ask what was going on when Andry met her gaze.

"Get in the car."

"Okay," Isla breathed out.

Andry stayed put for another second before shifting to let Isla move and slip inside. Andry shut the door, then let out another breath before she rounded the hood and got into the driver's seat. Isla was still completely lost. She held the silence, hoping for some kind of answer, but Andry pulled out of the parking spot and started driving without saying anything.

As soon as they were on Lincolnway, Andry shifted her hand

to Isla's knee, playing her fingers on the inside of Isla's thigh and pulling up her dress inch by inch. "Andry...?"

"I thought I'd be upset that you didn't tell me," Andry murmured, squeezing tighter on Isla's thigh. "But I'm not."

"You're not?" Isla released all the tension in her chest.

Andry slid her a look, one that was pure heat and pure desire. She hadn't looked at Isla like that before. Isla shuddered, her nipples hardening, and she had to shift in her seat when heat pooled between her legs, the stark and sudden memory of Andry's mouth down there running through her. Oh how she would love that again.

"No. Chris and I had our first real conversation last night, and I'll admit, I was put out a bit when she told me that, but she didn't do it to be mean. She did it to give me a heads up because you're one of my teachers."

Isla held still, Andry's sliding fingers against the inside of her thigh making it damn hard to think straight, but she knew she needed to concentrate on what Andry was saying more than what she was doing.

"I was holding myself back, Isla. I'm so sorry I did that."

"What?" Isla blinked, raking her gaze from Andry's hand up to her face as she pulled into her neighborhood.

"I was the problem when we...when we stopped before." Andry swallowed hard, tension in her jaw. Andry pulled into her driveway and put the car into park. She turned on Isla after shutting the car off, her hand still locked on Isla's bare thigh. "Come inside with me."

Isla canted her head to the side. "What?"

"I made a mistake marrying Chris, and it wasn't that we weren't committed to each other. It wasn't that I didn't love her, but I didn't continue to love her as she grew and changed. I wanted the Chris I met all those years ago in college. She was my first girlfriend."

"Oh." Isla's heart thumped hard. She looked out the front windshield, not quite sure what to say to that. She hadn't realized that Andry was so inexperienced with relationships, but she probably should have guessed that. They had gotten married so young. Still, she couldn't quite figure out why Andry was telling her this, especially with the touches on the drive back and that kiss against the car before they'd left.

"That's not who she is anymore. Hell, that's not who I am anymore." Andry sighed heavily and put her head into the back of the seat. "What I'm saying is the other night is my fault. I wasn't ready."

"But you are now?" Isla hesitated to even ask. She hadn't expected this out of the night at all, and to find Andry ready when she didn't think it would happen surprised her. "I went behind your back to find a job with your ex-wife and didn't tell you about it."

"I know." Andry sent her a sweet smile. "And that's honestly what did it."

"I don't understand."

"I know you don't." Andry reached up and touched Isla's chin, turning her so they faced each other. "I moved here because of Chris. I loved Montana and wanted to stay there, but she found a principal job down here, closer to her family, and wanted to move. I moved schools so that we wouldn't be working together. I did everything, and she didn't. You took the initiative to do something for me, I've never...that's never happened for me before. I was always the one making the sacrifices, and this isn't exactly an easy time for you. I know that. Staying would help you so much, but you're willing to take a risk for me."

"I am." Isla blinked clearly, knowing that it was true even if Andry seemed to be giving her more credit than she deserved. "I can't imagine someone not wanting to."

"When you don't say what you want, then it's easy to fall into those habits. I don't want her. I don't want anything like what I had with her, and that was my biggest hesitation when I decided to start dating again. I want something different, something more equal." Andry moved in swiftly, taking Isla's lips.

The kiss was full of pent up sexual energy, and Isla struggled to keep up, struggled to catch her breath. She threaded her fingers through Andry's hair and tugged. She groaned when Andry nipped her lower lip and slid a hand down her side, her thumb brushing against the side of her breast. Isla tried to get her brain to catch up with her body, but they were warring and struggling to keep up with each other. She gasped when Andry palmed her breast, squeezing gently.

"I know I stopped us the last time." Andry kissed a line across Isla's jaw to her ear, pulling her lobe between her teeth and scraping.

Isla shivered, not from being cold but from the forwardness of the touch.

"I won't this time if it's what you want." Andry's lips were at Isla's neck, sucking, teasing, enticing. "Come inside with me."

Everything in Isla told her to say yes, told her to climb across the center console and right into Andry's lap. She didn't want to wait until she got inside. She had wanted this for weeks now, and she was finally going to get everything. It was hard to breathe, her chest tightening at the memory of every touch Andry had done to her before, at the way her tongue had moved against her. Swallowing hard, Isla turned her head until their mouths connected again. She closed her eyes and poured everything she felt into that kiss—the tension, the settledness, the joy.

That was it...joy. Isla smiled when she pulled away slightly, her hand on Andry's cheek, her thumb swiping over Andry's moist and swollen lips. She grinned, pure and simple and without complications, and she was elated.

"Yes."

CHAPTER
Thirty-Four

ANDRY SHOT out of the car faster than Isla could keep up with. She giggled as she followed, shutting the passenger door with a loud click. She tightened her jacket with her hands as she strode quickly toward the front door in Andry's wake. Andry didn't stop grinning as she went, sliding her key into the lock.

As soon as the door was shut, Isla was in her arms again. Andry was voracious. She touched everywhere, her fingers sliding up and down and around Isla's body as she incited and left little wakes of pleasure as she went. Isla pressed their mouths together, shoving Andry's blazer off her shoulders and dropping it to the floor.

She did what she had wanted to do all evening and dropped her head down to press kisses to the opening between the buttons, sliding her tongue along the inside curve of Andry's breast and then scraping her teeth lightly. Andry groaned, her hands in Isla's hair, tangling in her curls and tugging.

Whatever barriers had been between them before were completely gone now. Isla had been wrong. She'd thought Andry hadn't held back but she had—she'd just been too damn blinded by her own desires to even notice it. This was Andry unhindered. Isla raised up on her toes, a smile on her lips as she leaned in and kissed Andry quickly. "If I had known finding a new job would do this, I would have done it weeks ago."

Andry snorted a laugh. "Timing is everything, Isla."

Isla traced a finger right where her tongue had just been. Andry hummed in pleasure, and it lit a fire. "I wanted to do that all night."

Laughing lightly, Andry shook her head. "I think our thoughts took a very similar path then."

"Did they?" Isla raised an eyebrow, her lips playing at a smile as she traced her finger in the same place again. "Because you very nearly had your fingers inside me in the car."

Andry groaned and pressed their foreheads together. "I did think about that."

Isla dropped her hands to the first button she came to and slowly undid it, revealing even more skin. "Why didn't you?"

"We needed to talk first." Andry kissed the side of Isla's neck, making a small circle with the tip of her tongue.

Isla shuddered, pleasure running through her, heat pooling between her legs. Andry had done that exact thing to her clit, and she couldn't wait to feel it again. She dragged in a breath as she undid the next button on Andry's shirt. "And did we talk enough?"

"I'm not sure I could ever get enough of you." Andry nipped, biting down and then sucking.

Isla gasped. She would have a mark the next morning for sure, and she would have to find a way to cover it up when she went to school on Monday. She bruised so easily when people did that, and Andry wouldn't know that yet. She said nothing as she pulled the next two buttons, finally undoing all of them and pulling apart the sides of Andry's shirt. She was greeted with gloriously hot and smooth skin.

"Please touch me," Andry whispered, sucking on Isla's neck again.

The angle was awkward, but Isla leaned back and moved her hands along Andry's hips to the small of her back. She dug her nails in slightly so there would be a bite when she dragged them back around. She wanted to give Andry everything that she had received before and more. She wanted this to be perfect and filled with laughter and joy just like it should be.

Isla let go of Andry enough to pull her jacket off and drop it to the floor. She moved her hands back to Andry's skin as soon as she could and tried to step out of her heels, but she stumbled. Andry laughed and caught her. They both stared at her feet as she tried to get the shoes off and step away from them. As soon as she had them off, Andry pulled her by the hand back down the hallway and toward the bedroom. Isla walked on her tiptoes as she went, her heart ready to burst with pure happiness.

Andry spun her around so she landed half on the bed with a bounce. Her hair settled on her shoulders while Andry grabbed onto the footboard and lifted a foot to untie the laces on her shoe, never tearing her gaze from Isla the entire time.

"Now that is damn sexy," Isla stated, so happy that she nearly forgot to breathe.

"What is?"

"You," she answered with a giggle.

Andry scrunched her nose as she threw her shoe into the corner of the room before undoing the other one. "Take your damn underwear off."

"My my, you are demanding." Isla winked as she wiggled on the edge of the mattress to get her hands under the sides of her panties and pull them off.

"That you already knew." Andry gave her a hard look that meant no funny business.

Isla freely laughed, dropping her underwear to the floor below. Before she even had a chance to figure out what was happening next, Andry knelt down and pushed up the edge of her little black dress, her mouth on her clit in an instant.

"Fuck," Isla crooned, falling backward onto the mattress while Andry held her in place. She bucked her hips wildly, lifting them and riding Andry's mouth with wild abandon. She put her heels on Andry's shoulders and pushed down, not because she wanted Andry to stop but because she needed something to hold herself steady.

Isla moved her hand to brush her dress to the side so she could see Andry's face. She looked so relaxed, so into everything that was happening. When her eyes popped open, Isla's heart skipped a beat. She struggled to breathe, the connection between them growing by the second. She groaned, her body jerking of its own accord, and she leaned into the feeling of losing control. They kept their gazes locked as Isla cried out, crashing through her orgasm as she struggled to drag in cold air to cool her overheated skin.

Andry stood up sharply and pulled the buttons at her wrists open before ditching her shirt and her bra. She reached under Isla's back and dragged her up and onto the mattress more before bending down and pressing their mouths together, this time just as heated as the last. Isla completely lost herself to it, covered by Andry, their clothes very much in the way of what she really wanted.

Reaching up, Isla pulled at Andry's pants until she managed to get them undone and down to her hips slightly. She moved her hand between the fabric and Andry, feeling heat and dampness. Fuck, she could do this every day and never get tired of it. Andry nipped at her neck again, in the exact same spot she had before, and Isla groaned, losing her concentration.

"Turn over," Andry whispered right into her ear. "Sit up, take this damn thing off, and turn over."

Isla's heart raced at the command, the control Andry had. Her lips parted as she raised her gaze to meet Andry's for a breathtaking moment. She stilled, never before seeing *this* Andry. She'd seen her kind and gentle with teachers and kids, she'd seen her hold boundaries with students and parents, compromise, work together, but this was pure control.

Moving slowly, Isla pulled her hand from Andry's pants and put her palm to the top of the mattress, pushing herself into an upright position. Andry sat back on her heels, her chest heaving with her deep breaths. Her gaze dropped to Isla's hands as she shifted to her knees and pulled upward on the hem of her dress, the little black dress that she'd bought years ago and had never worn before. She'd never had a reason to until that night.

Dragging the material over her, Isla centered herself as best as she could and waited for Andry's reaction. She had a feeling that it would be amazing when it did happen. With a deep breath, Isla sat on her knees in front of Andry with nothing on but her bra. She swallowed hard, her heart racing as she reached behind her and pinched the hooks. She dragged the straps down. As soon as she was unencumbered, Andry was on her.

Mouths together, hands exploring, fingers teasing and testing. Isla gasped, trying to keep herself upright and do exactly what Andry had asked her to do. Andry jerked back with a start, and Isla looked at her with wide eyes.

"How come you always end up with clothes still on and I'm naked?"

Andry let out a wry chuckle. "I like you naked."

Giggling, Isla shook her head and reached for Andry's pants again. "I'd like to at least experience you naked before I have to decide that."

"Your loss, but I'll get naked if you want." Andry kissed her quickly and shifted around onto her ass to pull her pants off all the way.

Isla watched with rapt attention as every inch of Andry's skin was exposed. Andry was amazing. Her legs were strong, the curve of her hips slight, but it led up to the curve of her breasts. Cuddling before with Andry mostly clothed had done nothing for Isla's imagination. This would give her months worth of dreams if she wanted.

Tentatively, she reached out and flitted her fingers along Andry's leg up to her hip and then to her breast, flicking her nipple teasingly with the tip of her pointer finger. "No wonder you waited to show me this."

"What? Why?" Andry's brow drew together, and she stilled her movements.

"I wouldn't have been able to resist you."

Andry's cheeks were bright red "Shut up."

"No!" Isla grinned, moving in to touch again. "I'm absolutely serious."

"You're not."

"I am."

"Jesus." Andry shook her head, but she had a smile on her lips. Isla was so happy to see it, and she couldn't stop from wanting to do it again.

Isla moved in, skimming her hand over Andry's breast and nipple. "Tell me how you want me to touch you."

"I want your fingers." Andry stilled, the words almost timid, but not quite.

Nodding, Isla lay down on her side and beckoned Andry to follow her direction. They lay down together, and Isla continued her slow exploration of Andry's body, touching and finding every little place that would cause some sort of reaction.

"What were you going to do to me?" Isla asked.

"Hmm? When?"

"When you told me to lie on my stomach." Isla tweaked Andry's nipple and earned herself a groan.

"Oh, that. Want me to show you?"

"Maybe, depends on what it is and what else we can do during it."

Andry laughed wryly. "Guess we'll just have to try that next time."

"There better be a next time." Isla moved her hand between Andry's legs and teased her clit first. She wanted to draw this out, take her time and make sure that Andry got just as much from everything she did as Isla had when she'd been the focus of attention.

When she pushed one finger inside Andry, she spread her own legs. Andry touched her, teased her, and Isla found a smooth and regular rhythm that Andry seemed to enjoy. They stared into each other's eyes, smiling as Isla continued to swipe her thumb across Andry's clit, the jerks and twitches becoming bigger and deeper as she continued. Before she knew it, Andry's lips parted, and she let out a breath as her eyes clenched and her body tensed.

Isla moved in and kissed her, lazily tangling their tongues as she kept her hand moving at an impressively slow pace. She wanted to drag out Andry's pleasure as much as possible before they switched things up again. Andry pulled away, and Isla squeaked when she pressed her hand more firmly between Isla's legs, rubbing quickly back and forth. Isla gasped, not realizing how close she had been to another orgasm until Andry really focused on her.

When she came for the second time, Isla wrapped an arm around Andry's side and closed her eyes to try and catch her breath. Her heart thundered, and her head spun from the unexpected exertion. "Don't ever let anyone tell you that you're not good at this."

"I never do," Andry murmured into Isla's ear. "Now, about that other thing."

"What other thing?" Isla dared herself to raise her gaze to meet Andry's.

Laughing, Andry pulled away and gave Isla's ass a good tap with the palm of her hand. "Get on your hands and knees, we're not done yet."

"What have I gotten myself into?" Isla laughed before turning over like Andry had told her to.

"The best night of your life."

"Apparently." Isla laughed until Andry smacked her butt again, then she was groaning and pushing backward. Andry wasn't wrong, and Isla was more than determined to figure out just how long they could last.

CHAPTER
Thirty-Five

ISLA STEPPED into Andry's office just as her phone rang. She juggled everything in her hands, unsure of what to set down first so she wouldn't drop everything. Putting the rolls of wrapping paper onto the table in the corner of the office, Isla fished her cellphone out of her pocket. She didn't recognize the number and hesitated to answer it, but something made her hit the button.

"Hello?" Isla straightened her shoulders and stared around Andry's office. It always felt a bit odd to be in there without her, but she had to be in order for this to work, and she still had a box of things to bring in from her car.

"Isla Walsh?" The woman's voice on the other line was clear and precise.

Andry frowned as she glanced at the clock on the wall. It was just after four, but Andry had a meeting that had taken her out of the school for the last part of the day. "This is she."

"This is Chris Murphey, from Irving."

"Oh." Isla's stomach dropped, her heart racing suddenly, and with Andry's scent filling her from being in her office, she knew she was doomed.

"I looked over your resume and talked with some of your

references, and you look like you know what you're doing. I was wondering if you'd like to set up an interview for that position." Chris was so precise and sure of herself.

Isla hadn't fully talked to Andry about moving schools, but if Chris had already talked to her for a reference, then surely she must have said something good about her abilities, right? "I would love to," Isla replied, her heart in her throat. This could be the one chance she had to do this the easiest way possible.

"Tomorrow at five work for you?"

Isla was going to make it work even if it didn't. "That'll be fine."

"I'll see you then." Chris hung up.

Isla spun around in Andry's office, her heart still racing, but the energy of anticipation building. She hadn't thought anything would happen from her earlier phone call, not after Andry had told her that she had talked to Chris. It hadn't come off like a good conversation. With her fingers trembling, Isla grabbed the first roll of wrapping paper to get started on what she could do until she needed to go back out to her car for the rest of the supplies. She only had limited time to get this done.

Taking the scissors and tape, Isla got to work on wrapping everything in the room that she could. She spent hours in there, with some people coming in to help when they could before leaving when they needed to. It was nearly seven-thirty by the time Isla stretched her back and stared at her handiwork. Tomorrow morning was going to be amazing, and Andry would have an explosion of laughter.

She grabbed the box she had gotten from her car and took the unwrapped pens and pencils out with her. It had helped to prepare as much of that as she could. It looked like someone vomited Christmas in the room. She'd even taken the time to decorate Andry's door, which had been forgotten in the all-school Christmas door decoration that the PTA put on every year.

With her job done, Isla cleaned up and slid into her car,

exhausted from the day. There was only another week until the holiday break, and everyone could feel it. The halls in the school buzzed with energy every day and the kids were restless. Teachers felt it too, and they only had a few more days to get through this week and next before a glorious two weeks off.

Isla started her car and stared at the doors she had just walked out of. If the interview with Chris went well, she could very easily not be coming back after the break, or maybe she would start at the beginning of the new quarter at the end of January. She had no idea, but this could be one of the last times she walked out of the school since she'd started teaching.

But it didn't feel bad.

It felt like hope, and she'd never thought of something ending quite like that before. It always used to scare her and drag her away, but this time was so different. It was because of where she was at mentally, all the work she had done in the past few months, but it was also because of Andry. There was no denying that. Isla's lips curled upward just at the thought of Andry, and when she glanced at her phone, she saw a few missed texts from her.

Andry had brought her so much joy. She answered the texts quickly and was about to settle her phone into the cup holder to head home when it buzzed loudly. Glancing at the caller ID, she saw Lynda's name, and panic reared its ugly head. Lynda rarely just called without warning, and if there was something wrong with Wil—when had she made that switch? Lynda holding such a close relationship with Wil meant that she would be the first to know everything and Isla wouldn't, but she'd eased into that part of their relationship without struggle.

"Hey," Isla said as she answered, putting the call through her car so she could drive and talk at the same time.

"Hey." Lynda's voice was clipped like it always was, somewhat aloof and cold, but Isla knew better than to judge her for that now. "Wil and I were talking about Christmas. Would you like to come down here?"

Instead of the usual pull of anxiety, Isla was elated. Thanksgiving had gone so well, and she couldn't imagine another holiday without her family around her. She'd finally found them after years of avoiding what was right in front of her. It was still going to take some work to smooth out all the awkwardness, but she wanted to put in the effort to do that. Wil was so happy with Lynda, and she'd come to find a different side of her stepmother all together, one she'd never known even existed.

"I'd love to."

"Come stay a night or two. There's a spare bedroom."

Isla couldn't stop the smile on her lips as she turned into the parking lot at her apartment. "Sounds perfect. Is Aisling coming?"

"For Christmas day. She has to work the next day, so she won't be staying the night, and she mentioned something about getting back together with her boyfriend."

Isla sighed heavily. She didn't like him, and it wasn't because she was being the overprotective big sister either. She just really didn't like how he treated her. Rolling her shoulders, Isla let out a sigh. "I hope she figures that one out quickly."

"Likewise."

Glad to have another commonality, Isla grabbed her bag, turned off her car, and held her phone up to her ear as she climbed up the stairs to her apartment. She had a chance to put more trust in Lynda, and where she would have hesitated before, she decided to take the risk now. "I have a job interview."

"Do you?"

"To teach second grade at another school. I'd start sometime around the beginning of the year." Isla put her key into the lock and stepped inside her warm living room.

"And this is what you want?"

"It is. I think I need to do it." She dropped her bag onto the couch cushion. "It'll be good for me to have some new school experience."

"It could be. This isn't because anything went sideways, is it?"

"No, the exact opposite." Isla smiled, remembering their first official date and everything that had happened that weekend. She'd loved waking up in Andry's arms, snuggling close to her all morning while they took a lazy day in bed. She especially loved wearing one of Andry's oversized shirts when they'd had coffee and breakfast.

"I'm glad for you. I'd love to meet her in this new capacity."

"Someday. She's got a kid about to graduate high school, so they need to spend as much time as possible together." Isla flopped onto her couch and put her feet up. "But someday, I promise."

"I'm glad to hear it. Oh, Wil wants to know if you'll help with cleaning. She says she and I will just argue if I help out."

Isla snorted and closed her eyes, shaking her head. "Yeah, I'll help. We can do it after Christmas."

"Perfect, I'll let her know. See you soon, Isla."

"See you, Lynda." She'd almost slipped up and called her mom, something she hadn't done in a very long time. Instead, Isla held that feeling in her chest and blew out a breath. Everything seemed to be moving right along, didn't it? Still, she had this feeling in the back of her mind that something was going to go atrociously wrong.

She was just about to get up and take a shower when her phone rang again. Isla shook her head. She never used to be this popular. When she saw Andry's name on the screen, she instantly smiled.

"Evening," Isla said, her voice low and seductive as she could make it. "How are you doing?"

"Not great," Andry muttered. "It was a long day and kind of pointless unfortunately."

Isla smiled. "That's why you get paid the big bucks."

"Being in administration isn't all it's cracked up to be."

"Oh yeah?" Isla turned on her side, curling into a ball. "Why'd you go into it, then?"

"Lots of reasons." Andry sighed, and Isla imagined she was

running a hand through her hair. "I wish you could come over tonight."

"I can't?"

"Katie's home."

"Ah." Isla's heart clenched. She wanted to be over there every night she could, and she'd been hanging on every word Andry said, hoping there would be an invitation of sorts there. She knew it was in part the new romantic interest that drew her toward it, but her relationship with Andry was so different from any other relationship she'd been in. "Is she still uncomfortable with this?"

"I... no, I don't think so."

Furrowing her brow, Isla stared at the dark television across the room from her. "So why couldn't I come over then?"

Andry groaned, and then her voice dropped to just above a whisper. "Because what I want to do with you involves being loud."

Isla's cheeks burned, but the smile on her lips matched how happy she was. "It was a good weekend."

"It was, and one I'd love to experience again."

Giggling, Isla rolled onto her back. "I mean, there's always phone sex."

"Oh my god." Andry's shock tickled Isla.

She had expected it, but it was still adorable. For someone who was quite forward and confident when it came to sex, Isla had a feeling that anything outside a bedroom wasn't her norm and that Andry would struggle with it. "We can always try it."

"You're going to keep me on my toes, aren't you?"

"I don't know why you ever thought otherwise, considering the history of our relationship together." Isla smiled to herself, remembering the first time she'd been brave enough to pull a prank on Andry. "Don't you remember?"

"Oh yes, I remember." Andry's voice was back to that low, seductive tone.

"It took me self-talking myself a hundred times over to play that first trick on you. I was so nervous." Isla shivered, remembering when she realized Andry was easy to scare and had the best scared face. Isla had hidden behind the side of the bus while she walked around it during a field trip one time only to pop out and shout "Boo!" The kids on the bus had gotten a huge kick out of it.

"Did it really?"

"Yes, I had so many opportunities before the bus to try something."

"You should have." Andry sighed softly. "I love when you do it."

Isla wrinkled her nose, knowing that when Andry walked into her office in the morning she was going to get another surprise, but she kept her mouth shut, not wanting to spoil the prank. "When can we go on another date?"

"This weekend."

"Yes." Isla's eyes were heavy. She hadn't realized just how worn out she was from that week, but it had been a busy one, and standing on her feet for hours wrapping up Andry's office had taken what was left out of her. "What are we doing?"

Andry growled low. "I think you know exactly what we're doing."

"Good." Isla gave a sleepy chuckle. "But what else are we doing?"

"Well, eating something, I'm sure."

"Andry..." Isla could barely open her eyes. "You already said we were doing that."

"Oh my god. Isla!"

Chuckling even through her weariness, Isla was happy to bring the smile to Andry and herself. She shivered and forced herself to get off the couch. She checked the lock on the front door and dragged her feet to her bedroom. "Andry?"

"Yes?"

Isla stopped cold. She almost said that she loved her. She almost let the words fly from her lips. She stopped herself just in time and bit her lip, staring at her bed with rumpled sheets and clothes on the floor.

"Isla?"

"I'm exhausted. I can barely keep my eyes open."

"Then go to bed." Andry laughed lightly. "I'm not going to keep you up."

"I wish you would, but not by talking on the phone to be clear." Falling back onto humor as her defense, Isla continued to stare at her bed. "But since I know that's not happening tonight, I'll see you in the morning at work."

"See you then."

Hanging up, Isla stripped out of her work clothes and flopped onto her bed naked, pulling her blanket over her. She closed her eyes, but sleep failed to find her. She couldn't stop thinking about those three damn words she'd almost said and just how true they were.

CHAPTER
Thirty-Six

ANDRY STEPPED into the main offices when the sun was still below the horizon, and she stopped short. She raised her chin, seeing her entire door decked out in wrapping paper, ribbon, and taped-on images of *The Grinch*. Was someone trying to say something about her?

She glanced around the main offices and furrowed her brow when no other decorations had changed since she'd been in the morning before. Her stomach swirled with the thought that she knew exactly what this was. With only a hint of trepidation, Andry put her hand on the door and opened it.

Everything in her office was covered with buffalo plaid wrapping paper. The books on her shelves, the pictures she'd hung on the walls, the desk, the chairs and table. Laughing, Andry stepped around her office, and set her coffee mug onto the top of her desk, her heart pattering away swiftly.

Her rolling chair was wrapped, taped perfectly around the back of it along with the arms, the legs, and even a little on the wheels. She shook her head in disbelief. This had probably taken hours, and it would take her even longer to get it all down. Andry swung her bag off her shoulder and dropped it to the floor, startled when it crinkled. Looking down, she found the mat under her desk had also been taped with buffalo plaid wrapping paper.

"I can't believe this."

"Believe it," Isla's voice startled her, and Andry jumped around with a hand over her heart.

It was a good thing she'd put her coffee down because she'd have spilled it all over herself. "What are you doing here this early?"

"Had a feeling you'd be in early, and I wanted to see your reaction." Isla had her arms crossed as she leaned against the doorframe, her lips curled into a sweet smile. "I'm pleased with the results."

"This must have taken you hours!" Andry stepped up to Isla and skimmed her hand down her arm to her elbow. She wanted to lean in and kiss her, share a moment of intimacy, but they were on school grounds.

"When you called last night, I'd just gotten home."

"No way." Andry's eyes widened. She turned on her toes and looked around. "Did you wrap everything yesterday?"

"No. I did some prep work." Isla shifted to stand and walk into the office. "Like the pens."

Andry's eyes riveted to the small container she kept on her desk with pens and pencils. The container itself was wrapped as was each individual pen. Her stomach fluttered. She reached for Isla's hand instinctively and threaded their fingers together. "I have no idea how you come up with all these insane ideas."

"Practice," Isla whispered, sliding in closer to Andry so that her breath fluttered against Andry's ear. "All good practice and imagination."

"And patience." Andry turned, their mouths nearly touching. A shiver ran through her, remembering Isla's salacious ideas of what they should do the night before. She wished she'd taken her up on the offer, but it seemed as though Isla had needed the rest after all this work. "You're amazing."

Andry gave in, planting a chaste kiss on Isla's mouth. Isla

leaned in like she wanted more, but Andry put up that boundary again, needing to keep it in place until they had their work life figured out. No one else was in yet, but it wouldn't be long until some started to come in for the day.

"Isla..." Andry trailed off, not quite sure what she was going to say. She stopped herself again, looking into Isla's baby blue eyes like her world was there. "...you're ridiculous."

"Some days." Isla grinned and squeezed Andry's hand, pulling away from her. "But I wanted to see your reaction in person."

Andry chuckled and shook her head. "I suspected something might be up when I saw the door. Why *The Grinch*?"

"Have to keep up the mean principal persona, don't you?" Isla laughed and leaned against the top of the table, her hands on either side of her.

The space between them was good, and Andry needed it too. She stayed put, right in front of the door. "I don't give off that vibe, do I?"

"Only to some." Isla winked. "Maybe you can try it out on me sometime."

"Isla!" Andry flicked her gaze to the outer offices, hoping that no one else was in yet to hear that.

Laughing, Isla rocked back on the table and shook her head. "You're too easy sometimes."

"Not all the time."

"Oh definitely not." Isla winked and stood back up. "But I've got a classroom to set up."

Isla walked by, ready to leave, but Andry caught her hand to stop her. She stared once again into Isla's eyes, trying to figure out exactly what Isla was thinking and feeling, not to mention what she herself was feeling. "Thank you."

"For pulling a prank?"

"For that and other things." Andry's cheeks heated.

"No one's ever thanked me for pulling a prank before."

Andry lifted her free hand, curling it around Isla's cheek and drawing her in closer. "There's a first time for everything." She brought their mouths together, this kiss tender and full of meaning. She didn't want to give this up. She had found so much lightness in Isla, in their relationship, and it made her smile nearly every time she thought about it. It'd been too long since she'd smiled this much. "Come over tonight."

Isla stiffened. "I can't, and besides, you said Katie..."

"I know what I said," Andry murmured. "But we're going to have to navigate that at some point."

"Not tonight," Isla whispered, her gaze downcast. "This weekend. I'm heading out to Denver for the holiday for at least half the week."

"Then we need to get together before you leave."

Isla nodded her agreement. "This weekend."

Andry didn't like that she'd have to wait, but it was Thursday, so it wouldn't be long. The door to the main office opened, the handle rattling. Isla jumped back, putting space between them, the entire mood shifting and the walls coming right back up as they should. Andry hated it as much as she understood it.

"See you around, Andry." Isla stepped into the main office before anything else could be discovered. She smiled at whoever it was and ducked out of the room. Andry was startled by the loud burst of laughter that hit her ears, and she suddenly remembered she was standing in the middle of a prank and not in Isla's arms.

∼

Friday morning could not have come quickly enough. Andry needed the time with Isla to figure out everything between them and just exactly what she was feeling. Her brain had been swirling with the longing look that Isla had given her in the office, but also the hiddenness of something behind it. She couldn't quite put her finger on it.

The halls were filling up with teachers and some students as they came in for the day. She was about to step out and do some face-to-face time with those who had come in, and she stopped short. Chris stood in the middle of the hall, her warm winter coat covering her shoulders, her dark curly hair fluffed around her shoulders. Andry raised an eyebrow, her stomach spinning in circles as they eyed each other over. Surely nothing was wrong with Katie—Chris would have called instead of just showing up. No, this was something else. Chris pointed toward the office, and Andry stepped back, waiting for Chris to join her.

"Morning," Andry said as a way of greeting and hoping she would get a bit more information from Chris about what was going on.

"Morning," Chris answered gruffly, her own travel mug of coffee clasped tightly in her fingers.

"This isn't about Katie, is it?"

"Unfortunately for you, it's not. This is business."

"Perfect," Andry muttered. She stepped through the main offices and into the still mostly wrapped office. She'd undone what she had to the day before but had left a lot of the wrapping job Isla had done up. She'd take the rest of it down after the holiday, liking that it added a bit of a Christmas touch to her office.

"What vomited in here?" Chris wrinkled her nose, but her eyes said absolute amusement.

"A prank, actually. I came in yesterday morning to find everything looking like this and more."

Chris let out a wry chuckle and shook her head. She shut the door behind her before turning on Andry. Andry's stomach twisted, having no idea what would cause Chris to visit her early on a Friday morning before school started.

"Aren't you going to be late?"

Chris canted her head to the side. "I will be, but this is a conversation we need to have, and like I said, it's business."

"What's going on?" Andry crossed her arms, planting her feet so she would be steady for whatever bomb Chris was about to drop.

"I didn't exactly ask you for a reference for Isla Walsh. I'd like it." Chris' gaze was unwavering, but her entire body said she was relaxed and that this wasn't an attack.

Andry swallowed the lump that suddenly formed in her throat. "She's one of my best teachers. Like I said before, I hired her right out of school. She's taught sixth grade every year she's been here except two when she taught third. She much prefers the older kids than the younger."

"So if I stuck her in second grade...?"

"She'd be fine, but her passion is the older kids." Andry dashed her tongue across her lips. "Why are you asking?"

"*Why* is a very good question." Chris raised an eyebrow in Andry's direction. "You know, it's really odd to have a teacher try to transfer schools in the middle of the year and break a contract. It doesn't usually bode well for anyone, but this is you we're talking about."

"We're talking about Isla." Andry clenched her jaw, trying to keep her fingers from curling into fists in fear that Chris would figure everything out.

"We are, and we aren't. Where's the poop, Andry?"

"What?"

"What's really going on? Why would she want to transfer? Because I asked her that at the interview last night, and she skirted around it beautifully. It wasn't until late last night that I realized she'd done it." Chris lifted her coffee and took a long sip, her gaze not leaving Andry's face the entire time.

"She wants to transfer to a new school." Andry bit the inside of her cheek, not quite sure how to bring this up to anyone, let alone her ex-wife. It would cause so many issues, not to mention they had already crossed that line. Her heart thundered so hard in her chest and neck that she swore Chris would be able to see it if she stepped any closer.

"But why?" Chris' eyes were dark, direct, and Andry knew

instinctively that she wasn't going to let this go. "It'll put you in quite a spot and you don't even seem upset by it."

Because she wasn't. Of all the things she had forgotten to act, upset was the one she should have, but she'd been so thrilled with the possibility of not having to hide anything that she'd completely forgotten to pretend to struggle with the decision.

"Andry..." Chris' voice dropped low, realization flashing across her face. She shifted around and looked at the closed door before coming in close, standing only a step away. "Did you sleep with her?"

Andry's cheeks were on fire. She cleared her throat, the weight of everything that had happened since the start of the school year resting on her chest and making it so damn hard to breathe. Chris locked their gazes together, and Andry was sure her heart was about to burst out of her chest. There was no hiding anything from Chris—ever.

"Are you *in love* with her?" Chris' accusation was simple, hushed words because no one had said it out loud yet.

Andry had to work hard to keep her gaze up to meet Chris', and she knew without a doubt that Chris could see right through her. If it had been anyone else with the job opening, they would have managed to slide through it, but Chris knew her too damn well. Straightening her back, Andry found her voice. "Yes."

"Holy shit." Chris rocked back on her heels, looked around the office, and spun on Andry with her head shaking. "You're an idiot."

You're one to talk, Andry thought as her heart sank. She didn't want Chris to be the first one to know. She didn't want to jeopardize anything, and yet she knew the decision not to wait until summer was flat out stupid. "I didn't plan it this way."

"You could lose your job."

"I know. That's why *this* is so important."

Chris sighed heavily. She set her mug onto the desk with a loud thud. "So you dragged me into it?"

"I didn't know she had applied until you told me, I swear, but it was something we had talked about needing to happen before the start of the next school year if we were going to continue our relationship, and this just...this just happened, Chris. I don't know what to say."

"Does Katie know?" That accusatory tone was back.

Andry blanched. "Yes, of course she does."

"And you asked her to keep it a secret?"

"No. I didn't." Andry dragged her hand through her hair. "I never told her to, but she's a smart kid, and she knows what this could mean for my job."

Chris rolled her eyes. "She didn't say a damn thing to me."

"Like I said, she's smart. And protective." Andry was still tense, every muscle in her body telling her she had just walked right into the fire of a hell she'd been narrowly avoiding.

"How did we end up with such an amazing kid?"

"Who knows?" Andry was about to tremble from holding herself together.

Chris paused, looking her over carefully. "You really love her, don't you?"

"I do." Andry's eyes filled with tears as the confirmed thought consumed her. "She's the one who papered my office."

Snorting, Chris laughed. "You're such a sucker."

The tension in the room eased somewhat, but that still left the rather large question of what Chris was going to do with this information and how much trouble she was going to be in at the end of it all.

"I'll hire her."

"What?" Andry shook her head in shock. She touched Chris' arm lightly, her eyes wide as she tried to figure out if this was some kind of joke or not.

"If you really think she's a good teacher and you weren't just saying that."

"I wasn't just saying it. I'll be losing one of my best."

"Then I'll hire her." Chris' lips curled upward into a sweet smile. "You deserve to be happy, Andry, and I know how unhappy I made you. If this is one thing I can do for you, then I'll do it."

"I don't know what to say." Andry took in short raspy breaths.

Chris pretended to think hard for a moment. "*Thank you* would do it."

"Chris... this deserves way more than simple thanks."

"Fine. It does, but don't say I never did anything for you." Chris pointed a finger at her as a tease before she softened and her entire face relaxed. "I just want you to be happy, Andry."

"Thank you." Andry smiled, all the pent up tension that had been there earlier completely gone. She swallowed hard and let out a loud laugh. She never would have guessed this was where the conversation was going to go, but she was so glad to see Chris. She shook out her hands, and Chris wrinkled her nose, that knowing smirk on her lips. "What?"

"You're stupidly in love. I remember that look."

"You're an idiot."

"Most days." Chris snickered. "But not today. Today *you* get to wear the idiot crown."

"With honor." Andry shook her head again, the adrenaline from being caught easing from her body rapidly and leaving her cold and off-kilter. She had never anticipated that Chris would be the first one to really know. "Today you're rather with it."

"You have certain tells."

"I don't."

"Oh yes, you do. Like right now, I can tell you're fallen hard for this girl, and I want to point out, she is a girl." Chris laughed, but it didn't feel like she was laughing at Andry. More like laughing with her.

"I fully understand there's an age difference."

"Right." Chris straightened her back and reached for her coffee. "I guess I have some paperwork to do."

"Chris?" Andry held her breath when Chris stopped right in front of the door. Their eyes locked. "Thank you."

"I would do this for you any time, and don't worry, I don't plan on reporting it."

With the door shut, Andry collapsed into her office chair and closed her eyes letting out a breath. Chris wasn't the villain today. In fact, she was the hero of the story. Andry picked up some papers on her desk and stared at them blankly. She might not ever get the Chris she'd fallen in love with back, but perhaps they could find a friend in the new Chris.

"Fuck," Andry cursed under breath. She had just told her ex-wife that she was in love with her girlfriend before she'd told her girlfriend. She was going to have to fix that mistake pronto.

CHAPTER
Thirty-Seven

STARING around her classroom with her hands on her hips, Isla debated exactly what she would take with her and what she would leave. She couldn't have been more excited for the holiday break, but that also meant she was one day closer to leaving her classroom behind and starting fresh somewhere else. Her mind had been spinning since she'd signed the paperwork the day before.

She would have to spend some quality time in her classroom in the next couple weeks preparing to take all her supplies with her. It would be a feat, but she was ready for it. A move in the middle of the year wasn't something she had ever planned for, but she was glad she had made that decision. Checking her watch, Isla left to collect her kids from their regular PE class.

The walk down the hallway was bittersweet. Within a month, she would have all new kids in an all new school, and she'd have to learn how to work with a new principal. Not just any principal, but Andry's ex-wife. Though that didn't seem to be too much of an issue so far, but once their relationship came out, it could become a problem. It was something Isla was willing to suffer through if she had to in order to be with Andry.

Isla smiled at her kids, already lined up and ready for her to take them back to the classroom. She walked at the end of the line, her feet dragging a bit. She hated to leave them, but it was a necessary change that she wanted to make. As soon as she stepped into the classroom, she stopped short.

A balloon was tied to her desk, just one simple red balloon with a black ribbon. Isla furrowed her brow, the kids already swarming around her desk as they tried to figure out what was going on. Isla clapped her hands to get their attention. They all looked at her for answers.

"What did we find?" Isla's voice rang clearly through the room.

One of the kids picked up a small mesh bag and handed it over to Isla. She stared at it as it rested in her palm, the small *Scrabble* letters inside clinking as they juggled in her palm. What in the world were these for?

"What is it?" Alice asked.

"No idea," Isla murmured back. Not one to waste time, she straightened her shoulders and looked around her room. "You know what time it is, so let's get to work, and we'll figure this out later, okay?"

The kids groaned but did as they were told. Isla spent the next hour going through the history lesson she had planned until it was time for a bit of a break. She knew the kids wouldn't be happy to leave without her figuring out what the bag was, but they had the holiday party in thirty minutes and needed to get ready for that. Isla got the kids' attention and told them to clean up and pack up for when the parents came in to help with the party.

While the kids were doing that, she sat down at her desk and dumped out the small bag, flipping all the letter pieces upward so she could see what the letters were. Alice was the first one to lean over her desk and watch what she was doing. Isla gnawed on her lower lip as she stared at the letters in front of her, trying to figure out exactly what it said. There was nothing in there other than the letters.

"What's it say?" Alice asked.

Isla raised her gaze and shook her head. "No idea."

Reaching over the desk, Alice moved some of them around, but there were so many and yet no words popped out at her, especially without context. Other students came over to try and help out. They spelled out a multitude of words, but none of them seemed to be right and not all of the tiles were used. As the parents started arriving to set up for the party, Isla had to give up. She'd try again later.

The party was wild and fun, but she was ready for the end by the time the bell rang. She helped her kids file out of the classroom with all of their goodies and bid them a happy holiday. She'd have to tell them when they returned that she wouldn't be there much longer, but she didn't want to taint their holiday plans. It was something that could wait.

Going back to her classroom, Isla scrubbed the tabletops and did some deeper cleaning as the parents who were still there finished picking up their stuff. Isla said goodbye to them and sent them on her way. Finally, she had a moment to sit back at her desk and figure out this damn message. She was nose deep in it when she looked up to find Andry standing in her doorway with her arms crossed and a smile on her lips. A quick glance at the clock told her she'd been there nearly forty minutes trying to parse out the puzzle.

"Figure it out yet?" Andry raised an eyebrow, her eyes crinkling in the corners.

"Is this from you?" Isla leaned back in her chair, stretching her back.

Andry sauntered over and put her hands on the desk, then lifted one and flicked the tiles around and messed up whatever Isla had done. "I see you haven't figured it out yet."

"What's it supposed to say?" Isla leaned in, lowering her voice. "The kids wanted to know before they left."

"Too late now, and I may have planned it that way." Andry winked, her grin growing even bigger.

Isla canted her head to the side and looked Andry over curiously. There was something up that she really wasn't getting, and that irked her. Pranks were her thing, and if this was... She stopped short at that thought. This was a prank, not a puzzle. Locking her gaze on Andry, Isla pursed her lips.

"Where's the trick?"

"What trick?" Andry grinned like the cat who caught the canary.

Isla was definitely on the right track to figure out what was going on. Andry stood up straight and crossed her arms again, right next to the red balloon. Standing up, Isla came around her desk and stepped in close to Andry, her own arms crossed as she faced down the prank that might undo her because she was failing it so hard. Lowering her voice to a soft plea, Isla whispered, "Andry."

Andry chuckled lightly and shook her head. "I'm hopeless against you when you beg."

Uncrossing her arms, Andry showed Isla her hand and the thumb tack that was in it. Isla's brow wrinkled in confusion while she reached for the purple tack and held it between her two fingers. Before she could ask a question, Andry grabbed the balloon and held it between her palms right in front of Isla.

Instantly, Isla saw the piece of paper settled at the bottom of the red balloon, small and folded up so it wasn't easy to see. "How did I miss that?"

"Because you weren't looking for it—and neither was I."

Isla met Andry's gaze, hesitating at the meaning behind what she wasn't saying. Reaching up, she took the thumbtack and pressed the point into the latex. The pop resounded throughout the classroom, echoing loudly into Isla's ears. The letter fell to the floor between them. Her breath caught in her throat, but she bent down and picked up the piece of paper, unfolding and uncurling it. It was a letter, handwritten in Andry's scrawl. Isla's heart skipped a beat.

Isla,

I never expected this when I hired you. I never thought in a million years that I would fall in love with you. Sometimes things happen when you least expect them and where you're not looking for them. And that's what happened to us. You complete me in a way I didn't even know I was longing for. You're brilliant, kind, and gentle-hearted, and you are so full of life that it's contagious. We found each other in our storms.

I love you.

Andry

Isla's breath caught in her throat. Her hands trembled as she stared at that last sentence. Her mouth went dry, and when she raised her gaze to meet Andry's, she was completely overwhelmed. Andry touched her shoulder and pulled her in, wrapping her arms around Isla and pulling her in for a hug. "I mean every word of that."

"Andry," Isla breathed out. She centered herself, pulling back to look deep into Andry's eyes. "I love you, too."

Andry grinned from ear to ear. Isla risked everything. She leaned in, pushing up on her toes and pressing their mouths together. She closed her eyes, reveling in the feel of Andry against her, in the freedom of the confessions, in the moments of hope they shared together. Her heart raced. She dropped the note to the floor and wrapped her arms around Andry's neck and held her tightly, keeping their mouths together, moving against each other.

Andry skimmed her hands up Isla's back, rubbing up and down and tangling in the ends of Isla's hair. Isla dashed her tongue out, needing more connection and touch. There was no hiding anything anymore, and Isla felt fully confident in that shift. She couldn't have wanted something more.

"We should stop," Andry murmured.

"In a second." Isla dove back in, taking what she wanted and giving as much as she could. Instinctively she knew they were on cameras, she knew anyone could walk by the windows and the door and see them, but she just couldn't bring herself to care.

Dragging in a deep breath, Isla pulled away with one last peck to Andry's lips and a smile on her face. Isla didn't step away. She wanted the closeness between them in this moment to remain, especially while she dropped the next bomb in Andry's lap. "I signed a contract to work at Irving yesterday."

"I know." Andry gave her a slow smile, her cheeks flushed. "I mean, I didn't know that's what you were doing yesterday, but I knew Chris was going to offer the contract to you. When do you start?"

"Beginning of the next quarter."

"So we have a few more weeks working together." Andry swallowed, and Isla could see the strain on her face, she just couldn't place why it was there. "It's going to be hard to keep our distance during that."

"Do we have to?" Isla whispered.

"Yes." Andry nodded and stepped away slightly, putting some space between them. "Because it's my job on the line now, and we don't have much longer to keep everything hidden."

"Right." Heat rushed to Isla's cheeks, knowing that she had pushed that boundary Andry had been so sure to set. "I'm sorry about doing that here."

Andry gave her a sweet smile. "Don't be. It was well worth it, and we have the next couple of weeks to spend together without being in the building."

"True." Isla bent down to grab the note that Andry had written her. She set it on her desk, never wanting to give up that letter. "But then what?"

"What do you mean?" Andry furrowed her brow, shoving her hands into the pockets of her slacks.

"What happens when I start at Irving and there isn't this—" she put her hands out around her to indicate the school "— problem anymore?"

"Isla, I love you. I'm not going anywhere, and as soon as you work at Irving, we can come out with our relationship if you want. I'm not giving us up any time soon."

She couldn't stop the smile from finding her. Isla brushed her fingers across her lips, remembering the passion behind their last kiss. "Does Chris know?"

"Yes." Andry sighed. "She didn't figure it out from your interview, actually. She said it wasn't until later that night that she realized you had neatly evaded her question as to why you wanted to move schools in the middle of the year."

"Oh?"

"Whatever you said did the trick, but we were married for seventeen years, and it's impossible to hide some things from someone who knows you that well. She paid me a visit last week and figured it out." Andry's shoulders dropped. "While you could hide it, *I* couldn't. Or maybe I didn't want to. I'm tired of hiding it just as much as you are."

"It really sucks." Isla laughed nervously. "But um...is Chris going to hold that against me?"

Andry met her worried glance. "No, I don't think so. She really is an excellent principal, and I think we've moved on enough from each other that she'll be able to separate everything out. I don't think she has a vindictive bone in her body."

"That's good to know." Isla relaxed instantly. "I won't lie... I'm nervous about moving schools."

"You'll do amazing." Andry touched Isla's arm. "You're a wonderful teacher and you have such passion for your kids. Not to mention the politics of the job haven't gotten to you, which is a miracle in and of itself."

"They do some days." Isla sighed. "So what do we do now?"

Andry grinned broadly. "Well, now I suggest you get your stuff together as quickly as you possibly can."

"Why?" Isla looked at Andry directly.

"Because Katie is spending the night at Chris', and I want to continue what you started." Andry openly looked her over, raking her gaze all over Isla's body.

Isla instantly warmed, tingles racing through her and settling between her legs. Just the thought of another full night with Andry was the perfect way to start the holiday break. She wet her suddenly parched mouth and drew in a ragged breath. "What do you mean *what I started?* You're the one who wrote that." She pointed at the letter on her desk.

Andry laughed and walked toward the door to the classroom. "You've got about ten minutes to get to my house before I come and find you."

"If that's a threat, you're going to need to find a different punishment."

Andry spun around at the door, an eyebrow raised. She contained all that energy neatly in her body, and it made Isla weak in her knees. "I'll get creative, don't you worry about it."

In an instant she was gone. Isla's breathing came in rapid gasps, and she shivered, completely aroused from one simple conversation. She never wanted to give this up. She quickly packed up her bag and turned off the lights in her classroom. Leaving the school was so much easier than she'd thought it would be because she knew exactly what she was doing it for, and she knew it was worth it. They were worth it.

CHAPTER
Thirty-Eight

THE NEXT SCHOOL YEAR...

THE KEYS WERE cold when Isla pulled them out of her pocket. She hadn't touched them except to slide the spare set into her jacket that morning when Andry wasn't looking, and she'd pretended to go to school even though she'd taken the entire day off. It had taken everything in her to plan this, and there were still so many things that could go wrong. Andry could easily walk into the wrong classroom or look out the wrong window and the entire prank would be spoiled. She parked on the street, away from the cameras placed around the school so that no one in the office would see her.

Isla slipped from her car and walked right up to Andry's. She got behind the wheel and parked next to her car. She started filling the back of Andry's car with kiddie ball pit balls that she had mass ordered online and stored at Chris'. It had to work, and it would be the prank of a lifetime.

She filled as much of the trunk and the backseats as she possibly could and then she texted her contacts inside the school to make sure that Andry was one hundred percent occupied at the moment, and after sitting in the car for another three minutes, she got the go ahead. *This is it.* There was no going back now, and Isla knew it would be the best prank of the year. She'd been planning it since that summer, so it would have to land perfectly.

Driving the car around the side of the school toward the side gate where the trucks dropped off the lunches, Isla waited until one of the janitors came out and unlocked it, holding the gate open. She lowered the window and grinned, greeting her prank accomplice—well, one of the many that this entire process was taking. Isla drove slowly through the playground to the small pad of cement in front of the classrooms, right where Andry had her class sit with their desks nearly a year before when their prank war had started.

She parked the car and ran to get the rest of the balls she had stored in one of the classrooms. It helped that she was still good friends with most of the teachers there. They were all in on this one. Isla checked her watch before she finished filling up Andry's car with the balls, shoving as many as she possibly could into the vehicle and climbing on top of the car to put them into the sunroof. It would be impossible to open the door and not have them spill out.

Isla's heart raced when she slid to the ground and checked her phone. She had five minutes to get inside and finish this entire thing. The end of the school day was fast approaching, and she had told everyone that there would be a very special intercom announcement right before the final bell. Her heart raced as she snuck inside, stopping short when her phone buzzed.

The school administration told her to hold on because Andry had started to come out of the classroom. Her heart was in her throat as she waited for the go-ahead to continue walking toward the main offices so she could get onto the intercom before Andry figured everything out. This was the last part of her prank, but at the very least, the car would be a good one. When the next text came through, Isla nearly ran to the front office.

Laughing as she skidded into the room, she stopped short in front of the microphone. She had thirty seconds, and she was out of breath. She had to do this. Shannon gave her the thumbs up and hit the button on the PA system. Breathing heavily, Isla spoke.

"Good afternoon, Elbert Elementary! I know I haven't met all of you, but I'm Ms. Walsh, and I used to teach sixth grade here. I have a very special announcement today, and I need you all to help me."

She could hear the cheers go up and echo down the halls. Isla grinned over the microphone at Shannon.

"Not everyone knows, but today is Dr. Murphey's birthday! Why don't we all walk outside onto the playground and give her a big Happy Birthday treat!"

The hallways erupted with noise. Isla grinned from ear to ear, giving everyone a few seconds before she started singing because she didn't want to miss the shock on Andry's face when she found her car, and she certainly didn't want Andry to skip the events outside and come into the office. She sang it twice until she saw that most of the school was outside surrounding Andry's car. Glo had made sure that she would be the last one out, and she had been the one to keep Andry occupied while Isla set up the car. As soon as Isla saw her through the window, she dropped the microphone and ran for the door to the playground.

Andry stepped out the opposite door and hollered out a laugh. She put her hands over her face and pointed at her car, then wiped at her eyes as tears of joy ran down her face. Isla grinned as she waded through the crowd to find Andry on the other side. As soon as Andry saw her, she pointed a finger in Isla's direction and shook her head.

"You're insane!"

"I got you good this time!" Isla shouted over the roar of noise from the kids.

"You sure did."

Andry was still laughing when the kids started chanting. "Open the car! Open the car!"

Andry's eyes widened as she turned to take a closer look at her car. "You didn't."

"I didn't what?" Isla winked and took Andry by the arm to lead her toward the vehicle.

They walked over to the car, and Andry couldn't stop shaking her head. She sighed heavily and wrenched open the passenger door, the balls scattering to the cement and all over the playground. The kids nearest to them picked some of them up. Isla laughed and clapped her hands, bouncing in her shoes.

"I can't believe you did this!" Andry laughed, grabbing Isla around the waist and spinning her so that their mouths met.

Isla stilled, a hand on Andry's arm and her lips captured by the person she had fallen head over heels in love with. The cheers surrounding them grew even louder, the kids screaming at them when Andry dipped Isla backward before breaking the kiss.

She leaned in and whispered directly into Isla's ear, "God, I love you. I had a feeling you would pull something today."

"Did you?"

"Oh yeah, so I planned for it." Andry stepped back from Isla and reached into her pocket.

Isla cocked her head to the side, her brow furrowing as she watched Andry in slow motion move from standing...to kneeling...on one knee. Her heart raced, cold washed through her before it was replaced with a sudden heat. Her eyes widened and excitement filled her in an instant. The small box in Andry's hand was blue, and when she opened it, a beautiful sapphire ring sat in the middle of it—the same ring she had bought with her dad for Lynda.

"Will you marry me?"

"Andry!" Isla fell to her knees and wrapped her arms around Andry's neck, giving her a huge kiss. "Yes. Of course, yes."

Andry kissed her again, holding her tight as she stood up and pulled Isla with her. She pulled out the ring and slid it onto Isla's finger, kissing it and the top of her hand before lacing their fingers and raising their hands into the air in a cheer. Everyone went wild.

Isla stepped into Andry's side, grinning broadly. She relaxed and put her head on Andry's shoulder and closed her eyes. This was everything she had ever wanted and more. She'd found the perfect person, the one who would love her at her worst, no matter what.

About the Author

Adrian J. Smith has been publishing since 2013 but has been writing nearly her entire life. With a focus on women loving women fiction, AJ jumps genres from action-packed police procedurals to the seedier life of vampires and witches to sweet romances with a May-December twist. She loves writing and reading about women in the midst of the ordinariness of life.

AJ currently lives in Cheyenne, WY, although she moves often and has lived all over the United States. She loves to travel to different countries and places. She currently plays the roles of author, wife, and mother to two rambunctious youngsters, occasional handy-woman. Connect with her on Facebook, Twitter, or her blog.

facebook.com/adrianjsmithbooks

twitter.com/adrianajsmith

instagram.com/adrianjsmithbooks

tiktok.com/@sapphicbookmaker

Also by Adrian J. Smith

Romance
Memoir in the Making
OBlique
Love Burns
About Time
Admissible Affair
Daring Truth
Indigo: Blues (Indigo B&B #1)
Indigo: Nights (Indigo B&B #2)
Indigo: Three (Indigo B&B #3)
Indigo: Storm (Indigo B&B #4)
Indigo: Law (Indigo B&B #5)
When the Past Finds You
Don't Quit Your Daydream

Crime/Mystery/Thriller
For by Grace (Spirit of Grace #1)
Fallen from Grace (Spirit of Grace #2)
Grace through Redemption (Spirit of Grace #3)
Lost & Forsaken (Missing Persons #1)
Broken & Weary (Missing Persons #2)
Young & Old (Missing Persons #3)
Alone & Lonely (Missing Persons #4)
Stone's Mistake (Agent Morgan Stone #1)
Stone's Homefront (Agent Morgan Stone #2)

Urban Fantasy/Science Fiction

Forever Burn (James Matthews #1)

Dying Embers (James Matthews #2)

Ashes Fall (James Matthews #3)

Unbound (Quarter Life #1)

De-Termination (Quarter Life #2)

Release (Quarter Life #3)

Beware (Quarter Life #4)

Dead Women Don't Tell Tales (Tales of the Undead & Depraved #.5)

Thieving Women Always Lose (Tales of the Undead & Depraved #1)

Scheming Women Seek Revenge (Tales of the Undead & Depraved #2)

Broken Women Fight Back (Tales of the Undead & Depraved #3)